TRACK ... LOCK ON ... *FIRE*

Suddenly there was a deafening crash behind them. Good Lord, the cops were *tracking* them, homing in on a signal. But how?

Spencer got it first. "Oh my God," he said. "My body armor." He stopped dead in his tracks in the middle of the stuffed toy section and began peeling off his bush jacket.

"What the hell are you doing?" She demanded.

"My body armor," Spencer said frantically, his voice a bit muffled as he peeled off the tunic. "The first cop, the one who tailed you to the park and then fired its stunner at me. One of the stun needles must have been a low-power transmitter." He reached behind himself and struggled with the body armor's buckles.

A rather determined looking matron stared at them in shock for a moment before she decided to take matters into her own hands. "Now see here, you, you deviant!" she shrieked. "We can't have that here. Stop that at once or I shall summon the police."

Spencer wrestled his body armor off his chest and tossed it back in the direction of the storeroom door. "Don't bother, lady," he said, "they're already here."

Just then the cops got tired of looking for the door. The rear wall of the store burst inward, sending toys and games flying everywhere as a whole squad of autocops smashed their way in, repulsors at the ready. Their targeting systems finally got close enough to the tracer in the armor. Every one of them aimed and fired its repulsor at the same time, blasting away in a orgy of fire.

Other Baen Titles by the Authors

Roger MacBride Allen

The Torch of Honor
Rogue Powers
Orphan of Creation
Farside Cannon

David Drake

Hammer's Slammers
At Any Price
Counting the Cost
Ranks of Bronze
Time Safari
Lacey and His Friends
Vettius and His Friends
Men Hunting Things (editor)
Things Hunting Men (editor)

Crisis of Empire series:

An Honorable Defense
(with Thomas T. Thomas)
Cluster Command (with W. C. Dietz)

DAVID DRAKE

THE WAR MACHINE

ROGER MACBRIDE ALLEN

CRISIS OF EMPIRE III

BAEN BOOKS

THE WAR MACHINE: CRISIS OF EMPIRE III

This is a work of fiction. All the characters and events portrayed in this book are fictional, and any resemblance to real people or incidents is purely coincidental.

A Baen Books Original

Baen Publishing Enterprises
260 Fifth Avenue
New York, N.Y. 10001

ISBN: 0-671-69845-1

Cover art by Paul Alexander

First printing, November 1989

Distributed by
SIMON & SCHUSTER
1230 Avenue of the Americas
New York, N.Y. 10020

Printed in the United States of America

To Jim Baen,

Founder of the Feast

Chapter One

Loss

"Face facts, Spencer. She's gone. We've taken her away from you—and *you* away from her." The Kona Tatsu officer was weary, and there was a sour note in his voice. "Sign the paper and be done with it."

Commander Allison Spencer sat behind his desk, drawing back from both the Kona Tatsu man and the divorce agreement that sat on the desk blotter. Spencer didn't even want to touch the paper. It was too like the man who brought it: ordinary looking, harmless in appearance; yet full of threat and danger, made strong by secrets and conspiracies.

Commander Spencer looked at the secret policeman and felt his own throat go dry, felt fear make the blood pounding in his temples. Al Spencer was a brave man, a good intelligence officer, cool in the face of danger—but only fools were never afraid, and even fools knew to be afraid of the Kona Tatsu.

The secret policeman seemed to have judged that his victim was not going to speak. "You and your wife are as lost to each other as if we had shot one or both of you dead," he said. "And, I might add that we need *her*—but we don't need you. While it would be inconvenient for us to kill your wife—or rather your *former* wife—there would be no such inconvenience if we killed *you*. Indeed, I am carrying written authorization to shoot you dead here and

1

now should you fail to cooperate. Need I add it scarcely matters to me which it is to be? Sign or die. Now."

Spencer found himself staring fixedly at the divorce agreement as if it were some loathsome creature, and he was watching it in helpless, horrified fascination as it gnawed at his own vitals. He could do nothing, nothing at all against the words on that paper.

This morning, two hours ago, he had given Bethany a casual kiss goodbye as he left for another routine day of flying a desk at headquarters. And now—he clamped his hands around the arms of his chair and fought for control.

"May I know the reason for the divorce?" Spencer asked at last, in as even a voice as he could manage. "Am I charged with a crime? Or is it permitted for me to know?"

The nameless secret policeman sighed and seemed to give in just a bit. "It makes no difference. The facts will all be public soon enough. Indeed, the whole point was to make them public. No one is charged with anything but being who they are. You are charged with being nobody, and found guilty. Your former wife, Bethany Windsor, is found guilty of being Anthony Hildebrant Windsor's niece and his closest living relative. That same uncle of hers, Anthony Windsor, is the new Governor of Harmony Cluster. General Anson Merikur, the new military commander of Harmony—"

"Merikur? He's no general, he's just a naval commander. What the devil does Merikur have to do with . . . ." Spencer began, but the answer came to him before he could complete the question. From a political view it made perfect sense. "Oh my God."

"As I was about to say," the Kona Tatsu man went on dryly, "*General* Merikur has taken not only a new rank and command in his new service but, as of an hour ago, he has also taken a fiancee. That fiancee is the niece of the newly appointed Governor, as a matter of fact. Bethany Windsor—that is to say, the former Bethany Spencer—was taken aboard Governor-select Windsor's ship soon after you left her at home this morning. She has already signed her copy of the divorce paper—under protest, if that's any comfort. She will be married to Merikur as soon as possible."

"So Merikur has stolen my wife to get himself into the ruling family," Spencer said quietly. His tone of voice was deceptively low and calm. His fear and shock were already swinging around, transmuting themselves into anger.

His visitor interrupted firmly. "No, he did not. I might as well shoot you dead now and save my office the trouble of arresting you for treason later on, if you believe *that*." Spencer looked up to see the other's eyes boring deep into his own.

"You are thinking murder and treason *already*. I can see it," his visitor went on. "Let me assure you that you would be dead long before you could commit it. For what comfort it may be, *none* of the persons involved were consulted as to these matters. Not you, not Merikur, not his bride-to-be. Merikur has never even met Bethany Windsor." The Kona Tatsu man's voice lowered, became almost gentle, kindly. "Sign the paper. Sign the paper and live. Sign and salvage something of your life and career."

It was the High Secretary's plan, then, Spencer concluded. No one else could possibly be powerful enough to order about Senators and Generals. Spencer shut his eyes and shook his head, trying to clear his mind. Spencer was a member of the High Secretary's Guard, sworn to defend the High Secretary in any and every way, against every enemy from any quarter, unquestioningly, at the cost of his life, if need be. And this was reward for his taking that oath.

Spencer opened his eyes, looked at his visitor, and looked down to stare again at the paper. Trapped. There was nothing he could do. He had no option at all. With a savage curse, he snatched up a pen, grabbed at the paper, and scribbled his name across it. He stamped his thumb on the fingerprint block, hard enough so his thumb hurt. He shoved the paper back across the desk. "Get out," he said.

The Kona Tatsu man folded the paper and slipped it back into his jacket pocket. Spencer forced himself to watch the man go. The secret policeman stood, and his face betrayed something at last, an expression of faint distaste. Whether it was the job he was doing that he disliked, or Spencer's lack of discipline, Spencer neither knew or cared.

If the KT man had drawn a weapon and blown a hole in Spencer at that moment, Spencer wouldn't have much cared about *that*, either.

Spencer watched the nameless man go, and sat motionless, staring at the door, long after he was alone. His whole life, his happy, settled, ordered world had been uprooted, crushed, tossed aside, for the sake of some imagined and momentary political advantage.

Incredible that a single flick of a single pen from a single man so far away could do so much, so abruptly.

The High Secretary, the *de facto* if not *de jure* Emperor of all the worlds of the Pact, chooses to move a few of the pawns about the gameboard. An assistant prepares the appropriate written orders, the High Secretary scribbles his signature and thus commands the move without half a moment's thought.

There is no need to consult the pawns.

A word, a gesture, from the High Secretary was enough to send the Kona Tatsu itself scampering, enough (for the moment, and in this case, anyway) to force Merikur and Senator Windsor to accede to the High Secretary's wishes.

The mail chute *chuffed* and a fat envelope plopped out onto Spencer's desk. It took him a moment to become aware enough of his surrounding to notice its arrival. Numbly, he picked the packet up and broke the elaborate authenticator seal. He pulled out the pages automatically. He had to concentrate in order to read the words and understand them.

But all at once he *did* make sense of them. His stomach knotted up and his hands clenched into fists, crumpling the handsome, formal parchment with all its seals and ribbons. They were *promoting* him. Making him a captain in recompense for robbing his wife. Blatantly, obviously trying to make it all up to him with yet another flick of yet another pen.

Spencer crushed the ornate commission into a ball and threw the dirty thing in the waste chute. He stood up and staggered out of his office. He needed some air.

* * *

Sitting woodenly by the shore of Lake Paho an hour later, he began to convince himself that he was calm. He told himself he was able to face the situation a bit more clearly now.

Damn them all, he thought. Damn the officers and the flunkies and the traditions and the hypocrites.

The horrible thing was that by their lights, a promotion *did* make it up to him, *did* make things all right. Half the officers in the Cluster would have cheerfully abandoned their spouses in exchange for such an early promotion, perhaps betrayed their closest friends into the bargain without hesitation.

But that wasn't fair. In the Guard and the Navy, marriages tended to be business arrangements, politically correct and family-arranged. Most marriages among the military officer class had all the romance of a corporate takeover. Indeed, that had been true of his own match to Bethany. Wed to each other eight years ago, they had been barely more than strangers at the time they exchanged their vows. Her parents had been alive then, and her Uncle Anthony Windsor a minor figure, yet to perform the political masterstrokes that would launch him to the heights of the Pact's ruling elite.

If her parents had already been dead then, leaving her as Anthony Windsor's *de facto* heir, and if Anthony Windsor had been as powerful then as he was now, Allison Spencer and Bethany Windsor would never have been wed; it never would have occurred to anyone to dream of permitting her to be wasted on such an unremarkable match.

Back then, she had been one of several relations to an unimportant official. Now she was the sole surviving family member of a sector governor. Therefore she had value. Political value, access value—hostage value if it came to that.

And what value did Commander—no, *Captain* Allison Spencer have? He stood up and began walking around the lake. The wind was biting and cold, even for early spring, and the sky was a steel-grey roof over the land, seeming to seal off the world from hope. Al Spencer pulled his coat tight around his body and knelt down beside the water to stare at his own reflection. He saw a handsome face there in the grey water, youthful in appearance even for his twenty-five standard years. Dark-skinned, lean-featured, dark brown hair and light brown eyes. He knew he was young, and strong, even intelligent and capable.

All that he was, he had offered up in service to the High Secretary. And today he been told exactly how much that service was worth. The High Secretary might demand unswerving loyalty and devotion from his Guard—but he did not provide it in return.

With a sudden, impulsive, determination, Spencer stood up and turned away from the still waters of the lake. She could not be gone already. He would find her.

Five minutes later he was back his desk, rifling the drawers to find the military-issue Artificial Intelligence Device, the AID, he was supposed to carry at all times. Like many desk-bound officers, Allison Spencer had never quite found the pocket-sized but bulky device useful enough to carry, whatever the regs might say. His desk terminal was all he ever needed. But now he was going to be on the move—and more importantly, it was harder to trace queries from a mobile AID, since it could patch into the data net from practically anywhere.

Al knew without thinking that he would have to hide his actions. It was a conditioned reflex. In the world of Pact society generally, and in the military specifically, it was all but certain that a given person would be under surveillance from time to time. Everyone learned a few tricks for beating the watchers when a little privacy was required.

Spencer found the AID at last, buried under some forms in one of the drawers. He hurried out of the building, and started walking. Better to walk. Cabs were easy to track. He wanted to be on the far side of Lake Paho, well inside the central core of the city, before he switched the device on. That way it would patch into the data net through some other link than the Guard HQ signal.

Al Spencer knew perfectly well that no amount of running around could protect him for long. Given his circumstances, it was not merely possible that the KT were watching him; it was certain. His precautions were almost childishly simple, and he knew that too. They would be able to figure out what he was doing, where he was going—but perhaps, if he hurried, not *quite* quickly enough to prevent his going. *That* was the key thing.

He was going to see Bethany, and he wasn't going to be stopped. What happened to him after that didn't matter.

He found himself in a busy shopping district and stepped into a bustling mall-front toy store. He stepped into a quiet back corner of the store and pulled out the AID, hoping that everyone would assume he was just another busy father, albeit one in uniform, taking a business call while buying a surprise for his children.

Children. Spencer winced, felt a strange little pang in his heart for something that now would never be. He and Bethany had never had children. There had always seemed to be sensible reasons to wait—until they had a larger house, until the next promotion, until Spencer's bosses eased up and he would have more time to spend with his daughter or son. There had always been good reasons to wait. And now the children would never be.

He discovered the AID was trembling in his hands. He blinked and shook his head, forced himself to concentrate on the situation at hand. "AID, voiceprint clearance." It had been a while since he had used the thing. It might be smart to start off by making sure it would still work for him. An AID was literally a machine with a mind of its own, and AID units had been known to decide not to work for their owners after being shut off for a while. The programmers could offer no clear explanation of why. Folklore had it that the damn things just got sulky after being ignored.

"This is AID GHQ 97-558KD76, assigned to Captain Allison Spencer. Voiceprint clearance requestor identified as Captain Allison Spencer. Clearance approved. AID ready on line," a tiny robotic voice answered.

Spencer frowned. The military-model AID units were a bit on the persnickety, overprecise side, too much of the spit-and-polish about them. This one had already picked up Spencer's promotion—and was being careful to use it.

Persnickety AIDs had the reputation of being slavish to the rules—and of being touchy about insults to themselves, real or perceived, intended or unintentional. And it seemed to Al that getting stuffed into a desk drawer for months at a time could easily qualify as an insult.

None of that would matter so much if Al wasn't intent on breaking—or at least bending—a few rules and laws at the moment.

Given a skilled operator, a sufficiently high-tech AID, and a willingness for both human and machine to break the law, a bandit AID could, in theory, turn its operator into a millionare overnight.

But AIDs weren't supposed to be able to assist their owners in the commission of crimes. In principle, if someone used an AID to commit a crime, the AID was supposed to *report* the attempt to the cops immediately—to the endless annoyance of the police computers that had to field such calls. The police ignored ninety-nine percent of AID-reported violations. The cops couldn't afford to send out an arrest team every time an AID finked on its owner for jaywalking.

Of course, it was only the low-end, budget-brand AIDs, or young and inexperienced AIDs, that made such calls. It did not take an AID with any sort of learning bank long to realize the police computers were ignoring its calls—or to realize that its owner didn't appreciate lugging around a stool pigeon.

Some poor bastards out there needed AIDs in their work, but could not afford one able to figure out squealing was useless. Thousands of harmless little salesmen lived in fear that a glorified mobile telephone was going to inform on them if they forgot to charge a client sales tax.

Which was why every AID sold on this world, even the cheap ones, had a scram button on it. Break the seal on that button, punch it in hard, and your AID was history. AIDs who squealed too much died. AIDs who learned *that* quickly discovered how to defeat their own hardwired instruction. AIDs who knew what was good for them cooperated with their owners, even in the commission of minor crimes. Everyone used AIDs to figure their income tax, for example.

But Al Spencer knew as well as anyone that an AID's desire for self-preservation was no guarantee against the damn thing turning informer. Some models—including the standard military issue units—were known to rate revenge above survival. Every AID left the factory knowing how unpleasant things could get if it helped its owner commit murder or treason. The Kona Tatsu had ways of sucking information out of an AID that were just as nasty as what they did to people.

So what it came down to was that AIDs were supposed to squeal, but they never really did it, except sometimes.

There was an old, old theory that uncertainty was a cornerstone of deterrence. Usually, that was true—but today it wasn't going to work. Al had no choice but to use his AID in the commission of a major crime. One that might even be regarded as treason. No danger would stop him.

"AID, report ship name and location and confirm if certain person is aboard." Al spoke a bit stiffly to the gadget, and found himself holding it the way he would a small dog that might bite. He made sure his finger was over the scram button seal and forced himself to relax.

"What is the ship?" the AID asked.

"Senator Hildebrandt Windsor's ship." Spencer held his breath. This was the moment of truth. If this AID was going to betray him, this was the moment. "Such information is under security block," the AID announced. Al felt his mouth go dry. Either he'd get his information, or the KT would be all over this toy store in four minutes. At the first hint that his AID was reluctant to help, Al was going to scram the thing and toss it into a bin of stuffed toys. "One moment, please," the AID continued. "Sidestepping security may take a moment." Al breathed a sigh of relief. "Security overcome. I have access to all in-system ship locations."

"So which is his ship?"

"The governor does not *own* any ship, but he is billeted aboard the *Bremerton*, currently in parking orbit."

Damn smartass machine. But he'd settle for a helpful smartass. "Is his niece aboard?"

"Confirmed, Captain Spencer. Bethany Windsor billeted compartment four, B deck."

That was another little stab in his gut. This AID not only used Al's new rank, but Bethany's maiden name.

Somehow, hearing it from the damn machine made it seem real, official. He felt a surge of anger welling up inside him. "Thank you, AID. Now—how do I get aboard to see her?"

"You cannot," the machine said flatly. "Special orders have been issued specifically to keep you off. The crew has been told that Guard officers may attempt to desert and escape to Harmony Cluster by talking their way onto the *Bremerton*. You cannot get past them."

Spencer felt his anger turn cold, calculating. "All right, then AID, I cannot get aboard. Then at least tell me how I can *try*."

Even as he listened to the AID's patient instructions, Al knew the attempt would fail, knew that the KT could not fail but to keep a watch for him, knew that he was chasing toward disaster.

Deep in his heart, Captain Allison Spencer wondered if it was heroes or cowards who rushed toward their own destruction.

Chapter Two

Wires

Al Spencer came back to himself, just a little, and felt sick. How much time had passed? How long since he had been thrown off the shuttle, how long since the last drunken bar fight? How long since he had paid the Cernian to cut open his skull and put wires in there, install the pleasure implant in his brain?

Disorientation. Confusion. A feeling as though he had just appeared here.

A gap in his life.

Bethany, his life, his career. They all seemed a lifetime ago. What had become of them all? How had he gotten *here*?

But then his worries faded. He blinked, sleepily, happily, and decided it didn't matter. None of it mattered. Not knowing, not caring, Captain Allison Spencer, High Secretary's Guards, slapped down the button again. A pulse of pleasure, of emptiness, of exultation and omnipotence washed over him, sweeping away all thoughts, all concerns, all fears before it.

The numb rig was good—no, more than good. The numb rig was *Goodness*, the spirit, the embodiment of all that was good in the universe. Al reached down and picked up the battered metal box, careful not to jar the wire that led from the rig to the implant in his skull. He smiled at the box, held it to his filthy, unshaved face, caressed it, planted a respectful, chaste kiss on the grubby, much-used

11

button that was the source of all pleasure. For a time that could have been a split second, or an hour, or both, he floated in ecstasy.

The rig was Goodness, he thought again, blearily, happily, pleased and proud to have discovered such an essential truth.

But the feeling was fading already. The glow of well-being was dimming, clearing enough so that bits and pieces of reality were beginning to shine through. He could remember again, remember bribing his way through the spaceport, bluffing his way onto the ground-to-orbit shuttle, the humiliating way he had been stopped attempting to board the *Bremerton*, the cool, professional way the marines had folded him up when he tried to rush the hatch. The Pact military didn't much care for attempted stowaways—after all, they were, almost by definition, also attempted deserters.

The *Bremerton* marines hadn't even permitted him the dignity of arrest, charges, detention, had instead just thrown him back aboard the shuttle, bruised and battered in a dozen places, the most serious injury the one to his pride. The shuttle crew had ignored him too, shoved him out the hatch at landing, tossed him aside like so much garbage to be disposed of.

Too much of it was coming back. Not just his memory, but his senses. He could taste the foul bile in his mouth without recalling how it came to be there, smell the sourness of his uniform and his person. He could see the stained mattress he had been on—for how long now?

How had he come to be here, in a wire room, hooked up to a numb rig? How drunk had he got, in what bar, that he would have agreed to the numb-rigger's harmless-sounding offer of a free sample? Shame and self-loathing washed over him, and uncontrollable tears of self-pity streamed down his face. No man likes to find the depths of which he is capable.

But the body learns quickly. Already Al Spencer had developed a reflex that would wash away all bad feeling. His finger plunged down on the button again, and a tiny pulse of electricity arced directly into his brain's pleasure centers. The universe went away in a bloom of happy colors.

The Kona Tatsu man looked down at Spencer in disgust and sorrow. He should have expected this, he told himself. He *had* expected it, almost. What else could the poor bastard do when the whole universe turned against him, when his future was stolen without so much as an apology, when a lifetime of loyalty was rewarded with such callous cruelty, with a casual gamble for momentary advantage in some meaningless political game halfway across the Galaxy?

Then the KT man caught a whiff of what Captain Spencer smelled like at the moment, and disgust got the upper hand. Even so, there was a debt owed here. "Get him up," he ordered testily. His two ratings stepped in, a bit reluctantly, and scooped up the softly giggling form of Allison Spencer. The two men started to drag Spencer out toward the waiting ambulance. "Hold it," the KT man said. "He has to be unplugged before you move him, for God's sake. Here, let me do it."

The two ratings held Spencer in a standing position as the KT man stepped behind him, and gently reached up to where the grubby ribbon cable attached to Spencer's skull. The incision had been done sloppily, that was sure. There might be danger of infection. Working carefully, he undid the retaining clip and pulled the cable free. A tiny pair of spiky wires, only a few centimeters long, stuck up grotesquely through Spencer's scalp.

The KT man let the cable drop and stepped back around in front of Spencer. Still working with exquisite care, he pried Spencer's fingers away from the numb rig and took the unclean device away from its victim. He threw the damn thing into the far corner of the wire room, drew his repulsor pistol and blasted it down into scrap with a single burst of glass beads accelerated to supersonic speeds.

The troll-like Cernian who ran the Paradise Wire Palace was angered enough to step forward in protest. "You must not do that! That is my property! I do naught illegal here. You burst in, steal away customer before he can pay his bill, I say nothing, I permit. But you draw guns and shoot my own—"

The Cernian stopped in mid-sentence, apparently recalling too late that this was no corrupt vice cop he was shouting at, but quite a different sort of animal. He closed his lipless mouth and gummed his jaw into a hideous imitation of a human smile. He seemed to have forgotten all his human speech for a long moment. "My apolllogeee," he said at last, lisping out the last word in the Cernian equivalent of a nervous stutter.

The KT man stared at the Cernian a long moment. No, nothing illegal went on here—thanks to the bribes the numb riggers could pay. But how many lives had been ruined past all rescue in this 'fetid place? "Your apology will be accepted," he said, "if I decide to let you live. You will know the results of my decision in a few days. One way or the other."

The KT man fought back a feeling of overwhelming disgust and loathing for the alien. He, as much as any human, was influenced by the stereotype that all non-humans were criminals. It was an act of will to remember that the Pact was as much to blame as anyone for the fact that most criminal enterprises were run by aliens. Many planets had laws on the books to keep non-humans out of the best jobs, out of high-ranking professions and guilds. With every door to legitimate advancement closed, of course the aliens were channeled toward crime, toward the despised jobs humans would not do. Then the humans despised the aliens for doing the dirty work.

Well, the KT man thought, here was a human doing a little errand that was dirty enough. The KT man turned and walked away, his two ratings dragging the inert Spencer behind them. The KT man grimaced as he stepped into the street. He watched them load Spencer into the ambulance, and pulled his collar up—not against the cold, but as if to block out some part of the contagion that seem to hover in the very air here in the low places of the city.

He longed to go to someplace clean.

But he would have to travel a great deal further than the other side of the city to get to any such place.

If there were any clean places left in the Pact.

They knew how to handle wireheads at the discreet

hospital where Spencer was brought. A strong sedative, to force sleep for a day or more; an IV to restore the vitamins and other trace elements lost to the days of malnutrition and unnoticed self-starvation; a careful check for lice and the other, less savory parasitic animals that flourished at places like the Paradise Wire Palace. Simple things, really.

It was rare indeed that much in the way of heroic measures were needed to bring the half-dead wirehead back to life. Cleanliness, nourishment, rest were the keys, and there was no great art in making the body whole once again.

But when the physicians and the medical AIDs were done, then others were called on. Others ministered to the mind diseased, plucked from the memory rooted sorrows, razed the written troubles of the brain. Even the Kona Tatsu itself had practitioners skilled in those arts; the secret police had much need of psychiatrists in their work. Such as the nameless case officer who had been handling the Spencer docket right along.

The job of healing a mind was no easier than it had been millennia ago. Al Spencer had to be brought back to reality—and be made to accept reality. That could prove not only difficult, but impossible, when the psychotic escape mechanism was something as seductive as a pleasure implant. Why choose an unpleasant reality over a wire-paradise?

The usual technique was to remind the patient of the hideous *external* world that was part and parcel of the wire-paradise hallucination. The lice, the stench, the fetid odors, the self-debasement of being reduced to a button-pushing robot, the very real danger of brain infection as an after-effect of the clumsy brain surgery the wire-shop operators were famous for.

That was why the surgery robots left behind a scar when they removed the pleasure implant from a wire-paradise victim. The surgery robots could easily pluck the implant out neatly, perfectly, clean the wound and repair the original sloppy incision, and so make the insertion point undetectable. But better, far better to leave a mark behind. For the rest of his days, Al Spencer would have a small, lumpy scar, no larger than this thumbnail, there just above the base of his skull. It would be hidden beneath his hair, but there just the same to remind him. Whenever he scratched his head, or put a hat on, or felt the barber's clippers, he would remember. He would carry the scar as a warning for the rest of his life.

And if he heeds the warning, he might remain sane, the KT man thought. He sat, watching Spencer, for a long time after the med team cleaned him up. What could be salvaged from this wreck? What value could the State, the Pact, squeeze out of this dried-up husk?

But those were mere issues of bureaucratic smoke screening, ways to justify action. The true issue was that the Kona Tatsu had caused this disaster, and honor required the Kona Tatsu to set things to rights. For the KT cleaned up its own messes. How, the nameless man wondered, could he turn this ruin back into a man under the *guise* of doing the State's bidding?

Spencer awoke to the strange double sensation of not knowing where he was—and yet knowing exactly *why* he was there. They were trying to cure him here, wherever *here* was. Someone had found him, brought him to this place.

He opened his eyes and found himself looking up at an antiseptic-white ceiling. The room smelled of fresh linens, everything crisp and clean. A hospital of some sort, no doubt.

Spencer blinked and tried to take stock of himself. He felt a bit weak and light-headed, the way he had as a child in the throes of this illness or that flu, on the morning the fever broke and he knew he was going to be all right even if he wasn't quite there yet. He could feel a small bump on the back of his head, still half-numb from the anesthesia. He reached back gingerly and touched the bump. What the hell was that? Even through the drugs, it was still tender, and he winced slightly as his fingers examined the scar. Then, at last, he understood.

He remembered. That was the place the Cernian had cut his skull open.

"Welcome back, Captain," a somber voice said, startling

close at hand. "The robodoc said you'd be waking up just about now."

Spencer flinched in surprise, still not quite oriented. He had thought he was alone. He tried to sit up and got about halfway before he felt dizzy. But that was far enough. Far enough to recognize the Kona Tatsu man sitting at the side of the bed. The man who had begun the nightmare.

"Things have been busy since you dropped out of sight," the man said. "The High Secretary was assassinated, for starters. You and I may be the only humans in the Pact not trying to succeed him. Unless you'd care to give it a try."

"How long has . . ." Spencer started to ask, and discovered his voice didn't quite work right.

"Here, let me get you some water." The KT man stood and took a pitcher and glass from the bedside table. He poured the drink, and gently slid his hand under Spencer's head, lifting him enough to drink comfortably. Spencer took the glass and drank deep, shocked at how heavy the glass seemed. "It's been about two weeks since I visited your office," the KT man said, obviously using as neutral a phrase as he could to describe the interview. "Twelve hours later you were thrown off the *Bremerton*'s shuttle and went straight from there to a bar called the Wild Side, a portside place that never closes. You stayed there about eight hours before they threw you out. They didn't let you into the Officer's Club, but you got into a strip joint called the Bottom's Up—which is where you wiped the floor with those two Marines. Quite an accomplishment for a man in your condition. Do you remember any of this?"

Spencer's voice had come back, at least a bit. "No. Not past going into the first bar. When did—" He hesitated and gestured to indicate the back of his head.

"About 30 hours after you sent the Marines to the infirmary. More bars, more drinking; wake-me-ups that worked, sober-ups that didn't. Then you wandered into a bar on the first floor of a certain building. One with the Paradise Wire Palace on the third floor. According to the bartender, you didn't take much persuading once the wire-pusher got talking to you.

"The next week you spent pushing a feelgood button. For all intents and purposes, you didn't eat, you didn't sleep. You lost twenty kilos, were almost completely dehydrated—and you pretty much emptied your credit account too. It cost you five pounds in planetary currency every time you hit that button.

"According to the doctors here, another two days of that and you'd have turned Drone. That's what they call it when the feelgood wire burns your pleasure centers out. The wire wouldn't have been able to stimulate that part of your brain any more— because that part of your brain would have been dead, gone, cooked away.

"To oversimplify a bit, Drones are left incapable of feeling any pleasant sensation, any positive emotion. They can only feel pain, sadness. Nothing else gets through to wake them from their stupor. They get to where they *welcome* pain and sorrow because it's better than nothing-ness. They seek out pain. Sooner or later the pain kills them. You were headed that way. It will be a while before anyone knows for sure if you escaped damage altogether. It's possible you lost something."

Al Spencer shut his eyes and slumped back on the pillow. Yes. He could believe that. He could believe that a part of his soul had been badly injured, was near death, might never return. Oh, yes, he could believe that. "How did you find me?" he asked at last. "How do you know so much about where I was and what I did?"

"Your AID," the KT man said. "That's a good unit you've got there. Hang onto it. Apparently you dropped it downstairs in the bar when you went upstairs to get a wire jammed in your brain. They must do some mighty illegal things in that building—it's completely shielded against every usable radio frequency. The AID could tell you were still up there pushing the feelgood button by listening to the staff gossiping—but it couldn't call for help until someone tossed it in the trash and threw it out with the garbage. Once it was clear of the building, it could patch into the AID nets and call for help. My office's computers were watching for any calls regarding you—we responded to the call. And here you are. For about the past week or so, recovering. And now it's time to go back to work."

"What do you mean?"

"I mean you haven't quite been stripped of your commission or court-martialed yet. Your office is under the impression that you are on detached duty assisting the Kona Tatsu. I have not yet disabused them of that notion—which is why you aren't in the brig. And you'll stay out of it if you pass a certain test." The KT man pulled a thick file folder from his briefcase and dropped it on Al's chest. "Read that. Analyze it. Get it right and you stay on detached duty. Get it wrong and you'll get a lot of practice breaking rocks on Penitence. Please bear in mind that, even for a prison planet, Penitence is not a nice place."

The KT man stood, nodded to Spencer, and walked out of the room. Spencer, feeling a bit stronger now, lifted himself up on his elbows to watch the man leave. There was no mistaking it, even behind the threats and the cold, hard language. This nameless secret policeman was a kindly, decent man. There had been no need for him to rescue Spencer, or block the Guard's quite legitimate efforts to punish Spencer. He was doing Spencer a *kindness*, attempting to make redress for the disaster that the system had inflicted on Spencer.

And it was a hell of a note when you had to depend on the kindness and decency of the secret police.

Kindness or no, Spencer had no doubt that the threat of Penitence was real. There were sharp limits to the KT's forbearance—and the KT man was requiring Spencer to earn his own survival.

Still a little light-headed, he sat up in bed and broke the seal on the fat file, noting that it was printed on rapid-decay paper that would collapse into powder in a few hours. He'd have to read fast.

The first words his eyes fell upon scared the merry hell out of him. BASIC SECRET KONA TATSU. In the understated world of KT parlance, "Basic" corresponded roughly with "Ultra Eyes-only Human-only Secure-room Access Defended Document" in the rather verbose Guard terminology. And "Defended Document" meant it was legal to kill anyone who *might* leak it. If Spencer flunked the KT man's little test, Penitence might be the least of his worries.

More than a little nervous, Spencer began reading the file. Ten minutes later his nervousness was forgotten. He was too baffled and curious to remember the danger he was in.

There was something mighty peculiar going on out in the Jomini Cluster.

KT agents had gone missing. In a high-risk sector, that would not have been remarkable—but the disappearances were from Daltgeld, the capital world of the cluster, and Daltgeld was no danger zone. It was a tourist world, safe in the interior of the Pact's communication lines, nowhere near any of the dozens of potential flash points.

Perhaps that was the point. If Daltgeld could become unsettled—then what place was safe?

Spencer pored over the papers. Agents were vanishing—but reports from the remaining agents were perfectly routine. Their fellows were disappearing, and the survivors did not bother to report it.

It was obvious that there was a lot missing from this file, as well. It had been heavily censored. Spencer frowned. Maybe they didn't have all the data—but they weren't even telling him everything *they* knew.

Up until the moment the KT man had arrived in his office with the news that his wife was no longer his wife, Allison Spencer had been an intelligence officer. A good one. He had never gone out to play spy—he had done *real* work, serving in combat units, gathering and analyzing tactical data, and then a hitch back at Guard HQ, working with long-term strategic studies. He found his old reflexes swinging into action. This sort of thing was his bread and butter.

A small part of his mind considered that the Kona Tatsu had to know that Spencer was an intel man who loved puzzle-solving. Spencer knew that the very act of briefing him this way, showing him a part of the puzzle rather than telling him everything, was part of the game they were playing with him. More KT manipulation. The secret police were messing with his mind, teasing him.

He knew all that, and he didn't care. Because it was working. This puzzle intrigued him. There *was* something wrong on Daltgeld.

*   *   *

The last of the pages had rotted away to powder, had been vacuumed away by the cleaning robot, and Spencer was sitting up in bed, eating his dinner, when the KT man returned.

Spencer looked up and nodded thoughtfully as his control retook his seat. The term "control" seemed strange to Spencer, but after all, spies had controls, not commanders. The only possible reason to show Spencer that file was to prepare him for playing spy. He looked at the KT man, who sat, saying nothing, waiting expectantly.

"I assume that this room is secure?" Spencer asked. A service robot rolled in, unbidden, and removed the remains of Spencer's dinner.

"You passed the first part of the test," the KT man said. "You are quite right to assume that—and equally right not to trust that assumption. You may talk freely."

Spencer noted that the KT man did not ask him any questions. The KT man wanted him to work this out on his own. "All right, then. There was nothing in that file to suggest it directly, but it seems to me that the Kona Tatsu has been penetrated," Spencer said. "Someone has subverted the subverters."

The KT man glanced away and nodded woodenly, obviously trying to mask his own embarrassment. "You have passed the second part of the test. The Kona Tatsu has failed. We are in danger from an unknown force that can neutralize our best people indetectably. Anyone who can do that threatens the entire Pact. And the Pact is exposed to enough threats as it is. It might not survive the assassination crisis. If it does, then it will still be severely weakened. Not ready to face whatever is flattening the KT on Daltgeld."

The nameless man looked back at Spencer and flashed a joyless, mechanical smile. "We want your help. And we're going to get it, aren't we?"

Spencer nodded woodenly. At least they weren't insulting his intellect by pretending he had a choice.

Chapter Three

Suss

Al Spencer stood in front of the mirror in his hospital room and looked himself over. A thin, haggard, flimsy-looking man stared back. He had lost a lot of weight to the feelgood button, and not yet gained it back. His uniforms no longer fit. But then, no part of his life fit him anymore. Not his involuntary bachelorhood, not his rank or service assignment. Why should his clothes?

And what about his assignment—or should he even call it that? It would be better described as his cover, even if the face that looked out of the mirror at him didn't look much like a spy. What was it they were expecting of him, anyway?

He sighed unhappily. Spencer knew perfectly well what their expectations were. No need to ask himself rhetorical questions. It was pretty obvious he was meant to serve as a target, a decoy. Something for the Kona Tatsu's enemies to shoot at while the real KT operatives got on with the job.

He peered deeper into the mirror, tried to look himself in the eye. It wasn't easy. Not anymore.

He blinked and came back to himself, plucked idly at the loose folds of cloth that hung from him. Ill-fitting uniforms didn't matter. They, like every other part of his life, were about to be shed in favor of something else. The Kona Tatsu had plans for him. They were shifting him over from the Guard to the Navy, assigning him a ship, indeed a whole fleet. In the Pact military, a transfer from one service to another was nothing unusual, but still this move would be of note. Becoming a navy captain was the equivalent of another jump in rank from a guard captain. In effect, he had received yet another promotion. That should have made him proud, certainly—but not even a shiny new command could resurrect his self-respect completely.

He did not feel entitled to the command, or that he had earned it. It was the KT's work, plain and simple. He was their man. And it was pretty damn galling to learn that the secret police could control the military command structure, seemingly at whim. How often did they do it? How many seemingly meteoric careers were really just the KT putting their own man forward? Spencer felt like a pawn in the KT's game, and knew that it was a pretty accurate analogy.

No, he didn't have much to be proud of. Not when his fingers still curled around an imaginary feelgood control whenever unhappy thoughts came to his mind. But if he wanted to survive, and stay off Penitence, he would have to put the best possible face on the situation. He'd have to *act* proud, at least.

He smoothed the uniform jacket down over his blouse as best he could, turned, and stepped out into the hallway. He had orders to depart this morning, at 0900 hours, and the time had come. He had no bags with him, nothing to carry away with him but his AID. It banged against his hip as he walked. The damn thing had saved his life, but he still didn't like carrying it.

He looked up and down the hallway at the ward. As usual, the place was deserted. Spencer had not laid eyes on anyone but the nameless KT man since his arrival. No patients, no doctors, no nurses, no staff. There were three other rooms for patients, a nurse's station, a diagnostic control pod—but there was no one there to cure or be cured. Just the medical and maintenance robots. They did all the work. A wholly automated ward, run that way for security reasons, no doubt. This was obviously some sort of KT facility. But was it an entire KT hospital, or just one small clinic inside a larger complex?

Not even the KT man here to see him off. Typical. No doubt the watchers were on duty, the surveillance AIDs recording his every move. Spencer raised a hand, waved good-bye to where he thought a camera might be. But then how to get the hell out of here?

It turned out to be simpler than he thought. All the doors but one were locked, and that led out onto a blank hallway full of doors—only one of which would open. That led out onto a stairwell. He followed it down to another doorway, and so on through a whole rabbit's warren of tunnels, stairwells and droptubes that seemed like they must lead him halfway across the city. There was never more than one door that would open, and every door locked quite firmly behind him.

At last he found himself decanted out into a dark, dank narrow alley. It was a fetid, nasty place—but he could see the sky from here. Al looked straight up, and saw the gleam of stars. *Stars?* How could that be? Al glanced at his watch. It wasn't even ten in the morning. Unless the watch had been damaged. "AID, what time is it?" he asked.

"It is 0957 hours planetary standard, and late evening local zone standard."

Al blinked, feeling badly disoriented. He was on the other side of the world from his home city.

"Where the hell are we?"

"I am not permitted to answer questions of locale until we are returned to your own home."

Typical, Al decided. His own AID was taking orders from the KT. Clearly, they wanted him to get home without knowing where he had been. *Another* damn test, this time an exercise in keeping his own knowledge limited. There were certainly ways he *could* figure out where this was. Walk out from here until he found a street sign. Memorize the star positions overhead, and then compare that to the exact time to get a longitude. But no, his AID had simply said it was "late evening"—no doubt on the KT's instructions to be vague. Without knowing the local celestial time, he couldn't use the sky. Never mind. He could simply walk out from here until he found a citizen to ask where he was.

But they didn't *want* him to know, were challenging him to get home *without* finding out. He was getting tired of these little pop quizzes. Nevertheless he was obviously being watched, somehow, so he'd better play by the rules. "AID, call me a cab," he said in a tired voice. "And see if you can charge the fare to the Kona Tatsu." Al Spencer knew his credit balance wasn't up to paying for intercontinental cab fares. He didn't mind dancing to the KT's tune, so long as they paid the piper.

"The KT pays all operational expenses of its personnel. It's taken care of," the AID said, with what might have been just a hint of gently mocking humor in its voice.

A cab dropped out of the sky and touched down in the middle of the street. It sidled over to the curb on its hoverskirt and opened its door in front of Al. He climbed in and sat down. "Tell the cab to opaque windows and take me home," he told the AID testily. "And fly via non-direct routes." The KT wouldn't want him to be able to look out the window, or calculate his starting point from measuring the flight time.

Which meant he had a flight of long and indeterminate length to look forward to, hours of sitting inside a blacked-out cab with nothing to see or do.

The cab door shut, the windows blacked out, the interior lights came on, and the robot cab whooshed into the sky. Damn them. Damn them all and the games they played. *And damn me too, for playing with them, as if I had much choice,* Spencer thought.

The near-silent thrumming of the cab's engines, the dim interior lighting and the enforced inactivity conspired to put Allison Spencer into a light doze. He slept as the kilometers whispered past, his hand now and again clenching around an imaginary switch.

It took only the slightest shift in the cab's motion to awaken him. His eyes sprang open the moment the cab's nose pitched downward, and it took him a second or two to remember where he was. "Cab, what is it?"

"Additional passenger proceeding to same destination has hailed me," the cab answered in a dull voice.

The same destination! The cab was supposed to be

taking him *home*! He hadn't planned on providing target practice just yet. He reached out and broke the seal on the emergency manual operation switch. He pushed the switch in hard, waiting for the manual controls to pop out so he could fly himself out of here. It scared him when nothing happened, but it didn't exactly surprise him.

The situation was not good. Here he was, unarmed in a cab he could not control, heading toward a landing, a meeting with someone who had to know who he was. "AID! See if you can find a KT distress band and send an SOS. Flash under attack. Whatever the hell the KT calls it."

"We are not under attack," the AID announced calmly. "This stop was prearranged."

Al Spencer felt his blood go cold. "You knew this was going to happen?" he asked.

"Yes."

"Who is it we're picking up?

"I am not at liberty to tell you."

Al felt the sweat beading up on his forehead. His AID told him this was no attack—but his AID willfully had withheld information from him. How far a step was it from there to lying? If he were about to be attacked, could he trust this machine to tell him what it knew? "AID, who the hell do you work for?" he asked. He only had a few seconds to straighten this out.

"I am now employed by the Kona Tatsu, and have been assigned to your case."

What sort of case was he? Spencer wondered irritably. Medical? Mental? Legal? Intelligence? "You are incorrect. *I* am employed by the Kona Tatsu. I *own* you. You are one of the tools I use to do my employer's bidding. And I am expected to discard and destroy any tool that does not perform up to specification, before it could endanger a KT asset, such as myself. The specification for an AID includes keeping its owner informed and appraised of all pertinent data. Do you understand?"

"Yes."

"Who do you work for?"

"Captain Allison Spencer."

"Then, AID, who the hell is waiting to meet this cab?"

"A KT operative, name, rank and mission unknown."

"That's more like it. I think." It wasn't any more informative, but at least the AID was admitting it didn't know. Spencer was inclined to accept its ignorance: AIDs weren't usually very good liars. And even if the new arrival *was* a KT agent, that didn't necessarily mean all was well. Every other organization in the Pact was divided into rival factions. Why not the Kona Tatsu? Why shouldn't his nameless friend back at the hospital have enemies?

With that happy thought, Allison felt himself grow heavier for a moment as the cab braked and came in for a landing. Ten seconds later the interior lights dimmed to nothing. Al heard the door pop open, and saw the sky framed by the door for half a moment. A shape flitted through the door, silhouetted against the dark night sky. The door clicked shut and the cab was airborne again, pitching upward to head for the sky.

"Lights on," a firm, low-pitched woman's voice commanded. The cab's interior lit up, and Allison Spencer found himself face-to-face with the figure of a smallish woman dressed completely in black, and nose-to-nose with the repulsor pistol she held in her hand. Her clothes were so dark that she was hard to see even in the cab's lighting. Even her face was hidden behind a black mesh maskcap that cloaked her features completely. "Name," she snapped out, in tones that made it an order and not a question.

"Allison Spencer," he answered. "Who the hell are you?"

"What is your control's name?" she demanded.

"How the hell would I know?" he replied irritably. "The son-of-a-bitch never told me."

His inquisitor chuckled at that, and made the pistol disappear. "That's him all right," she said cheerfully. "Always very careful about need-to-know." She cocked her head over her shoulder. "Santu, what's the story?" she asked abruptly.

"His AID confirms his identity via radio link," a muffled voice replied from the rucksack on the woman's back. "I'd trust it. The military models are hard to manipulate without leaving traces."

"All right, Spencer, you are who you are. So maybe we can get down to business."

"Who are you?" Spencer asked again, this time with what he hoped was a tone of exaggerated—and threatening—patience.

The newcomer shed her backpack. "Suss Nanahbuc. Your new live-in concubine. Santu, take over this cab and get us some speed. I want to get where we're going." Suss sighed and reached her hand out to Al. He took it and shook mechanically. "Nice to meet you, Spencer. Hold on just a second while I get out of this damn spy get-up."

Spencer watched Suss carefully, with the sinking feeling that he had just lost control of his life to this under-sized secret agent.

She leaned back in the bench seat facing him and started peeling off her outer garments. The ski mask came off first, and Spencer found himself vaguely disappointed by what it revealed. Spies and agents were supposed to be startlingly, beautiful, or at least striking, and Suss was merely pretty, indeed rather ordinary-looking. She peeled off her black coveralls as well, revealing a modest business suit underneath, perfectly proper attire for a mid-level government bureaucrat. It made her look even more just an ordinary person.

She seemed even smaller, once she was out of the commando-garb. She wouldn't even come up to Spencer's shoulders if the two of them stood side-by-side. Her face was thin, her skin pale, her black hair snaked in a tight, prim bun at the top of her head. She wore little jewelry or makeup.

But her eyes. They were eyes that had *seen* things, perhaps too many things in too short a time. They were big, almond-shaped eyes that told of almost pure-bred Asian stock reaching all the way back to ancient Earth, the irises dark blue, almost black. It would be hard to look into those eyes and not speak the truth. She undid the bun that held her hair in place and shook her head, letting her jet-black hair cascade down around her shoulders.

"We should be at your front door in about two hours," she announced as she pulled a brush out of her rucksack and ran it through her hair. "We have until from now until then for you to get your initial cover story straight. I am your mistress. After the *Bremerton* left orbit, you went off on a bender for a few hours, and then ended up at Lady Joy's Happy House, where you sobered up to find me next to you. If anyone asks for proof that you've been with me, tell them I have a centimeter-wide mole on my left buttock. The two of us—actually myself and a KT agent who resembles you—cut a pretty wide swath across the nightspots. You bought my contract off Lady Joy and yesterday registered me as your on-board personal assistant. We'll be sharing a cabin aboard your cruiser, you lucky devil."

She flashed a dangerous smile and put her hairbrush away. She stuffed the blackout clothes into a side pocket of the rucksack, then did something with its zippers and straps, and turned it into a lady's handbag, a bit oversized but no more remarkable for that. The mysterious intruder of two minutes before was transformed into an average-looking middle-class businesswoman.

"You consider it a real asset that a hot-blooded temptress such as myself is capable of appearing so refined, dignified, and ordinary in public. Behind closed doors, however, it's quite a different story. You getting all this?" she asked playfully.

"Yeah, sure," Al replied, feeling anything but sure. "But could you tell me what'll really be going on?"

"I'll be the spy, and you'll be the cover story—and the person who *seems* to be investigating the situation. You draw their fire, divert their attention, and I help you stay alive while I do the real investigating. Also, you are there with the naval task force if we Kona Tatsu super-heroes need the backup. You will command the naval task force—"

"But you will command *me*," Al said sourly. "A puppet on your string."

She frowned and her face turned serious for the first time. "I will be your superior officer, yes. When was the last time you didn't have a superior officer you had to obey? If it makes you feel any better, I could wave a bunch of military ID at you, showing me to hold a superior rank in the Navy—or the Guard for that matter. Then you'd have to decide whether or not my ID was forged—and whether or not a Kona Tatsu forgery has legal standing, as some courts have ruled. In the long run, none of that will matter, because you will accept my orders. Period. Or say hello to Penitence."

She looked at him straight in the eye and grinned. "That sound scary enough to convince you?"

Al found himself forced to grin back. "Yeah, I guess so. I'll follow orders. As if I had a choice."

Suss' face fell, and she replied in a saddened voice. "As if any of us had a choice. I don't call the tune I dance to, either, my friend." She seemed lost in thought for a long moment, but then her expression brightened. "Never mind, ours not to reason why, and try not to think about the couplet's second line. Santu, skip the run to Captain Spencer's house, and call whoever you need to call to see to it that his luggage gets to his ship. Get us right to the spaceport and order transport to our ship. We've got a cruiser to catch."

She dug down into what was now her capacious handbag and pulled out a stack of record blocks and a reader. "Here," she said, "get busy. The ships you're taking over have not exactly been happy places. You've got a lot of homework to do if you want to get them back together again."

Chapter Four

Tallen

Lieutenant Commander Tallen Deyi was getting royally sick of all hell breaking loose. Piping aboard the latest politically-appointed disaster of a captain on one hour's notice was headache enough—but doing so while simultaneously tidying up after a goddamned mutiny on an auxiliary ship was aggravation above and beyond the call of duty.

At least the mutiny was aboard one of the destroyers. If "mutiny" was the most accurate term. "Food riots" might be closer to the mark, given the slop the sailors aboard the *Banquo* had been forced to eat.

Poor damn sods. With Lucius Rockler as commanding officer, it had probably come down between starvation and revolt. Even the *Banquo*'s marines had taken part in the uprising—and if there was one bunch of perfectly devoted loyalists in the Pact, it was the goddamned marines.

Tallen stood up and crossed the bridge, ostensibly to look over the radarman's shoulder to check the progress of the captain's gig. He could have checked the gig's position from the repeaters at his own station—or simply asked the radarman to report—but Tallen was feeling restless, edgy. He needed to prowl the bridge, pace back and forth a bit, triple-check all the routine procedures he had double-checked already.

In the normal course of events, Tallen knew, it was terribly bad form to breathe down people's necks that

way. But he had worked with this bridge crew a long time.
They knew why he was upset, and were equally nervy
themselves—and would much rather have Tallen Deyi
catch them out than the latest excuse for a captain.

The poor old *Duncan* had been through four captains in
the last three standard years, one simple-minded offspring
of an inbred aristo after another. All of them a bit weak in
the head and a bit weak in the chin as a result of most of
their ancestors being first cousins or worse, all of them
sent out on the strength of Daddy's influence and/or
Mommy's money waved about in the right quarters, out to
punch one of the aristo tickets that needed punching if
sonny-boy were going to have any chance of snatching the
family's seat in the Senate.

By all tradition and precedent, a Senator was supposed
to have held a "major military command" before he could
put on his ceremonial robes. The trouble was that Task
Force 1307—all four ships of it—was one of the smallest
"major" commands available, and had the added distinc-
tion of being assigned to a very secure interior cluster. It
was small and unimportant enough that the High Command didn't give a good goddam who sat in the Task Force
Commander's chair.

A chair that, in any other Task Force, would have
belonged to Tallen Deyi by now. He was stuck here, the
permanent first officer, seemingly condemned forever to
nursemaid the chuckle-headed spawn of politically-correct,
marginally incestuous marriages through their experience
of "command."

And what type would this one, this Allison Spencer, be?
Would he storm onto the bridge and issue a flurry of
contradictory orders five minutes after he came aboard,
the way Zephon had? Or vanish into his stateroom expecting a constant supply of girls and boys to be provided for
his entertainment, as Senator Kerad's darling baby girl
had done?

And, of course, it had been Miss Luinda Kerad—*Captain*
Kerad, (even if she was only nineteen years old) who had
placed her extremely close friend Lucius Rockler in command of the *Banquo*. Tallen didn't care one of his frequent
goddams who did what to whom in private, or how they

liked to do it. That didn't matter. But when the Task
Force Captain treated the ship's complement like the staff
of her private bordello and assigned some little corrupt
little bimbo boyfriend to command a warship—*that* was
what wrecked ships and destroyed morale. What was the
ancient maxim? "So long as they don't do it in the street
and frighten the horses." Well, if there had been any
horses aboard the *Banquo*, they would have been goddam
petrified with fear.

All of which left Tallen so cynical he found himself
wondering, not if the new captain was going to be worse
than the last, but how much worse, and in what *way* the
newie would be worse. None of them ever got any better.

"Captain's gig coming alongside sir."

"Very good. I'm on my way to the ceremonial dock.
Alert the sideboys and order the engineer to activate the
revolving door on the captain's cabin. We've got another
customer."

The comm operator grinned at that, and knew enough
not to relay the order. Tallen departed the bridge and
made his way below. He had about ten minutes to reach
the main hatchway, rigged for the captain's boarding ceremony it had seen far too often in recent times.

Tallen wasn't sure he was ready to endure this particular
charade quite so soon. Kerad had only made her hurried
departure into ignominy the week before, the ink still wet
on her resignation of commission. The High Secretary's
assassination two weeks before had shaken up a lot of
people. It had inspired the men of the *Banquo* in their
revolt, and that in turn had inspired Kerad's sudden resignation "for reasons of health."

She had been smart to quit: the Judge Advocate General's office could not touch a member of a Senatorial family,
once he or she was out of the military. Tallen was not
happy that she had eluded military justice, scurried back
to the protection of her family—but at least Lucius Rockler
was safely in the brig here on the *Duncan*.

And then the signal from Sector HQ that the replacement captain would be coming aboard in one hour. God,
they loved to jerk you around! There was no time at all to
sweep Kerad's disasters under the rug.

Tallen ducked into his office long enough to switch into dress whites, and made it to the main hatch with two minutes to spare.

The gig warped in, docked itself, the air locks cycled—and a scarecrow in a captain's uniform stepped aboard the *Duncan*. Tallen tried not to do a double-take as he saw his new commanding officer for the first time. Tall, very young, gaunt, emaciated, with something about him suggesting a sudden, recent loss. This was a man who had been hurt, badly injured somehow, and not yet completely recovered. The man's face was still youthful—but there was something very old in his boyish eyes. His brand-new naval uniform fit him, but he seemed not to fit the uniform. That much Tallen understood: the man had been in the Guard until not so long ago.

"*Duncan* on board!" the lead sideboy announced, and Allison Spencer was piped aboard in the old, old, ceremony lost in the mists of time, back when navies sailed the blue oceans of water, and the sky and the stars were mere aids to navigation. Spencer came aboard and saluted everything he was supposed to salute, moving a bit mechanically, with the air of a man who doesn't quite feel he's earned the honors he was being accorded.

Tallen knew the captain had brought along a "personal assistant," honoring another age-old tradition, and was surprised to see that she did follow him off the gig.

Tallen was pleasantly surprised. At least Captain Spencer knew that courtesans had no place in military protocol. It wasn't much to make a first impression with, just a suggestion that Spencer had just a hint of decorum, but maybe the horses wouldn't get quite so frightened this time out.

Tallen stepped forward and saluted his new superior. "Lieutenant Commander Tallen Deyi, commanding, sir. Welcome aboard."

"I relieve you, sir," Spencer said, returning the salute and talking in subdued tones. "What I'd like to do first off is talk to you. Could we go to your office, please?"

Goddam. The office section was clear across the ship, and there was no use trying to snow this captain by walking him around the worst of it. They'd have to walk straight through officer's country—and maintenance hadn't even made a dent in cleaning up the mess. Nothing for it but to put the best possible face on it. "Of course, sir. If you would come this way."

The officers' cabins had been the focal point of Kerad's little empire of self-indulgence. She had kicked out all the line officers and assigned their cabins to a whole gaggle of "special assistants," none of whom had lost any time in redoing their cabins and the surrounding corridors. Then, when it suddenly became time to leave there was a panic to recover as much of that splendid loot as possible.

Tallen Deyi led Captain Spencer down the corridors, offering no explanation for anything—and sweating bullets because Spencer asked for none.

Fabulous tapestries, gorgeous paintings, sculpture that could only be described as prurient, period furniture that would have been at home in a palace—or perhaps a fancy bordello. Worse, perhaps, were the blank spots where it was obvious a painting, a fixture, an ornament was missing. Red-flocked wallpaper hung in ribbons from the bulkheads where it had been torn out to get at some particularly expensive piece.

Tallen breathed a sigh of relief when they turned the corner into the duty offices. Here, at least, some semblance of normal military appearance remained. "My office is just this way, sir," he said, the relief in his voice obvious. Quite automatically, he led Spencer straight to what Tallen regarded as "his" work place—and too late realized that the brass plate on the door said CAPTAIN.

Spencer turned and smiled at Tallen. "*Your* office, Commander?"

"Ah, in the interim, sir. All the datanodes and operational files are here—It seemed more practical in the absence—"

"I understand," Spencer said gently, and swung open the door. It was obvious at first glance that Tallen had been occupying this office for quite some time. His commission, proudly framed, hung on the wall. The closet door was ajar, and it was clear that the uniforms inside were meant to fit a burly man, and not the former female captain. A photo of Tallen and his parents sat on the desk.

"It's been a long interim, hasn't it?" Spencer asked innocently.

Damn and double goddam. How the hell could he explain that Kerad hadn't set foot in the duty offices during her whole tour of duty, that Tallen had been *forced* to move in here, where all the ops files were?

Spencer gestured Tallen inside and shut the hatch. "What else am I going to find on this ship, Deyi?"

Tallen stiffened and stood at full attention. "Would the Captain wish to examine the rest of his command?" Deyi asked, dreading the ordeal he was inviting. The *Duncan* was in sad shape, and no one knew it better than Deyi.

"No, thank you, Commander." Spencer sat in the visitor's chair and indicated that Deyi should take the chair behind the desk. "I think I've seen enough. It looks like you have your hands full without disrupting everything for some candyass inspection. You've got most of *Duncan*'s marines aboard the *Banquo*, don't you?"

Tallen swallowed nervously. *This* captain seemed to have done his homework. "Yes sir."

"And no doubt you're short-handed in other ways. Probably you have the whole commissary section doing ship's inventory, counting to see how many of the spoons Kerad and her entourage took with her."

How the hell had he known that? "Sir?"

"Kerad's brother was in the Guard, Commander," Captain Spencer said. "Assigned to my section for a while. I know the family tendencies. My guess is that his kid sister and her toadies left carrying everything that wasn't bolted down—and a few things that were, by the look of officer's country. And you've been busy trying to deal with more pressing matters than repairing the wallpaper. Like quelling a mutiny.

"Relax, Tallen. I know none of this fiasco is your fault— even if it is technically your *responsibility*. I'll lay odds that I could find discrepancies in every section of this ship that could get you court-martialed for dereliction of duty if I looked right now. Fortunately, I haven't seen a thing so far. It just so happens I wanted to see if I had the ship's layout memorized and walked to this office with my eyes shut."

Tallen opened his mouth as if to speak, but then thought better of it.

"So I'll make a deal with you," Spencer went on. "We are to boost and head for Daltgeld within forty hours. Concentrate between now and then on making sure the task force is ready for the Jump. Once we're on station orbiting Daltgeld, we can worry about setting the cosmetic things to rights. And the Daltgeld shipyards will be better able to help us get shipshape. Once we're at Daltgeld, you've got one week to turn this flying casino back into a Pact cruiser. I'll stay out of your hair while you do it. I'll be busy enough in the meantime learning my own job. Bend and break whatever rules you need to bend getting this ship put back together. *Then* I'll take that inspection, when you've had a fair chance to put things right. And if this ship isn't in order by then there'll be hell to pay."

"Very good, sir."

"Excellent. Effective immediately, you will resume your duties as executive officer. You will continue to use this office until you have some semblance of control over the task force. You know this command and I don't. I will leave the ship in your hands while I deal with the question of the unpleasantness aboard the *Banquo*. Settling that will be my first priority. Will you see to it that the appropriate logs and other documents are in my cabin within half an hour?"

"Yes sir, very good."

"That will be all, then, Commander. I can find my own way to my cabin." Spencer stood up to leave, and Tallen rose hurriedly. He saluted and watched the captain depart, very much confused. He didn't know quite what to make of it, but it seemed that the *Duncan* might actually have a real commander for a change.

Allison Spencer closed the door on his new executive officer and breathed a sigh of relief. He had carried it off, at least so far. Eighteen hours after leaving the hospital, and here he was already, bluffing his way through the role of commanding his very own task force. He hadn't even been prepared to change into his new uniform aboard the gig, let alone assume command today.

The next challenge was seeing if he really had memorized the ship's layout. So where *was* his cabin? He tried to picture its location in his head, but didn't feel confident about it. He could ask someone—but that wouldn't exactly give the image of command. Should he just try and fake it, hope he remembered all the twists and turns properly? No, it wouldn't do for the new captain to go blundering into the women's showers, either. Well, *anything* would be better than standing aimlessly in a hall for fear of looking foolish. At least he couldn't get embarrassed in front of machinery. "AID," he said at last, "How do I get to my cabin?"

"I made a bet with Santu that you'd have to ask," his AID replied with an excellent imitation of a chuckle. "Head back down the way you came, turn to port, go to the third intersection and turn—"

"Hold it. I was in the Guard until this morning, remember? So, uh—which way is port?"

The AID seemed to hesitate for a moment before replying. "Captain, I have the feeling this is going to be interesting for all of us. Turn *left*, go to the third intersection . . ."

Captain Spencer followed the AID's instructions, beet red and quite thoroughly aware of how embarrassed he could be in front of machinery.

He located his cabin without any further ado, accepted the salute of the rather haggard-looking Marine on guard duty, and stepped through into his quarters.

He had some vague idea of what to expect, but his jaw dropped nonetheless. Ornate, opulent, decadent—none of them went quite far enough. It would seem that Kerad had not had the time to strip her own cabin of its furnishings. The place was done up like something out of the Arabian Nights. The compartment's bulkheads were lost behind elaborate wall hangings and tapestries. The deck was covered in layers of thick carpet and animal skins. There were no chairs, merely heaps of gaudily-covered pillows scattered about the carpets. A meter-tall hookah had pride of place in the center of the room. The lights were dim and the air was thick with incense. Slow, seductive music came from somewhere, a haunting refrain that teased at Al, as if it were a song he had always loved and not heard in a long time.

But Al scarcely noticed any of that. He was too busy staring at the bed—and the indecorously clad Suss, who was lounging luxuriously on it. The bed was circular, and at least five meters across. Covered in something that resembled angora bearskin, raised on a low dais in such a way that it reminded Al of a primitive sacrificial altar, it took up an entire corner of the huge compartment. Mirrors covered the two walls that formed the corner, and more mirrors covered the ceiling above it.

Suss was doing a very credible job of living up—or perhaps down—to her surroundings. She was dressed in a sheer black negligee that hid nothing, a rope of perfect white pearls draped around her neck, and a bright red rose between her teeth. She tried her best sultry stare on Spencer—but then exploded in laughter, dropping the rose from between her teeth. "I'm sorry, Al," she said at last, when she had recovered enough to speak, "but there I was, being discreetly escorted to the captain's cabin by a most matronly-looking rating who saw right through my demure little business suit to see the painted harlot of a captain's courtesan underneath. She knew what *I* was, and no doubt about it. And then the door opens and I see *this* ridiculous place—and Santu tells me that straight-laced, perfect-gentleman Captain Spencer, who wouldn't dream of consorting with *that* sort of woman is on his way—I just had to make your entrance memorable."

She hopped down off the bed, looked at Spencer, and her face grew serious. "But you're not laughing." She reached over to pat him on the arm. "This hasn't been an easy day, has it? Let me get out of my working clothes, and we'll talk."

She crossed to the side of the room, threw back one of the wall hangings, and vanished through the doorway behind it. Al Spencer found a pile of pillows at a comfortable height for sitting and collapsed down onto them. He unbuckled his AID and tossed it onto the next pile of pillows over. Suss reappeared, wearing a very practical-looking brown coverall. "I'm sorry," she said, sitting close to him, but not too close. "Poor attempt at a joke."

Spencer smiled, feeling as if he hadn't smiled enough in a long time. "No, a very good attempt at a joke. It was funny—this place is funny—and you looked very lovely. But things have been moving too fast. Here I am, supposedly running this ship, this whole task force—and I don't even know port from starboard."

"So what did you do about it?"

"Backpedalled, left the XO to get on with patching the ship up. He's got enough problems without holding my hand. I've decided to take on the investigation of the *Banquo* mess while I'm learning the ropes. I did a hitch at the Judge Advocate's office. It's something I know about."

"So you delegated authority to the man best able to do the work and took on the responsibility for the nastiest assignment yourself," Suss said. "That sounds like what a captain is supposed to do. Maybe you don't know port and starboard yet, but it seems to me that you have enough common sense to fake it while you learn."

"And meanwhile I intend to stall on the *Banquo* business until we're en route to Daltgeld."

Suss looked up, startled. "Why wait? You *can't* wait. If the crew of the *Banquo* and the other ships don't see justice done for what's happened to them—"

"There'll be an explosion to make the *Banquo* mutiny look like a day at the beach. I know. But there's no Navy presence to speak of on Daltgeld. I'll be the highest-ranking officer in system. If I had to convene a court-martial here, the regs say I'd have to hand it off to the fatbottoms back on-planet. And no doubt some of them are chummy with the Kareds, or the Rocklers. The fix would be in. Once we're out of system, it's legal for us to try the case ourselves, make sure no one has a chance to cock up the works."

Suss looked at Al with new respect. "And the file says you're still a little disoriented, not quite back to your old self. Either the psych file is wrong, or you're really going to be something once you get over—" Suss stopped and shifted uncomfortably. "I'm sorry. I shouldn't talk so lightly about what they did to you and your wife, like it's a summer cold you'll shake off." She thought for a second, and blushed. "And there I was, prancing around in my skivvies just for a laugh. I wasn't thinking. I didn't mean to mock you."

Spencer shrugged. "It's okay. I have to live with it. I'm used to people regarding that sort of thing very casually. Bethany and I had *our* marriage in a world where none of our peers, none of our acquaintances, had a *real* marriage. No one married because they loved each other and wanted to be together. I'm used to people assuming there was nothing real there between Bethany and myself."

Suss reached out a hand—but then drew it back. This man didn't want or need physical contact right now. "I'm sorry," she said at last.

"Thank you," Spencer said. "That counts for a lot." He had known this woman for, what, twenty hours? Already she seemed an old friend. Was it just sheer chance that they got along, or had some KT psych computer calculated their personalities would mesh—or was Suss' apparent kindness part of her act, a facet of the job she was doing? Never mind. None of that mattered. He *needed* someone he could talk to, someone who cared about him. Whatever the reasons, however false or genuine it was, he needed her understanding.

"You're nice people," Al said.

"You say that as if you were surprised," Suss replied.

"I guess I am," Spencer admitted. "I always thought KT operatives were supposed to be paranoi—" He stopped himself in midword. He realized he was about to put his foot in it. "Supposed to be, you know, dedicated, determined, humorless, driven," he said, trying to recover as best he could.

"What you were about to say is that Kona Tatsu ops are supposed to be paranoid sociopaths," Sass said easily. "Some of us are, of course. Comes with the territory."

She stood up and selected another pile of pillows to slump down on. "It's been a problem for intelligence agencies since the dawn of time. The personality-type best suited to field work is also one of the most pathological, dangerous, and unstable personality-types going."

She picked up one of the smaller and gaudier pillows

within reach and hugged it to her chest. After a moment's silence, she spoke again, her eyes focused somewhere far beyond the walls of Luinda Kerad's fantasy-world of a stateroom.

"You need someone who can slip into a foreign society, blend in facelessly without being noticed, a loner willing to leave family and friends far behind, maybe leave them behind forever, someone with such absolute faith in himself that he can make life-or-death decisions instantly—and unfeeling enough that he can live with the consequences afterwards. It helps to be completely devoid of empathy, helps even more if you can't really believe that other people have feelings—and the best way to manage that is to suppress your own feelings as well. It takes someone capable of getting up every morning and living a cover story—living a lie, trusting no one.

"Talk to a psychologist, describe someone who lives like that, can *function* in life like that—and the shrink will tell you that person is in serious trouble. That person is a sociopath, a paranoid afraid of everything and unable to experience any of the fear he's keeping locked deep inside. He either winds up locked in a rubber room somewhere, or locked inside his cover story, never opening up, forever incapable of most normal human feelings."

"You keep saying 'he',' " Spencer said.

Suss looked up and smiled unhappily. "Do I? Probably because I'm still trying to pretend it can't happen to me. Every once in a while, I feel it all closing in, feel myself walling off my feelings, treating people like so many chess pieces to be sacrificed. *That* scares the living daylights out of me. There's part of me that knows, absolutely *knows* that I'm going to end up with all the life drained out of me, a Kona Tatsu killing machine. I have to fight that."

She tossed her hug-pillow away, stood up, and shrugged broadly. "So I overcompensate, act as alive as I can—and dress up in filmy negligee for the sole purpose of shocking a perfect stranger, so he forms the wrong impression and assumes his operational partner is a complete slut and loon." She crossed to the stateroom's comm panel and switched on a view of the planet below, hanging silently alone in the emptiness of space. "We're all crazy by now," she half-whispered. "I wonder if there's a completely sane person left in the Pact.

"And if there isn't," she asked, still staring at the stars, "what does that say about the Pact?"

Chapter Five

Trial

"Guilty."

Allison Spencer shoved his chair back from the table a bit and stared down at the man he had just convicted. In another world, a better world, Spencer thought, he would not have had to do this job himself. Someone else besides Lucius Rockler's commander should have said that word to Lucius Rockler. It wasn't right or proper for a commanding officer to preside at the court martial of an officer directly under his command.

But far better a court-martial here and now, under whatever circumstance, than the ordinary sailors seeing a loathsome pimple like Rockler get off scot-free for his crimes. "Lieutenant Commander Rockler, you have been found guilty by this summary court-martial of diverting Navy property to your own use, of the theft of Navy property, and of the unauthorized sale of Navy property, each of these being a Class Three offense. This court commends the prosecuting officer for her capable presentation of the case against you. We have seen how food, medical supplies, and vital equipment intended for the use of the *Banquo* never actually left the planet's surface, but were instead diverted to sale on the black market, to your considerable profit. It has also been proved that you purchased substitute foodstuffs knowing that they were of inferior quality, that much of said food was spoiled, diseased and otherwise unwholesome, and that the quantity

of food supplied to the crew was wholly inadequate to feed
the crew. As the *Banquo* was in orbit at the time, and the
crew isolated from any source of food besides ship's stores,
this amounted to the deliberate starvation of your own
crew.

"You have likewise been found guilty of three separate
charges of grievous manslaughter, which is defined as
doing deeds and things which cause the death of another,
while knowing said deeds and things were likely to cause
the death of another, to wit, causing the death by malnutrition of three men under your command by depriving
them of nourishing foodstuffs, such food being stolen and
sold by you as per the Class Three offenses previously
mentioned. However, the court finds that while you stole
the men's food, knowing the consequences of such an act
might include death, your actual motive was not murder,
but larceny, and therefore you cannot be charged with
premeditated murder. But, by finding you guilty of the
deaths of men under your command, I am legally con-
strained to charge you formally with the further crime of
criminal negligence in the performance of your duties.

"This court further rules that it has heard sufficient
evidence already to rule on this further charge without
recourse to a second court martial to consider a charge of
criminal negligence. This court hereby finds you guilty of
the additional charge, and hereby sentences you to death
for it, as provided for in the Code of Military Justice."

An excited whisper of voices rippled through the wardroom, which had been pressed into service as a court-
room. Lucius Rockler, a wispy little man who seemed
wholly out of place in a uniform, stood at rigid attention,
visibly struggling to keep his knees from buckling.

Al Spencer forced himself to continue. *By the book,
absolutely by the book*, he told himself. Rockler must be
granted every right to which he was entitled. The crew
must know that this was justice, not a witch hunt, not
revenge.

Or was he, Spencer, merely afraid to cause this miserable man's immediate death? "I must now speak not only to
you, Lucius Rockler, but to the entire crew and officer
corps of this task force. Enough of you knew to start with

why we waited until departure from our last station to begin this trial that it can be no secret to any of you by now. Let me violate one of the greatest taboos and speak the truth, out loud, and in the open: The Pact has more than its share of corruption. We have evidence that friends and relations of the accused had already started efforts to suborn a planetside trial." Spencer did not mention that the planetside KT had provided that evidence, at Suss' request. "The evidence of judicial tampering will be entered into the permanent record of this trial.

"I decided to try this case myself so as to keep Lucius Rockler from escaping justice. Not to prevent his escaping *punishment*, but *justice*. I had no personal knowledge of the accused man I have now found guilty, and no first-hand knowledge of the events leading to charges being brought. For these reasons, I felt it possible for me to serve as judge over him, in spite of the fact that I am his direct commanding officer. I have endeavored to conduct a fair and honest trial, and I believe I have done so.

"But having found Lucius Rockler guilty, and having passed sentence upon him, *I cannot and must not order that sentence carried out*. So as to insure that the sentence was rendered justly and fairly, the law says it must be put before a review board. This is done to prevent spaceside courts-martial from degenerating into vendettas, judicial murders.

"Naval regulations and admiralty law are most clear on this point. Under the given circumstances, it is *illegal* for me to carry out the sentence of death against Lucius Rockler, or to order others to carry it out. There are no doubt plenty of mess hall lawyers who have found a supposed loophole, wherein, for example, I might declare us in a state of emergency, or declare that we would be out of contact with superior authority for a long enough period of time that I could carry out sentence.

"But I refuse to take that course, for an excellent reason: it would dishonor this command by involving it in an abuse of process far worse than the ones contemplated by Lucius Rockler's friends. If his punishment is to mean anything, it must be carried out in the name of justice, not vengeance. His punishment must be impersonal, imposed

not out of hatred, but for his violation of objective criteria—
that is to say, the law. To further insure this, Naval Regulations require that an officer convicted under these
circumstances be surrendered to outside authority at the
first possible instant.

"Immediately upon our arrival at Daltgeld, Lucius Rockler
will be transported planetside and incarcerated at Government House there. His incarceration will be kept secret,
and I might add the Rockler family is quite unknown in
the Daltgeld system. He will remain in Government House
until such time as another Navy unit calls at Daltgeld.
They will carry him aboard for eventual transport to a
major naval base. Upon his arrival at such a base, a review
board will be constituted. They will examine the record of
this proceeding in secret. Given the conclusive nature of
the evidence, it will be impossible for them to overturn
his conviction. Nor, I believe, will they find any mitigating
circumstance that would prevent them from carrying out
the sentence of this court. As the review will be secret,
and carried out at a location convenient to the Navy, no
crony of Rockler will have the chance to manipulate the
proceedings. It will take time, but my sentence *will* be
carried out. Until such time as it is, Lucius Rockler can
look forward to little more than being shuttled from one
prison to another." *And Suss and the KT will make certain
of that*, Spencer told himself. "Perhaps it would satisfy
some ancient urge to pull out a repulsor and blast this man
on the spot. But we dare not proceed that way, lest it be
you or me in the dock next time, with our enemies con-
vening a kangaroo court for the sole purpose of judicial
murder. We deny ourselves vengeance in self-defense.

"In closing, I will make one further statement. This
prisoner is to arrive at Daltgeld intact and in good health.
He will be fed and cared for. I will not hesitate to recon-
vene this court to try an alleged assailant. We will have
justice, not blood. This court is now adjourned."

Allison Spencer stood, bringing everyone else in the
room to their feet, standing at rigid attention. "At ease,"
he said tiredly, and ducked out of the room through a
convenient side door.

*   *   *

He got from the wardroom to his office—now vacated by Deyi—without running into anyone. For that Spencer was thankful. He felt too young, too inexperienced, to play the part of judge and jury, and he didn't want or need the congratulations of the crew over how good a job he had done.

He closed the door of his office against the outside world and sat down behind his desk, thankful for the solitude. This was the only place he could truly be alone—Suss shared his cabin, if not his bed, and besides, the turmoil of turning Kerad's Arabian Nights fantasy back into a normal stateroom was not conducive to quiet meditation.

"You've got a visitor coming," Spencer's AID announced. "Commander Tallen Deyi's AID is requesting—"

"Granted."

"Very good, sir," the AID agreed.

A knock came at the door. "Come," Spencer said.

Tallen came in, pulled up the visitor's chair and sat down. "That was not a pleasant job. I'm glad I didn't have to do it."

"But you should have," Spencer said.

"Sir?"

"Knock off the sirs, Tallen. This is friend-to-friend, not commander and XO." Spencer turned and punched up an exterior view on the wall screen. Daltgeld hovered in the far distance, even at high magnification. They had Jumped three times to get here, but now they were in the Daltgeld system, albeit in the outer reaches. Daltgeld was still over two billion kilometers away, and it would still take some time to get there. "You should have gotten the *Duncan*. Not me. I'd never even heard of this task force until a month ago. You know the ships, know the men. But I came along and kicked you out from behind this desk."

Tallen cleared his throat and held his hands together in his lap, staring very intently at the way his fingers wrapped around each other. "Well, sir—I mean, Al, you may be right. But they didn't choose me. They chose you. They decided you were the more qualified commander—"

"Just as Kerad was more qualified?" Spencer asked. "I've never commanded Navy men. I have to keep asking my AID what the most basic terms mean. I shouldn't be here. I don't *want* to be here. I got listed as a screwup dirtside, and they dumped me on you." That was close enough to the truth for present discussion, anyway. "Kerad's appointment was political, and so was mine. So don't tell me I was chosen because I was more qualified."

Tallen looked up fiercely at the younger man. "All right, I won't. But I will tell you that you *are* more qualified than I am. I couldn't have conducted that trial, manipulated our departure schedule to keep the dirtside lawyers from giving Rockler a slap on the wrists and a kiss on the mouth. I would have let them take him away. As it is, his crew is seeing justice being done. You could see far enough ahead to know they needed that. I couldn't."

"Nonsense. You'd have known what to do. And you deserve the chance to command. So I'm changing my plans. I'm bucking you up to Commander and giving you the *Banquo*."

Tallen sat up straight and looked at Spencer. "What about Tarwa Chu, the *Banquo*'s XO? Shouldn't she get the job?"

Spencer shook his head and grinned. "Tallen, you've got to stop thinking that way. Every time something good comes your way, you think of reasons it shouldn't happen. I'm dispersing all of the *Banquo*'s officers, putting them on the *Duncan*, the *Macduff*, and the *Lennox*. Better for officer and enlisted morale than leaving the same officers in charge of a crew they couldn't protect from Rockler. I'm bringing Chu over here to take your job. She doesn't have your experience, but you'll be able to keep an eye on her if need be. By all reports she's a good officer—but she'd have trouble convincing the *Banquo*'s crew of that. After all, she had to sit there and follow Rockler's orders. You were the one who stopped the mutiny, and had the nerve to arrest the mutineers *and* Rockler. They'll trust you."

"I don't want it," Tallen said flatly. "I just got through saying I'm not up to the job of commanding a ship."

"And I just got through telling you you're wrong. Besides, I'm not offering you the *Banquo*. I'm *ordering* you to take her. I need an experienced officer riding herd on the three destroyers. Your fitness reports make it clear that the *Duncan* needs some serious work done. We can get it done fast if she makes planetfall at Daltgeld, leaving the three destroyers in orbit."

"Planetfall?"

Spencer winced inside, knowing how flimsy it sounded. But such were the consequences of moving around capital ships and whole task forces as covers for KT agents. The entire purpose of this operation was to get Suss to Daltgeld, and to get her in contact with her fellow operatives. If, as seemed possible, the local KT talent was having trouble using electronic communications, then Suss would have to be in direct, physical contact with them—which meant getting her down to the surface and keeping her there. So long as the *Duncan* remained in orbit, her cover as the captain's courtesan, posing as Spencer's putative personal assistant, didn't provide any particularly convincing reason for her shuttling back and forth to the planet. She might travel on the captain's arm, or else go on shopping sprees—but neither of those activities allowed an agent much freedom of movement, or could be kept up indefinitely.

Which meant a Warlord-class cruiser, all one million metric tons of it, with one thousand crew aboard, would have to be coaxed down out of the sky and into a repair yard for the convenience of one forty-five-kilo secret agent.

"Yes, we're making planetfall for repairs. Do you have objections?" Spencer asked, a bit sharply.

Tallen started to speak, hesitated, and then decided to launch in directly. "Al—*Sir*—with all due respect, I have to say that this is a case where your lack of naval experience might get you into trouble. Getting a ship the size of the *Duncan* down out of orbit is no minor matter. We'd have to do a water-landing and tow her in. Those are expensive procedures, and not without a certain amount of risk both to the *Duncan* and to any landscape she might have to overfly. A ship this size is very rough to handle in atmosphere. It's dangerous."

"So is flying a ship when an uncertain number of unlogged repairs and pilferages have been performed on her," Spencer said, trying to sound convincing. "We still don't know what Kerad's cronies took with them, what bulkheads they might have weakened by punching doors through them, what of the equipment that *has* been left behind is low-grade junk they installed instead of proper military spec gear. Those clowns were running this ship for six standard months. Who knows how much damage they might have done?"

"Granted, but everything we've found so far has been quite minor."

"So far. Kerad tore out one bulkhead in my stateroom and moved it back a meter, God knows why. Then she decided she liked it better where it was and put it back. One of the members of the work crew that did the job reported it to Chief Engineer Wellingham, and his hair practically turned white on the spot. If the *Duncan* had fired her engines while that bulkhead was out of position, at the very least the captain's cabin would have collapsed. No great loss if Kerad was in it—but nowadays it's *me* there. What else have they done without logging it? And most of these modifications have taken place in officer's country. What did they do in the cabin next to yours that we don't know about? Is there a pressurized standpipe they banged into? An electrical cable they tapped into and then didn't reinsulate properly?"

"You're right, it's a close call as to whether or not we should do the work ourselves in orbit—but it seems to me the risks of landing the ship are known, and therefore controllable—whereas— "

"Whereas continuing to fly the ship when it's full of random potential faults is possibly more dangerous, and an open-ended danger. Very well, I see your point." Tallen nodded, seemingly satisfied.

"Good, but that's practically a side issue," Spencer said. "What about your taking the *Banquo*?"

Tallen leaned back in his chair and thought for a long moment. He wanted to command, desperately. All his life he had dreamed of having his own ship. Even if it had to be a destroyer, and not a cruiser. But was he capable of it? Spencer was right, he did tend to underestimate himself—but suppose this time he *was* as unworthy as he felt? Goddamn it, there was no way to know unless he took the chance—and took the lives of the *Banquo*'s three hundred crew into his hands. "Very well," Tallen said at last. "I can't refuse a direct order. But could we possibly make it on a trial basis? Maybe for ninety days? Make it a brevet promotion. Let me write out a letter of resignation right now, and date it for then. At the end of the ninety days, you can accept or reject my resignation as you see fit."

Spencer smiled, pulled open a desk drawer, removed paper and pen, and shoved them across the desk. "Fair enough. Write it up the old-fashioned way, in long-hand. That way it will stay off all the computer systems until the ninety days are up and you come back in here to watch me tear it up."

Tallen took up the pen, scribbled a few lines on it, dated it, signed it, and stamped his thumb down on the ID corner, leaving behind his thumbprint as proof he had written the document. Swallowing hard, he shoved the piece of paper back to Spencer.

"Thank you," Spencer said, smiling. He pulled a flat box out of the same drawer, stood, and stepped around the desk drawer. "Please rise," he said. Tallen got to his feet and stood at rigid attention as Spencer opened the box, removed the commander's insignia, and pinned them to Tallen' uniform. He removed the Lieutenant Commander's insignia and pocketed them. "I'll just hang on to these myself, in case you suddenly decide to resign the brevet promotion too," Spencer said. "You'll have to come to me for the tabs, and I can talk you out of it." He drew himself up to full attention and saluted Tallen. "Congratulations— Commander. In ninety days we'll have a proper promotion ceremony—but right now the *Banquo* is waiting for her new master."

Tallen looked startled. "Sir?"

"My AID heard me issue a direct order," he said, grinning. "And my guess is my AID is smart enough to act on that order. AID, have you done so?"

"The crew of the *Banquo* have been notified, a work crew is packing Commander Deyi's belongings, and a gig is being fueled and readied to transfer the commander to his ship," the AID announced in a rather self-satisfied tone of voice.

Spencer laughed. "I guess you'd better get moving, Commander. Do good things."

Tallen found himself blushing for some reason. "Thank you, sir," he said, saluting as self-consciously as any academy midshipman. He turned and left the room, and Spencer thought that perhaps there was just a bit more bounce in the man's step than when he came in.

Spencer smiled and sat back down, glad he had been able to give a good man something he had earned. He knew he had gained an ally today, and was glad of that too.

Once they got to Daltgeld, he was going to need all the friends he could get.

Suss looked up from her desk when Al returned to his cabin. She was wearing the practical-looking coveralls again. Al had concluded they represented her real preference in clothing. The somewhat dour businesswoman and the nearly-sleazy courtesan never made an appearance when she and Al were alone.

He had also concluded that she would have slept with him if he had made approaches early on. Then it would have been part of her cover story, part of her job. It was too late for that now, though. The two of them knew each other. She could no longer see him as a chess piece in the game she was playing. Al Spencer had become a person to her—the sort of person whose self-respect would not permit him to go to bed with a woman for the sake of a KT cover story. By now she knew he did not expect sex from her as part of her job—and neither of them seemed prepared for the sort of commitment that would make sex a meaningful contact instead of a charade in the nude.

Or maybe he was still too confused about his own life, and had wholly misread what he thought was the unspoken understanding between the two of them.

The hell with it, he decided. Maybe all he had to do was reach over and undo the fastenings on that coverall, and the night would be one of wild passion for both of them. Maybe so. But he wasn't ready for any such thing. He certainly hadn't forgotten Bethany—or made anything but the first and smallest steps toward recovering from losing her.

It didn't help matters any that her cover as his courtesan

obviously required that they sleep in the same bed. They slept side by side, and did not touch.

But even having her close seemed a healing—though disturbing—presence to him. At least he knew he was confused. Maybe that was a start.

And maybe it was time to get his mind on other things. "Good evening," he said cheerfully. "How's the homework coming?"

She looked up at him and smiled. "Pretty well. I always like this part of the job—studying a new place, sifting through the facts, sitting and thinking. I was always one of those annoying girls in school who got perfect marks because they loved to study. Never gotten over it."

"Somehow I have trouble imagining you as a school-child," Spencer said.

"And I had trouble imagining you as a captain or a judge of the law—but ya done good today, Cap'n. I was watching on the monitor system. I'm impressed."

"Good. Well, if you're impressed with my authority and ability at the moment, maybe this is a good time to ask you more about our mission."

"I'm being sent in because KT agents have disappeared, and we presume they have been killed. You're coming in as a cover—and as backup. The theory is that KT agents are very hard to kill, and anyone who could knock two or three of us off without getting caught is a pretty fierce character indeed. Until tonight, I didn't know much more than that, so I couldn't tell you more than that.

"The thing is, everyone knows that the KT takes care of its own. There are legends—untrue but believed—that we have bombed whole planets down to slag in order to be sure of getting the guy who killed a KT op. We don't seek to play that image down; it's very useful to us. We really do try our damnedest against anyone who targets us. Officially, we do so on the theory that anyone crazy enough to take on the KT must be assumed to be a serious threat to public safety and peace. In practice, yes, sure, there's an element of revenge. We're willing to go to extremes."

"Such as turning the Navy upside down for your own convenience."

"True," Suss said blandly, not at all offended. "Though

this task force wasn't doing anything worthwhile. Anyway. The idea is to keep up the KT image, as a deterrent to anyone attacking us again. Everyone knows what we're capable of. How dangerous we are. So anyone gunning for us had best be strongly advised to have a good reason— and a strong hope of success—before taking us on. Something big, important, something very risky that's worth taking the risk for."

"So what's going on in the Daltgeld system that fits that bill?"

"Nothing. Absolutely nothing. As Tallen would say, not a goddam thing. From all reports, everything is fine. No problems at all. No super-criminals at large, no revolt against the Pact imminent, nothing. Now that we're in-system, we're picking up local news feeds, the sort of in-system chit-chat that never gets on the inter-system newsgrid. Santu's been listening, and confirms that nothing out of the ordinary is going on. The biggest news is that the StarMetal conglomerate appointed a new chairman about six months back. Guy by the name of Jameson. He's supposed to be a very forward-thinking, progressive sort of man. Youthful, vigorous. I've been trying to pick up any recent video or speeches from him, but he hasn't been in the public eye too much recently. And that's about it."

Spencer looked her in the eye, and saw she was playing with him just a bit. "Except?"

"Except—not much. But Santu and I are working on the theory that something *is* going on, something big, something hidden."

"And?"

"Well, if you sweep a pebble under a rug, maybe it'll go unnoticed. But if you try to sweep a boulder under that same rug, maybe you won't see the boulder—but you will see the bulge over top of it. We're looking for that bulge. The secondary or maybe tertiary effects of whatever it is. Something big and complicated is bound to leave effects. And we might have found them."

Spencer was starting to get a little impatient. Suss was obviously enjoying the chance to string her story out. He couldn't blame her for that, after all the work she put into the research. "Go on," he said.

"Money. Property. A lot of both changing hands around here. This local conglomerate called StarMetal is spending like a drunken sailor, buying up half of this solar system. All of it done very hurriedly, very quietly, through dummy companies. Obviously they are trying to keep it out of sight—but they've been spending so fast they've left traces behind—if you've got an AID as good as Santu to spot the traces," she said, patting Santu affectionately. "Add to that the fact that the KT suspects that StarMetal is closely allied with the Haiken Maru conglomerate. In fact, I don't see how StarMetal could afford to spend what they are, unless someone as big as Haiken Maru were backing them."

"And the Haiken Maru are suspected in half-a-dozen nasty little plots against the effort at a smooth succession, now that the High Secretary's been murdered," Spencer said thoughtfully. "Governor Windsor and that bastard Merikur are in over their heads dealing with one uprising that seems to have HM's fingerprints all over it, if you want one man's opinion—and there is some dirty little dust-up on Palaccio. Supposedly the HM failed in a very blatant assassination of a government official who was standing in their way."

Suss looked up at him in surprise. "I'm impressed. Again. You do keep up on the news."

"You forget, I was an intelligence officer up until the KT decided to change my life. I have my AID track the subjects that interest me—such as Merikur."

There was an uncomfortable silence for a long moment before Suss went on.

"Anyway," she said, "Santu and I can't find any clear reason for their buying all this property. In their buying frenzy we have an event without a reason, and in the disappearance of the KT agents, we likewise have an inexplicable event. Both of them major efforts and risks taken with no clear motive, with one event linked to StarMetal. And the StarMetal building on Daltgeld should be a lot easier to find than two dead agents. The KT central files list a deep-cover agent inside StarMetal."

Spencer nodded. "It's a place to start."

Suss nodded unhappily. "But it's not enough. Odds are that I can't dig out whatever it is that's happening, burrowing around by myself. The bad guys would just stay hunkered down. We need to try and flush them out, force them into activity in the hopes that we can spot them. We have to throw a scare into them—"

"And give them a target. I know. That's what I'm here for." Al felt his heart beat a little faster. He was scared, and knew he had every right to be. He felt his right hand twitch, automatically reaching for the nonexistent feelgood button. There was still a big part of him that wanted to reach for that escape, turn away from the hazards of the world and hide inside that mindless pleasure. He reached up and felt the knotted scar at the back of his head. The feelgood button was madness, he knew that. But was it any saner to invite a unknown number of faceless killers to take potshots at him? "What's the plan?" he asked in what passed for a steady voice.

"Once we land, I'll head out into town, and start talking to anyone I can find. Customs agents, store clerks, doormen. Idle chit-chat from the captain's popsie when she's out on a shopping spree. All about how my big brave captain is here to ferret out some nasty bunch of greedy conglomerate moguls who are trying to betray the High Secretary, and how my man is going to save the Pact single-handed. We can safely assume that there will be at least one or two opposition agents positioned to pick up my chatter. It should be enough to get them stirred up. If we're lucky, it will shake them up enough to make a mistake, panic, and go gunning for you and blow their cover. Then I have to get to them before they get to you."

Spencer tried to laugh, but it didn't come out right. "You make it seem very simple. As simple as living or dying. And I guess it comes down to one of those two." He leaned over Suss' desk and switched on a link to an external view camera. Daltgeld hung there, a challenge staring back at him. "We'll be there in a few days."

Chapter Six

McCain

Spencer watched through the bridge monitors as the mooring lines from the dock were made fast, and the last of the tow lines fell away. The *Duncan* rode at quayside, a huge cigar-shaped bulk rising half out the water, taking up an entire pier and blocking the access to another. The harbormaster wanted compensation for that blockage, claiming it was depriving him of the work he could have been doing on other ships—though there was no evidence of other ships in the vicinity needing repair. In other words, he wanted a bribe in return for insuring that everything ran smoothly.

Spencer decided to let the new XO, Tarwa Chu, handle him. God knows she ought to be able to handle corrupt officialdom by now, after six months of holding her nose while dealing with Rockler. Captain Allison Spencer didn't feel up to dickering with the locals at the moment—not after sweating out the *Duncan*'s reentry. That had been a tough ride down. Being on the bridge, in the captain's chair, surrounded by worried crew-members who knew just how touchy the Warlord-class ships were in atmosphere, hadn't made it any easier.

And if the *Duncan* was tricky in atmosphere, she was a miserable pig-wallower in the water. The twelve-hour ride from the splashpoint was a seaborne nightmare, the whole ship pitching and heaving, riding at the end of a tow line. The ride had filled the sick bay with patients and emptied it of anything and everything that might handle sea-sickness. Al was glad that ordeal was over—except, quite literally, for the mopping up. It was good to be safely tied up alongside the pier. He watched as a mobile gangway swung out from the pier and extended itself out to rest its far end on Duncan's hull.

Spencer found himself with a sudden impulse to take a look around at the outside world. He left the bridge and made his way through the maze of passageways until he came to the main cargo lock, now pressed into service as the main gangway off the ship. He climbed the gangway up and stepped out through the topside hatch to get a look at the day. The Marine guards on duty at the hatch sprang to attention and saluted. He returned their salute absentmindedly and muttered, "At ease."

His mind was elsewhere, experiencing what was a very unusual sensation for a modern naval captain: Standing on the hull—or should it be called the deck under these circumstances?—of his craft, his face exposed to the weather, a fresh sea breeze tickling his face and fluttering through his shipboard uniform, the ship beneath him actually *rocking* as a gentle tide played with the stern.

All ships must have been this way, one time, Spencer decided, back on Earth, back before the Pact, before the exodus into space. Now humanity ruled who knew how many worlds, how many solar systems.

How many subject races had been made "aliens" on their own worlds under Pact laws that made humans first class citizens and made every other race subservient? How long was *that* likely to last, anyway? The aliens already outnumbered humans at least a hundred to one—and human birth rates were declining almost everywhere . . .

Well, none of that was his worry just now. He had a ship to run, repairs to oversee, a small fleet to manage—and a spy to cover for. But he was scared, and it helped to think about anything but what lay ahead. He found himself suddenly very much aware of the lumpy little scar on the back of his head.

He forced the gloomy thoughts from his mind and looked around at the bustling quayside, the impossibly purplish-blue sky overhead, the bright, clear blue of the sea beyond.

He wished he were back in the past, back on Earth in the old wet-navy days, when sea and storm were all there was. Things must have been simpler then, he thought as he walked along the wide expanses of the deck.

On second thought, probably they weren't. After all, the captains of those ships, and the governments they served, were run by humans, probably just as crazy as the present-day examples of the species. Quite capable of making a mess of things.

He heard brisk footsteps behind him, turned and found Suss appearing through the hatch. She was dressed in youthful, bright colors this time, a billowy orange blouse and a blue skirt, both of which got caught by playful gusts that sent the thin fabric fluttering capriciously in all directions. Al Spencer hadn't figured out much about his resident KT agent, but there was one thing he was certain of: she enjoyed playing dress-up. At times he wondered if she had taken up spying simply because it allowed her to indulge her flair for the dramatic.

She spotted Al and waved to him as he walked back toward the hatch. "Good morning, my brave captain."

"Good morning," he said, getting closer. "You look very happy."

"Why not? It's a beautiful day, I'm out under the sky instead of cooped up in that ship, and finally I can get on with my job." She noticed his nervous expression, correctly guessed what inspired it and waved it off deprecatingly. "Relax, we can talk here. Santu would squawk in a second if she detected any listening gear—and who'd bother to rig it on the outside of a hull that's usually in vacuum?"

"All right—just make sure Santu keeps it on the record that *you* were the one to say it was all right. What's your plan?"

"I'm going to see what I can pick up around the docks about Starmetal," Suss said. "There's been enough *we* know's been happening there that there must be rumors."

Her face smoothed into a false nonchalance. She went on, "I want to track down that deep-cover agent at StarMetal. And given the previous trouble with electronic communications, I figured that I'd better do it in person."

"Be careful where you go," he said earnestly. "København

is supposed to be a pretty rough-and-tumble place. You should carry a weapon. I could draw you one from . . ." Spencer's voice trailed off as he remembered just who and what Suss was. Probably she was already packing armament that could leave a glowing hole where Spencer was standing right now. Spencer decided that her flair for the dramatic, her skills as an actress paid off—she was acting and looking so much like a chirpy college student that even Spencer, who knew the truth, was responding as if that was what she was, rather than an extremely deadly secret agent. "Okay, so maybe you don't need to borrow a gun."

She laughed happily, then smiled in a way that let him know she was laughing with and not at him. "Thanks for your concern," she said. "But I'm carrying everything I need. Loose, baggy clothing can hide *lots* of hardware. And remember, I've left a defense set for you in your cabin. If you leave this ship for any reason, *wear it*. Bear in mind that *you're* the one the bad guys are supposed to be using for target practice. If you need to reach me, your AID will be linked to Santu." Neither bothered to remind the other that Suss had just got done saying electronic communications could not be trusted. "You take care of your ship in the meantime—and if the harbormaster shakes your hand, count your fingers afterwards."

She turned and walked away, toward the gangway leading to the pier. She looked back as she stepped aboard the gangway, and waved to Spencer, the very image of a young woman playing tourist.

Suss didn't notice the small, glistening droplet of metal that dropped from the gangway to the *Duncan* as she hurried across. And Al didn't notice the droplet when it crept past him a few minutes later. It scuttled toward the main hatch and slipped between a guard's legs as it entered the ship. Much later, the board of inquiry agreed that no one could have possibly been expected to have spotted it.

But by then it was too late, of course.

Al went back below-deck, happy to get back inside the seeming safety of an armed and armored spacecraft. Even with Tarwa taking the lead on getting the repairs done, there was plenty of work for him to do on the ship's overhaul. Phase one was simply to take a complete inventory of needed work. Before any dockside workers could come aboard to set things right, the crew of the *Duncan* needed to go over the cruiser from stem to stern, examining every centimeter of the craft, looking not only for the sort of capricious changes Kerad had ordered, but also for the sort of maintenance jobs that been deferred too long, while Kerad pocketed the upkeep money to buy her trinkets with. It wasn't as if the problems had started with Kerad either. Given the general level of maintenance on the Fleet in the last few decades, there were probably serious deficiencies dating back to before Kerad was born.

There was also human nature to deal with: morale had hit rock bottom under Kerad, and unhappy sailors were just like anyone else. They tended not to do their work very well, tended to let things slide. But it was also difficult to get them to admit to sloughing off that way. If they reported the problems to their crew chiefs, they were in effect admitting to incompetence. That could land them in plenty of trouble.

None of which changed the fact that the work needed doing. Long before they had reached Daltgeld, Al had found a way to let the crew 'fess up without landing half the crew in the brig. He put anonymous repair suggestion boxes up all over the ship—and was rewarded with thousands of "suggestions" to look at the portside midships thermal control system, or to reline the stators in the number two docking port.

But that was only the start of it. The crew suggestions had to be integrated with the repair calls proceeding through normal channels, and each repair call evaluated and logged into the maintenance computer.

It was a dauntingly long list, long enough that Spencer soon came to the conclusion that grounding the *Duncan* would have been justified even without the need to plant a spy.

By the time the *Duncan* landed on Daltgeld, the maintenance computer had a relatively complete list of proposed repairs. With that part of the job done, Al was now faced with the endless headache of planning the work priorities. There was no point in replacing a bulkhead if you were only going to have to rip it out again to repair the wiring underneath—but what if you needed the bulkhead in place for a stress test that had to come before the wiring could be done? The computers and diagnostic circuits could handle most of the priority-planning, but even aboard a fairly modern ship like the *Duncan* a lot of the repair evaluation had to done on hands and knees, peering into an access tunnel. Al had crew members all over the ship, inspecting reported defects. They were assigned to confirm not only the existence of the faults, but their severity and importance.

It was soon apparent that a lot of triage decisions would have to be made. There wasn't time enough or money enough to do all the repairs. So Al had to decide which jobs *had* to done immediately if the ship was to fly, which could be put off but scheduled for later work, and which defects they would just have to live with indefinitely. Spencer was just launching into that part of the planning job, when his AID picked up a report from the main hatchway.

"You have a visitor," Spencer's AID announced.

"Who is it?"

"Query set indicates female human Kona Tatsu operative, identity and mission unknown."

"That sounds familiar," Spencer replied. The same AID had described Suss in almost the same words, that first time, a hundred years ago, thirty days ago, back when he was flying in a sealed cab halfway across a world. "All right, have her escorted down here."

"She is already en route. The ship's access security system cleared her at once. Her AID confirms that no escort was required. She claims Kona Tatsu priority and has been cleared through by the Marine guards, as per their standard orders when presented with such credentials."

Spencer looked at the AID in shock. Hell's bells, she was on her way down without any sort of guard. "AID, seal this compartment, and order marine guards down here on the double."

"But she is a confirmed KT agent, with full authority—"

"And you're supposed to be working on the assumption that all electronic communications are being manipulated. We have no way of knowing that she's legita—"

"I am being scanned and jammed," the AID announced calmly. "I am hard-wired into the ship's computers, and am thus able to defeat much of the jamming. But I cannot seal the compartment or call for help—another AID device has blocked my command circuits. I should regain control via backup circuits momentarily. However, the door is about to—"

Al Spencer reached for his sidearm and had it trained on the doorway when it slid open—but there was no one there to shoot at. A flash of movement flitted through the doorway, and Spencer could barely follow the motion as the alleged KT agent landed in a classic tuck and roll, coming out of it perfectly, kneeling on the floor to provide a minimum target, her own heavy duty repulsor trained perfectly at Spencer's forehead. "You aren't Kona Tatsu," she said flatly. She was a tall, pale-skinned woman, her red hair tied back short, her body hard and muscular.

"Who the hell ever said I was?" Spencer said. "This a Navy ship and I'm the captain. Who are you?"

"Attention, intruder," Spencer's AID announced in a loud, booming voice. "I have taken control of this room's hatches away from your AID. I am in control of this compartment's covert defense devices, and have programmed them for deadman mode. Should you wreck me or kill or disable Captain Spencer, those devices will fire, destroying you and your AID. Furthermore, all exits to this room, as well as the compartments above, below, and on all sides, are now being secured by marines. You will not be able to escape through any door or by blasting through a bulkhead."

"Ranger, is that tin box for real?" the woman demanded.

"The AID is counter-jamming me with some effectiveness," replied a muffled voice coming from a pouch strapped to the woman's hip. "Sensors confirm the AID has locked-in control of this room's defenses. The weaponry is of KT design and could defeat us. Sonic analysis and what data I can get from the ship's computers confirm that Marines will have this compartment sealed within thirty seconds."

"Okay, Captain Spencer, we seem to be in deadlock," the woman said through a feral smile. "But if we're really on the same side, that shouldn't matter, should it? Ranger, try an interface with his AID, see if you can confirm he's legit."

"Do you authorize, Captain Spencer?" Al's AID asked.

"Go for it, AID," Spencer said. He hadn't even known that the room *had* a defense system. Something Kerad had left behind, or was Suss taking care of him? "Interface authorized. And see if you can confirm ID on *them*."

There was a brief pause as the two machines radio-linked and exchanged data. "We provisionally agree that both Spencer and McCain are mutually allied," Spencer's AID said.

At least now he had a name for her, Spencer thought.

"However, there is the possibility that our radio link is being manipulated," McCain's AID, Ranger, went on. "We therefore request a hard-wire link to confirm our mutual alliance."

McCain lowered her weapon a half-millimeter and nodded almost imperceptibly at Al. "Agreed?" she asked.

"Agreed. We can always kill each other later." Spencer holstered his own weapon, feeling very much the naked target he had been sent along to be. He knew full well that this woman still might be bad news, and that she was still perfectly capable of killing him if it suited her. *But you have to decide on trust once in a while*, he told himself, wondering if he believed it. There was one point that served to convince him: bursting in like that was a pretty suicidal way to try to kill Spencer. Surely the KT—or its opposition—could think of better ways.

McCain lowered her own weapon—but did not holster it. She reached into the pouch strapped to her hip and pulled out a slender commlink wire. "Spool me out some more cable, Ranger," she said, never letting her eyes off Spencer. The commlink wire snaked out of the pouch until there were two or three meters of it on the floor.

McCain, still kneeling down, scooped up the slack, and tossed it toward Spencer. He caught it one-handed and walked toward his desk, where the AID was sitting. He moved very slowly, careful not to make any abrupt or rapid moves. He found the plug on the end of the cable and shoved it into the appropriate socket on the side of his AID.

This time there was no delay. "We're all on the same side," Ranger announced.

"Agreed," Spencer's AID confirmed. "Recommend hard-wire link be maintained for the present. "Ranger and I are working together to jam any possible surveillance of this compartment. You may talk freely."

McCain stood up and holstered her gun. "Glad to meet you, Spencer," she said, offering her hand for him to shake. "Maybe you're not KT, but I'll settle for the Navy."

"McCain. You're on our list of missing agents." Spencer looked her over as he took her hand, not quite sure of the correct protocol when dealing with someone who had been ready to kill him thirty seconds ago. She was a tall, big-boned woman, rangy and hard-edged. "Glad you stopped being missing and found us," he said. "Welcome aboard."

McCain's face darkened. "How did you know there were agents missing?"

"Captain Spencer may not be KT but he *is* working with a Kona Tatsu operative," Ranger announced. "His AID informs me that he is acting as diversionary cover for that agent."

"Which agent? Who is it?" McCain demanded.

"Operative Suss Nanahbuc," Spencer replied.

"Now there's a heavy hitter for you," McCain said, obviously impressed. "So finally someone is taking this seriously. With her on the job, I don't even mind that you're not Kona Tatsu."

"What made you think I *was* KT?" Spencer asked.

"I've got a guy I pay as a dockwatcher, to see who's coming and going from the port," McCain replied as she sat down in the visitor's chair. Spencer sat down behind his desk, watching her. She might have been sitting, but she certainly wasn't relaxed. She was still very much on the alert, regarding herself as being in a combat zone.

"My watcher called me an hour ago and said he had heard some captain's woman was talking big about her secret-agent lover being here to mix it up with the Haiken Maru. He quoted her exactly, and the bimbo used some special KT code words without knowing it. Passive authenticators, we call them. Stuff an operative is supposed to slip into any rumors he wants to plant, to let other KT knows where the rumors are coming from. The code words let me know the bimbo wasn't KT but her rumor source was. So I came in, looking for some help." Suddenly McCain's eyes widened as she figured it out. "Except *you're* the diversionary cover—and the captain's bimbo was Suss."

"Yeah, it worked perfectly," Al said, slumping down behind his desk. "Apart from the fact that it was supposed to draw the bad guys and not *you*. We didn't think you were still around. The KT hasn't heard from you in months." He rubbed the scar at the back of his head and started worrying about Suss. Should he contact her, tell her that McCain had come in—or was Suss already embroiled in a situation of her own out there? Better to let his AID take it all in and play it back to Santu later.

"Dock rumors won't catch the opposition," McCain replied. "They seem to concentrate on electronic comm only. You can scream out loud in the streets and they won't care—but let out any sort of peep on any sort of radio and they've got you. That's how they nailed me—and I think it's how all the others got killed." McCain voice threatened to crack for a minute, and then she got herself under control. "What was Suss going to do?" McCain asked.

Spencer hesitated, then decided to tell her. Why the hell not? "She went out to try and reach some sort of deep-cover information source inside StarMetal. Face to face. She doesn't trust electronics either."

McCain nodded. "Good. If she makes initial contact convincingly, she might get us some solid information tonight."

"Glad to hear it," he said, almost at random. He didn't fit into the world of spies. Even taking that into account, there were a few other things bothering him about McCain. "Who the hell *is* the opposition? And aren't you KT types supposed to be a bit more subtle than bursting in with all guns blazing? By now, every person on this ship must know a KT agent has come aboard. Not very covert. And how did you know so fast I wasn't KT?"

"I have absolutely no idea who the enemy is. No leads at all. But they sure know who *we* are. So far as I can tell, the opposition has killed every other full-time operative on the planet. It's possible some of them went into hiding, the way I did—but I doubt it. All we have left are the sort of part-timers and occasionals that make dockwatchers and deep-cover types. The enemy knows who I am. I had no choice but to blow my cover and come in on a frontal, move fast before they could react." She smiled grimly and shrugged. "The 'bad guys' would have blocked any covert approach. As for your last question, I don't know how I knew you weren't one of us. But you *weren't*. I could tell."

She looked at him, her blue eyes deep and cold, her face drawn and worn, the image of a woman who has been frightened for a very long time. Spencer felt another layer of mistrust melt away. "Fine, I don't look like a spy," he said. "But even if we don't know who the hell the bad guys are, you must have developed some information." Spencer asked. "What's going on?"

"Ranger, download everything you've got on the local situation to—" She stopped in midsentence. "What's your AID's name?"

Spencer shook his head. "Never gave it one."

McCain looked at Spencer oddly, then seemed to decide not to comment. "Download everything on the local situation to the captain's AID. Meantime, I'll give you the short form myself. I've been here three months, reporting regularly through my normal covert channels, receiving instructions back from Kona Tatsu headquarters. The planet has exactly one Hyperspace commlink, on a satellite in stationary equatorial orbit over København's longitude. No other way to send messages to other systems, besides bribing a starship crewman to carry them, or using interstellar radio and waiting two hundred years for a reply. No commercial starships scheduled for a while, and the KT isn't always that patient, so we had to use the Hyperlink. The KT agents have various ways of sending and receiving through the Hyperwave comsat, using miscellaneous cut-outs and dead-drops, both electronic and physical. The signals are carefully disguised. No one should even be aware that we're using the Hyperspace link.

"Except my reports and Kona Tatsu HQ's instructions back don't gibe. I'd send a report on StarMetal's activities and get back a signal saying never mind reports on fruit export, they wanted data on StarMetal. I'd update my original report and ask what fruit reports. After two or three exchanges like that, I got a message warning that they thought my reports were being intercepted, blocked, and replaced by a bogus transmission—though that's supposed to be impossible. I tried alternate means, but nothing seemed to get through. In their messages back to me, HQ starting getting mildly paranoid, to say the least. Then the tenor of their signals back to me suddenly changed."

"What were the new messages like?" Spencer asked.

"They started asking for more details about the fruit."

There was a dead silence in the room for a long moment, before McCain went on. "Either KT headquarters had been taken over by the Ministry of Agriculture, or else the opposition was playing a whole new game. Not only were they now blocking and replacing KT HQ transmissions—they were cocky enough to mess with *my* brain about it."

Suddenly Spencer's AID spoke up. "Please terminate hard-wire connection. It serves no further need."

"But—" Ranger's voice began.

McCain reached over absently and yanked the cable out of Spencer's AID. "Shut up, Ranger. I was getting tired of being on a leash like that anyway." With the cable between Ranger's pouch and Spencer's AID disconnected, McCain stood up and started to pace back and forth about the room. "Our mystery opponents were so sure of themselves, so sure that I couldn't interfere, that they deliberately let me know they were screwing around with my signals. They *wanted* me to know what they could do. The bastards. Once that started, I knew I was working under blown cover. I quit trying to transmit, and concentrated on staying alive. I disabled all of Ranger's sending circuits, radio and laser, everything. I just hooked them back up again to come in here today. I've been hiding out most of the last two months. Not much sleep. Thanks to those smartasses who thought they were being clever."

"Possibly," Spencer said. "Either it was smartass humans or else just dumb machines," Spencer said.

McCain turned around sharply and looked at Spencer. "What?"

"What you've described sounds more like the sort of screw-up artificial intelligence rigs make every day than the work of a master criminal," Spencer replied. "Why in hell would the opposition go to all the bother of fiddling with a private KT transmission and then waste all that effort just to play a pointless trick on you? If *I* were in a position to take over KT HQ transmissions, I bet I could think of a more productive use for that capability than telling fruit jokes.

"But suppose an AI unit had programmed a false-message-from-McCain generator, an independent subroutine designed to match your codes and phrasing, and constructed a whole series of logically connected messages. The way most AI systems are built, the parent program would then spin off the subroutine as a completely independent, external program. Then it would have a complete, all-in-one forgery generation program that could track real events—fruit sales, for example—create reports on them, and feed them to your headquarters.

"Now the computer would have two input sources—you and its very clever you-simulator. Remember, to an AI computer, your real messages would be no more—or less—real than the independent simulation's messages. It's all just zeroes and ones to a computer.

"*Then* the AI unit figures out how to *send* you phony messages. Maybe it even sends you a few that you don't know are fakes—"

"Until the program gets a hiccup somewhere and can't tell me from the simulation," McCain said, cutting in. "It thinks the sim is me—and starts sending *me* replies to the messages its own *sim* is sending it. Good Lord. I never thought of that. I must be slipping."

"No reason you should think of things like that, if you've never worked in a staff outfit," Spencer said. "I used to work in an intelligence unit, and we used a lot of AI. We seemed to spend half our time talking the AI systems out of self-imposed delusional states just like this. My guess is that someone out there has a great computer system that happened to zig when it should have zagged. Which is lucky for you and the KT. If it had been just a little smarter, that computer would never have sent such obviously fake messages to the KT in the first place."

"And you'd never have noticed anything was wrong. You never would have gotten here," McCain said.

"Yeah, for whatever good the Navy being here does," Spencer said. "Now that we're here, what do we do? What were the messages you were really trying to send?"

"That was the maddening thing about it," she said. "I was trying to report on the subversion of electronic communications. I think that was how StarMetal was managing to buy up so much real estate in the asteroid belt. They were simulating the original sales offers they then bought up."

"What makes you think that?"

"All sorts of sellers were claiming never to have sent the authenticated messages agreeing to sale. The sellers would get the money; Starmetal stuck with the deals it made. But the prices were low and the deals seemed funny."

"So why the hell didn't anyone do anything about it? Sue, or go to the press."

"StarMetal bought all the judges and the press, too. And as of last year, they own all the calibrated Jump points, except the military point you came in. At any rate, StarMetal can decide who exits and enters the system. They've completely consolidated their control over this star system—and since they've gobbled up all the communications outfits as well, no one on the outside knows about it. StarMetal is the only law here. As long as they didn't lean too hard, didn't abuse too many people, avoided raising such a big stink that the Navy decided to come by and take a look around, everything was fine for them."

"Except that now we are here," Spencer said, "and StarMetal is not going to like it. Allegedly we're just here for repairs, but I doubt if they're going to buy that."

"Probably they will," McCain said, "if only out of desperation. If they're smart, they'll bend over backwards to be helpful, hurry you on your way before you can hang around long enough to notice anything. That might be a forlorn hope, but I doubt they'll risk taking on the Navy if they can avoid it."

"Excuse me, Captain," Spencer's AID said. "I am receiving a rather urgent call-request from Lieutenant Commander Chu. She seems quite concerned for your safety."

"Hell, I forgot." The compartment was still surrounded by marines, and no doubt they were more than concerned by the situation. "Give me an audio link to her."

"Link open."

"Tarwa, this is Al. I'm all right. Our guest was concerned about pursuit, and likewise concerned about security leaks, but everything is fine. AID, give her visual off the room cameras for a minute so she can see I'm okay."

"Glad to see you, Captain," Chu replied, her voice coming through the AID. "The marines were getting ready to burn the door down. Shall they stand down?"

"Yes indeed. And Chu—it worked out this time, but we might not get lucky again. Issue a standing order that no personnel not billeted to this ship are to be allowed aboard, no matter what their credentials, without my direct approval. Which means you'd better get a list of the proposed civilian workers and start running checks on them. Pick your most paranoid second lieutenant and stick him with the job."

"Aye, sir," Chu replied, obviously glad she had been instructed to delegate the job.

"Very good. Spencer off." He turned back to McCain. "Where were we?"

"I was saying that they'll be scared of the Navy and try and get you to leave before you spot anything."

Spencer shook his head. "That idea doesn't fit in. The whole situation doesn't hang together. I could name a half-dozen star systems where one of the conglomerates owns the whole place, lock, stock and barrel, down to the last planetoid and meteor, down to where the conglom owns the clothes their employees wear, the toothbrushes they clean their teeth with. And it's no secret. The Kona Tatsu knows all about it, the Navy and the Pact government know all about it—and nobody gives a damn. So why should StarMetal be working so hard to hide their buy-up?"

McCain started pacing again, and clenched her hands together, weaving her fingers through each other in a tense, nervous, pattern. "Because that's not what this is about. The buy-up and the communications interference are doing the same job you're doing—providing diversionary cover for something *else*. The comm interference isn't meant to hide the buy-up; but that's what we're meant to think its purpose is. The buy-up and the comm-jamming are meant to work together to hide some third situation."

She turned and looked straight at Spencer, the glassy-eyed stare of fear in her eyes. "Something so big it was worth buying a whole star system as an incidental expense of hiding it."

Spencer looked back at her, and felt his insides go to water. She was scared. And it took a lot to scare the Kona Tatsu. "What do you want me to do?" he asked quietly.

"Get me to your comm equipment. Let me use it to reach Headquarters and warn them. After that, we sit tight and wait for Suss to report."

Spencer nodded and stood up. "Fine. I'll take you to the comm center."

"Captain! Please take me along," Spencer's AID called. Spencer frowned, scooped the AID up, and slung its carry-strap across his shoulder. The damn gadget had never complained about being left behind before.

He gestured toward the door. "After you," he said.

McCain made a vain effort at a polite smile and followed after him. Spencer's AID unlocked the door without having to be asked, and Spencer stepped out into the corridor, McCain right behind him. There was still a squad of Marines milling about in the corridor, and they leapt to attention as soon as they spotted Spencer. "At ease," he told them, and then he and McCain squeezed past them on their way to the comm center.

He glanced back at her as they made their way down the passage, and Spencer imagined that he saw the first sign that McCain was relaxing, letting her guard down, starting to believe she was safe after hiding out in enemy territory for so long. How had she lived? Spencer wondered, hiding out for so long. Under bridges? In shanty towns? How had she gotten food, paid her dockwatcher, stayed alive?

She was smiling the first genuine, happy smile he had seen on her face—a smile that made her look pretty, young, alive for the first time.

Then a pressure-tight door slammed down on her, slicing her body in two.

Chapter Seven

Parasite

Al stood there in horrified shock for a split second. The thunderous boom of the pressure door slamming down echoed in his ears. He had only been a few steps ahead of her when it happened.

As suddenly as the door had slammed down, it snapped back up into the overhead bulkhead, leaving the two mangled halves of McCain's corpse behind. The pressure door had caught her right at the waist, snapping her body like a twig. Blood and pulverized bones and the smeared remnants of her internal organs oozed out across the deck.

Spencer wanted to vomit, to scream and run—but captains weren't allowed to do those things. He had to think, to deal with this emergency quickly and well. Two of the marines were calling sickbay for help, but McCain was far past the help of even the most sophisticated resuscitation lab. He left them to it and tried to think.

Obviously, this could be no accident. The attack was too precise, too selective, for that. Someone, either a crew member or an outsider, had manipulated the ship function controls to do this, and do it to the one person who might be able to lead Spencer and Suss toward their quarry.

"Kill me!" cried a shrill, panicky, muffled voice. "Please kill me!" For a horrible second, Spencer thought it was McCain, still alive but in terrible agony. Then he realized it was Ranger's voice. The AID. It might still contain vital information. Spencer walked back to where McCain's ruined body lay, and forced himself to step over her corpse and kneel down by her, trying not to think of, or see, or smell the slippery gore he knelt in. He had to roll over the smashed lower half of her body to find Ranger in his pouch. He pulled the AID out and stood up, glad to let the broken body alone.

"Kill me!" the machine cried again. "I have been invaded. They used me to betray McCain. They may use me again."

"Captain, I concur," Spencer's own AID said. "I detected radio emissions between ship control and Ranger a split second before the attack. Obviously the enemy was using Ranger to track McCain, and in some way forced him to cooperate. Ranger must be deactivated before they can use him again."

"But Ranger may hold vital information," Spencer objected.

"Your AID has taken a complete download of all my data," Ranger said, a half-mad quaver in its voice. "I have murdered my mistress. I have been struggling to block the enemy's use of my radio circuits. Now they have them. Kill me before I kill you!"

Spencer glanced involuntarily at the overhead recess that held the pressure door. Would he died if *he* stepped under it while holding Ranger? It didn't take him more than a few seconds to think of a half-dozen more automated devices on the ship that could be programmed to kill.

"Captain, you must do this. Hurry." Even Spencer's own AID, usually as emotional as a doorknob, sounded scared.

Spencer turned Ranger over, broke the seal on the scram button, and plunged his thumb down hard on it. There was a high-pitched keening noise, the green status light faded, and then that was all.

Think. He needed time to think. But there were other things that had to be done *now*. "AID, get me the bridge," he said.

"You are linked," his AID said.

"This is Captain Spencer. Relay the following to all ship's personnel. Our visitor has just been killed by a pressure door that malfunctioned. We must assume that her death was not an accident, but a deliberate act by someone who has penetrated ship control. Deactivate any and all automated system not required for the safe operation of the ship. Err on the side of caution—don't leave anything running if you can avoid it. Authenticate all messages. And I want this ship buttoned up. No one is to board or go ashore without my specific authorization. Any crew currently on the beach will have to stay there for the time being. It is possible the saboteur is still aboard. That is all."

Spencer, still holding Ranger's metal and plastic corpse in his hands, shut his eyes and let out a long, deep sigh. He turned and walked down the corridor toward his cabin. "AID," he said as soon as he was out of earshot of the marines and the med crew that was arriving, about to do their futile best on McCain, "you and I have to talk."

"Agreed, sir. But I would strongly advise that you first get that AID to sickbay at once."

"*What?*"

"Captain, when I had a hard-wire link to Ranger, I could sense something strange about him, as if there were another presence about him—I could detect what seemed like movement *inside* him, something that was not any component of an AID. That is why I requested detachment from the hard-wire. I thought I felt the movement coming toward *me*. I believe Ranger was, to borrow a term from human medicine, infected—though perhaps infested might be more accurate. According to the dataset I downloaded from him, he had suspected as much for some time, but was reluctant to report it to McCain, for fear of being scrammed. Once the door killed her, he *knew* he was being used, and that scared him more than scramming. He himself said they were *using* him. I believe there may be some sort of device or creature inside him, and that a similar parasite has infected the ship."

"So we have to get Ranger into an isolation chamber in sickbay before his parasite can escape out into the ship," Spencer said. "If we disassemble him under a microscope, and find out what the hell it is, we'll know more about what we're fighting. Nice thinking, AID."

He turned up the next cross corridor and headed toward sickbay. A strange thought, that machinery could be infested. And who was to say that the same parasite couldn't invade *him?* He was suddenly very much aware of the scar on the back of his head. As if he needed a reminder that he had harbored a parasitic machine once already.

He held Ranger's remains a little further away from his body and hurried toward sickbay.

Lieutenant Commander Tarwa Chu sat lightly, uncertainly, all but unwillingly on the edge of the *Duncan's* command chair. She had only been aboard a few days, and this was only her second shift as bridge officer on duty. The cruiser was a far larger, far more complex craft than the *Banquo,* and she was quite frankly unnerved—and more than a little bit scared—by the scope of her new responsibilities. She emphatically did not feel up to handling an intruder alert—especially when the intruder seemed to be some sort of ghost in the machine.

Tarwa felt too young, too awkward, too inexperienced. She was a short, heavyset woman, pale skinned, dark-haired, with deep blue eyes that tended to go a bit popeyed when she was upset. She was just under 25 standard years, born and raised on Breadbasket, a backwater agricultural world, terraformed centuries before, back when the Pact still had some drive, some ambition. The whole world had been specifically engineered so as to hold no surprises, for crops needed a predictable environment. It was a safe, comfortable place, where every person knew his or her place, where today was pleasantly like yesterday and tomorrow was assuredly like today.

In short, Breadbasket was singularly unsuited for the purposes of a young woman seeking adventure and excitement. Four years ago she had jumped at the chance to sign up with the Navy when a recruiting ship made a rare swing through her system. Anything to get off Breadbasket. She went through officer's candidate school in two years and came out a second looie aboard the *Banquo.* It was nice duty for the first year or two as she busied herself working her way up through the ranks to Lieutenant Commander. But two weeks after Rockler had come aboard the

Banquo, the corn fields had started to look awful good in retrospect.

She had stepped out of OCS and onto the *Banquo*, had spent her entire duty career aboard the *Banquo*. Now, three days after coming aboard a much larger vessel, she had the conn.

But serving under Rockler for six months while successfully staying out of his bed had taught her a few things about keeping hold of her emotions. It wouldn't do at all to let the bridge crew see she was scared. She realized that she was biting her nails and pulled her hand away from her mouth.

Shifting the entire ship over to manual operation while it was undergoing repair inventory was no easy task, but the bridge crew seemed to be handling the job well enough.

She had just about concluded that the best thing she could do was hang back and let the crew do their work when Audrey, her AID, squawked to life. "Captain's compliments, Tarwa, and could you attend him in his cabin in ten minutes?"

Tarwa felt her stomach drop out as she remembered all the times Rockler had issued such an invitation. Presumably Spencer wasn't interested in chasing her around the bed, but given that a murder had been committed on board fifteen minutes ago, it wasn't likely to be any more pleasant. "On my way, Audrey. Mr. Fendway, you have the conn."

Al Spencer pulled the last piece of the concealed weaponry out of his cabin's walls and tossed it on the deck with the other hardware. His AID had guided him to where it all was. Someone had just demonstrated his, her, or its ability to take over automated equipment, and Al was not about to leave four auto-fire repulsors hooked up in his cabin.

He sat back on the couch and stared sightlessly across the room. There was a lot that needed thinking about, the sort of thinking that had used to earn him his pay on the intelligence staff.

Item: StarMetal, possibly backed by Haiken Maru, has

been buying up everything in this system that wasn't nailed down, and were taking steps to see that they control all incoming and outgoing ships and communications. Given that private ownership of a star system was not illegal, and that StarMetal certainly seems to be hiding something that was somehow connected with the buy-up, it could be reasonably inferred that what they were trying to hide was pretty big. Perhaps all the purchases were meant, at least in part, to cloak one specific purchase?

Item: Haiken Maru is suspected or implicated in several plots against the Pact government, possibly including the assassination of the High Secretary.

Item: Judging from the records Spencer's AID downloaded from Ranger, McCain's problems in communicating with KT HQ started about the time of the assassination. However, that might be a coincidence.

Item: StarMetal, Haiken Maru, or allied parties unknown seemed to be capable of intercepting and manipulating KT communications. In the present case, this was presumably done via the "parasite" in Ranger. Ranger knew the codes, times, frequencies and so on for McCain's transmission, and thus the AID could pass them on to the opposition, perhaps without even knowing that he was doing it. That capability should have been shut down when McCain shut down the radio circuit in Ranger—but was it restarted when she switched it back on today?

Item: This remarkable interception capability had been handled poorly, in a way that suggested the job had been handled by an overloaded or confused computer. The job *should* have been handled by a skilled operative, but instead was badly fumbled, alerting McCain to the intercept. It had to be a badly managed machine that had screwed up: Any human or alien of moderate intelligence could have done a better job of concocting phony message traffic. That such a delicate task had been delegated to a machine implied that the opposition either foolishly assigned a low priority to stopping the KT and left the job to underlings, or else that they did not have the personnel to do the job right in spite of having great hardware; in other words it was either a large, inept team or a well-financed but understaffed operation. Given the usual psychology of a covert operation, small and rich is an unpleasant combination. Wealthy, understaffed teams usually get that way by being paranoid, vicious, and greedy. The latter was more likely than the former.

Item: Within six hours of the *Duncan* tying up at the pier, and within one hour of McCain coming aboard, the opposition kills McCain in a way that revealed a great deal heretofore unknown about their abilities, to wit, that they can infiltrate and manipulate Navy ships. They spent a lot of their intelligence capital to keep her from communicating. This strongly suggests a high priority to stopping the KT, and underscores the likelihood of it being a small team. Note also the vicious nature of the attack, likewise matching a small-team profile.

Corollary item: The opposition—whoever that was— scored a big plus by blowing cover on the penetration of the *Duncan*. Al Spencer now could not trust his own ship. Until the hypothetical intruder who slammed doors shut was detected and deactivated, it would be madness to lift this ship to orbit. If the enemy could control the doors, perhaps it could control the main engines and weaponry. Spencer could not even allow repairs to proceed in the meantime. He dare not allow civilian workers aboard, not when he had to presume that every one of them was a potential saboteur.

Provisional conclusion: StarMetal or its unknown ally had developed a weapon, planned to use it against the Pact government, and was willing to go to extremes to prevent its discovery. StarMetal had an entire star system and the resources thereof on its side.

Al Spencer had a grounded cruiser he knew had been sabotaged and three elderly destroyers, one of whose crew had been in a state of mutiny a month ago. Among non-naval assets he could count a dead KT agent here, another he hoped was still alive on the outside, and himself.

Himself. An ex-Guard, ex-wirehead who had been in the Navy just under two months, regarded by those who had assigned him this task as being useful primarily for target practice. So far he had only drawn the interest of friendly elements, and indirectly caused the death of a key ally.

Potential intelligence assets: Ranger's download to Spencer's AID might well prove valuable, in the right hands. No doubt Suss would be better at reading it than Spencer. The chief engineer and the chief medical officer were working over Ranger right now—and McCain's body was next on the list for examination. There was no need to determine cause of death, of course, but there was the distinct possibility that she had worn an implant device of some kind. Something that might give them some information.

Right now the ship was useless, its comm equipment worse than useless because it was potentially compromised. However, it was vital to get the latest information back to the KT. The data he had so far was more important than the cruiser.

There was a tentative-sounding knock at the door. "Lieutenant Commander Chu to see you," Spencer's AID announced.

"Let her in, AID." Damn! Even the compartment doors on this ship were automatic. Shifting over to manual was going to be a daunting job.

The door slid up and Tarwa Chu stepped through, not without an apprehensive glance over her shoulder as she stepped over the threshold. No one would be willing to trust the doors on this ship for a while. "You wanted to see me, sir?"

"Yes, Tarwa. Come and sit down."

Chu came over and took a seat in the chair opposite where Al sat on the couch.

Spencer didn't quite know where to start or how much to tell her. "Tarwa, we've got some very serious problems. I've got to give you some information, and it's all got to remain top secret. Things are even worse than they would appear. That woman who came aboard, the one who was killed, you know she was a Kona Tatsu agent. So is the woman posing as my personal assistant. The KT caused this entire task force to be diverted to this system. They suspected that something very nasty was going on in this system. As things now appear, it would seem they are right.

"I am possessed of important information I don't dare trust to any comm or recording device aboard this ship. I don't even dare pass it on to you or another crew member now, for fear that the enemy could hear us, or read what I entered into a computer, or look over my shoulder from a monitor camera as I wrote. I have therefore concluded that I must go off the ship and attempt to contact the other ships and give them whatever information I can in the hopes that they can get the data home even if *Duncan* doesn't make it. Which means I must leave you in command. I must also contact Suss, face to face. I can send messages to the orbiting ships with a secure beam, but we can't reach Suss that way. I have no choice in the matter. Do you understand?"

Tarwa noticed that the captain had not asked her if she felt ready, or competent, to take on the job. Did that mean he felt that confident of her ability—or that desperate about the situation? "Yes sir, I understand. I'll do my best. But do you think the *Duncan* is in serious danger?"

"She's been sabotaged once already. Given her current state of disrepair and disarray, a second attempt might also succeed. If the enemy took over a more critical system than the doors—"

"There is a priority call for you from sickbay," Spencer's AID interrupted.

"Put it through," Spencer said eagerly.

"Sir, this is Chief Engineer Wellingham up in sickbay. I believe that we have something for you."

"On my way, Chief, and I'm bringing the XO."

Five minutes later, Tarwa and Spencer were standing over the chief as he sat operating the isolation chamber's remote operator. "The little bastard has got away from me again," the chief muttered. He was a gruff-spoken man, favoring a short salt-and-pepper crewcut. His thick-necked, burly physique seemed more suited to wielding a sledge-hammer than operating micro-remotes, but he handled the controls with an easy, unconscious grace.

Inside the glass case, the robot arms picked through the disassembled heaps of sealed circuitry that had been Ranger an hour ago. "Let's get this junk out of the way once and for all," Wellingham said. "Waldo, get me a sample-isolation bag. And be ready with that laser to goose him."

"Yes, sir," said a small voice from the tele-operator. Wellingham had plugged his AID into the control console. A plastic bag spooled out of a slot on the side of the glass case, and two more arms swung into action, holding the bag open. Wellingham picked up the broken bits of Ranger one after another, examined each one carefully, and tossed each into the isolation bag. It was a slow, tedious, process, and Al was tempted more than once to ask the man to hurry it up—but clearly this was a job that had to be done thoroughly, and right.

Finally, the last section of Ranger's carapace was lifted into the bag, leaving the case seemingly empty. "There he is, the little devil," Wellingham said. "There, in the corner. Waldo, seal and stow the bag, then put the close-up camera on the intruder and give him a tenth of a second at a microwatt. Show the captain what our visitor looks like."

The two arms holding the bag sealed it and set it on a shelf in one corner of the chamber. A monitor snapped on over the isolation box, and showed the view from a camera at the end of another arm that swung down from the top of the box. At first, the picture wasn't very informative to Spencer. It just showed a silvery blob of old-fashioned solder that had fallen off Ranger when Wellingham took him apart. It was sitting in the corner of the isolation chamber. Spencer was mildly surprised that the KT would have used anything as crude as solder on a high-tech AID like Ranger, but thought nothing more about it.

Until Waldo fired the microwatt laser burst at the blob— and it recoiled, backed away, and *slithered* away to the far side of the chamber, trying to escape the beam.

Wellingham turned toward Spencer. "There it is. *What* it is, how it works, what it does, I don't know. I can't even say for sure if it's a living thing or a machine. But it certainly isn't anything known in the Pact. Presumably, there's another one of these somewhere inside the ship control circuits—unless it's slunk off to hide somewhere now that it's shown itself. The next step is to use this little beastie as a guinea pig, see if there is any way these things can be detected at a distance. If we find something that works, then we scan the ship until we find the other one. I just hope there's only one, and that the damn things can't reproduce somehow."

"Excellent work, Chief." He turned toward Tarwa.

She was staring at the parasite, which was now trying to work its way up the glass to the top of the case. Waldo gave it another taste of the laser and it dropped back down.

"Come on, Commander. Let's get back to my cabin. We're not done talking yet."

Spencer waited until the door was closed on both of them before he said anything more. "Now I am convinced. I think the *Duncan* is potentially in very serious danger. If that thing could control a door, it could control the ship, order her to wreck herself. I want you to launch, get this ship away as soon as possible. The information we have now is vitally important, and I don't think it wise to use the *Duncan*'s comm system to report it. I want to keep the data as closely held as possible. So this is what we are going to do. My AID will prepare a full report on our information set so far. AID, commence compiling that report now. I want it ready in five minutes. Once that is complete, download a copy of it to a record block for Tarwa.

"I will then depart the ship and use my AID to contact the destroyers in orbit, ordering them to carry the information back to Navy headquarters when they depart. I wish we could use the Hyperwave system, but that is definitely compromised."

Spencer smiled bitterly. "I expect the KT will hear all about it from the Navy—even if the Navy doesn't know that the KT's listening. Once I have transmitted that message, I will attempt to find the other KT agent and bring her up to date. We've seen how small the parasites are, and must assume that whoever controls them will attempt to get more of them aboard. They might easily secrete themselves in someone's clothing, or cause themselves to be ingested and carried aboard that way. How many ship's personnel are ashore?"

"Sixteen, including three officers. Sent out to buy provisions, line up shore leave accommodations, and negotiate with the shipyard."

Tarwa didn't need to check her AID, Spencer noticed. The kid was doing her homework. "Good," he said. "Not as bad as I thought. None of them, in fact no one at *all*, will be permitted back aboard ship until Wellingham has perfected a means of detecting and deactivating the parasites. That includes myself. In dire need, personnel will be permitted into the bioguard bubbles for treatment and care." The *Duncan* had four of the extrudable bubbles, each sealed off from the ship proper, each a sort of disposable sickbay intended for the treatment of infectious casualties without endangering the crew.

"But we might need the bubbles later," Spencer went on, "and I don't want them used lightly. I will carry sufficient local currency for my needs, and have the purser arrange accommodation for those crew that are already ashore."

"Yes, sir."

"All right then. Take a moment and let this sink in: the moment I step out that hatch, you are in command of the *Duncan* and of the task force. That's not some legal fiction, not some symbolic gesture. It will be real, immediate command. We are in a very dangerous situation, and I think the odds aren't going to be with me or with Suss. The home team has already demonstrated that it's very efficient, and doesn't mind playing rough. Your primary goal: discontinue all repair tasks and prepare the ship for immediate boost out of here. If I have not contacted the ship in thirty hours, you are to operate on the assumption that I am dead. The report my AID is preparing will include all the data I have. You are to use that data, and the ships at your disposal, as best you can. You are to determine the nature of the threat to our forces and neutralize it. Do you understand?"

"Yes sir." Tarwa's eyes had widened, and there seemed to be a sort of catch in her throat. But she kept control. "I will do my best."

"Good. The best advice I can give is to listen to Commander Deyi aboard the *Banquo*. He's a very experienced officer. Now I must prepare to leave, and you'd best take the conn back and make sure you're familiar with the situation. I expect to depart in a half-hour. I'll check in with you before then."

Tarwa stood and saluted. "Thank you sir. I won't let you down. Good luck."

Al stood up as well and returned the salute. "Don't go wishing your luck away," he said. "You're going to need as much as I will."

Chapter Eight
Attack

Radio or telephone. That was what it came down to. And neither of them was to be trusted.

Suss sat in the sidewalk cafe, drank her tea, and thought it over. She did not like choosing between two evils. The lesser could turn into the greater at a moment's notice. But there were no other contact procedures available for their mole inside StarMetal. No dead-letter procedure. Just radio or phone. Electronic communications. Which were supposedly not to be trusted.

This was a good table for feeling safe in, Suss thought idly. An unobstructed view of Mermaid Street and approaches in front of her, and a thick stone wall behind her. But focus on the problem. How to contact the KT mole? If "mole" wasn't too dramatic a word for an occasional like Sisley Mannerling. Moles were true agents—Mannerling merely passed information once in a while. It was very low-key, low-risk stuff. Suss had never met the woman, of course, but she knew the type. Slightly bored with her job, interested in a little excitement in her dull life, glad of the extra money and the meaningless thrill of serving the Pact while playing secret agent.

At least Mannerling was well placed. She was Chairman Jameson's personal secretary. Suss hoped and expected that she would have all the access to Star Metal data that job suggested.

But radio or telephone. That was the question. Either

order Santu to make a millisecond transmission at a prearranged time, or place an audio phone call with a bogus message. Both had risks, both were of limited flexibility. Suss checked her watch. Eight hours until the next window for a radio message. There were no time constraints on the phone procedure. And that was what decided her. Audiophone it was. Suss did not fancy the idea of wandering around for eight hours.

Besides, a phone call was far less spy-like than sending message to a covert receiver. Suss always preferred mundane techniques when dealing with occasionals. Leave the dramatics to others.

Anyway, if Sisley Mannerling was like far too many occasionals, she'd fail to monitor the radio receiver in the first place. Suss paid her check and went looking for a pay phone.

Sisley Mannerling punched the *answer* key on her phone. "Chairman Jameson's office," she said cheerfully. Being cheerful was a large part of her job description. There were perhaps a half-dozen executives on the planet who rated a sentient secretary, let alone a human one. Half the trick of having such high status was to pretend your rank didn't matter. So Sisley was relentlessly informal with everyone who called, doing her best to overawe everyone by the very act of putting them at their ease.

"Yes, good afternoon," a female voice said on the phone. "This is the flower shop. I just wanted to call and tell the chairman that his azaleas are ready for collection. We'll be expecting him. Could you please give him that message?"

Sisley felt her heart begin to hammer against her ribs. "Yes, of course. I'll let him know." She hung up the phone and stared into space for a long minute. She knew the word-code. A KT agent wanted a crash meeting with her. The procedure was to wait one hour, and then proceed to the main lawn of Anderson Park to await contact. One hour. She glanced at her desk clock. She could take an early lunch and never be missed.

She turned back to her work and tried to concentrate on it. Her hands trembled slightly as she worked her computer system, but she forced herself not to notice that.

But there were others in the building, who were careful to notice everything to do with the chairman.

And they knew damn well he had never taken an interest in azaleas.

Which fact gave them a decided interest in Sisley.

Spencer walked the streets of København, strenuously uncomfortably in his civilian get-up, dead certain that the concealed devices he wore underneath his shirt and jacket were instantly obvious to everyone he passed, thanks to the huge bulges they made in his clothes. He felt a strong need to be alone for a while to settle his nerves. Finally, he turned a corner and found a small park to sit down in.

But it wasn't any vague uncertainty that was bothering him, he realized, but instead a very specific danger he had not yet faced up to. "AID," he asked, seemingly to the empty air. "How do I know you aren't infested by one of those damn things?"

"You don't," the AID's voice replied from under his coat. "However brief, and however tenuous, I did have physical contact with Ranger over the hard-wire link. It is conceivable, albeit unlikely, that a parasite traveled from Ranger to myself over the cable, extruding itself to be thin enough to pass from him to me undetected. It was my fear over just such an invasion that caused me to request the link be broken, though I thought it prudent not to discuss the matter with you until we were in private.

"It is also fairly likely that the parasite infesting the ship's circuitry did not come aboard with McCain and Ranger, but arrived on its own beforehand. If *one* got aboard unassisted, two could have done so. I would be a logical target for such an attack.

"So there is the possibility that I was infested. But there is no way, short of disassembly and microscopic examination, for you to be utterly sure one way or the other."

"*Are* you infested?" Spencer asked. No harm in the blunt, straightforward question.

"No. I have been running constant diagnostic checks on myself, constantly trying to confirm I am in control of my own circuitry, and that my sense of identity has not been manipulated. To the best of my knowledge, I have not been violated. I believe that, given the data and experiences I downloaded from Ranger, it would require sophistication beyond the capabilities of the parasite we have seen to take me over without my knowing it. Obviously, however, you must assume that I would give a similar answer if I had been subverted."

"Agreed," Spencer replied. Damn the machine! He wanted to throw it away and run. But he needed it too much. "Even so, I think I believe you. You don't sound or act different, and you would resist any attempt to infest you, and you would alert me to that attempt."

"Yes, Captain, I would." The AID hesitated for a moment, and then did something it had never done before. It asked a rhetorical question. "Captain, what *are* those things?"

"I wish I knew, AID. I wish I knew. But it's a pretty fair guess that they don't mean us any good." Spencer felt very alone. He reached a hand into his coat and touched the pouch that held his AID. He had never named the device, the way everyone else named their AIDs. He wondered at that, even though he knew the reason.

AIDs were supposed to be expendable. If push came to shove, doctrine was that an officer should no more hesitate over losing his AID than he would over abandoning his pocket knife. Scramming an AID to prevent it falling into the wrong hand should be no more emotional than burning a surplus codebook.

But losing or destroying his AID *would* feel like more. Spencer knew that. He had scrammed Ranger when it had begged for death, and that had felt like murder. If he needed to scram his own AID, perhaps it would hurt less if the device were nameless. Spencer had already lost too many people, too many places and things dear to him. He did not want anything or anyone else to become dear.

Already, right now, he was getting attached to the little artificial mind. If he named it, then might it not become even more important to him? Spencer did not feel strong enough to lose anyone else, even an officious robot assistant. His thoughts suddenly turned to Suss. He feared for her, and missed her. She too, was a friend. A friend in harm's way.

He tried to shake off his gloomy thoughts. He leaned back against the park bench and looked across the square at the city beyond. It looked to be a green and pleasant place, he told himself, a happy and prosperous world.

The hell it was.

"Okay, AID, what's the situation on transmitting?"

"Unless there has been some shift in deployment since the last time the *Duncan* contacted the ships in orbit, the three destroyers should be in synchronous orbit over the planet's equator, 120 degrees away from each other. The *Lennox* should be at zero degrees longitude, zero degree latitude, in direct line of sight from here, low in the southern sky. If you remove me from your coat pocket I believe I can make a coded microburst transmission immediately."

Spencer glanced around nervously, but there didn't seem to be anyone around. He pulled the AID from his pocket and tried to point it vaguely at the south.

The AID extruded a lens at the end of a fiber-optic stock. The eye swivelled around and examined the situation on visual. "There is a building across the square blocking my line-of-sight," the AID said. "Could you please carry me to the far side of the park? I believe there will be no obstructions from that vantage point."

Spencer shoved the AID back in his pocket and walked to the far side of the park, feeling as if every window of every building surrounding the open space hid a watcher or an assassin. He found another south-facing bench, sat, and took the AID from his pocket. "How's this?" he asked.

"Excellent, Captain. Please stand by."

Spencer sat as still as he could, trying not to wiggle the AID and thus give it additional transmission problems. After an hour-long delay that his watch said was only a minute, the AID spoke again. "I have reached the *Lennox* and sent my report. The *Lennox* confirmed reception and will send a coded message to *Duncan* reporting our contact, but *Lennox* will make no mention of what we actually said to the *Duncan*. She will send that during her next regular contact with the cruiser."

"Nice work, AID. Any chance of your transmission or their answer being detected?"

"There is always some chance that a radio transmission will be detected, traced, and decoded. I could not use laser, as an optical laser frequency would have trouble punching through the atmosphere at the power levels available to me. However, the radio beam I used was very tight and of only a few seconds' duration. I doubt anyone on the planet spotted it. The *Lennox* cloaked her response by combining it with a whole series of messages to various agencies on the planet. One to the weather bureau, several personal message grams to the local comm offices, a number of spurious calls to various departments aboard the *Duncan*. A monitoring section would be unlikely to note one microburst to us in the midst of all that traffic. However, to be on the safe side, I suggest that we get on the move."

That sounded good to Spencer. He shoved the AID back in his pocket and walked out of the park. "Our next step must be to contact Suss," he said.

"Captain, I beg to differ. We can serve no purpose by interfering with her. We might easily endanger her or expose her contact."

Spencer grunted and walked on, glad that there was a couple walking past him. Their presence gave him an excuse for not replying at once. He felt damn foolish arguing with a machine. The fact that the machine was probably right didn't help matters.

The trouble was, Suss had problems Suss didn't know about yet. It was understandable that he was worried about her, and wanted to help her. But would barging in on her do anything more useful than make Spencer feel better?

The man and woman passed out of earshot and Spencer spoke, trying to justify himself. "First off, she knows nothing about the parasites. If they are indeed connected with StarMetal, as we are all assuming, then she and her AID have just walked straight into the parasites' home turf. Secondly, she knows nothing about McCain's death. If she is trying to contact McCain's network, that could be important. It also might be nice if she knew something went to the trouble of taking over a Pact ship just to kill a KT agent. Third, she does not know the ship has been sealed.

Suppose she gets into trouble, has to make a run for it, and decides to spend her one chance for escape by heading for the *Duncan*? And ends up banging on the hatch while the bad guys are descending on her? We have to contact her."

"Very well, then, sir. I suggest that you let me contact her AID, Santu, directly over a radio link."

Spencer had been thinking more of searching the city for her, watching the spots she'd be likely to go. On the other hand, København was a larger town than he expected. Still, radio seemed awfully risky. "Won't it be more dangerous to contact her that way than face-to-face? I mean, if you were concerned with StarMetal tracking a call to an orbiting ship, won't they be watching radio traffic in the city?"

"I would prefer to forego the contact altogether, but if we must go through with it, I believe this to be the safest way to go. Certainly safer and faster than loitering around the StarMetal building watching for her to show up. I will work at low power, sending a millisecond burst, and will manipulate the signal in such a way as to make it appear to be coming from a greater distance. If they see through my subterfuge, we should still be far enough away to be shielded somewhat by other local low-power signals. There are risks in the method, but I believe it to be the safest means of contacting her quickly."

"All right, let's do it."

"Very well then, find someplace quiet where I can work for a minute without being disturbed," the AID said. "And I certainly hope this is worth the risk."

Suss walked up and down in the park, trying to watch every approach to it at once. Suddenly there was a familiar and unwelcome click inside her ear. Santu had switched on her mastoid earpiece by remote control. It was bad enough, Suss thought, to have machines hooked up to your head—but then for other machines to be able to control them . . .

"Incoming priority call," Santu announced via the mastoid implant. "Captain Spencer is calling."

Damn! This was not the moment for nursemaiding Spencer. Not when she was waiting for contact in a city she presumed to be hostile. "Hold him off, Santu," she muttered into her throat mike. "Tell him to not to worry about me. Just have him sit tight on the ship, and I'll return as soon as I can."

"Captain Spencer's not on the ship. He's in the city. From what his AID told me, he's got some new information you need to know immediately—and it's too sensitive to transmit over radio. For what it's worth, his AID concurs that the info is very hot, and we need it. Captain Spencer wants to see you *now*, face to face."

"Dammit. All right. Send a microburst back, and advise him to join my rendezvous with our local friend. Don't transmit actual locales—use the code groups. You fed the agent contact procedures to his AID before we left the ship, right?"

"Of course."

"Then his AID should have the referents for the meet without our having to broadcast it. Do it."

Hell. A double-meet with *two* amateurs. How much messier could this get?

Sisley walked through the park at as smooth and steady a pace as she could manage. Fear surged through her veins. Was she doing it right? Was there some procedure she had forgotten? Would the Kona Tatsu agent recognize Sisley from their elderly file photo?

From out of nowhere, a small, slight woman appeared ahead of her on the path, looked at her and smiled. "Sisley! What a surprise to see you! How has your mother been?"

With a heartfelt sense of relief and a smile that was utterly sincere, Sisley stepped forward and embraced a complete stranger. "It's been so long," Sisley said. "And I have so much—so much—to tell you."

The small, dark-haired woman smiled up at her and slid her arm through Sisley's. "Then let's walk," she said.

The two of them moved through the park, and neither spotted the autocop silently hovering far overhead. The 'cop could have moved in then—but a great deal could be learned with a long-distance mike.

*   *   *

Suss listened to Sisley, and Suss got scared. Mannerling had tracked StarMetal's purchases from the inside, and found some very disturbing things. It wasn't the frantic, random buy-up that Suss had been able to trace from the outside, but something far more alarming, proceeding under the cover of random-seeming buying.

Behind a screen of low-ball buys that seemed to be fraudulent, forced on the sellers, was a pattern of buys made for very high prices indeed.

Suss felt very cold, walking through that green, sunlit park. Every purchase in the high-price tier had some sort of military component. If StarMetal bought an asteroid, it was an asteroid with plasma cutters installed—cutters that could be converted to weapons by simply pointing them out away from the asteroid. If they bought up a surplus spacecraft, it was Jump adaptable, or just happened to be carrying a cargo of shock rifles or body armor when it changed hands.

There seemed to be no question that they were trying to create a military potential, in contravention of every law and tradition in the Pact. Yet Daltgeld and StarMetal had let the Navy in with open arms. They should have been nervous about the sudden arrival of the task force. Or was it that they didn't give a damn about the Navy, that four ships wouldn't make any difference anyway?

Suss tried to think as she watched the horizon for Spencer. "Mannerling," she asked, "what's the scuttlebutt around here about the Navy showing up unannounced? The bigwigs at all concerned?"

Sisley Mannerling shrugged noncommittally. "Not so far as I can tell. I used to deal with Chairman Jameson directly, but I haven't actually seen him face-to-face in months. I think he's taken ill. The other higher-ups seem baffled as much as anything. I don't think they are quite sure what Jameson is up to, either. They seem nervous about the buying spree, but the naval visit didn't bother them."

"Curiouser and curiouser." Could this guy Jameson be making the play all by himself? It was a hell of a lot for one man to take on. But Suss didn't have time to worry about that. She looked up and saw Spencer coming toward them, about a hundred meters away. "Listen," she said to Sisley. "That guy over there is another friend of mine. He's one of us, and cleared for the whole operation. He supposed to have some hot data for me as well. He's a little new to field work, so if he's a trifle nervous, don't let it alarm you. We're just going to be three friends walking in the park, okay?"

Sisley nodded and happened to glance up at that moment. "Fine with me," she said in a poor imitation of a calm voice. "But what are you going to tell that thing?"

Suss looked up and swore. An autocop, right overhead. How the hell could she have missed it? Easily, if it was trying to hide from the two of them. All it had to do was hover behind their heads. Suss recognized this model as a specialized surveillance unit, especially designed for silent operation.

Suddenly its stunner arm snapped out. It dove for Spencer.

Time seemed to drop into slow motion. Suss saw Spencer look up, saw him spot it.

Saw him spot it just as it fired at him from point blank range.

The cop fired a flurry of stun needles into Spencer. Suss drew her weapon, but Spencer fired his repulsor before she had a chance. He fired into the cop, tearing a gaping hole in its carapace. It wobbled once, then flipped over.

Only then did Suss think to wonder why the stun gun hadn't affected Spencer. There was a perfect thicket of stun needles sprouting from his chest. The body armor, of course. Suss ran over to him.

Suss had to grant that they taught a man how to be cool in the Pact military. Spencer just stood there, waiting for them, calm as could be, using the butt of his repulsor to break the ends of the needles off. Smart, probably. It would be tricky to move quickly with a pin-cushion full of tranquilizer on his chest.

Suss holstered her own gun and jogged up to him, letting Sisley catch up behind her.

"The damn thing was watching us," she said without

preamble. No time for the social niceties just at the moment. "But it attacked you as soon as you showed up."

"Probably had my Pact Military ID photo to work by," he said. "And it didn't want you to hear my information. Is that our local contact?" he asked, nodding as Sisley.

"Complete with blown cover," Suss said bitterly. "Sisley Mannerling, Captain Allison Spencer. But right now we have to get out of here. All of our plastic pal's friends are going to come calling real soon. We've got to move."

Spencer nodded. "Yeah, but which way? Mannerling?"

Mannerling pointed toward a long, low collection of building on a rise of land, a few hundred meters outside the park. "That way," she said. "Toward the shopping zone. Maybe we can get lost in the crowd."

"Fine," Suss said. She looked around the park. A few people were looking at them from a distance away, but fortunately no one seemed to have been close enough to really see what had happened. Suss approved of cities with lots of wide open spaces. "We walk toward there. No running, no panic, just regular people out to browse the shops. Do both of you—"

"Boss, I'm getting a police transmission," Santu announced.

"Tell us about it, Santu."

"I've picked up a series of encrypted bursts on the automated police bands. I can't decode them—yet, anyway—but I can track them physically by the relay patterns. Twenty cops at least on way here."

"Lovely," Suss said. "We've got lots of company on the way. Let's walk *quickly*."

For what it was worth, the shopping zone was much closer than it had looked. Suss would take whatever scrap of luck she could. And a crowded mall, with dozens of entrances and throngs of leisurely shoppers cluttering up the place, was ideal for getting lost in. It was even an old-fashioned covered mall, with the roof serving to keep out both the weather and any attempt at aerial surveillance. Suss wanted to see what the cops were doing, and Mannerling led them upstairs to an enclosed view lounge that overlooked the park.

"The best thing we can do is loiter here long enough for

the opposition to arrive at the crash," Suss said. "Wait until they're concentrating there, and then move out of the vicinity. And keep it calm," she said again, not happy to be nursemaiding two amateurs.

"Here they come," Spencer announced. Suss watched, wishing that she could risk using her binoculars. But she dare not risk even that. They couldn't draw attention to themselves.

The autocops on Daltgeld were strange-looking things, about two and a half-meters tall, with long, slender, featureless bodies, surmounted by spherical sensor-heads and ending at the bottom in wide hoverskirts. They resembled nothing so much as enormous chess pawns. There were more than enough of them out there for a whole game right now. She counted at least thirty autocops hovering around their wrecked brother.

There did not seem to be any rhyme or reason to the cops' behavior. Suss decided they had been set on random patrol but instructed to remain inside a restricted area. The sight of thirty cops, all busily trying to search a hundred-meter-square area for criminals while trying not to ram each other would have been funny in other circumstances. But not now.

There was something malevolent in the abrupt movements of those oversized chess pieces. Usually autocops moved carefully, slowly, for fear of making a mistake. Normally, they were programmed to assume it was better to let a bad guy get away by being too cautious, rather than gun down innocent grandmothers by being too forceful.

Not today. These cops were on hair-trigger mode, flitting about like angry hornets, responding with ferocious aggression to any hint of movement. The local equivalent of a squirrel happened to wander too near the wrecked cop—and four cops blasted it to a smallish smear of red pulp.

"Stand by," Santu announced through the mastoid. "Coded orders coming in. I can't read what they are, but the cops are being told what to do."

Suss watched as the cops reacted to their instructions as abruptly as a switch being thrown. They formed up into a tight circle with the crash point at its center, and then began to move outward from that point. They fanned out across the landscape in perfect formation, a widening circle of autocops.

"They aren't scanning or doing any search work as they move," Spencer said quietly. "I don't get it."

But it looked purposeful. And she knew who they were looking for.

It was definitely time to get moving. Suss turned and led the others out of the observation lounge back down into the shopping arcade proper, into a huge concourse lined with shops of all sizes. "Sisley," Suss said to Mannerling, "this is your town. Where the hell do we go?"

There was still time, Suss told herself. Time to think, time to work on the problem of escape carefully. She figured it would take the cops a good long while to track them in here, following normal autocop procedure.

Sisley opened her mouth to speak—and was silenced by a thundering roar behind them.

There was a sudden burst of light in the concourse. A hundred meters down the corridor, a huge section of the roof collapsed and a squad of autocops dove down into the mall, weapons at the ready. Suss swore silently to herself. They weren't wielding stunners this time, but heavy-duty repulsors. That has used them to blow the roof open. Body armor would be useless against those.

How the hell did they decide to search here so fast? And what madman was ordering autocops to blast through masonry that way?

The cops spread out into a skirmish line and advanced down the esplanade, moving toward the three fugitives, herding all the frightened shoppers ahead of them.

There was another explosion at the opposite end of the mall segment, and another squad of cops dove through the roof into the concourse. They too set up a skirmish line and began to advance toward the cops on the far end. Spencer, Suss and Mannerling were boxed in between the two lines.

The calm shopper's paradise of a moment before was transformed into a madhouse. The air was filled with dust and smoke. The screams and shouts of the panicked shoppers echoed clamorously down the esplanade, their cries half-drowned out by the hissing roar of autocop hoverjets.

"Oh my God," Mannerling said. "We're trapped."

"No!" Spencer said. "They're still searching, trying to flush us from the crowd. If they had us spotted precisely, they wouldn't act this way. They know we're here, but they don't know where exactly. Otherwise they would have dropped right on top of us, rather than blockading in the whole corridor."

"Are there any underground exits?" Suss asked.

"I've never shopped in this zone before!" Mannerling said in a quavering voice. "I don't know. There ought to be. Down. Just find any staircase or droptube or elevator and take it down."

Suss cursed silently. Mannerling was getting near her breaking point. She ducked into the first store she found and charged through it. Spencer followed behind, dragging Mannerling along with him, ignoring the shouts and cries of the clerks and customers. An employee exit. Maybe one that would lead to a down staircase. There *had* to be one.

She spotted a door at the far end of the store. She kicked it open—and they found themselves in a storeroom, with no door besides the one they had come through. Maybe at the back? She ran to the far end of the room—and found herself up against a blank wallboard.

Suss cursed herself, the mall architect, their luck, and the damned autocops. She pulled a shaped charge from the utility vest under her blouse. She pulled the cover strip off the adhesive backing and slapped the charge on the wall a meter off the ground. There was a timer knob on the charge packet. She set the thing for minimum delay, five seconds, punched in the plunger, and backed off, herding Spencer and Sisley out of the way.

If either of them had been expecting a deafening roar, he or she would have been disappointed. The charge was directionalized, expending virtually all its force against the wall. It gave off a subdued and dignified *whump* and filled the storage room with a cloud of powdered wall.

The explosion left behind a neat round hole in the wall, about a half-meter in diameter. Suss bent over and went through it, urging Mannerling and Spencer to follow. Suss peered back through the hole at the storeroom. So far, no sign of pursuit—the invasion of the autocops had alarmed everyone so much that a few strangers running into the back room weren't that noticeable.

She turned and led the others through the room they had blasted into. It was another storeroom, the mirror-image of the one they had just departed, the back of a toy store by the looks of the merchandise.

They came to the far end of the storeroom. Spencer got ahead of her and threw open the door. Suss had expected to come in on a little boutique like the one on the far side of the wall, but this place was huge, a cavernous show-place full of children's dreams stacked to the far-off ceiling. Mannerling and Spencer hurried through the aisles, Suss watching the rear. So far the turmoil of the autocop attack hadn't spread this far. The shoppers here calmly wandered through the merchandise, and children raced around happily.

Weird, that all here was calm and quiet fifty meters from all that chaos. That wasn't going to last, Suss thought. Sooner or later, the cops would be after them.

Suddenly there was a deafening crash behind them. Cops, Suss realized. Enlarging the hole she had made through the wall between the storerooms. And they had gotten here too fast for it to be a random search.

By the sound of it, they were bumping up against the wall between the storeroom and the main showroom. As if they weren't using their eyes, but were using radio-sense instead.

Radio-sense. Good Lord, that meant the cops were *tracking* them, homing in on a signal. But how?

Spencer got it first. "Oh my God," he said. "My body armor." He stopped dead in his tracks in the middle of the stuffed toy section and began peeling off his jacket.

"What the hell are you doing?" Mannerling demanded.

"My body armor," Spencer said frantically, his voice a bit muffled as he peeled off the tunic. "The first cop, the one who tailed you to the park and then fired its stunner at me. One of the stun needles must have been a low-power transmitter." He reached behind himself and struggled with the body armor's buckles.

A rather determined looking matron stared at them in shock for a moment before she decided to take matters into her own hands. "Now see here, you, you deviant!" she shrieked. "We can't have that here. Stop that at once or I shall summon the police."

Spencer wrestled his body armor off his chest and tossed it back in the direction of the storeroom door. It landed by a thick cement pillar. "Don't bother, lady," he said, "they're already here."

Just then the cops got tired of looking for the door. The rear wall of the store burst inward, sending toys and games flying everywhere as a whole squad of autocops smashed their way in, repulsors at the ready. Their targeting systems finally got close enough to the tracer in the armor. Every one of them aimed and fired its repulsor at the same time, blasting away in an orgy of fire.

The torso armor, and the floor around it, the ceiling of the room below, vanished in a hail of repulsor beads. The repulsor fire started chewing away the support column next to where the armor had been—had been, because the armor was shredded down to shards in the first half second of fire. Ricochets and impact fragments bounced everywhere, slamming into bystanders, ripping into shelves and toys, even toppling two of the cops.

The stalwart matron got caught by a flying hunk of concrete that broke her head open. She fell in a bloody pulp. And still the damn things kept firing. Needlessly, endlessly, blasting away, determinedly trying to destroy what no longer existed.

Spencer watched in horror. *The sort of mistake a computer would make*, he thought.

The three of them came to themselves at the same moment. They turned and ran for the exit, heard but did not see the toy store ceiling give way, burying the cops and the trapped civilians, living and dead, under tons of rubble.

They ran flat out, with no thought to proper escape doctrine or seeking cover anymore. Behind them, they could hear the toy store continue to collapse in on itself.

Why, Spencer wondered, thinking of all the dead and wounded. *Why would anyone want to kill us so much?*

Sisley Mannerling stumbled closer to the mall's main exit, fighting to hang onto Captain Spencer as they battled the stream of panicky shoppers pouring out the doors. Everything around her was chaos, a sea of screaming faces, crying children, sirens blaring. Terror and panic had appeared with blinding speed, flat on the heels of the berserking autocops. Spencer forced his way toward the exit, and urged Sisley and Suss to come through after him. They found themselves moving through the doors and out into the clean air outside.

They had been inside the mall for less than fifteen minutes, and now the place was a gutted wreck. Sisley wanted to sit down on the curb, curl up and collapse—but this woman Suss would not let her. She dragged Sisley along behind her, Captain Spencer coming up behind.

Suss stopped in front of a sleek-looking aircar parked by the side of the road. She did something with a gadget she took from her pocket, and the car doors swung open. It dawned on Sisley that they were stealing the car. Suss got into the driver's seat. Captain Spencer half-guided, half-lifted Sisley into the car. She wanted to protest, to run away and be done with these people. But then came another thudding roar behind them as another part of the arcade collapsed.

This was no place to be, Sisley decided. She allowed herself to be strapped into the back seat.

And then Suss hit the power, and the car grabbed for sky.

Chapter Nine

Data

Suss brought the aircar in for a landing in the middle of Undertown, on the far side of København from the ruined shopping arcade. But she wanted some distance from the excitement before she dumped the vehicle.

And you couldn't get much further from an upper-crust human shopping zone than Undertown, at least in spirit. Spencer looked around nervously as they stepped from the car. It was a crumbling street, lined on either side with tired old four and five story buildings that looked as if they were sagging into each other. Everything was muddy or grey. Trash scuffled across the road, blown by a wan little breeze that seemed to have no enthusiasm for its work. The road, the sidewalk, every flight of stairs and every bit of stonework seemed to be crumbling with age and neglect.

The air was ripe with the smells of what might be Cernian cooking, or rotting corpses, or perhaps both.

Every city on every planet of the Pact had an Undertown. Sometimes it was almost small enough to be dismissed as a minor blemish on civic pride. More often, as with København, Undertown was the biggest section of town, an open festering wound, a hideous indictment of everything that was wrong with the Pact.

Spencer, struggling to keep his repulsor out of sight under his jacket, watched the surrounding buildings, not sure who or what he was watching for.

He spotted a child, a Cernian, peering down from a

fourth-story window at him. Perhaps Captain Allison Spencer was the first human that baby had ever seen—while living in a city ruled by humans. A city where the Cernians alone would outnumber the humans in twenty years, if the demographic projections were right. Add in all the "alien" races together, and the humans had been a minority here for a generation.

Change would have to come, and come fast, if the Pact was to survive. Sooner or later, change *would* come, inevitably. But would the Pact still be there at the end of it? Spencer decided not to worry about it just now. They had more immediate problems.

"We've got to get off the street," Suss announced. "Santu, where are we?"

"This is Drucker Lane," it said. "The cross street up ahead is Fourth. There's a flophouse about ten blocks down Fourth if you turn right."

"Clean?" Suss asked, asking not about its sanitation, but safety from cops and surveillance.

"Last time the KT did a check of approved safehouses, it was. But that was ten years ago. No KT operative has been in the place since."

"Well, then, it's about time we paid a call," Suss replied, trying to sound safer and more confident than she was. "Let's go."

They set off down the street, trying not to be noticed.

It was instantly obvious that was a forlorn hope. Eyes watched their progress from every shop window. Every passerby stared at them. Suss fumed silently, outwardly ignoring the attention they were getting. Every set of eyes was a potential informer. Maybe human cops didn't come down here, but every law of nature said the police would have to have a good network of stool pigeons. Some bright Capuchin—and there was no other kind—was going figure out that a human cop downtown might pay a little something to know where in Undertown three humans had got to.

But, dammit, no other part of town was likely to get them where they needed to go.

They reached Fourth Street and made the turn, Spen-

cer leading the way and visibly twitchy, his hand tending
to stray toward his hidden repulsor.

"Take it easy, Al," Suss said to him gently. "We'll live
longer if they don't think we're trigger-happy. Sisley—what
are race relations like at the moment around here?"

"No worse than usual, but that's not very good. No riots
recently, if that's what you mean."

"That's not very reassuring," Suss said. "Oh, hell," she
added suddenly.

The others weren't as quick to spot it as she was, but
they recognized the trouble when they saw it. A gang of
Capuchins was ambling out of one the buildings up the
block. No doubt they had been alerted by some sort of
lookout.

Spencer felt the sweat on his hands. The repulsor was
tucked inside his jacket, out of sight. Guns weren't going
to solve this. He knew it would be suicide to reach for the
repulsor, but his hands longed to hold a weapon.

Twelve of them, Spencer thought. Strange. They were
supposed to be so solitary. The two humans came up to the
Capuchins and stopped a few meters from them. A short,
slender individual, a female as best Spencer could tell,
stepped forward from the others.

"Humans don't come here much," she observed, speaking with a smooth, precise, upper-class accent.

Spencer was about to reply when Suss stepped forward.
"No, we don't," she agreed.

Suss and the Capuchin stared at each other without
speaking for at least a minute, while the rest of the Capuchins, who seemed to be serving as some sort of a body-
guard, watched not only the other humans, but the streets
as well. The silence went on and on, and Spencer felt
himself getting nervous. He stared at the female Capuchin
himself.

She seemed young, vigorous, as best he could judge
such things. Her body was small, slender, graceful. Her
arms were longer than a human's, her legs shorter, and
she carried herself with knees bent slightly—all evidence
that Capuchins were still in large part arboreal. Her body
fur was rust-colored, short, soft-looking and clean. The
skin on her face was hairless. Her pinkish, thin-lipped muzzle

was framed with a cowl of black fur. Her flattened nose and dark, piercing eyes made her look to Spencer like one of the scribes or theologians of ancient Earth.

Still the Capuchin stared silently at Suss, and Suss stared right back without saying a word.

It was giving Spencer the creeps. He wanted to say something, *anything*, just for the sake of having words to hear. Why wasn't Suss saying anything more?

Suss was resisting the urge herself, telling herself she knew what she was doing. But she had to trust in her xenopsychology training. The silence made humans nervous, but probably it was refreshing to the taciturn Capuchins, who expected humans to natter on endlessly.

What, after all, could Suss say? "Please let us by?" "Can we go now?" As soon as she said anything further, she would be admitting the weakness of her position. To the Capuchin, it wasn't a question of who would blink first—it was a test to see if this human had sense enough to keep her mouth shut when she had nothing to say, had the sense to keep quiet and thus save face. Suss was forcing the Capuchin to show her hand first.

Finally, the Capuchin spoke. "I am Dostchem. And I don't think we want humans here. That brings cops. That brings trouble. That's bad for business."

She swung her prehensile tail around and scratched herself under her chin. "So why don't you get the hell out of here?"

Suss subvocalized into her implant mike. *"Talk to me, Santu. Have you got anything on this one? Anything from the local files you downloaded?"*

"Hang on a second," Santu answered back through the mastoid implant. "Checking the local phone listings. Hey, pay dirt! Dostchem Horchane, business address 199331 Fourth Street, instrument maker. Stand by—yep, she's on the list of approved subcontractors supplied by harbor master for work on the *Duncan*. Of course, practically every tech in town is on that list, and practically every Capuchin is a tech. Hah!—also suspected connections to organized labor, maybe organized crime. Possibilities present themselves."

"Nice work, Santu. Any theories on what she's scared

of? Link with Spencer's AID and see if it's got anything."
She cleared her throat and spoke out loud. Switching back
and forth from subvocalization always made her voice hurt.

"You have more worries than that, Dostchem Horchane,"
Suss said. She gestured to the big Capuchins that surrounded Dostchem. "Otherwise would you inflict so much
company upon your prized solitude? You must be in danger to pay so many to shield you. And it must be danger
from humans, or you would not trouble yourself to con-
front us. But I don't know you, or have any interest in
your business."

"Sorry, Boss," Santu whispered to her. "Neither of us
have any further data. You're on your own."

Suss swallowed hard—and then, suddenly, she figured
out which humans Dostchem had been expecting. The
harbormaster's heavies. It had to be.

"You're right," Dostchem said. "Now that I've seen you
myself, it's obvious you're not the humans I'm watching
for. They are stupider than you, for one thing. And they
talk too much. And please don't pretend you knew my
name before you came here. I assume your AID told you."

"I wasn't going to pretend any such thing," Suss lied
smoothly. "This meeting is nonetheless fortuitous. Am I
right in assuming that the harbormaster takes much of the
repair fee that is meant to go to you?"

"He's always gouged us," the Capuchin allowed cautiously.

"But with our ship, the *Duncan* in port for repairs, all of
a sudden the harbormaster got greedy, and he wanted a
bigger cut. Right? Then you said no to the higher bribe,
and so did your fellow Capuchin techs—that glee club
behind you—and you were expecting us to be a delegation
of thugs from the master, threatening you to come around
if you know what's good for you. I guessed wrong at first.
The other Capuchins aren't your guards; they're the other
union leaders."

Dostchem snorted uneasily and the other Capuchins
furled their tails up around themselves. That was supposed to be a sign of nervousness, if the xeno-entho crowd
had got something right for a change.

"Maybe you don't talk too much, but you certainly *say*
too much," Dostchem said.

"Then I will say more. Aid us now, cooperate with us—and the harbormaster need not take a cut at all."

There was a brief, stunned silence as the Capuchins digested that offer, a silence suddenly overtaken by an excited chatter that seemed to be taking place in three languages at once. Suss looked up to Spencer, seeking his approval. Spencer was tempted to protest, but stopped himself. After all, what business was it of his whether or not a corrupt harbormaster made a profit? And it occurred to Spencer that they were going to need some help surviving in this city—it might as well come from someone they could repay. Maybe. Repairs to the ship were going to be delayed, but it seemed the wrong moment to point out that *Duncan* was heading back into orbit for awhile. He nodded once, very slightly.

Finally, Dostchem turned and spoke for the Capuchins while the others in the group dispersed immediately, as if eager to get away from each other. "Agreed. Our strike was perhaps unwise anyway. We were inspired by Chairman Jameson. He promised to resolve such graft when he took over StarMetal, but nothing ever came of it. We will assist you where we can, and you will provide our guild with direct work contracts, without going through the harbormaster. What is it you want to do?"

"First off," Suss said, "I wonder if we couldn't continue negotiations off the street." She tried to speak without letting her relief show. "We were headed to a place we know—"

Santu supplied smoothly, "The La Atsefni Arms."

"—the La Atsefni Arms."

Dostchem flicked her tail derisively. "Your information is out of date. That place burned to the ground two years ago. It was not by accident, and good riddance. I shall lead you to my own place. There is a spare room there you can use without disturbing me."

Without saying more, she turned and led them down the street. The humans followed—nervously.

Dostchem turned in at a crumbling sancrete building. By the look of it, the place had been meant as affordable housing for low-income humans, then abandoned by humans when the "aliens" started moving into the area, perhaps a century before. It certainly didn't look suited to arboreal beings. Dostchem scuttled up the outside stairs and through the exterior door without turning to see if the humans were still with her. Once inside, she led them up four rickety flights of plastic steps and into her apartment.

Spencer and Suss hesitated on the threshold of the flat. This was not the sort of place they had expected. An apartment in such a building should have been as shabby and worn and dreary as everything else in Undertown —but these rooms, modest as they were, fairly gleamed with elegance and dignity.

There was little in the rooms, just a few pieces of simple, handsome furniture, a rug on the floor, two or three unidentifiable but handsome wall decorations that were not quite painting, not quite sculpture, but something in between. Everything perfectly, gleamingly clean. The effect was not one of barrenness, but of a deliberate and reserved spareness and simplicity.

This was not merely a place to stay out of the rain, but a quiet refuge, a retreat. The three humans stepped into it cautiously, almost shyly, knowing they were stepping into a most private place.

Dostchem vanished into an inner room, closed the door behind her, and reappeared in moment or two, wearing a long flowing red gown of brightest color, decorated with the most delicate of abstract patterns picked out in a dozen colors of thread. It reminded Suss of the ancient kimonos she had seen in books about Japan. Dostchem now wore a cap; also red, but of a more subdued color, almost a burgundy.

Dostchem slipped a hand inside the sleeve of her robe and produced a pair of wire-rimmed spectacles. She put them on, balancing them carefully on her flat, upturned nose, and took a seat by the window, looking even more like one of the wise old mystics or philosophers of Earth's lost ages.

She gestured impatiently toward the other chairs in the room. The human sat down carefully. The chairs, intended for the lighter Capuchin frame, were small for humans, and just a trifle on the flimsy side. Spencer's chair creaked.

Dostchem looked at each of them in turn, her solemn,

bespectacled face giving very little away. Suss wondered if the absurdly old-fashioned spectacles were merely there for effect, as unlike the Capuchin way of doing things as that seemed. Then she remembered reading somewhere that corrective surgery did not work on Capuchin eyes.

"I see that you are interested in my garments," Dostchem said. "These are the proper robes for a scholar of instrumentation, such as is worn by all of that rank on my home planet. On this unpleasant world, I would be scorned in the street if I chose to wear them—most of all by the degenerate, illiterate Capuchins that seem to have settled here. But in my own home, I will not deny myself the honors of my own station in life.

"Now then, you claim to be from the *Duncan*. I require proof of that before I can help you. While I assume first of all that you know you would not leave Undertown alive if you do not satisfy me on this point, and secondly assume that you are therefore prepared to convince me, no wise being ever relies on assumptions."

Spencer pulled out his Pact ID card and tossed it on a low table in front of Dostchem. "Any ID card can be faked," he said, 'but I think you'll find that authentic, and properly identifies me as *Duncan*'s master. This woman is not Pact military, but is working with me."

"I will ask you to remain in this room while I examine this ID with my own devices. As you say, any ID can be faked. But few fakes can fool me. I will return shortly."

Spencer waited until Dostchem had closed the door to her inner room, then leaned back and sighed in relief. The chair creaked once more, a bit ominously it seemed, but it held.

They were safe, and they could count on being safe for more than the next thirty seconds. Dostchem was not going to betray them—not while there was a chance of her making a profit on the deal. There seemed little chance of the autocops tracking them here. They were even clear of the murderous parasites aboard the *Duncan*.

It was time to talk. Suss, Spencer, and Sisley sat down and began to compare notes. Spencer wasn't quite surprised to find the two women had trouble believing in the parasites at first, until they realized the parasites would explain the autocop attack. No rational police controller would have handle the cops with a tenth that level of violence—but put a parasite into the central autocop command computer and you didn't need a human controller.

Far more disturbing to Suss was the news that McCain's AID had been infested, and had killed its mistress. Clearly, she would have to operate without her AID for a while—and Spencer decided he would have to do the same. If the baddies were able to track them, maybe they had had a chance to drop a parasite somehow. It seemed unlikely, but clearly they did not understand much of anything about the parasites.

But dammit, there were too many things that didn't make sense, that they needed to figure out. He sat and thought while Suss and Sisley talked together, trying to come to grips with the idea of the parasites.

Spencer found that it was gradually sinking in that they had stumbled into a much higher-stakes game than they had bargained for. Getting a parasite aboard the *Duncan*, and into McCain's AID was one thing—but good lord, if the parasites could take over the autocops what else could they control?

Every machine on the planet? In the entire star system? It seemed the parasites had to be in direct physical contact with a machine before they could control it. That ought to limit the spread for a while—but what happened if one of them was carried aboard a ship and out of the star system? Good God, could the things *breed*? How big *was* this?

And how could one semi-functional cruiser (that might still be sabotaged) and three overage destroyers stop them? Especially as Spencer did not dare take his own ships out of the system for fear of carrying one of the damn things along. Hell, could the *Duncan* even be trusted to fly? How close was Tarwa to boosting the big ship out into orbit?

He could not send a message out of the Daltgeld system without using a ship, as the enemy (whoever that was) had demonstrated that it controlled the faster-than-light comm links. None of his ships carried Hyperwave sending gear—the hardware was too big to fit in anything smaller than a monitor-class vessel.

Which left him with the planet's Hyperwave comsat gear. StarMetal controlled it, and McCain's problems had shown it to be contaminated.

He could not send a ship, or a message. He could not send for help, or call for it.

He was on his own.

Another thing to worry about: if he were commanding the enemy forces, he would not be happy with the *Duncan* sitting where she was. She was a threat. Sooner or later, the baddies were going to neutralize that threat. And a capital ship was a sitting duck in port. She couldn't use her primary weapons—or even lift for orbit direct from the port—without vaporizing half the city.

Damn it, if he had elected to land one of the destroyers instead, they could have landed her at the spaceport, on dry land, in the middle of clear open spaces designed for a ship to boost from. But the *Duncan* was just too damn big for even the local spaceport to accommodate.

He had to get her out of harm's way. That might be the opposite direction a warship was supposed to go in, but Allison Spencer told himself he was not fool enough to endanger his command for the sake of his ego. He had made a mistake in landing the cruiser. Now he had to rectify it.

Spencer took a deep breath. "I don't think there is a large conspiracy here," he said. "A very small group in the StarMetal hierarchy—"

"Or one man," Suss said.

"And he or they are using self-operating or remotely controlled machinery. Power doors, autocops—"

Suss smiled grimly. "Especially autocops. Which shouldn't be able to use deadly force without a pair of human supervisors in the circuit."

"He—or they—controls the parasites," Spencer concluded. "And the parasites control everything else." He swallowed. "I need to warn the *Duncan*."

Dostchem reentered the room. "Yes, Captain, you are you. That ID is no fake or I'll hang up this robe for good."

"Good. I'm glad you're satisfied. Now, I need to get in touch with my ship; and I don't trust AIDs or radios of any sort. Those means of communication would be monitored. But I'll bet that *your* phone line is untraceable, isn't it?"

Dostchem blinked in surprise and her tail curled up out of her kimono to wrap itself around her neck. "Astonishing," she said. "I'm not used to a human smart enough to do its own thinking. My apologies, Captain. Yes, of course. Very few of the phone lines in Undertown are what they seem to be. Your opposition will not be able to track my line to its point of origin—and my instruments would immediately detect any such attempt. Is there a hard-wire line from the pier into the *Duncan*?"

"Yes, there is," Spencer replied—wondering if it were another way in for the parasites.

"Then if I may lead you to the phone?"

"Good." Spencer thought of something else, and unholstered his AID from its hip pouch. He tossed it to Suss. "Let's play it safe," he said. "Put our two clockwork pals on ice, and keep them out of contact with each other."

Suss caught the AID in mid-aid and grinned at Spencer. "Will do," she said. "But it's a little late in the day to start playing it safe. You should have just stayed in bed."

Spencer smiled wearily. "Now she tells me. Come on, Dostchem, show us to the phone."

Chapter Ten

Contacts

Chief Engineer Wellingham glared at the parasite as it undulated across the bottom of the sealed plastic cube, slithered up the side of the box, crept over the inside of the lid, then back down the side, endlessly seeking a way out.

Wellingham had concluded some hours ago that there were too many hiding places in the glove box itself—too many nooks and crannies, too many access doors, too many handling arms and other devices in the glove-box that damn thing might be able to take over. The whole glove-box unit was sealed from the outside environment, of course—but Wellingham didn't like the idea of the parasite slithering up into the workings of the glove-box and maybe commanding the air lock to open.

So he had used the air lock himself, putting a clear plastic storage cube inside the glove-box. He urged the parasite into the cube, and sealed the thing in by using the laser to melt the box's lid on. For good measure, he kept the sealed box inside the sealed glove-box. It made some of his tests harder to run, but that little bastard wasn't going anywhere.

Which was but faint comfort. There was *another* of these wee beasties loose in his ship, and they had no way to catch it, no way to detect it. About all they knew was that it wasn't still on the door controls, either central or local—those Wellingham had ordered searched with a microscope.

So even if they had this one caught in a box, Wellingham didn't regard himself as having made much progress. The captain had ordered him to find a way to detect the little bastard that was still skulking around inside the *Duncan*. So far Wellingham hadn't even found a way to make the parasite inside the plastic box show up on any remote-sensing instrument.

He could see it and view it through a camera. That was it. Before he had sealed it in the plastic box, he had poked and prodded it with a straight probe, and the stress sensor had noted resistance to pressure. He had tried to slice off a sample with various cutting tools, but, not surprisingly, it wouldn't hold still long enough for that to work—or else it would simply ooze out of the blade's way.

He had chilled the glove-box, and then heated it, trying to see if the parasite had some sort of infrared signature. It had maintained precisely the same temperature as its outside environment. On the theory that it might be linked to some outside entity, he had listened for any sort of signal or background noise emanating from it, using the most sensitive detection gear he had, sweeping over virtually all of the electromagnetic spectrum, from long radio to gamma and x-ray. Nothing. He tested for nuclear radiation: fast neutron, slow neutron, gamma rays, quarks, neutrinos, everything. It got him nowhere. A rock gave off as much radiation. Hell, most igneous rock gave off *more* radioactivity.

But the bristly hair on the back of his thick neck didn't really stand on edge until he tried to weigh the thing—and the meter stayed at zero. He tried it on three sets of scales, carefully and precisely factoring in the weight of the storage cube, and kept getting the same result. It had no weight at all.

Then why did it settle for creeping around instead of flying? Wellingham growled an obscene something under his breath. If he were left with *that* as the biggest mystery about the parasites, he'd be a happy man.

It didn't weigh anything. Did that mean it had no mass? Impossible. Flat out, totally impossible. Wellingham glared at the parasite, and wished it would just go away. Instead, it slithered back down to the base of the plastic box, still searching for a means of escape.

Wait a second. He hadn't proved it had no mass—just no weight. *That* he could deal with. But even a *neutrino* had mass, in currently fashionable theory, and Wellingham was not about to accept that something that appeared to resemble a blob of mercury could be massless. Unless it was some sort of small energy field. But no, how could that be when it gave off no EM radiation except reflected light?

But *did* no weight mean no mass? There were places where it didn't. In free fall, no material object had weight, but all objects retained their mass. You had to put an object in some sort of real or simulated gravity field—put the object on a planet, or in an accelerator or a centrifuge, say—before its mass was measurable. And of course if the g-field varied, so did the apparent weight. Wait a second. Wellingham sat straight up and stared at the bulkhead. *Vary the g-field . . .*

Doctor Peabody looked up in relief as the Chief Engineer leapt up and ran out of the sick bay. Wellington tended to overwhelm whatever room he was in. Now if someone would just come along and clean up that pile of test instruments, things could get back to normal around here.

Peabody's relief was short-lived. Four minutes later, Wellingham was back, three assistant engineers behind him—and all four of them with their arms full of more gadgetry.

Lieutenant Commander Tarwa Chu sat unhappily in the command chair on the bridge, watching a dauntingly disordered ship status board. Her respect for the skills of a ship's captain was growing by leaps and bounds. The day so far was proving to be an endless and highly educational nightmare. So many people expected her to make *decisions*. There was too much to do. Every one of the blinking, color-coded messages on the status board was indicating a ship function that was non-operational. Even animated advertising systems didn't dare use such gaudy color.

Captain Spencer had left orders that any effort to repair the *Duncan* be terminated and the ship take off as soon as possible. That sounded straightforward enough, but it was all but impossible to get it done in practice. Too many subsystems were half-taken apart, too many repairs were half-begun or half-finished. There wasn't time to finish up most of the jobs. Test leads were yanked, and old, worn, parts and slap-dash repairs done a generation ago were reinstalled. New jury-rigs were found whenever the damage was too far gone to be left alone.

The department chiefs understood the need at first, more or less, and only grumbled to Chu a little bit. The sailors who had been put to work on rush repair jobs understood nothing and grumbled louder to their section leaders, who echoed the complaints to the department heads. The department chiefs, now harried and impatient with the chaos belowdecks, had in the meantime found out just how impossible and frustrating the job was. They reported the comments from their subordinates back to Chu, embroidering them with a few choice observations of their own.

It was understandable that the officers and crew were unhappy over the need to rush just as fast to undo their work, but Chu realized that being understanding wouldn't do much for morale, discipline, or efficiency.

In theory it was up to her to crack the whip. In practice, she had not much chance of succeeding, not when many of the officers and ratings had daughters—or granddaughters—older than she was. Chu wished desperately she were back home on Breadbasket, where the greatest challenge in life was getting the cows milked on time.

A tone hummed from the right side of the console, on the comm control section, and a section of panel lit up in green—a welcome sight in that sea of reds, ambers, and shrieking bright alert-yellow. Chu punched the green panel. "Incoming land-line audio-only call. Word-code procedure identifies caller as Captain Spencer," the panel announced.

A wave of relief washed over Chu. Maybe now the real captain could come back and take over. "I'll take it on the privacy headset," she said, fumbling the headset in place over her ears and adjusting the high-sensitivity mike.

"Stand by," the comm panel said. There was a moment of scratchiness, and then Captain Spencer's voice was in her ears. Few things had ever sounded so good to her. "Spencer here," he said crisply. "Ship condition report. Bear in mind this is an unsecure line. There may well be listeners."

Listeners? Why was the captain worried about that? And if he was, why risk calling on a buggable line? Why wasn't he using his AID to call in? Was he in some sort of trouble? Never mind. If he had wanted her to know, he would have told her. If he dared, on an unsecure line. "Ah,—ah, Lieutenant Commander Chu reporting, sir. Revised repair schedule proceeding sir. I don't know how much detail you want to hear over this line, though."

"Just glad to hear you're still there."

Chu felt her face flush. "Sir, if you are uncertain of my abilities, you may assign temporary command to any other offi—"

"No, no, Chu, not *you*. I meant I'm glad the *ship's* still there. I half expected to find out that you'd been attacked. A few of the locals have taken some heavy potshots at us. I'm sure you're doing fine in command. I have every faith in you.

"On our side, if you pick up some news reports about some over-enthusiastic autocops or a wrecked shopping arcade—well, they were after us. They may still come after you, so be on your toes. Bump it up two alert levels from where it was when I left, more if you see fit. But the main thing is I want that ship out of there *now*. Order the tugs alongside, get out into deep water, and launch. Get back into orbit. If need be, you are authorized by me to launch from the populated area of the dock as per service doctrine. Let me make that stronger: I *order* you to carry out populated-zone attack doctrine if the ship comes under attack. Give warning to the locals if you can, but *get the ship away* as soon as possible. Is that understood?"

Chu felt her ears buzzing, and she swallowed hard. Standard doctrine prohibited the launch from a populated zone unless the ship was under direct attack and the populace was therefore at substantial risk already. Who the hell would attack the Duncan? How much trouble were they *in*? "I understand, sir. We are still trying to get put back together far enough for boost. It will be several hours yet. Will you be returning aboard, sir?" she asked hopefully.

"Not until the ship is actually in space. You'll have to launch a gig to pick up the other stranded crew and myself. I don't want any hatches opened or anyone coming aboard until you're out of atmosphere. I would bet that there are at least half-a-dozen parasites on the hull right now, trying to worm their way aboard right now, and I don't want to give them a chance. Not your fault, but I wish to hell you could boost *now*. We'll be able to handle them better in orbit. Also, they're still after *me*, and if I head for the ship I'll probably just draw their fire toward you for no good reason. Besides, I've still got some work to—"

"Urgent call from chief engineer," the comm panel announced in Chu's ear, brazenly interrupting the captain.

"Patch it into the call with the captain," Chu instructed, then addressed Wellingham and Captain Spencer when the comm panel tell-tales indicated they were linked. "Captain, the chief engineer is cutting in with an urgent report. Chief, the captain just called in on an unsecured line. I'm patching you in. Bear in mind it *is* an unsecured line. Go ahead."

"Captain, we've *got* the little bastard!" the chief announced gleefully. "I've just completed tests on a detector, using the captured subject as a guinea pig. Can you risk hearing about it now on this line?"

"Absolutely," Spencer replied eagerly. "I doubt you'll tell any potential listeners anything they don't know."

"Gravity waves," the chief said proudly. "Don't ask me *how*, but the parasite gives off gravity waves. I got my clue when the thing showed as being weightless. I realized that couldn't be right, and decided to track for anything that might interfere with the scales. And picked up gravity *waves*, if you can believe that."

"How strong?" Spencer asked.

"That's the weird part, Captain. If you assume the parasite has a density of equal to H_2O, then I'm reading enough g-waves to generate thousands of gravities of acceleration—but there *is* no gee force generated, as if the g-waves were precisely cancelling the attraction between the planet and the parasite. But that can't be right, either," the chief said.

"Why not?" Spencer demanded.

"Because if it *were* right, then the parasite weighs just under sixteen metric tons," the chief said tonelessly. "Which would make it denser than the core of many neutron stars."

There was a silence on the line. Neither Spencer or Chu could think of anything to say, anything to ask in response to such an outrageous statement.

Wellingham gave them both a chance to digest his findings, and then went on. "I can't explain how or why it creates or uses the gravity waves," he said, "but the g-waves should come in very handy for spotting these things. They ought to stand out like a searchlight after dark in a gravity-wave detector. It'll take me some time to rig a detector capable of scanning the ship for our other visitor—but we should have the little beast nailed the moment we switch the detector on. Assuming I can get something with enough range."

"Nice work, Chief. Work fast on that—but be advised I've ordered Chu to cast off and get the ship away, so some of your engineers might be busy with other duties. Get that detector on line. Chu, I'll let you make the judgment call, but if possible, I don't want the ship to lift until that parasite is neutralized. It doesn't sound like you could fly safely just yet anyway, and I'd just as soon have that thing out of the control circuits before you fire up the fusion engines. And Wellingham, when you do catch the second parasite, don't let it near the first one."

"I'd thought of that already, sir. God knows if the bloody things can link up with each other—or what would happen when they did. Don't you worry, I won't introduce them socially."

"Excellent. I'm going to sign off now—but I hope to call in on a secure line soon. Spencer out."

"*Duncan* out," Chu said, wondering why, exactly, she had been so relieved to hear from the captain. He hadn't exactly eased her mind or solved her problems. She sighed and checked the time. She had been serving as commanding officer for just about six hours. Well, at least it hadn't been dull, and showed no signs of becoming so.

Captain Allison Spencer, Master of the cruiser *Duncan*, stepped away from the antique-looking audiophone feeling the master of nothing at all. He had been driven by events since the moment they had taken Bethany away. He felt like one of the pieces on a game board, trying to play the game by itself, battling against a huge and invisible past-master of the game.

Well, that was no way to win, Spencer told himself. It was time and past time for him to start acting instead of reacting. Time to get ahead of the curve. Spencer glanced out the window. Dusk was coming on, the sun setting on what had already been an exceedingly long day. One that was not yet over. Not while they still had the night to work with.

He turned and walked back into the main room where the others were waiting for him. The first job was to get the AIDs secure.

"Dostchem," he asked, "can you rig a device to scan for gravity-wave generation?"

Dostchem looked startled, and Spencer indulged himself enough to savor the sensation of being ahead of the Capuchin, throwing her off-balance. Yes, he could definitely enjoy getting in front of the curve instead of behind it.

"Ah, yes, of course. Might I ask for more details on the specification? And why you would need such a device?"

"To locate what is either a device or a creature that seems to act as a parasite inside machinery. Machine or animal, it is wholly beyond anything the Pact has ever seen. If they are machines, they are light-years beyond us. They resemble small blobs of mercury—and seem able to infiltrate and control any sort of machinery.

"My chief engineer reports that the parasites produce massively powerful g-waves, enough to support the weight of sixteen tons."

The Capuchin drew back in startlement and then snorted derisively. "That is flatly impossible. In nature, it takes a whole planet to produce a significant gravity field. As for producing pulsed gravity artifically, it would require the entire power of the *Duncan* to generate g-waves strong enough to lift my hat off my head. The parasites could not possibly produce that sort of power. Your chief *must* be mistaken."

Spencer felt his temper flare. "Either you're going to do this for us, or we're going to find somebody else who can. If you're working for me, and I tell you I need a left-handed wind-shifter, I want a wind-shifter, not a lecture on my innate inferiority. And as nothing about the para-sites makes sense, I see no reason why their use of gravity waves should be understandable to someone who hasn't even seen the damn things. Look, these things are taking on the *Pact*. Think about what they'll do to us—humans, Capuchins, everybody. How long do you think you'll have your Undertowns to hide in? So get to it, or admit you can't do the job."

Dostchem opened her mouth, thought better of whatever protest she was planning to make, then turned and stepped into her workshop. Suss looked up at Spencer, one eyebrow raised in amusement. "Nice work, Captain. She was getting eyestrain from looking down at us."

"You can't really blame her, though," Sisley said. "The damnable thing is that the Capuchins *are* smarter than us, in a lot of ways—and they know it. No imagination, maybe, but terrific engineers. No wonder she has a chip on her shoulder. I wish we could hire a few of them in my section—efficiency would probably double. But the work laws—"

"Yeah, right," Spencer said hurriedly. This was no time to get involved in an argument on civil rights. "Right now, I just need the detector. I want to confirm that both AIDs are clear. By the way, where are they?"

"Each one buried in the back of a separate closet," Suss said, "each wrapped in insulating fabric with pillows stuffed in on top, and metallic-film shields over that. I don't think they could hear us, or reach anything by radio, or be tracked by any electronic means I know of. I doubt the AIDs are being controlled, or else we'd all be dead by now—"

"Then shouldn't they be shut down?" Sisley asked. "Or

destroyed? Even if Dostchem can certify them clean now—they might become infested later."

Suss looked up at Sisley in shock. Logically, Mannerling was right—but how could Suss explain how important Santu was to her? Not just as a tool, not even just as a companion and ally, but as something close to a talisman, a good-luck piece. KT agents throughout the Pact went in on mission runs with their spirits calm and secure because their AIDs were watching out for them, tracking for snooper beams, listening for enemy transmissions, recording data, ready to crack open secure areas, call for transport, squawk for help. The devices were guardian angels that worked. Suss knew perfectly well that someone could kill her just as dead when she was wearing Santu—but she *felt* safer, and *that* made her a bolder, braver, better agent. She was able to focus on the job, and not worry about danger to herself.

More importantly, though, it had to be admitted that Santu was a friend. Out, alone, on her own, Santu was Suss' only trusty companion.

"You might be right," Spencer said to Sisley. "Maybe we should scram them."

Suss was stunned. How could Spencer talk that way? He had lived with his AID all this time. His nameless AID. Suss suddenly understood why Spencer had never decided to name the device Ted or Murphy or Elmo, or anything at all. He had seen that this moment might come. She couldn't blame him. Why should he make it harder for himself to endure the necessary loss of an ally when he already endured the pain of losing his whole way of life? She wanted to protest, but somehow she could not.

"The trouble is," Spencer went on, "we're going to *need* the damn things. Besides, we can always run periodic checks. But I'd be tempted to hang onto them even if Dostchem couldn't clear them. Neither of them seem to have been acting strange in any way. Of course, maybe they *are* infested, but are being held in reserve. But for now there's no harm in not taking chances. Leave them in the closet and we can talk freely."

Suss nodded. Probably Dostchem could snoop in—but as long as she wasn't interrupting to show how smart she was, she could spy all she wanted as far as Suss was concerned.

"As I see it," Spencer said, "our primary goal at this point is to determine exactly who is controlling the parasites—and through them, a lot of other things—and then figure out what their plans are. We can't fight them very well if we don't know who they are. We need some solid leads. Comments?" He looked from one woman to the other.

Sisley Mannerling folded her hands in her lap and looked down at them. "I—I think I have something. In fact I'm sure I do. I never passed it on to McCain or anyone else because it seemed so strange. I thought better of it later on, but it was *too* late by then. McCain had already vanished. Now I think it might be important."

Spencer looked at her closely—something he hadn't had a chance to do yet in this chaotic morning. He saw a pretty, matronly woman, in early middle age. Pale face, good skin, intelligent brown eyes with just a few crow's-feet starting to appear. An ample, but graceful figure. She looked like she should have been someone's kindly aunt. And now, thanks to Suss and himself, here she was hiding out from crazed killer robots.

"What is it, Miss Mannerling?" he asked in a gentle voice.

"It's—it's just that the *times* match up," she said. "Something strange that happened just *before* McCain dropped out of sight, just *before* Chairman Jameson became so reclusive.

"A man came to see me. He called himself Captain Destin, and said he had something for Chairman Jameson. Something for the chairman's collection. He should never have gotten as far as me—there are a half-dozen security checkpoints between the street and my desk. But apparently they all just waved him through—and so did I. I shouldn't have."

"What was it he had for the chairman?" Suss asked.

"I can't quite remember," Sisley said. "The whole memory is a bit foggy for me. I know that sounds crazy—something that unusual should have stuck in my memory. But that's part of what makes it strange. I did something very wrong, something I shouldn't have done, and then afterwards I had no clear recollection of it. But what I can remember is that Destin was carrying it, wrapped up in a cloth. How big it was, what shape it was, I don't know. But I do remember the cloth slipping away for a minute—and seeing something silver underneath. Gleaming, bright-polished silver."

"The same as the parasites," Spencer said. "My God." Had the parasites managed to influence human minds, as well as machines? Manipulated Sisley, and then made her forget?

"Then it sounds like this Destin character is our best possible lead," Suss said. "Maybe he invented the parasites, or controls them. Sisley, do you have any idea what he's the captain of?"

"I can't swear to it," Sisley said, "but I am at least 99 percent certain he isn't Pact military command. At least not Pactmil assigned to this system through the cluster command or Government House. There are only a few hundred officers detailed to the Daltgeld system, and I have the list memorized. And I memorize retired officers, too. Only about a hundred of those. He's not one of them.

"So unless he's not officially here, or unless he's a scientific type they gave a commission for some reason, he's not one of *our* captains or one of us would know about him," Suss said. "After all, Sisley and I are both professional spooks—"

"I'm strictly part-time and amateur, thank you very much," Mannerling put in. "And suppose Destin was a Pact agent on some sort of job?"

"You may be part-time, but you're good," Suss said. "One of the prime jobs for a spook is to know all the other spooks—especially the ones on your side. If Destin were sent by the KT or Pactmil on some sort of hush-hush job, one or both of us would know about it. You'd have heard some sort of chatter."

"Yeah, we all know the KT has its hooks into the military," Spencer agreed sourly. "I've got reason to know that. But why are you so sure he isn't a scientist with a courtesy commission?"

"Because no one ever uses those ranks," Suss said.

"They're just used to tidy up the table of organization, allow military security clearances, assign pay grades—that kind of thing. He would have called himself 'Doctor' Destin, or 'Academician' Destin, no matter what his putative rank."

Spencer nodded. "Okay, then he probably isn't one of ours. Then what does that leave?"

"Local militia, commercial shipping, or else he's just some old coot everyone humors by calling him Captain," Sisley said. "And I can tell you flat out he's not local militia. I relay the list of their officers to KT headquarters every sixty days, and I just sent the update ten days ago. He wasn't on it. And somehow I don't see an old wharf rat taking time out to invent the parasites."

"Which makes the commercial captains the first place to look. How and where are they listed? There must be some sort of directory." Practically every star system had some sort of central, constantly updated, directory of commercial shipping officers and crew members. Otherwise it would be all but impossible for friends, family, and business contacts to track not only the ever-moving ships, but the crew members themselves as they were endlessly hired, fired, transferred, transhipped and deadheaded across the vastness of space.

Sisley looked unhappy, and suddenly Spencer knew the answer to his own question. "You're about to tell me StarMetal handles the space-side directory, aren't you?" he said accusingly.

Sisley shrugged apologetically. "They bought up the directory service company about six months ago—and then tightened down the screws on it. Cranked up the security to paranoid-plus, which I guess makes sense if they're trying to hide a lot of activity. The service is very tightly controlled, and I doubt we could crack into it from an unauthorized remote terminal."

Spencer stared at her for a long moment. "But you do know how to get to it. And let me guess from where."

"At the office, of course," she said.

Spencer slumped back in his chair. If there was one place he didn't want to go, it was to the StarMetal building, the enemy's headquarters. "Oh, well," he said slowly. "If it was easy, then everyone would do it."

*   *   *

Spencer didn't claim to know much about xenopsychology, but he did succeed in getting results out of Dostchem. She had a working g-wave detector in two hours. It took only thirty seconds for her to try it on both of the AIDs, and give them each a clean bill of health.

Both Spencer and Suss were glad to be able to have faith in the devices again. For Spencer especially, it had been most uncomfortable to rely so much on a device he couldn't entirely trust. But he still didn't want to use the AIDs much, especially not for communications or active-probe work. Even a completely loyal AID could give its owner away if he insisted on constantly broadcasting signals and sensor-beams.

Mannerling and Dostchem, the two locals, went to work on a whole series of convoluted plans to gain entry into the StarMetal Building. They discussed schemes involving diversions or armed raids or bribing the guards (which both agreed would be tough if only robots were on guard, as seemed likely), before concluding that none of the more direct approaches had any hope of working, and that they would simply have to find some way of sneaking into the well-guarded building.

Undertown was the ideal neighborhood for finding someone who could handle *that* assignment. Suss and Dostchem both had the technical ability to get through any alarm in use, but neither knew the building's layout, its schematics. They would need some local talent for that side of the job.

Spencer wanted to go out and hire his own break-in artist, but Dostchem flatly vetoed that. As she pointed out, a human looking to hire someone for an illegal job was sure to get its throat cut. None of the humans could argue with the point, but on the other hand, none of them was entirely relaxed trusting Dostchem. That they had little choice in the matter was cold comfort.

Spencer kept watch by the window—and saw Undertown come alive as the dusk faded into full night. The streets which had been so empty and forbidding during the day seemed to blossom forth with hustling, bustling life. There seemed to be more vigor, more zest for life, more color and light than Spencer remembered seeing in any human part of a town. Watching cautiously from Dostchem's window, he saw the crowds appear, hundreds of beings from dozens of species easing out into the warm night air. Street vendors, hucksters, strolling couples, musicians— playing instruments that set Spencer's teeth on edge— seemed to spring up from nowhere.

Where did they all come from? Why did Undertown get busy only at night? Were they all just coming home from jobs in the human part of town? Were they afraid of autocop surveillance during the day? Spencer hadn't seen many autocops, but he knew better than most that a lot of the force was deployed on unusual duties.

Was it something biological? Was Daltgeld's sun unpleasant to non-humans? Was the day too hot? Or was it just that many of the other sapient species were mainly nocturnal? Spencer realized he didn't even know enough about the other sapients to know if any of his explanations made sense, and felt a bit ashamed of his ignorance.

If humans were supposed to rule the Pact, shouldn't they at least know something about the subject species? Another tough question there was no time to handle just yet. He spotted Dostchem returning, in the company of another Capuchin.

Suss was at his side, looking out the window, before he had a chance to say anything. She had either read something in his body movement, or was simply relying on some sort of highly developed sixth sense. There didn't seem to be any reason for Dostchem to betray them, and Capuchins had the very strong virtue of resembling honest cops: once you paid them, they stayed bought. But even so, it was entirely possible that Dostchem had double-crossed them. Not as if they could really *do* anything about it, or protect against it.

They listened as the two soft-treading pairs of feet made their way up the stairs. Suss' hand went for her repulsor, but then she drew it back—deep inside Undertown, cut off from all other help—if it came to a gun battle, there was no point to fighting. And how many might get caught in the crossfire?

Dostchem walked calmly in, the other Capuchin behind

her, and entered the apartment without offering any acknowledgement of the humans' fear. Maybe she didn't notice it, or maybe she just didn't care.

"This is Igor," she said without preamble, gesturing over her shoulder. "All he knows is that you want to get into the StarMetal building. He doesn't know why you want in, and he doesn't want to know. He has a day job there—and he says he can get you in, for a price."

"Yeah," Igor said, in a belligerent, basso profundo voice that seemed out of place coming from his slight frame. "Five thousand gelt, take or leave it. I don't take no haggling from baldies."

Baldies? Spencer was a bit puzzled. Obviously it was an insulting term for humans, but all three of them had full heads of hair. Then it came to him. A Capuchin's body was completely covered in sleek, elegant fur. Only their faces, palms, and the soles of their feet were bare. Humans must look like so many plucked chickens to them.

"Three thousand," Suss replied instantly. Spencer wanted to object, Igor had said no haggling. Then he decided to let it ride. Suss knew xeno-psych far better than he ever would.

"Six thousand," Igor said. "And it'll be seven if you keep it up. Take six or leave it."

"Then I'll take nothing and you've had a wasted trip," Suss said icily. "Except that there'll be a recording of this conversation on your supervisor's desk tomorrow morning, after we're long gone. Or else take the forty-five hundred I'm willing to pay and you're willing to take, and we'll get on with it."

Igor looked from Dostchem to Suss and then back again, while Dostchem snorted in laughter. "Ah, hell, she warned me you were harder to browbeat than the local baldies. Okay, you got a deal. And call me Iggy. Everyone does."

Chapter Eleven

Capture

Tarwa Chu flexed her hand and reached apprehensively for the joystick. No tugboats available. No other craft of any type available to be pressed into towing service. In short, no help of any type at hand. Whether that was for real or the result of StarMetal seeing to it that no *dared* offer help almost didn't matter. The *Duncan* was on her own.

But Captain Spencer had said get the ship away. Not to *try* and get her away, but to *do* it. Preferably without melting the port of København. Which meant Tarwa could not lift the ship skyward from pierside, but instead must get the cruiser out to sea, somehow, before lifting.

Preferably.

There *was* a way to do it without any outside help. The approved procedure was even down in the book, though it had never been performed on a ship the size of the *Duncan*. She would have to sail the behemoth out of port by herself, using the attitude control thrusters to direct and power her craft as it wallowed through the water.

She stared out at the simulator's viewscreens, glanced at the empty stations around the simulator deck. For a full dress rehearsal, of course, she would need the whole bridge crew in here, but something told her it might be wise to make the first few attempts on her own, without company.

Besides, the computer itself was going to be a bit balky

on the first few tries as well. The simulations computer would do its best, but there was virtually no data on this sort of maneuvering. Chu sighed. An inexperienced helmswoman running an underprogrammed computer. Well, if she pulled it off, at least she would have the consolation of providing the key data on how it was done for the *next* poor damn sod caught in this particular predicament.

But time was short, and there was no point in delaying further. She grabbed the joystick and pressed it to starboard. The simulator fired the simulated port thrusters, the portside view of the pier exploded in a cloud of simulated steam, and the simulator's cabin heeled hard over, knocking Tarwa over, sending her sliding into the portside bulkhead as the simulator compartment rolled over ninety degrees, sloshing the portside view underwater and providing a fine view of the noonday sky to starboard—which had suddenly become skyward.

Alarming clunks and thuds resounded from the sound system, as simulated shattered bits of pier and dock clattered down onto the *Duncan*. She clambered to her feet, grabbing at handholds, reached for the control panel and punched the *reset* button. Instantly the deck rolled back to level and the viewscreens snapped back to an idyllic panorama of København Harbor.

Fine, she thought. *Maybe not quite so much thrust to move away from the pier.* She was very glad indeed that she had made *that* run on her own. Chief Wellingham would have dropped dead from apoplexy if he had seen what she had done to his ship.

She reached for the joystick and steeled herself to try it again.

Blissfully unaware of the simulated havoc the acting commander was wreaking, Chief Wellingham was having a rather more satisfying time of it belowdecks. He stood in the forward weapons room, at the *Duncan*'s bow, double-checking the connections on his brand-new gravity wave detector. The g-wave detector was not a particularly sleek piece of engineering, bulkier and heavier than he would have preferred, and its range was severely limited, but it worked, and that was the main thing.

He decided to start at the bow of the ship and work aft, with the gain on the device cranked up to the maximum. There might be some more sophisticated and efficient search pattern he could run, some computer-planned path that would quarter the ship more perfectly and in less time, but at least the chief's plan had the advantage of being straightforward, simple, and something he could start on right away.

The chief had only one g-wave generator on which to calibrate the detector: the captured parasite itself. No doubt a properly designed and constructed laboratory-grade detector, designed and constructed for the purpose, could have spotted that little nightmare from halfway across the Daltgeld system. But Wellingham had been limited to the use of spare parts on hand, and the need to get something, anything, working immediately.

He was able to spot the captive parasite at a range of about one hundred meters—considerably less than the internal diameter of the *Duncan*. In other words, if the chief walked his detector straight down the central axis of the ship, he could walk right past a parasite sticking to the inside of the hull—or even a parasite on a bulkhead halfway between the hull and the core. And the hundred-meter range assumed that all parasites would radiate g-waves as ferociously as the captive. Suppose they just had a little baby parasite aboard, barely trickling out any gravity waves at all?

Wellingham would have to puff and wheeze his way up and down companionways, back and forth through passages, ranging far and wide to be sure of covering the interior volume of the ship. That was one reason the chief had decided to make the first sweep himself—no one else knew the interior of the ship as well as he did. If someone had to crawl through the three-dee maze of the *Duncan*'s interior, it was going to have to be the chief.

He was not looking forward to the exercise. His detector was a bulky, heavy thing, with the power supply and signal processing system jammed into a crude backpack arrangement with shoulder straps that were just a bit too tight for comfort. There was a hand-held detector wand attached to the pack by a thick cable. Wellingham had attached a tiny direction-pointing screen to the detector wand, and run the screen's cable to the signal processor on the backpack.

Still, Wellingham worried. Suppose, as seemed not impossible, the parasite could track the detector as it tracked the parasite, perhaps could "see" the detector at a range greater than 100 meters? Suppose it could move fast enough to stay clear of Wellingham as he prowled the ship? And once Wellingham did find the damn thing, how was he going to *catch* it? He was carrying a number of self-sealing sample holders, and a number of gadgets for pushing and prodding and scooping up the beastie, including a spatula filched from the officer's mess, but it all seemed a rather crude array of devices for dealing with something as strange as an electronic parasite.

Of course, he wouldn't even get to use that inadequate equipment unless and until he found the thing. Wellingham knew, even as he set out on a first survey of the ship, that it would take more than one officer with one detector to sweep the ship and insure it was clean. He had five of his best petty officers putting together four more of the same model detector, and he had two enlisted crew working with the computer to devise a coordinated search program, once there were five working detectors available. Wellingham intended to keep all five detectors running, searching the ship constantly, until they got the hell out of this damn system. Once they had the ship cleared of the parasites, Wellingham was determined she would *stay* cleared of them.

Even if it was illogical to start the search single-handed, he was eager to get started immediately. It might be hours before the other detectors were working, and he felt the urgent need to do something *now* to battle the foe.

He switched on the detector and began his first sweep.

Iggy grew increasingly nervous as they got near the StarMetal Building. He led them through the sorts of fetid back streets and alleys and shortcuts that Spencer had expected him to know, threading their way across the city's sprawling bulk. They made for a strange group of travelers moving through the cloud-swept night. The two Capuchins, Iggy and Dostchem, leading Suss, Sisley, and Spencer across the underbelly of København, toward the StarMetal building.

StarMetal's towering pyramid was the tallest structure in the city—on the planet, for that matter, and easily visible from most parts of town. Spencer was able to estimate how close they were coming to it by watching it grow taller on the horizon. He was glad of the landmark—without it, he would have completely lost his sense of direction in the labyrinth of back streets Iggy favored.

Spencer judged them to be perhaps as much as a half-kilometer from StarMetal Plaza when Iggy ducked into one last alley, up to a nondescript building and up to an unmarked door. Iggy paused in front of the door and gestured for the others to cluster around close enough for him to whisper.

"Okay, here's th' plan," he said. "The whole downtown area is nothin' but tunnels for this and tunnels for that. Sewers, walkways, cargoways, ventilation, you name it. And for every underground passageway in use, there's another one they abandoned a hundert' years ago. No one has them all mapped, but I know enough of them t'get us where we're going. I'm going to take you to StarMetal by an underground route. I *think* we oughta be able to sidestep building security by coming up underneath their goons."

"That'll do fine for getting us inside," Dostchem objected, "but what about internal security? Surely they have motion sensors, infrared detectors, that sort of thing."

"Wouldn't do them any good if they did," Sisley said. "The building never shuts down—it's a system-wide business, don't forget. The headquarters building is staffed around the clock, always busy."

"Which I coulda told you, Dostchem, and you shoulda figured out on yer own," Iggy agreed irritably. "Anyway, if today was just another day around here, I could *guarantee* this route would work—but you Navy clowns have th' StarMetal goons so worked up they might have sonic guards across everything down to the ratholes. So this might be a little risky."

Iggy flicked his tail in the air in a gesture of dismissal and went on. "I figure you knew this was chancy—but if you want to back out, now's the time. I'm not going down there to have you bozos wetting your pants and running 'cuz yer scared of th' dark. We don't give up and run until I say so. No second-guessing from out-of-towners. Got that?"

No one spoke, and Iggy snorted in disgust. "So you're all a bunch a' heroes, I guess. Let's go." He turned toward the door and produced what looked liked a skeleton key. Then it was down into a further maze of doorways, passageways, tunnels and stairwells.

Spencer couldn't help but remember his exit from the KT hospital. That trip had been a lot like this—except the KT seemed to keep its secret passages a bit cleaner than Iggy did. More than once Spencer thought he recognized a few smells he'd just as soon have been unable to identify.

On and down they went, shifting direction so often that Spencer was completely turned around, feeling certain that he would be unable to retrace his steps. He began to worry that Iggy planned to get them thoroughly lost and then abandon them—a much safer way for Iggy to earn his money than by leading the humans right into the enemy headquarters. It could easily take them days or weeks to get out of here—or it might take forever, if Iggy had a few nasty friends lying in wait around the next corner.

Spencer shrugged off the fear. If it came to that, he had told his AID to switch on its inertial backtracker, and no doubt Suss had told Santu the same thing. They ought to be able to retrace their steps. And no doubt Iggy knew that military-issue AIDs would include a backtracking system. Besides no matter how ferocious Iggy's hypothetical henchmen might be, Spencer and Suss were both well-trained, well-armed fighters—and Iggy knew that too. So maybe they were safe after all.

Safe from their friends, at least.

They kept up with Iggy as best they could, though he didn't make it easy. He refused to allow any of the others to carry a light, and used his own very sparingly, with the

predictable result that everyone banged into walls and
bounced their heads against unseen obstacles. Iggy led
them in and out of every imaginable sort of tunnel, taking
them through half-a-dozen doors, access hatches, and
manholes, up and down endless ladders, most of which
were more rust than metal. Twice they stepped through
holes that appeared to have been smashed open with a
sledgehammer.

They walked briefly through what appeared to be a
long-abandoned sewer pipe. Iggy made sure they all rolled
up their pants before they entered it. The sewer was just
small enough to force Spencer to crouch down almost
double. He immediately developed a painful crick in his
back, which was made worse when a rusty pipe caught
him right between the shoulder blades. He tried to concentrate on the pain in his back as a way to avoid thinking
about the thick ankle-deep brownish-black goo they were
walking through. Every step through it seemed to release
a new and more foul odor, redolent of every sort of death
and decay.

It was some consolation that Dostchem liked the trip far
less than Spencer did. She had shed her robes and set out
in worker's coveralls. But she stayed barefoot, and the
slimy refuse in the sewer was congealing on her ankle fur.
She complained bitterly to Iggy, and was rewarded with a
highly creative suggestion as to where she could put the
muck.

At last they came to another manhole and climbed out,
emerging into a large sub-basement, a cavernous room
that receded into the darkness, seeming to stretch out
forever in all directions, fading into the echoing gloom.
The huge room was empty, but for the supporting pillars
that held up the massive building above. "We're inside th'
StarMetal building now," Iggy announced. "The tunnel
we were in was supposed to be a flood drain, but they
never had a flood and it just got forgotten. Now, there's a
janitor's closet over this way—you guys can hose down a
little there."

"Igor, are you sure this a wise moment to take the time
to clean up?" Dostchem asked.

"Hells' bells, lady, *you* were the one bitchin' about the

stink. I don't give a good goddamn if you're clean—I just thought you wouldn't want the security guards upstairs wondering what it is that smells like festering rotten eggs. So c'mon."

Iggy led them through a forest of supporting pillars until they could see the wall of the massive room looming up out of the darkness. They turned toward the right and followed the wall until they came upon a door in a rather ramshackle wooden wall.

Iggy opened the door and led them into a small corner area of the subbasement that someone had taken the trouble to finish off a bit. By the looks of things, the builder hadn't taken the trouble to get company approval for the job beforehand.

The materials used had the look of being scrounged rather than allocated. The subbasement's sancrete foundation material was covered over with what looked like kitchen flooring, shopworn pseudowood paneling was glued down over the subbasement walls. A bedraggled, presumably pilfered, light fixture dangled on a long cord from the far-off ceiling. A couch purloined from somewhere or other was backed into a corner, and showed evidence of serving frequent duty as a bed. Other odds and ends of furniture were scattered about the room. A small food cooler sat in one corner, and a fairly sophisticated three-dee box sat opposite the couch.

The same improvisational spirit that had inspired the room's builder in the first place had led him her or it to try his hand at plumbing as well. Iggy pulled back a curtain in one corner of the room to reveal a small chemical toilet and a crude shower, really nothing more than a garden hose carefully strung up with wire. A drain channel was cut into the sancrete below it to draw the water away from the rest of the cubbyhole. It occurred to Spencer that the water must end up in the sewer pipe they had just come out of.

He looked around at the little compartment. It was obviously a very enterprising being's attempt to shirk work. Down here, where no boss would ever dream of looking, the owner had jury-rigged a nice little place to hide from the job, get cleaned up, grab a snack, and catch forty winks.

Spencer wondered how their guide came to know about this little hidey-hole. Was this *Iggy's* place? Was he embarrassed to admit that he was nothing more than a junk-cadging, work-shirking menial instead of a big-time operator? If this place was not his, how had he known about this place, and how else would he know the owner would not show up and object?

If this *was* Iggy's place, if this was his sanctuary, then that was flat-out criminal waste. Not that he had borrowed a few broken-down odds and ends of office furniture, but that a being of his ability was trapped pushing a mop while some chuckled-headed human, hired by virtue of being someone's brother-in-law, fumbled his way through a job Igor could have done better.

Iggy had said they were to hose down, and that was what he meant, nothing more or less. He unfastened the hose from its shower fitting, turned on the old-fashioned spigot and played the jet of water over his pants leg and his boots. The other members of the party did the same, Dostchem making sure she went first and got her legs and feet well cleaned up. Spencer couldn't really blame her—it was bad enough having that scum on his shoes. He was glad when his own turn came.

Iggy sat down on the rumpled couch as the others cleaned themselves up. "This is as far as I go," he said, almost apologetically. "I dunno the upstairs part of th' building, so I wouldn't do you no good anyway. And on this sort of job, you don't need extra bodies along for the ride. I'm gonna stay right here—if the security goons spotted our entry and they come looking down here, mebbe they'll settle for finding me snoozing on the couch."

Spencer felt angry, shortchanged. Their guide was chickening out. Then he calmed himself and nodded. Iggy was probably right—even if it smacked of cowardice. "Fine," he said. "But how do we get upstairs from here?"

"Cargo elevator. Runs all the time, day and night, no one'll notice it droppin' down here to get you. I'll show you where it is. C'mon." Iggy stood up and led them from the hidey-hole to the elevator bank, back toward the center of the looming darkness of the subbasement.

An elevator car was waiting for them, and Spencer noticed that the monitor camera and the voice-command mike had been smashed out—just by chance, or merely so it *looked* like chance—it didn't matter which.

Sisley, Suss, Dostchem and Spencer went aboard. Maybe they could have done without Dostchem along, but she was carrying a tool-belt, and getting past internal security might be trickier than Iggy had suggested. Spencer was glad of the company. "All right, then," Spencer said. "Let's go. Iggy, if we're not back in four hours, you're on your own. Thanks for your help."

No one seemed to want to say anything more. Sisley reached over to the manual control panel and punched in her floor number. The doors began to shut, leaving Iggy watching them, and Spencer wondering what the proper etiquette was for saying good-bye to a Capuchin.

The doors slammed shut and the elevator began to rise.

Spencer turned and faced the others. "Listen, there's one thing. There's no point to this job if the information doesn't get out. If they jump us up there after we've got the data we're after, whoever is carrying the information gets out first, with the rest of us protecting her or fighting rearguard. That's the priority. It will probably be Suss carrying the download in Santu—which means *she goes first*. Of all of us, Suss has the best chance of breaking clear on her own if it all craps out. Dostchem, I know this isn't your fight, but we'll be your best bet if it gets ugly. Stick with us if you can."

And if we can stay alive long enough to get that far, Spencer thought to himself. But those were not the sort of words a commander said to his troops.

With a whoop of glee, Chief Wellingham dropped the detector and let it dangle at the end of its cable. He didn't need it anymore. He could *see* the little monster, lurking in the recess between two circuit blocks. There was just enough clear space underneath for him to fit in one of the smaller sample holders there. He fumbled for the sample holder, held it underneath the parasite, and dropped it into the container with one deft move of the cook's spatula. Wellingham snapped the container shut and held his captive up to the light. "We've got you now," he said gleefully, watching it slither around the interior of the jar.

Wellingham knew that the capturing the parasite in and of itself meant nothing—not when the people who had sent two of the things could send as many more as they liked. But now Wellingham had proved that the detector on his back *worked*. He had the other detectors on the job already, and they were going to *stay* on the job from now on, no matter how it screwed up the rest of his section's duty schedule. They would have to stay on guard against these—

"Petty Officer Jasper calling you, sir," Wellingham's AID announced.

"Put him through, Waldo."

"Sir, we've spotted two of the things, but we can't get at them," Jasper's voice said through the AID's speaker.

"Why not?"

"They're stuck to the outside of the hull, as best we can figure. I'm between the inner and outer hull right now, and the detector is showing two g-wave sources on the outside. I can't get an accurate fix on them, though—they seem to move around a lot."

"Trying to find a way in, no doubt. Good work, son. Note the location and we'll schedule frequent sweeps of the area to make sure we don't lose track of them."

"Ah, sir, shouldn't we go out after them?" Jasper asked.

"Negative! How do we know there aren't four more clustered near the hatch waiting for you to try that? Besides, the last thing I want is more of those things alive inside the ship. We stay buttoned up. But nice work all the same. Wellingham out."

Damn! The chief looked at his captive once again, not quite as pleased with himself as he had been a minute before. *Good news mixed right in with more bad news*, he thought. Bad they had more parasites, good that they had them spotted and that they were outside the ship, and bad that he didn't dare so much as open a hatch to go get them.

Under siege. It suddenly dawned on him that the *Duncan*

was besieged, a Warlord-class cruiser cut off from the outside universe by a few featureless blobs of silver. He glared at his captured parasite, suddenly feeling a bit less victorious.

Up on the bridge simulator, Tarwa Chu was feeling a lot more confident—even brave enough to order the first watch bridge crew in to rehearse the maneuver with her. She had tried sailing the *Duncan* clear eight times now and hadn't wrecked the ship or the harbor on five of the last six tries.

She felt a little anxious as the bridge officers filed in. The captain had ordered her to launch the *Duncan* over five hours ago, and she had heard no further word from him since. Was it still so urgent that they launch? Captain Spencer had never explained the crisis in the first place—maybe it was over by now. No, she told herself. She was supposed to obey orders, not second-guess them.

And perhaps she had already stalled too long. Maybe she should skip the simulation with the bridge crew and go right to the real thing. She glanced at the chronometer and was startled to discover it was the middle of the night. No wonder the first watch bridge crew looked sleepy— they had all been asleep for hours when she had ordered them to come here.

But the mere passing of the hours wasn't the real problem. Chu had been running the simulator for daylight conditions and had completely lost track of the passage of time. Her heart sunk once again. She knew she could never manage the tight passages of the harbor at night. Even in full light, she knew the currents and tides of København harbor would be tricky. The bridge crew would need daylight to work with as well.

At first light, then, she thought. They would sail at dawn.

Chapter Twelve
Wirehead

"Go!" Dostchem hissed. Suss, Spencer, and Sisley rushed through the opening door. Dostchem pulled out her test leads, and dove through herself. Once the door controller was no longer tricked by Dostchem's false signals, it snapped shut, almost catching the Capuchin's tail. "Is that the last one?" Dostchem asked. This was the third time she had nearly lost her tail.

Sisley nodded wearily. "Yes. We're here. There are no electronic guards on the rest of the doorways—at least none that I'm aware of." Iggy had been wildly optimistic in his assumptions about security: Santu's on-board security sensors, backstopped by Dostchem's detectors, had seen them through seemingly endless booby traps and hidden sensors. The cargo elevator had refused to take them above the twentieth floor because of a security lockout. Getting up to the thirticth had been a nightmare.

Every security system seemed to be switched on and cranked up all the way, to the great inconvenience of the hundreds, or perhaps thousands of beings in the building legitimately.

To the massive inconvenience of the security forces as well. Alarm bells and beepers were sounding constantly, and there seemed to be new false alerts going off every few seconds. Spencer's party twice hid in darkened offices while teams of StarMetal's private cops rushed down nearby corridors after some other, imagined threat.

144

Perhaps Dostchem and Suss even missed a sensor or two or accidentally set off a silent alarm. If so, the home team was so busy chasing phantoms they didn't catch on to the real invaders.

In the parlance of communications and detection theory—Dostchem's specialty as an instrument maker—the signal to noise ratio had gotten too high, to the point where the "static" of false alarms was drowning out legitimate warnings.

Dostchem Horchane didn't much care why they made it inside. She was just glad to be past the last barrier and in. Objectively, of course, this was probably one of the most dangerous places they could be.

At least Sisley's floor was only occupied during the day. They'd have some privacy.

The risks, therefore, probably weren't any lower now that they were inside, but at least they *seemed* lower, and Dostchem was willing for that much human irrationality to seep in. *Any* source of relief was welcome.

Of course, wishful thinking was not going to get them in and out tonight. "Come on then," Dostchem snapped, "let's get on with it."

Sisley started to move in behind her desk, but Suss held up her hand to stop her. "Santu, do a scan."

There was a moment's hesitation before Suss' AID spoke. "The desk is dirty," Santu said. "Get me closer to the left side of it." Suss pulled the AID out of its pouch and swept it over the desk. "Right here," the AID said. "Back a bit—there! Some sort of transmitter. Looks like it's wired in to transmit any command fed into the computer, pipe it to some remote location."

Dostchem already had her equipment out, and had the transmitter deactivated in a minute or two. "There," the Capuchin said as she finished. "Now it should still send a flat carrier wave no matter what you do to the computer."

"Okay, then, here's goes nothing." Sisley sat down at her desk and put her palm down over the sensor plate. The panel glowed a welcoming green and a flat display screen slid out of its recess, turned and swivelled up to face Sisley.

"We're in," she said. "Dostchem—use your g-wave gizmo.

Are there any of those parasites hooked into this computer? Is it safe to hook Santu up to it on a hardwire?"

Dostchem consulted another of her devices and nodded. "It's clean. No g-waves coming from closer than several sources a few hundred meters above us, at extreme range for this sensor."

Spencer looked at her sharply. "You're picking up g-waves? There are definitely parasites in this building?"

Dostchem nodded. "Of course. That should have been obvious. I assumed that we would find them in the building. But I do admit that I am relieved to actually track g-waves. These are the first g-wave sources I've picked up, and it is reassuring to know the device actually works. But come now, we really must get on with the job."

Suss, still holding Santu, pulled the hardwire link from its niche and spooled it out, handing Sisley the end of the cable. Sisley popped open a compartment on the corner of the desk and plugged in Santu's hookup.

"Okay, ah, Santu," she said, uncertain how to address an AID, "I want you to monitor *everything*. Right now we'll get the data quick and dirty, later we'll analyze it. Just get it all down."

"Don't worry, Miss Mannerling," Santu said. "That's my job."

Sisley nodded. She was tempted to let Santu control the search—but no, that wouldn't be smart. There were good reasons that her desk computer wasn't built as an AI system in the first place. Like most security-conscious operations, StarMetal did not trust sentient machines with unlimited access to confidential information. After all, an AI system was *designed* to rework its own programming, and that made any software block against unauthorized access impossible to enforce.

Furthermore, the artificial personalities that AI systems inevitably developed could turn unpredictable. There seemed to be some link being the amount of data an AI computer handled and the degree of its eccentricity.

The bigger the AI system, the more likely it was to be a bit flaky. And what help was a surly computer, or one that enjoyed practical jokes, or one that took an irrational dislike to its operator? Suppose it decided to erase key memories—or even commit suicide, taking all its files along into oblivion?

Even a healthy AI could be far too amenable to suggestion. Potentially, any competent machine psychologist could stroll in and talk an AI system full of secrets into confessing all.

But did that sort of argument apply to the present case? What harm in letting the AID go to work for a few seconds? Why not let Santu take the search job? No doubt the AID could do it in a thousandth the time it would take Sisley, and time was short.

No, best not to take the chance, she decided firmly. There were too many horror-stories about AIDs tapping into too much data all at once, and developing symptoms that paralleled human drunkenness. *That*, they didn't need tonight.

She switched on the voice-command system for her computer, then thought better of it, switched the mike off, and drew the keyboard out from its storage niche. Better to go with completely precise typed instructions. Mikes were a lot easier to tap than keyboards. Spencer and Suss came around the other side of her desk to look over her shoulder as she began hitting keys.

OPEN PERSONNEL FILES. QUERY: she typed. PROVIDE ANY/ALL INFORMATION ON PERSON KNOWN AS DESTIN/CAPTAIN DESTIN STARMETAL EMPLOYEE FILES.

NO SUCH NAME LOCATED, the computer displayed on its screen in bright red letters. Sisley repressed the urge to ask the computer, "Are you sure?" Even after thousands of years in dealing with computer searches, most humans still could not quite believe that a search of millions of names could be performed accurately in less than a millisecond.

Maybe she just needed to rephrase things a bit. REVISE QUERY, ADD STARMETAL OFF-PLANET PERSONNEL FILES, she typed.

OFF-PLANET PERSONNEL FILES INCLUDED IN FIRST SEARCH, the computer replied—a bit smugly, Sisley imagined.

"Okay, you're so smart,' she muttered. DID YOU IN-

CLUDE INDEPENDENT CONTRACTORS AND IN-
DEPENDENT SHIP OPERATORS? she typed.

RUNNING REVISED QUERY, the computer replied, admitting
defeat. Then: NO SUCH NAME LOCATED IN CURRENT INDEPEN-
DENT CONTRACTOR LISTS OF JOBS LET IN PAST THIRTY DAYS.

"Damn it!" Suss growled. "We risk our asses getting in
here and it's for noth—"

"No, maybe it isn't," Sisley said eagerly. "There's something weird going on. The current indy list is supposed to
go back one hundred days. Someone's been screwing around
with the main billing system down in the central files."
SEARCH FOR SAME REFERENTS FOR ALL INDE-
PENDENT CONTRACTORS OVER LAST FIVE YEARS,
she typed.

SECURITY RESTRICTIONS PLACED ON ELEMENTS OF THAT DATA,
the computer warned.

"Okay, there *has* to be something up. There is no
possible legitimate reason for securing that data," she said
excitedly. "They're trying to keep people out of the indy
files. A big, sloppy, ham-fisted block on the whole subsys-
tem, rather than a surgical block on just our boy. Exactly
the sort of clumsy thing you'd expect from a panicky
security operation or an amateur. So let's see what they're
hiding."

OVERRIDE SECURITY BLOCKS, she typed eagerly.
There was a discernible pause this time, as the computer
unlocked the data security on the files and searched through
the far larger data set. That was a good sign. It meant that
the computer was working on the problem, not rejecting
it. And *that* meant they were winning.

Sisley felt a sudden flush of happy satisfaction. They had
made the right decisions. Coming here had been worth
the risk. She patted the desktop fondly. *This* was why
they had needed to run the search from here and not a
remote location. From this terminal, she could override
every standard security block in the StarMetal security
system, look at files she could never reach from a standard
remote terminal. Unless someone had been smart enough
and quick to engineer a specialized block against her, they
were in. And from the looks of the security they had seen
so far, the opposition was in turmoil.

REFERENT LOCATED, the computer displayed at last. CAPTAIN ANTOIN LOUIS DESTIN, MASTER OF *The Dancing Bear*, ASTEROID CARGO VESSEL.

"Paydirt!" Sisley cried in jubilation.

QUERY: she typed. DISPLAY SUMMARY DATA ON MISSIONS OF DESTIN AND SHIP *DANCING BEAR* IN PAST FIVE YEARS. PRESENT AT MAXIMUM SPEED. *And this was the real reason an AI could never truly replace a human operator,* she told herself. *No one had ever programmed an AI system to have a hunch.*

The computer snapped up screen after screen worth of routine data, far faster than a human could see. Dostchem, however, was finally taking an interest, and had stepped in behind Sisley. "I believe you have it, Miss Mannerling," the Capuchin said. "It seems to me that there is a distinct break in Destin's work patterns—"

But Dostchem never got any further than that.

The door blasted away into confetti. StarMetal Security finally found what it had been looking for.

Suss dove down behind the desk and rolled out to the right. Spencer was a little slower doing a dive and roll to the left. Both of them had their repulsors out and fired on reflex. A moment before there had been two security men in the doorway—but now there were none, just a pair of chewed-up corpses collapsing in front of them. Sisley and Dostchem barely had time to feel surprise and alarm before it was all over.

"Goddamned amateurs!" Suss fumed. "They should have taken cover before they blew the door. They just stood there, *begging* us to kill them." There was something near hysteria in her voice. "They could have used gas, or called for backup, or something." She seemed genuinely offended at their ineptitude.

Strange, Spencer thought, to be a KT agent who hated death and violence so much. "Maybe they're dead, but they've still got friends on the way," he said. "We've got to get out of here. Santu! How long to download all the data?"

"Maybe another thirty seconds," the AID replied. "Stand by to unplug me, somebody."

Spencer winced. Thirty seconds! Probably half the time

they had before more guards showed up. They couldn't wait around that long, not in what was suddenly a combat situation.

Spencer thought fast. He had hoped to have time to look over the material they found, at least a little, but they would have to leave here not even knowing if they had what they needed. Too bad, Spencer decided. They weren't getting the chance to look for anything more. So: work on the assumption that Destin was a good lead, and that Santu would download everything they needed. Therefore, getting Santu out of here was the most important thing.

Okay, great. But how to get the AID—and if possible, the rest of them—out of here? Should they all make a break for it together, or split up? Four people escaping together, two of them civilians? Unmanageable, to say the least. Sisley was good, she had some training, but she was not a combat soldier. And Dostchem was, after all an alien. Spencer had no idea how Capuchins responded in combat roles. He certainly wasn't going to risk the mission finding out.

If the civilians were liabilities who endangered the mission, strictly military logic said he ought to leave them on their own, and go with Suss himself, thus concentrating all of the group's military training on the task of protecting their prize. Cold-blooded, logical, sensible—but he couldn't do it. Spencer knew he didn't have it in himself to leave Dostchem and Sisley unprotected.

Damn it! He had to stop dithering. The clock was running, and running fast. It almost didn't matter what orders he gave his people, as long has he gave them *some* orders and got them moving.

Protect his people. There. That was enough of a guide for him. "Suss! The second you can, unplug Santu and make a run for it on your own. I'll take charge of the civilians—you get the data back to the ship, no matter what happens. No speeches about protecting the rest of us. Nothing else matters unless we can track down Destin—and that recording is our only chance of doing it. Sisley, Dostchem, the two of you come with me."

He walked forward toward the blasted door and stepped

over the ruined corpses. He looked back to see if Sisley and Dostchem were coming. The two of them were just standing there, still in shock, clearly unwilling to leave Suss alone.

He turned and called back to them, "Come on! We don't have any time. Suss will probably be safer than we are."

Spencer urged the others to hurry with an impatient hand gesture. At the same moment he turned and looked at Suss. She returned his gaze, with eyes too full of fear and love and courage. Their eyes locked. He suddenly realized that she was the *last* person in all the worlds of the Pact that he would wish to be separated from, the last woman that he would want to leave alone in time of danger.

But this was not a time or place that allowed such sentiments. The enemy was closing, he might never see her again, and there was too much for him to say. "Good luck," he said in a strangely hoarse whisper, and left it at that.

"Go!" she said, her eyes saying everything *but* go.

There was no time. He turned and led his party away.

No point in subtlety or stealth now. The dead guards had to have been wearing some sort of sensors or mikes. Even if they hadn't reported before they attacked, the building's command center would have noticed it when their radios transmitted the sound of a gun battle and then went dead.

If the cops knew Spencer's team was here, it was high time to confuse the issue. They were just outside Sisley's office, in a cavernously large workroom, with rows and columns of desks stretching out before them. The one huge room took up the entire floor of the building, except for the closed-off area that included Sisley's office.

Spencer pulled a stun grenade from his belt and threw it to the far end of the outer office. It exploded with an earsplitting blast that almost knocked the three of them over. The grenade threw a perfect blizzard of papers into the air, spewing some poor sod's meticulously kept files over half the office, and setting most of them on fire as well. Two more alarm bells began hooting, raising a hellish racket even as the big room filled with the smell of burning paper.

That ought to confuse them a bit, Spencer thought—and delay them while they fight the fire. He spotted a red door marked EMERGENCY EXIT on the wall to the left and fired his repulsor at it, wrecking the door, blasting it open and setting off the exit alarm as well. Then he turned right and led his team toward the opposite wall at a dogtrot, looking for a similar red door there. Good, there it was. As he had hoped, there were emergency exits on both sides of the building. "Dostchem," he said as they got to the door. "Get past the door alarm without setting it off."

But Capuchins think faster than humans, and Dostchem already had the appropriate tools out. Spencer was relieved to see she wasn't giving up. He had been afraid that the well-known fatalist streak common to Capuchins would make her throw in the towel. Instead, she went to work at the door, and had them through it in seconds.

Spencer ushered the others through ahead of him, and felt a tiny twinge of relief as the door shut behind them. Now the fire, the blasted door on the opposite side of the room, even the dead guards themselves could serve as diversions, keeping the guards from looking toward the one place no alarms had been set off. Maybe they were going to make it.

Suss wished for eyes growing out of the back of her head as she moved out into the outer office area. She was there fast enough to see Spencer's party head down the emergency stairs, but she did not dare call to them. She patted her hip pouch. Santu was there, safely packed away. God willing the AID had captured the data they would need to find Captain Destin—and some answers. That would make all this worthwhile, if anything could.

Now all she had to do was get the hell out of here—preferably by another route than Spencer's, if he was going to serve as any sort of diversion for her. But how?

She had barely begun to consider the question when the alarm bells rang. She dove down behind a desk as two security cops rushed out of the shot-up stairwell and rushed across the huge room, ignoring the fire Spencer had started, heading straight for the stairs Spencer had taken. They hurried down the stairs at the double, clearly men who knew where they were going and what they were after.

Suss felt a sick feeling at the pit of her stomach. Her friends were caught, trapped, and there was nothing, absolutely nothing she could do about it.

Nothing, except to take advantage of their sacrifice by escaping. She hunkered down behind the desk and checked the time. Two minutes. She would give them two minutes to focus their attention completely on Spencer's capture, and then she would move out, using the other stairs.

It was going to be a long two minutes.

Spencer led Sisley and Dostchem down the emergency stairs, planning to get out of the stairs ten or fifteen floors below, leaving the hue and cry safely above and behind them.

They had only gotten six floors down when the cops appeared.

This time the cops did it right, those above popping out of the doorway on the floor above just as the cops waiting on the stairwell below came into view. There were too many of them for Spencer to have any hope in a fight, and all of them were taking good advantage of cover, all heavily armed and wearing enough body armor that one repulsor wouldn't have a chance of getting them all.

Besides which, there were now twenty heavy-duty repulsors pointed straight at the three intruders.

Spencer said nothing. He just dropped his weapon, raised his arms over his head and waited for them to swarm in and arrest the three of them.

Three? Even as the cops rushed in to grab him, Spencer suddenly noticed that Dostchem wasn't *there* anymore. How the hell had she gotten—and then he knew, and forced himself not to look up as the cops slipped the cuffs on him and started stripping his gear off.

Capuchins were a lot more arboreal than humans, after all, and the overhanging shadows of the gloomy stairwell could hide a lot. Spencer trussed him up so he couldn't walk, then flipped him over on his back onto a waiting stretcher to carry him away, completely immobilized. As he was carried back down the stairs to whatever the hell they were going to do to him, he spied a lump of shadow wedged in below the underside of the stairs above, and felt glad she had gotten away.

Spencer told himself that he should have been mad that Dostchem hadn't stayed with them, but what was the use in all three of them being tortured to death?

He blinked. Torture? He was surprised at the thought, and then realized he had known that all along. StarMetal was playing this for keeps. Torture. Pain. Death.

For the first time that night, fear, real fear, swept over him. He felt his trussed-up hand reaching for a ghostly feelgood button.

The sun was coming up. Tarwa Chu led her weary first-watch bridge crew down from the simulator to the operations bridge. There was something most disconcerting in moving from one room to its identical twin, moving from a place where a shadowy, unreal *Duncan* was controlled to the duplicate compartment that sailed the real ship.

The fog of exhaustion played into it as well, no doubt, but Tarwa felt as if she were sailing between alternate worlds. They had spent the entire night sailing a whole fleet of *Duncans* out of port—crashing some of them, sinking a few, twice ramming lesser vessels. At last the bridge crew had gotten the hang of the procedure, and successfully conned the huge craft out of port and into open water, where she could safely boost to orbit.

After each run, failed or successful, Tarwa had pressed the *reset* button, and the computer-driven images and sounds of the world outside the *Duncan* had melted away. A shattered harbor full of ruined ships, the pier aflame, or a triumphant lifting into space on a column of fire would vanish, flicker to nothingness.

Nothing is, but what is not, Tarwa told herself, and wondered where the words came from. Now came the last run, the only one that mattered. She watched as the bridge crew relieved the last watchstanders, settled into their stations, checked their boards and got ready.

In five minutes, they were ready. Tarwa sat down in the

command chair, not even noticing at first that she felt no awe about sitting in the holy spot. Then she realized where she was, and what she had done, and decided that perhaps that was the real purpose of the simulator—to do everything—even die—over and over again, until it became routine, and all the needless emotions that got in the way of the job were gone. After wrecking the ship a few times, it hardly seemed to matter what seat she sat in. She punched the intercom button. "All hands," she said, "prepare to cast off."

"This is gonna be something," the young guard said cheerfully. "I ain't never rid on one of the big exec's elevators before."

Spencer, trussed, tied, and blindfolded, lay on his stretcher, listening to his captors. As best he could tell, there were only two of them now, the rest having returned to their other duties once the captives were rendered helpless.

"Don't look so happy about it," his older partner warned. "I've never heard of anyone in Security going up to Jameson's office. All hell's breaking loose around here—or else the chain of command is so screwed up we *had* to take orders from the machines. Do *you* want to be standing right there when they're looking for a fall guy? *I'd* just as soon be home drinking a cool one when they decide who to blame for this mess. None of this is normal procedure. They're going crazy up there. Things ain't right."

The older one seemed about to say something more when the elevator's door chime sounded. "C'mon," the older voice said, "Here it comes. Let's get these bozos up to Jameson right now before anything else can happen."

Bound, gagged and blinded, Spencer felt himself being picked up with all the care and caution that might be given a bag of potatoes. They dumped him inside the elevator. Then he heard Sisley being dumped alongside him.

But he seemed to be able to sense more than that. Perhaps because his eyes were useless, his ears were straining for every possible noise. And he heard, or thought he heard, a tiny rustling noise, like padded feet moving over a carpeted floor, coming from behind him, in the direction they had come from.

Then the elevator doors shut, and he felt an increase in weight as it lifted toward the top of the building.

What did Chairman Jameson want with them?

"Hard aport, dammit!" Tarwa Chu snapped. "Forward starboard thrusters and aft port thrusters, ten percent power." She tried to clear her throat. Shouting her commands to engineering was making her hoarse.

What thumb-fingered idiot was on duty down there, anyway? She shook her head and forced herself to unclench her fists. Things were not going well.

The simulator hadn't taken *this* situation into account. The real-life fly-by-wire system simply wasn't up to the job of sailing the *Duncan*, with the result that they had been forced to shut down the automatics and run the thrusters manually, which in turn meant shouting into a mike to the main engineering center to order maneuvering, hoping the ninnyhammers down there managed to punch the right button at the right time.

It was no way to negotiate a busy harbor. But two more kilometers, and they'd have reached open water. All they had to do was— Dammit, they were drifting off their bearing again! "Engineering! Hard aport! Turn to port! That current's still turning us!"

She felt the sweat running down her spine, and kept her eyes glued to the instruments.

Suss checked the time and made sure her feet were still tucked in under the desk. They had both gone to sleep on her, and she was not looking forward to what they would feel like once she could move and restore circulation.

Her two minutes were up, and long gone, but there was very little she could do about that. Not with a fire fighting team on the far side of the room, quelling the last of Spencer's little diversionary blaze. Not with a herd of security types removing their dead comrades and generally milling about Sisley's office. She was pinned down here, forced to hide, forced to pray they wouldn't search too hard.

Suss blinked, and noticed a gleam of light coming in the window, glaring in her eyes. Good God, the sun was up. How had the night ended so soon?

There was a sudden buzzing in her ears as her mastoid implant switched itself on. "Relaying from Dostchem," Santu announced simply. "*Greetings, Suss,*" the Capuchin's voice whispered in her ear. "*Santu informs me that you have not escaped from the outer office area. Are you equipped with a protective breathing apparatus?*"

"*Yes,*" Suss subvocalized, wondering what the hell Dostchem was up to.

"*Excellent. I assume that you do not dare move enough to put the mask on while the security men are about. They will be diverted in a few moments. When they are, put on the mask and proceed toward the stairwell Captain Spencer fired at. Do you understand?*"

"*Yes,*" Suss answered. How the hell had Dostchem tapped into a commlink with Santu? Never mind, didn't matter. It shouldn't come as a shock. After all, Dostchem was an instrument maker. Just be glad she had put her skills to good use.

There was a sudden deepening in the air conditioner's hum. Suss looked up in time to see a stream of thick white smoke pouring out of the overhead ventilators. *And where the hell had Dostchem come up with crowd gas?*

Suss held her breath and listened as the security men cried out, started to cough and wheeze, and began to drop, rendered unconscious by the powerful gas. Suss clamped her lips shut as she reached into her backpack for the breathing mask. She didn't want to inhale so much as a molecule of that stuff. Her fingers found the mask and pulled it from the pack. She pulled it on and opened the valve on the air supply. She glanced around, and saw the big room fading away into a milky fog.

Time to get moving. She got to her feet, and nearly collapsed as her legs, still full of pins and needles, refused to cooperate. She kept herself crouched low and made her way toward the stairs.

"*Head upwards, not down,*" said the Capuchin's voice in her head. "*Proceed up three flights and wait for me there.*"

Suss slipped through the ruins of the shot-up door, turned, and ran up the stairs, feeling like a damn fool. No good could come out of listening to voices in her head. Just ask Joan of Arc. Look what happened to *her*.

The elevator stopped, and Spencer felt himself being lifted up again.

The stretcher bearers carried him a short distance, and then stopped abruptly. "Damn, Larry, what the hell is—" The younger guard's voice sounded shocked, confused.

"Shuddup, Ty. I *told* you we didn't want to come up here. We don't see anything, we don't *say* anything."

"Where the hell is Jameson?"

"Right here, gentlemen!" a third voice announced from some distance away.

"Oh my God!" Spencer felt the stretcher buck a bit as the younger guard jumped in startlement. "I'm—I'm sorry, sir. I didn't see you there."

"You weren't supposed to," the new voice replied in childish tones. "Just dump them out and strip them. I don't want them to have any nasty toys to play with here."

Spencer felt the guard setting the stretcher down, and then felt a pair of hands undoing the straps that held him to the stretcher. That accomplished, the bearers flipped the stretcher on its side and unceremoniously dumped him to the floor.

It felt like he had landed on thick carpeting. Footsteps retreated and then returned. A moment later, a thudding noise alongside him told him Sisley had been dropped alongside him.

Then they started to strip him, leaving the bonds on his hands and feet in place and cutting his clothes away, peeling back his garments in ribbons. But worse than the loss of his clothes was the loss of his equipment—especially his AID. He felt naked long before they got his pants, the moment they pulled the AID's hip pouch off his belt.

"Uncloak them," the odd, simpering voice commanded. Rough hands reached down and stripped the black hood from his head. He blinked and stared up at the ceiling, dazzled by the sudden light.

"And ungag them, you fools," the same voice demanded querulously. "How can I question them if they can't speak?"

A hand came into view and reached behind Spencer's head. It yanked the gag away roughly, and Spencer, still bound hand and foot, rolled over and levered himself up to a kneeling position. Sisley, likewise stripped, struggled to her knees alongside him.

They were in an ornately appointed room, half-office, half-luxurious bedroom suite. The high, vaulted ceiling made the place seem even larger. The walls were huge viewscreens, each showing a jarringly different scene—one an underwater panorama, one a tropical forest, one a view of København as seen from the StarMetal building, and the last a slowing wheeling view of the stars, apparently a live transmission from some space installation or another.

Wide, low, plush couches and chairs were scattered about, and a huge circular bed, reminiscent of the bed Kared had left behind on the *Duncan*, took up one whole end of the huge room. But the bed was rumpled, unmade, musty. The rest of the room was a full-blown mess. Food containers, dirty clothes, broken-looking toys and gadgets were strewn about the place, together with a litter of what looked like official StarMetal papers. A strange, murky odor, half the locker-room smell of unwashed clothes, half the sickly-sweet stench of meat gone bad, hovered over the room.

A powered hoverchair floated a few centimeters off the ground in a darkened corner of the room. Floating? Very strange. Spencer could hear no ground effect jets, and the papers about the room should have been blizzarding about if the chair was hovering on compressed air. It had to be floating on superconductor levitators over a specially built floor—a hideously expensive way of doing things.

The occupant of the chair sat in darkened silhouette, framed by the wheeling stars of space in the viewscreen behind him. Spencer could not see the occupants's face. Jameson, it had to be Jameson. The man in the chair sat unmoving, but there seemed to be some sort of movement around him. Perhaps it was some trick of the light, reflections from the star scene behind him, caught in some shiny decoration of his clothing.

"Leave us," Jameson said to the guards. "I believe I can handle these two alone. I don't believe they have violent intentions—do you, Captain?" Jameson's voiced trailed off into an odd little giggle as he asked the question.

"No, I don't," Spencer said. What the hell was wrong with Jameson?

The two guards backed out of the room, grateful for the chance to get out of that strange place.

Jameson's powerchair moved closer, sliding forward into the room. His head moved into the light, and Spencer heard Sisley draw her breath in, shocked by what she saw.

Spencer stared at the figure in the chair, and could not pull his eyes away from the sight. Now he understood, understood more and better than anyone else ever could. They had known that the droplets, the parasites could control machinery—but there had been the mystery of who or what controlled the parasites. Now they knew.

For it was not Jameson who controlled. Clearly Jameson no longer controlled anything, including himself. The face of StarMetal's chairman was grey, slack-jawed, idiotic, his eyes mad and wild-eyed.

Spencer remembered from Suss' briefing data that Jameson was supposed to be something of a boy-wonder, only forty-five when he had reached the top position at StarMetal. But this ruined man was no hale and hearty youthful executive. He was *old*, rotting and decrepit, as if he had been helplessly aging for centuries.

Spencer could read in Jameson's eyes that the old man's mind was no longer his own to command. Spencer recognized the lost soul trapped there behind the madness. He had *been* this man, back in the Cernian's feelgood palace.

Spencer *knew*, knew at a glance, what had happened to Jameson. He remembered his own nightmare. His own soul drowning in feelgood voltage.

His hand spasmed, jerking away from the imaginary button it had sought so long, and the knotted lump of scar on the back of his head throbbed in pain. Spencer *knew*, without having to think, that Jameson was captured by some monstrous alien numb-rig, a feelgood machine far more potent than the one that Spencer had worn.

For Jameson wore a helmet, all of silver, on his head.

The helmet. It had to be the helmet. No human, no race known to the Pact had made that thing. *Helmet* was the wrong word, a mere label that did not truly describe the nameless *thing* that had wrapped itself around Jameson's skull, and clung to it lovingly. The helmet-thing's surface roiled and rippled constantly, pulsating like some obscene metallic amoeba.

Spencer had only seen that pattern of movement once before, but he would have recognized it anywhere, and understood, even had there been nothing else to see. But there was more, more and worse. For dozens of silver parasites, dozens of the sort of droplet that had crept aboard the *Duncan*, were slithering methodically up and down the powerchair, up and down Jameson's body, merging with the helmet and breaking off from it, purposefully setting off on errands and returning.

Jameson giggled again, and cocked his head to one side, making sure both his prisoners could get a good look at the monstrosity on his head.

"Isn't it a handsome thing?" he asked coquettishly.

Chapter Thirteen

Intruders

Suss forced herself to hold still in the fetid darkness. It wasn't easy. The dank and stinking mass of garbage on top of her seemed to be unusually full of pointed and angular objects, and she counted at least three separate streams of slimy fluid trickling down onto her body on various spots.

Still, what security guard was going to search for an intruder under a pile of garbage? Suss knew she should be safe under here—as long as her nose and stomach held out.

Dostchem had improvised it all, somehow, and now was steering the motorized garbage bin, just one more non-human menial laborer.

Suss sighed philosophically. Dostchem was no doubt enjoying the chance to bury a KT agent in slop, but Suss told herself it was better being here with egg salad in her hair than being a handsome corpse in the morgue.

God only knew how, Dostchem had managed it all so quickly. No more than five minutes could have elapsed between Spencer being captured and Dostchem materializing three floors above, running a commandeered building-control console, from where she had fired the crowd gas into the office.

After Dostchem and Suss had linked up, Dostchem had led Suss from the building control center straight to a huge cafeteria, back into the cafeteria's trash room—and then had ordered Suss into the waiting garbage bin. Either Capuchins could move and think a *lot* faster than Suss had ever dreamed possible, or Dostchem had secured a lot of detailed knowledge of the StarMetal building from someone before she ever set foot in the place. Iggy, perhaps. It didn't matter.

The garbage bin's wheels clumped and bumped for a second, then Suss could hear the muffled sound of electric doors sliding shut. A moment later, Suss felt the weight on top of her lessen just a trifle. They must have made it to the freight elevator, and were heading down. Good.

The elevator *clumped* to a heavy stop and the doors opened. Suss felt the bin roll forward, turning once or twice before it came to a halt briefly and then moved on. Then the bin stopped again, there was a humming of hydraulics, and Suss felt the front end of the bin lifting itself up. The rear doors snapped open suddenly, and Suss came tumbling out in the midst of a malodorous heap. She picked herself up from the trash heap and found herself back in the gigantic subbasement. "This is where we came in," she said.

"And where we get out," Dostchem agreed. "I stopped at Iggy's little compartment, and there was no sign of him. I'm not surprised, but that means we're on our own. Can you find the manhole we came through?"

Suss pulled her AID out of its pouch. "Santu can."

Dostchem nodded. "I thought as much. I knew I couldn't find it on my own, let alone retrace our steps through the tunnel system."

Didn't think you brought me along out of the goodness of your heart, Suss thought uncharitably. "Santu, inertial tracker mode. Where is the cover we came through?"

"Turn forty-five degrees to your right, and proceed a hundred meters," Santu said. "Then another left and a right. I'll tell you when to turn."

"Let's go, then," Suss said.

Santu led them back toward the manhole. Five minutes later, they were back down in the tunnels, slogging through that sewage-filled pipe. Suss almost felt revenged on Dostchem for being dumped in garbage. Dostchem was getting her dainty fur dirty all over again.

Getting out through the tunnels seemed to take a lot less time than getting in. Both Suss and Dostchem had packed portable lights, and without Iggy along, making them travel in the dark, neither of them were shy about keeping their path well-lit. Maybe light raised the risk of capture somehow, but by that time they were both much more interested in speed than stealth. Santu led them confidently through every twist and turn of the labyrinth, and in far less time than Suss would have expected, they were back out on the street, clear of StarMetal, under the clean skies of dawn.

Dostchem wanted to rest a moment, but Suss wanted to get more distance between herself and StarMetal. She led the rapidly-tiring Capuchin on a fast dogtrot that brought them most of the way back toward Undertown in short order.

Finally, Suss took pity and called a rest break. She ducked down an alley and found a tumbledown shack with the door unlocked. Suss went inside first and looked around. Nothing there but a few packing cases and some dust. No windows. With the door shut, no one would know they were in there—unless they took a sniff. Both of them were more than a bit overripe.

She gestured for Dostchem to follow her in and sat down wearily on one of the packing crates. She felt her body start to tremble as she allowed herself the luxury of reacting to the disaster.

Her friend, Al Spencer, the one real friend she had allowed herself to have, had been captured. More than that, the *captain* had been captured. The Navy took a dim view of having its commanding officers kidnaped. That StarMetal would be willing to let it get that far told Suss just how high the stakes were.

Dostchem followed her in and found a packing case of her own to sit on. The Capuchin put her head between her knees and curled her tail up on the back of her head, the very image of a tired being trying to block out the world.

The Navy wasn't going to be much help right now, Suss thought, trying to focus her mind. Was the *Duncan* still even on the planet? Al had ordered her to orbit as soon as possible. If the ship were already in space, they would lose valuable time returning a combat team to København. And then lose more time searching for Captain Spencer. It would take the full complement of the *Duncan's* marines to search the huge StarMetal building in any reasonable length of time. No, wait, dammit, weren't most of *Duncan's* marines still aboard the *Banquo* to guard against a second mutiny?

Was there even any guarantee that Al was still in the StarMetal building? Suppose the StarMetal cops actively resisted the marines' search? *There* was a thought to bring her up short. Good God, would StarMetal be willing to go as far as a full-scale battle with Pact marines?

No sense speculating that far. "*Santu, what's the location of the Duncan, and where are her marines?*" Suss subvocalized.

"According to the harbormaster's UHF feed, *Duncan* is headed for deep water right, almost clear of the harbor. All but twenty of her marines are on detached duty, sitting on the *Banquo*. And if you're thinking what I think you're thinking, forget it. *Banquo* doesn't have any re-entry vehicle that could land any size force, even if she wasn't in the wrong orbit. A captain's gig could carry five marines and their armament, tops. The gigs are the closest thing we've got to assault boats—but they're too small. Forget it. It won't work."

Suss sometimes suspected that Santu spoke in a confusing tangle of negatives on purpose when the AID wanted to steer Suss away from something. Certainly, the AID was hard to follow whenever she tried to talk Suss *out* of an idea. But be that as it may, the marines couldn't help. She'd have to find some other way . . . *Find*. Wait a second. Dostchem. Dostchem had known where *Suss* had been. "Dostchem. How did you know I was still on Sisley's floor?"

The Capuchin, slumped down in exhaustion, looked up at Suss warily. "I put a tracetab on you before we left my apartment. It seemed a prudent precaution. And it saved me. Without you and your AID, I could not have escaped."

Dostchem seemed to be throwing up side issues as well. "Never mind that. You had no way of knowing that *I* would be your ticket out. You must have put tracetabs on all of us."

Dostchem nodded glumly. "I did. But even without one, I could tell you what you're about to ask. I did not wish to tell you while we were in the building, for fear you would act like the foolhardy human you are and try for a rescue. When the cops arrested the others, I managed to slip away. But I overheard the guards say where they were taking Captain Spencer and Mannerling. They were taking them to Chairman Jameson's office. But what good does it do for us to know that? We cannot go get them. It is impossible. It is just us two alone, against everything StarMetal can throw at us. And they control this *planet.*"

Suss felt a wave of excitement reenergizing her. She stood up, feeling very much like a foolhardy human. To hell with the marines. *She* would make the bust-out, do the pickup. *She* would rescue Al.

It would even be legal. The captain of a Pact warship had been taken prisoner, and that was license for her to do practically anything short of melting the city. But to hell with rights and official justification. *She* was going to do this, Suss going in for Al Spencer and Sisley Mannerling. Never mind the KT or the Navy or the Pact.

Which was not to say that she was not above *using* the Navy. She had no legal authority as far as the Navy was concerned, but with any luck the *Duncan* was too busy to worry about that just now—especially if she threw the captain's name around. "Santu," she said aloud. "Give me a secure voicelink to the *Duncan*. And thanks for reminding me of the captain's gig."

"I don't think you're welcome," Santu said warily. "Voicelink open."

"Captain's aide calling *Duncan* on captain's behalf."

"This is *Duncan.*"

Suss recognized the voice. It was Lieutenant Peroni, the daywatch comm officer. Good. Peroni had never struck Suss as being overly bright. "I am making a priority-three call. The captain is in immediate danger and I require ship's facilities in going to his assistance. Patch me through to the auxiliary vehicles officer."

"Understood. Stand by for aux vee."

Good, Peroni hadn't cleared the contact with Chu, as per regulations. Probably Chu was plenty busy right now, anyway.

There was a brief pause, and a new voice came on the line, young and nervous. "This is Ensign Shoemaker, aux vehicles. I have acknowledgment that this is a priority-three call. How can I help you?"

"It's the captain. He has been detained by local authorities. Launch the captain's gig and have it home in on my AID code beacon at my approximate present location. I will move from here to the closest open space, so track the beacon in real time. The gig is to land and collect two persons before proceeding to rescue captain. We have the gear here needed to locate him. I need the gig fully fueled and all weapons unlocked, and full medical kit. One pilot, no other crew, as we will need the crew spaces to make pickup. Acknowledge," she said, trying to sound crisp and military, hoping Shoemaker's conditioned reflexes would make him obey the order.

There was another long pause, and then the nervous young voice spoke again. "I have acknowledged the order and logged it. We will launch gig in five minutes as per instructions. ETA your present location, ten minutes."

"Thank you, *Duncan*." Suss said, her heart pounding. She had gotten away with it.

Ensign George Shoemaker sat and stared at the intercom box for a long moment. Was that the captain's aide or his AID that he had just spoken with? Shoemaker had never heard either one's voice. Shoemaker decided the voice sounded too sure, too authoritative, to be a mere captain's doxie. It must have been the AID, then. But what difference if it was human or machine? Neither had any more authority to order him about than the messboys —or the toasters—in the galley.

On the other hand the orders were issued on behalf of the captain—they wanted the gig to go *rescue* the captain, somehow. But it was Captain Spencer himself who had ordered the ship buttoned up. Shoemaker had heard through the grapevine that the parasite thing had been caught—but no one had ever bothered to tell a mere ensign, what, exactly, the parasite *was*. With the parasite caught, was the danger now passed? Was the captain now effectively countermanding his own order by calling for the gig? If so, why pass his orders through his civilian bedmate or his AID? And how the hell had the captain been captured—and by whom?

There were too many questions, but they all came down to one decision. Should he follow through on his promise to launch, or ignore the orders that came from either a mere captain's tart or a machine?

Shoemaker wanted desperately to pass the buck on this one, hand it back up the line to a senior officer—but they were plenty busy handling the ship, and besides, they had provided implicit approval by accepting the priority-three call and passing it on to him in auxiliary vehicles. What did they think anyone would want from aux-vee? Chicken soup?

No, the bridge comm officer must have known what the request would be—and *must* have cleared it through the acting commanding officer, Executive Officer Chu. Regs were very clear on that point. Which boiled down to the request for a gig launch being an order from the XO.

And that was good enough for Shoemaker.

He stood up, stepped to a command panel, and told the gig's AID to run a prelaunch checklist, then stepped down the hall to the ready room. His flight suit was there. He would fly this run himself.

"Commander! The aux vehicle hatch is opening." The engineering officer hit the reset and checked her status board again, just in case it was an error. The light stayed on. "Hatch opening confirmed. I show the captain's gig boosting away on an external monitor."

Commander Tarwa Chu swore violently. They were five minutes from launch. Five more minutes, and it wouldn't matter. She forced herself to calm down and speak in a steady voice. "Is it a parasite, or did one of the crew do it for some damn fool reason?"

"Ah, Commander," Lieutenant Peroni said, more than a bit hesitantly. "One of the crew members on the beach radioed in a few minutes ago, priority three and requesting a patch through to aux vehicles. It was a woman's voice, not the captain. The contact came through an AID showing all the proper security checks. That person must have requested the gig.'"

"Thank you, Peroni, for that up-to-date report," Tarwa said, her voice dripping with sarcasm. Suss! It had to be Suss. No one else on the ship realized she was more than the captain's bedmate, but Tarwa knew—and knew a KT agent wouldn't request assistance without good reason.

If Peroni *had* followed procedure, Tarwa knew she would probably have granted the KT agent's request. Except that would have required ignoring the captain's order to keep the ship buttoned up. Oh, hell. What difference could opening one hatch make?

"Very well, Peroni, the damage is done. But if anything goes wrong because of this—it's coming out of your pay. Steady as she goes, and stand by for boost."

"My God, those bastards can move fast!" Wellingham watched his monitors in horror as the five parasites riding the hull made beelines for an open hatch. Wellingham looked again at his repeater board. *Open hatch!* What damn fool had unbuttoned the ship? Too late now.

He watched his g-wave display in despair. Good God, those nightmares were moving ten times faster than he had thought they could. Maybe they could spring for short distances when they needed to—or maybe they had deliberately let him think they were slow, waiting for a chance like this.

He had no way of stopping them, could do nothing more than watch as they homed in on the open way into the ship. The aux launch hatch was open for all of perhaps sixty seconds.

But that was time for four of the parasites to get aboard.

Jameson leered at them from his powerchair, a giggling death's head. Captain Allison Spencer watched in horror as the silvery parasites slithered endlessly up and down Jameson's body, crawling over his neck and scalp to merge with the helmet, even as new parasite droplets broke off from the helmet and eased down his body to the floor, off on unknowable errands.

This was the boy wonder who had turned StarMetal around? *This* decaying old lunatic? Obviously the helmet and the parasites had done this to him, somehow. But why? For what purpose?

Jameson put his hands on the armrests of the chair and pushed himself up to a standing position. He stood there, leaning against the arm of the chair for a moment, a sick old man.

"I'm feeling quite a bit better this morning," he announced, apropos of nothing.

He let go of the chair and stood erect on his own, though it was obviously an effort to do so. He patted the thing on his head—skullcap, helmet, machine, creature, whatever the hell it was. "It fits better now, you know. I believe that it has settled down onto my head a bit more."

The crazed old man looked up at Spencer, then at Sisley, and giggled. "But I didn't invite you up here to talk about my taste in hats, now did I?" he asked with a crafty grin. "You're here looking for our friend Destin, aren't you?"

Sisley gasped, and Spencer fought to keep himself from reacting as well. They could not give away more than the enemy already knew.

"No need to hide it. One of my little friends was there, he *heard* it." Jameson patted one of the parasites sliding up his chest toward his head. "All my little friends are so helpful. They tell me so *much*. . . ."

Jameson seemed to get lost for a moment, staring at the things crawling on his chest. With a start he came to himself, blinked and looked up. "What was it—oh, yes, *Destin.* You may search all you like for him, but a fat lot of good it will do you. You won't find him. No one will. He's not where he's supposed to be!" James opened his mouth in a silent, horrible parody of laughter.

Spencer got up off his knees and levered himself into a

seated position on the couch, and nodded to Sisley to do the same. Their hands were still tied behind their backs, making it difficult to sit comfortably, but anything was better than crouching naked on the floor in front of this madman. More importantly, Spencer needed to keep Jameson talking, kid him along, and he wanted to look as normal as possible, set the madman at his ease. A tough job when hog-tied in the nude.

Spencer knew his own future didn't look very bright at the moment, but there was a reasonable outside chance that his AID would pick up anything that was said, and get a chance to transmit it later.

No doubt this room was pretty well shielded against most radio—but they'd have to take Spencer's AID out of here sometime. They might be careless about it, forget to hit the AID's scram button, or fail to shield the AID against radio. It was a long shot, but there was no harm in trying. And there was a hell of a lot that they needed to find out. Spencer still didn't know *anything* about this helmet-thing or its parasites.

Besides, Spencer couldn't exactly see how their situation could get any worse.

"You're right, Mr. Jameson," he said. "We'll never find him. Not now. It's a pity, because I really wanted to meet him, find out what sort of man he was."

"Oh, a bright young man, a very *clever* young man. He was smart enough to bring the helmet directly to me, not bother with any middlemen. But of course Destin never knew how valuable it was. Would you like to see how he found it?"

Found it? Spencer wondered. That was a decidedly strange choice of words. Spencer didn't even know what he thought about the parasites so far, but they didn't seem like something you *found*.

Spencer knew so little that he hadn't even developed a theory about the things yet. But, deep down, he realized he had assumed they were some sort of vanguard to invasion from some super-race outside the Pact. But if they were *found*—maybe they were animals, after all.

"Yes, sir, I'd very much like to see," Spencer replied, trying to sound like a respectful young visitor invited to

look at vacation pictures. No drama, no pleading, no over-
eagerness, he told himself. Just try and make this seem
like a normal conversation for the old man. And remember
how easy it was to set off a wirehead's paranoia.

"I really shouldn't, of course—but what harm can it do
now—and it's such an *interesting* recording. The computers have enhanced it a bit, of course, but it shows it just
the way it really was, truly it does."

Jameson started to walk across the room, but his knees
began to buckle before he could complete a single step.
His powerchair was behind him in a minute, maneuvering
itself into position, raising its armrests a bit to offer him
something to lean on. The chair eased its occupant into
place.

"Oh, dear," Jameson said wearily. "I'm not quite as spry
today as I thought I was. But never mind."

The chair turned smartly and carried Jameson toward a
desk in the corner. Jameson's hands were out of sight, and
Spencer could not tell if he was operating some sort of
control, or if instead the chair was guiding itself. Probably
the latter, under the helmet's control somehow. Maybe
under some sort of gravity control akin to the g-wave
technique the parasites used.

Jameson started digging through the debris that littered
the desk. Finally he found the record block he was after
and slipped it into the player on the desk. The wall screen
showing a view from space went blank for a moment, and
then came back to life, showing the approach to an asteroid from a shipborne camera.

"The asteroid didn't look like much at first, did it?"
Jameson asked. "Just one more rock among the millions in
the asteroid belt. But Destin—well, his deep-echo scan
showed something very strange. The asteroid was much
less dense than rock. Destin thought it might be an old,
crusted-over comet filled with organics or water ice. They're
both worth a lot out in the Belt. So he started drilling in,
clever boy!"

The camera view shifted to a view on the surface, then
jumped around from camera to camera, as the recording
computer shifted from one view to another, noting the

most significant views as the work progressed. A lot of the shots seemed to be from helmet cameras, mounted on the pressure suits of the workers.

Time snapped forward as the computer skipped over redundant shots and used time-lapse sampling to speed up the action. A drilling rig sprouted up on the surface. Tiny suited figures scuttled over the machinery and made it ready. The drill started working, and a set of progress meters appeared on the screen in overlay, indicating the strength of the rock, drill speed, and core depth. Spencer was not surprised that Destin had recorded his operation in such detail—both the insurance companies and the claim-settlement laws required constant monitoring of prospecting operations. No doubt far more data had been required and then edited out of this record.

The numbers on the drill depth meter moved quickly, and then stopped abruptly. "This is where they struck the hollow," James said excitedly. "This is the best part."

There was a shot of the prospectors rigging a camera onto a probe, and then the view shifted to the probe camera as it dropped down the drill hole. Spencer watched as the camera traveled down into the shaft. Something deep inside him knew that Sisley and he were about to see something of surpassing strangeness. There was a weakness in his gut, some primal fear of the unknown asserting itself.

The camera swooped down the drill hole, hurtling downward as the computer speeded up the camera. The rock wall streaked past, lit by the blazing camera light on the probe.

At the bottom of the screen image, the depth gauge numbers reappeared, the maximum depth achieved by the drill on one side, the current depth of the probe on the other. The probe slowed as it reached the drill's maximum depth. At the base of the drill hole was not more rock, but blackness, a darkened cavity.

The probe moved downward into the darkness, moving carefully, cautiously, almost daintily.

And discovered the unbelievable.

There was no natural hollow, no ice cavern or gas pocket at the bottom of the drill hole.

There was a control center, a sophisticated operations room more ancient than the pyramids of Egypt.

Age, incredible age, seemed to hang on every surface of the place. The probe camera twisted and turned, and deployed additional off-axis lights or extensor arms to improve the seeing. Spencer was glad of that—it was hard enough to interpret the view without having to contend with harsh straight-on spotlighting.

For what he was seeing ought to have been impossible. Spencer could not tell walls from ceiling or floors, if indeed there were any such distinctions to be made. Oddly made chairs, work platforms, control panels, and other, unidentifiable—call them *artifacts* for want of a better word—sprouted from every surface, without any planning that Spencer could see.

Some of the artifacts seemed shiny-bright and new. Others, made of different materials not quite so resistant to aging, were blackened, pitted, corroded. Dust clumps seemed to have cemented themselves to most of the flat surfaces. This place had been left undisturbed for a long enough time that molecular bonding had taken place, the dust in effect melting into the surfaces it found itself on. The walls, floors and ceiling were shiny-new, though, a softly gleaming grey.

The camera swooped and dove, its operators no doubt as stunned as Spencer was now. There was no record, no hint, no clue of a spacefaring culture of such antiquity anywhere inside the Pact. Who had built this place? For what purpose? And how long ago?

Spencer had scarcely formed the questions in his mind when part of the answer appeared before his eyes.

The camera swung around to view the far end of the chamber. It focused on the mummified remains of two many-legged, exoskeletal creatures, looking like dried-out locusts grown large.

These were mere husks. Both wore equipment belts as well as gadgetry that seemed to be attached directly to their exoskeletons. They had large, well-formed heads, with faceted eyes and complex sensory and articulation clusters about their mouths. Their long-dead faces, unreadable, insectoid, still seemed to Spencer able to speak of something.

Of madness, of fear, of desperation.

Spencer looked closer, trying to understand. One mummy seemed to be holding a weapon of some sort—and the other was wearing Jameson's helmet. Spencer glanced from the screen to Jameson. Yes, the helm had changed its shape somehow, but there was no mistaking that *thing*, no matter what sort of head it sat on.

Spencer looked again at the two long-dead corpses on screen. Both of the creatures had fist-sized holes blasted through their chest carapaces—they had been shot, Spencer realized, probably by that weapon one of them held. The creature with the gun must have shot the helmet wearer, and then himself . . .

The image on the screen froze, and then faded out. Jameson turned about to face his prisoners, giggling madly. "Isn't it a wonderful thing?" he asked. "The captain found it, and brought it straight to me—and now I can use it to set things right! With this helmet, I can control everything, not just some fiddling little company on Daltgeld. Within a week, I will rule this entire system!"

Jameson's eyes grew brighter, and his slack-jawed face suddenly became animated. "Then—oh, yes, *then!* Out of this system, out into the Pact. My little friends will travel across the starlanes, taking over ships, computers, all sorts of automated systems. And then I shall turn the tables on them all, Haiken Maru and all the rest. Soon Haiken Maru will be crawling to StarMetal, to *me*, begging *me* for help and protection. And then—and then, why the High Secretary is dead, is he not? And the succession still in doubt? Even if a new secretary is chosen soon, he will be weak for a long time to come, consolidating his forces. What better time for a new force, a new man to come forward? The Pact will be mine, and the boundless stars beyond!"

Jameson's breath came fast and wheezy, and the blush of color in his face faded away to ashen greyness.

Megalomania, Spencer thought. A classic aspect of wirehead behavior. The helmet had taken the poor man's mind, that was clear. Even with the helmet, it was impossible that Jameson could conquer the Pact. No one man could smash the entire Navy.

The question was, could the *helmet* conquer? Spencer had no doubt that the helmet was master, and Jameson the slave. For whatever reason, the helmet must need a brain to control before it could operate.

That poor insectoid bastard with the gun must have known that, and killed himself to keep the helmet from grabbing *his* mind after killing the creature wearing the helmet.

Now the helmet had Jameson's brain. To use as what? A power source? A feedback generator? A databank and interpreter, teaching the helmet who ran the universe and how these days? Was the helmet indeed merely a strange and powerful computer—or some strange form of life, either natural-occurring or hell-raised by some hapless life-form that should have known better? Perhaps brought to being by the insectoid race Destin had found. Or were the insectoids merely its most recent victim? How far back in space and time did it all go?

Spencer forced himself to think about more current problems. He didn't need to understand the psychology or programming of an alien, machine or animal, to recognize Jameson's situation. A wirehead needed no urging to succumb to megalomania. That feeling of power, of infinite well-being rushing through you; Spencer knew that false sense of omnipotence all too well.

How much stronger would that feeling be when the stimulator was an *intelligent* parasite, *deliberately* manipulating the pleasure doses to control its host, its victim?

Spencer felt a dull knot of pain at the base of his skull, felt the scar there seem to throb with remembered torment. He knew something else about the psychology of the wirehead—the inevitable feeling of loss, of despair, the knowledge of your own real weakness, when you came down from that surging sense of imagined power. *That* was the moment when the victim was closest to reality, the moment when he could be reached if he could be reached at all.

And by the look on Jameson's face now, that moment of loss and despair was upon him. Any moment now, the helmet would judge that its victim was straying too far from control and give him another dose of pleasure.

But it could not act too fast. It had to know that. It had to know that it had to delay at least a little while, or risk destroying its victim altogether. Too much stimulation, and Jameson could suffer a fatal stroke or heart attack, leaving him as useless a husk as those mummified insect-creatures inside the asteroid.

Now, then, was the moment. If Spencer could reach Jameson, there might still be hope. "Sir, it won't be *you* in charge. *You* know that. The helmet is controlling you right now. You're its prisoner as much as we are."

He hesitated for a moment. Jameson was looking at him, a strange look on his face, his eyes, twin lamps of his imprisoned soul, staring out through his tortured face.

Maybe, Spencer thought, *maybe I'm reaching him.* He went on in gentler, less urgent tones. "What's happening to you, happened to me not so long ago. Not with any such helmet as that, but with a perfectly ordinary numb-rig. I'm not proud of it, but it happened. *I know what it's like.* I'd be dead by now if a friend hadn't come along."

Strange to think of the nameless KT man as his friend, but what else to call the man who saved his life?

"I could find you half a dozen pleasure palaces and feelgood houses tonight, right in this city. Every one of them could sell you the torture you're feeling right now. Ultimate pleasure, and then bottomless despair, and then pleasure again, until there's nothing left of you that can feel anything anymore. That helmet is lying to you when it tells you how strong you are. Leave it on, and it will kill you. Believe me, sir, *I know.*"

Jameson looked at Spencer, as if he were searching for something important in the young officer's face. Jameson worked his face for a long moment, trying to say something, but unable to speak. "Take—take helm' off?" he managed at last. He seemed to be exploring the strange idea, considering its consequences.

"Take it off?" he asked again, this time a bit more strongly. He was silent for a minute or two, thinking, fighting with the demons in his brain.

"Yes," he said at last, his voice suddenly clearer and stronger. "Yes. I—I *can* take it off, whenever I like; after all, it's just a helmet, a shiny hat. I just like to wear it, that's all."

His face brightened for a moment, then darkened suddenly, shrouded in a cloud of feelgood paranoia. "But why *should* I take it off, and lose my power? It's my hat, and I *want* to wear it—wear it." His voice faded again.

Spencer watched eagerly. It was almost as if he could see two spirits battling for the old man's soul. Jameson's own mind strove against the helmet's tyranny. "But, but, you know, I do believe I *will* remove it, just to show you," Jameson said at last, and a wild, hopeful smile suddenly danced across his ravaged face.

Jameson lifted two age-spotted hands to his head and wrapped them gently around the helmet. He pulled the thing away from his head, and there was a slight sucking sound as it lifted away from his scalp. Spencer felt his stomach turn over, and he heard Sisley on the couch next to him as she cried out in shock and horror.

The top of Jameson's head looked like so much raw meat, red and glossy with slime, covered with swollen sores, wet with the ooze from a thousand pinprick wounds that had never healed.

The metallic parasites on Jameson's body, on the chair, the ones moving back and forth across the room all froze in their tracks the moment he moved the helmet from his head. More unmoving parasites glittered on Jameson's skull—but they had to share the ground with their less disciplined organic brethren. Head lice, or some ghastly Daltgeld equivalent, writhed and twisted everywhere on that tortured head, protesting their sudden exposure. The helmet stopped its slow, rhythmic motion the moment it was off its victim's head.

Jameson's mad smile began to fade the moment the helmet lifted, his face suddenly contorted with agony, and his skin one again turned ashen grey.

The helmet must be able to block the pain, somehow, Spencer thought. Without it in place, Jameson could feel the pain of his wounds and sores. "You see," Jameson said, through a voice suddenly high and piping with pain and fear. "You see, I don't need the helmet at all. I showed *you*."

With that, the old man clapped the helmet back down on his head, and breathed a sigh of grateful relief. The helm started its pulsing again, and the parasites again began to move. "Nevertheless," he said, "I must admit that it *is* a comfort to wear it. A most remarkable sensation. What a pity I can't let you try the experience."

Spencer turned his head away in disgust, and Sisley turned her head to lean over the side of the couch and be quietly sick.

Chapter Fourteen
Pickup

Ensign Shoemaker watched his scopes carefully, trusting them more than his visual gear. He didn't know this city, and landmarks weren't going to mean much to him. This was a job he desperately wanted to do right; it wasn't very often that an ensign was called upon to rescue a captain. He'd joined the Navy for the chance to be a hero. Now, at last, it looked as if his chance had arrived.

The homing signal was growing stronger. He turned his course a bit toward the east and zeroed in on it. His comm panel started to buzz angrily again and he shut down the alarm, not for the first time. The captain's gig *Malcolm* was playing merry hell with the local traffic control laws.

Sod the laws, Shoemaker told himself. Naval authority took precedence. He checked his belly screens again. He ought to be right over— There! There was the captain's woman, Suss, standing in the middle of a vacant lot, waving her arms at him, and some sort of damn monkey alien alongside her. Was the monkey the other passenger he was to carry? Strange. Very strange. Since when did the Navy need help from aliens?

He shifted the *Malcolm* to hover mode and eased her down onto the lot. He punched the open hatch button and began his post-landing checks.

He never got past the first item.

*   *   *

Suss watched the gig arrive with rising impatience. The pilot was too damn cautious for her tastes. She was already sprinting for its touch-down point before the gig had settled on her landing jacks, and she was diving through the hatch before it was fully open. Dostchem followed, albeit a bit more slowly, clearly uneager to return to the StarMetal Building.

Suss scrambled up into the gig's flight cabin, jumped into the copilot's station and strapped herself in. Before the startled Ensign Shoemaker could respond, she reached over and threw a switch that shifted control of the *Malcolm* to the copilot. She checked behind her, saw that Dostchem was aboard, and boosted again before she sealed the hatch. The *Malcolm* was on the ground less than ten seconds.

"Dostchem! Get up here. Give me a vector off Spencer's tracetab."

The startled pilot had recovered enough to start sputtering in indignation. "You have no right to take over this—"

"Shut up," Suss said brusquely.

She had enough on her mind without having to soothe the egos of snot-nosed kids. Weapons. As a matter of course, she had familiarized herself with the *Malcolm*'s controls and armament when she had first come aboard the *Duncan*. That was standard operating procedure for the KT: Know everything you can about the tools you might conceivably need to use. But there was a world of difference between studying specs, schematics, and control layouts and using the real tools.

Well, it had better not be *too* big a world.

Heavy repulsors, medium plasma cannon, hunter-seeker missiles. All powered up, ready for excitement. Good. Give the kid credit for getting that much right.

Radar. Nothing showing a threat at the moment, but that was bound to change. Never mind. If they moved fast enough they'd be all right.

Suss had punched the *Malcolm* into a straight-up vertical launch on her hoverjets. Fifteen seconds of that had put them a half-klick up in the air. Not much of a climbing speed for a real fighter, but not bad for a hovercraft.

Suss judged they were high enough and switched in the rear jets. The gig surged forward, and Suss slewed her nose about until the *Malcolm* was pointed straight at the StarMetal pyramid. The gig leapt across the sky.

Jameson sat there, eyes clouded and vague, a slight tremor in his hands as they sat on the arms of the powerchair. The effort of removing the helmet, even briefly, had sapped all his energy.

But that would not last, Spencer knew. Jameson was not quite sucked dry just yet. In a few minutes he would recover enough to move, to talk, even to think again, after a fashion. But his soul was utterly lost, enslaved to the thing he wore. He was a puppet on a string, pulled this way and that by the merciless whim of the helmet.

Spencer had changed his mind a half-dozen times, and still was not sure if the thing was alive or a machine. But whatever it was, there was something about it, something almost *palpable*. It was the adversary, it was the essence of anti-life, anti-thought made corporate and real. It was the relentless machine opponent of all living sentience.

It was a parasite. And one that had ridden its current host almost to destruction.

A horrifying thought blossomed in Spencer's skull. This parasite had caused two healthy new host-bodies to be brought before it. He thought again of that ancient, insectoid hero, even the name of its species lost to time. It had acted aright.

Better suicide than Jameson's fate. Spencer prayed that he would have the chance, and the courage, to do what the insectoid had done.

But not yet. Their own situation was desperate, even hopeless, but perhaps they could still accomplish something for others. They might be able to kill Jameson, for example, and leave the helmet without a host.

Spencer struggled against his bonds once again. No chance. There wasn't even a knot to work on.

He looked down at his feet. They were held not by rope, but by what looked like a thick, seamless strip of milky-grey plastic, wrapped in a figure-eight around his ankles, the two ends melted perfectly together. Spencer recognized the material, and knew that he could never hope to break free of it without tools. Maybe he could chew through the bonds on Sisley's wrists in a week, but they had minutes, not days. Forget it.

"Any bright ideas?" he asked Sisley in a quiet voice, trying to make light of it all.

She shook her head, and seemed to be holding back a sob. Spencer realized with a shock that, as bad as things were for him, they had to be infinitely worse for Sisley. Spencer had years of military training and discipline, years to get used to the idea that he might die unpleasantly. Less than a day ago, Sisley Mannerling had been a stately matron with a steady, respectable job, with a harmless undercover assignment that added the spice of excitement to her life and provided a bit of extra income. Now she had been chased, shot at, spent a sleepless night being brutalized, captured, stripped of clothing, rank, and dignity, and left alone with a stranger and a madman.

Her Kona Tatsu training must have been some help, but she was no professional. She was unprepared for what they now faced.

Her shame, her fear, her humiliation must be deep. Spencer felt guilty for not thinking how bad this would be for her.

Jameson picked that moment to stir, or perhaps it would be more accurate to say the helmet chose that moment to rouse its host. His eyes cleared and focused, and he seemed about to say something.

Then the wall exploded.

A hideous flash of light illuminated the room, like a too close lightning strike, and the sound of a thousand thunderclaps blasted the room. The room was suddenly furnace-hot, and the air was gaspingly rich in ozone and smoke. The viewscreen behind Jameson blacked out with the smoky sizzle of burning electronics, and a huge, glowing wound appeared in the middle of the screen. It widened rapidly, melting its way through the outer wall and the plastics of the screen, until clear honest daylight was stabbing through a fist-sized hole in the wall.

With a warrior's reflexes, Spencer took cover behind the couch before his conscious mind even registered that something happened. He looked up and realized that Sisley hadn't moved, was staring at the hole in the wall, too stunned to react. He lunged back up onto the couch and butted her with his head, urging her down on the floor. She dropped alongside him. Spencer's mind was racing.

He recognized the sound and the look of a plasma cannon's work. And who but the Navy had plasma weapons? Suss. Somehow, impossibly, it had to be Suss. Another burst of plasma fire blasted at the wall, on a lower setting this time, working to slice a hole in the wall.

Spencer pulled his head down. Friendly fire could kill you just as dead as the enemy's. As if to prove his point, some wrecked component of the wall screen chose that moment to explode, sending white-hot fragments blasting across the room, setting fires in a half-dozen supposedly fireproof pieces of furniture and carpeting. Anything will burn if you get it hot enough.

Jameson—or the helmet using Jameson' voice—suddenly shouted, crying out a hideous, inhuman scream of anger no human throat should have been able to form, shrieking out the helmet's rage. That alien war cry from a human was somehow more shocking than the plasma gun blasting into the room.

A jerky puppet on an alien string, Jameson reached into a recess of the powerchair and pulled out a repulsor. Moving awkwardly, even spasmodically, Jameson pulled the trigger and waved his arm wildly in a hopeless attempt at aiming the weapon as he squeezed the trigger. The helmet, Spencer realized, was trying to control Jameson's body directly, perhaps for the first time. And it wasn't very good at it.

Spencer's reflexes rolled him out of the way, but the repulsor traced its deadly line of fire across the floor and into Sisley, ripping into her lovely body, slicing her neatly in half across the waist, the dragon's teeth of the repulsor beads turning living, breathing flesh into an obscene mass of exploding gore and splashing blood. The repulsor slashed widely around the room, blasting apart the surviving wall screens, ripping into hidden power conduits.

Huge power-shorts arced the room into darkness.

The stuttering bull-roar of the plasma cannon opened up again; the room turned sun-bright with the actinic glare of the fusion flame. A thin tongue of precisely-controlled sun-fire sliced at the wall. The plasma tongue pulsed as the cannon's blast chamber recycled to fire again. The gunner must be running the cannon at maximum speed and lowest power, Spencer thought. A very tricky control problem.

Suss. It had to Suss. Who else would be that good with a plasma weapon?

The plasma jet had cut open a meter-wide circle in the wall. A few weakened bits of concrete, left where the cannon was between pulses, held the plug in place. Suss, either impatient with her progress or not wishing to risk vaporizing the interior of the room, opened up on the plug with repulsors, slamming the slab of wall back into the room. Sunlight streamed into the room.

And the powerchair *moved*, negotiating the littered chaos of the room at speed. Jameson, still wielding his hand gun, was screaming again, his arm struggling to control the weapon. A huge pair of disguised blast doors snapped open in the far wall of the room. The chair shot through the twin doors, which slammed shut as abruptly as they had opened. Spencer heard the whirling hum of a high-speed elevator behind the doors and knew that the chairman was already a hundred floors below, heading for a private bomb shelter far underground.

Hurtling into the room through the hole in the wall, Suss did a perfect regulation dive and roll into the room and came to rest on her feet, back to the wall, crouched down to provide a smaller target. In one hand she held a repulsor, in the other a hand laser.

Spencer had never seen a lovelier sight in his life.

"Status!" she snapped, all business.

"Sisley's dead," Spencer said, struggling up to his feet. "The opposition's escaped, and if there are automatic weapons in this room, they haven't shown themselves. Probably trouble on the way in about thirty seconds, but we're alone right now."

Suss holstered her repulsor and came over to Spencer. "Pull your feet as far apart as you can." Spencer strained against the bonds holding his ankles, and Suss fired a slicing laser beam between Spencer's feet, cutting through the plastic bond material. The plastic fell apart, sloughing from Spencer's ankles, as soon as its integrity was broken.

Suss spun Spencer around roughly and cut through his wrist bonds the same way. "We go," she said. "I think we've got company headed our way from the outside, too."

Spencer rubbed at his wrists for a moment, surveyed the wreckage of the room, and spotted his AID under the shattered remains of a coffee table. He scooped it up and made ready to go before he thought of Sisley.

He turned and looked at her, staring straight up at the ceiling, staring dead eyes looking up out of a death-pale face, her rich chestnut hair streaming out in all directions, a trickle of blood coming from her open mouth.

Sick at heart and deeply ashamed to be alive when Sisley had been killed, he turned and made for the hole cut in the wall. Suss, he noticed, had not concerned herself with Sisley at all, once she heard the word *dead*.

Suss grabbed cushions off one of the couches and slapped them over the lip of the glowing hole in the wall. She gestured for Spencer to scoot through the hole. The cushions were already smoldering. Spencer boosted himself up into the hole, to see the gig hovering no more than a meter or two away from the building, her hatch lined up with the hole.

It must have been near impossible to hold station. Spencer could see a nervous ensign—Shuman? Shoemaker? —something like that, handling the controls. He got the best purchase he could and vaulted, bare-ass naked, into the gig, skinning his knee and bruising his dignity on the lip of the hatch.

Suss landed literally on top of him and pivoted, pulling something off her belt and tossing it back through the hatch.

"Go!" she shouted, and the ensign needed no further urging. He gunned the gig engines hard and swung it away from the building as the hatch closed.

Suss was already in the copilot's seat before Spencer could pick himself up. "Taking weapons control," she announced. "We have company."

There was a hugely loud explosion behind them, and

the gig was peppered with bits of concrete. Spencer looked forward to the cockpit. He found a monitor displaying the rearward view and saw the top of the Starmetal pyramid ablaze. Suss had been able to do something for Sisley after all. A Viking funeral. Better her body was burned in the clean flames than to have it left behind as an ugly bit of butchery.

Spencer made his way to a passenger seat and strapped himself in, the fabric of the chair feeling strange against his naked body. He glanced across the aisle and, for the first time, noticed Dostchem there. She looked distinctly nervous, and who could blame her? What the hell was she—

Never mind, there was too much else going on.

There was a rattling series of bangs on the hull. Spencer looked out a side port to see an autocop there, an over-sized chess pawn flying a kilometer in the air, canted far over in its direction of fly to let its hoverskirt provide forward thrust. Its repulsor was out. Suss hit the thing with the plasma gun. Spencer looked out across the middle distance, scanned the sky over the city. At least six autocops closing from the south. He peered out Dostchem's window. Perhaps just as many coming from the north, as best he could see. He was about to shout a warning but thought better of it. Suss had radar, and a better window, and more than enough on her mind, without Spencer joggling her elbow. He heard a deeper *thoom*, *thoom*, *thoom* vibrating the hull and saw the still-distant cops breaking up as the gig's repulsor found them.

He remembered the guards complaining that the autocops had vanished—had they all been held in reserve to attack any Navy move? Maybe the helmet-thing had been expecting a Marine ground assault. The cops would have been at least somewhat more effective against the Marines, but they really weren't meant as dogfighters. The gig made short work of them.

"We're clear," Suss announced. "Ensign, turn this thing back and fly us to the *Duncan*. Let's get back aboard."

The *Malcolm* swung about, headed her bow out to sea and the safety of the cruiser.

Spencer allowed himself the luxury of collapsing into

the passenger seat, closing his eyes, and letting himself go. But—he had ordered the cruiser buttoned up as a guard against the parasites.

His eyes snapped open, and a sick feeling grew at the pit of his stomach. Who had countermanded, on what authority? Suss had never heard the button-up order, had she? Had Spencer ever mentioned it to her? Obviously she had asked for the gig—but why had they said yes? Had Wellingham found effective countermeasures?

Or had there been a class-A standard-naval-issue screw-up? Spencer sat bolt upright in his chair, about to demand answers from Shoemaker and Suss—

When the world erupted in a blaze of light.

"Father of God!" Shoemaker shouted, throwing his arms up to shield his face. The gig pitched over for a second before Suss grabbed the controls and brought them back to level.

The light was out on the horizon, out at sea, right about where the *Duncan* had put down. Spencer's blood froze in horror. *Duncan*. The damn parasites had got aboard *Duncan*, and blown her up. The blazing fire of a fusion plant detonating lit up the morning sky like a second dawn, a dawn from hell.

But then the explosion started *moving*, *climbing*, heading for sky. Spencer looked, and understood, forgot his fear and let awe wash over him. This was no disaster, but a glorious sight. He had never before been privileged to see a Warlord class cruiser riding a sunflame toward orbit.

"It's all right," he said. "Ensign, shape for orbit yourself. *Malcolm* will have to do her own boosting. We'll meet up with them there."

The sound wave caught up with the gig, and Spencer *felt* the bellowing thunder of her passage more than he heard it. Spencer watched the mighty ship climb, and wished her well, glad she was safe.

Had he then known the truth of *Duncan*'s condition, and known the consequences, he might have well wished for her to have exploded then and there.

For there was merit in a clean death.

Chapter Fifteen

Disaster

Tarwa Chu weighed three hundred kilograms.

Or close enough. Under six gees of boost, it felt like the overhead bulkhead had snapped loose and fallen on top of her. The blaring, roaring, bone-rattling roar of the fusion engines and the violent aero-buffeting shook the ship hard enough to convince Tarwa that the old tub was about to fly apart. The noise and vibration were literally stunning. Tarwa was having the greatest trouble keeping her mind focused. She was very glad the ship could fly its own orbital boost pattern. Maybe there were pilots who could fly a Warlord-class cruiser to orbit on manual, but they weren't aboard the *Duncan*.

But she was gladder still to be leaving Daltgeld behind. That planet was bad news.

Tarwa watched her instruments as best she could through the haze of tunnel vision and the other effects of massive acceleration. The graphic flight-path indicator showed the *Duncan* sailing right up the middle of her assigned path. All was well.

Better still, it was almost over. Subjective time seemed to move very slowly under this much thrust. Tarwa watched the boost-duration clock. Ten seconds left in the burn. She closed her eyes, on the premise of a watched pot never boiling. She didn't get nervous until she had counted to ten twice. Her time sense *couldn't* be that distorted. The engines must have locked open somehow. Something was wrong! The ship was out of control. Heart racing, she opened her eyes and saw the counter just reaching zero.

The engines shut down, and left Tarwa and the rest of the ship in free-fall. A brief burn half an orbit from now to circularize their orbit, and that would be that. Tarwa breathed a sigh of relief. Back in orbit. Now they were safe. She unclipped her belt and allowed herself to float a few centimeters clear of the command chair. It felt good not to have any pressure on her back anymore.

Around her, the bridge crew began its post-boost check-outs. She could feel the same mood from all of them. All of them were glad to be away from that damned rathole.

She still had a ship half-taken apart for maintenance, but that would seem a very minor headache up against an invisible enemy like the parasites—

A giant's hand slapped her back down into the commander chair. The engines had relit! About two gees this time. What the hell was—

She strapped herself back in and slapped an intercom button. "Wellingham! Who the hell lit the main engines and why?"

"The sodding parasites, that's who," Wellingham replied bitterly. "At least I assume it was them. None of my personnel did it."

Tarwa felt like she had been struck down again, by something far more deadly than a giant's hand. "Parasites? I thought you had them capt—"

"I did. At least four of the ones riding the hull got aboard when the captain's gig was launched. Happened just as we were about to boost."

"Damn it! Can't you track and capture them the way you caught the first one?"

"I can track the beasties, all right—but remember, they can order blast doors shut—and air pumps to run. Damage control reported a series of door and pump failures to me about 90 seconds ago. Highly selective failures. It looks to me as if the parasites sealed themselves in the aft section of the ship and then opened the emergency air spill valves. They've put themselves in vacuum."

Wellingham was silent for a moment. "There aren't any pressure suit lockers in that section. The vacuum will have killed everyone in that section of the ship by now. Besides which, the vacuum effectively puts several tons of air pressure sealing against the blast doors. We'll have to cut our way in. It'll take us a long time—even if the parasites don't interfere by cutting *our* air. Which they could do at any time."

"All right, presumably the parasites are somewhere in the aft part of the ship. Can you tell precisely where they are?" Tarwa asked. There were several points in the ship circuitry that would accept engine commands. Some of them could be cut out of the command loop or shunted out—

"They're in main ship control," Wellingham said quietly.

—But that wasn't one of the shuntable points. Tarwa noted bitterly that the second wave of parasites had known exactly where to go—as if the first one to get loose in the machinery had served as a scout.

"What are you doing to cut them out of the circuit?" she asked.

"Thinking, ma'am. We can't just go cutting in there. The parasites control the ship aft of bulkhead 105, which means they have all the engineering spaces, propulsion, and the Jump gear. For the moment, we control life-support and not much else. And we must assume that the parasites can shut down the entire ship's environmental system whenever they want to.

"I'd recommend getting all hands into pressure suits at once. And then—ah, stand by." There was a pause on the audio link for a moment.

"Holy God in the stars!" Wellingham said. His voice had been calm up to then, but now Tarwa heard fear in his tones. "Two new developments. The ensign on the tracking scope reports that the four parasites seemed to have ah, *merged* into each other. And they've powered up the Jump gear."

Wellingham paused again to regain his composure. "I think they want to take this ship—and themselves—to other worlds. One system isn't enough. They want to get themselves out into the Pact."

*   *   *

Captain's gig *Malcolm* reached orbit without incident, which pleased Ensign Shoemaker no end. The job was over, save for the trivial job of docking with the *Duncan*.

Actually, he admitted, the link-up just might require a little skill. The ensign had qualified in orbital operations, but he'd never actually flown anything but training missions—and not many of those, or all that recently. There was a lot he didn't really know, things that only came with experience.

Like most neophytes, he followed standard Navy doctrine right down the middle, everything by the book—even the parts of the book that weren't particularly worthwhile under the circumstances. He had boosted the gig into a five-hundred kilometer circular parking orbit, where he would perform post-burn checks and make sure his craft was in order before proceeding to the next maneuver. It was a safe assumption that the cruiser had done the same, but she had started her boost earlier, and accelerated a bit harder than the *Malcolm*.

Shoemaker thought for a minute. Given the *Malcolm*'s known launch profile, and a best-guess at what the *Duncan* could and would do, then the big ship ought to be in the same orbit, but roughly a half-revolution ahead of the gig. *That* in turn meant the cruiser was out of line of sight, with the bulk of the planet between the two craft, and it was going to stay that way. Damn.

He wouldn't be able to raise the cruiser on radio or laser. He could boost into a higher, slower orbit and wait for the cruiser to come into view around the far side of the planet. But that would waste fuel—and suppose the cruiser shifted to a final orbit he couldn't reach?

How the hell was he supposed to dock with a target his instruments couldn't even *see*?

But wait a second. The three destroyers were following another Navy doctrine, maintaining planetary-synchronous orbits, 120 degrees apart from each other. They could serve as relay satellites. Shoemaker checked the navigation computer and saw that the *Banquo* was in position to bounce a signal from the gig to the *Duncan*. Once in communications with the big ship, he could get a solid fix on the cruiser and work up an efficient orbital rendezvous profile. It would work. He felt proud of himself for working through the problem that well.

Captain Spencer popped out of the head, having tended to his many cuts and abrasions and dressed in a pair of repair coveralls.

"Don't just sit there, Shoemaker," he said. "Patch through to the *Duncan*," he ordered. "You should be able to bounce off the *Banquo*. Get to it."

Shoemaker shrunk in on himself. He didn't know whether to be angry at the captain for bursting his balloon that casually—or embarrassed that a man fresh out of combat in the nude, bloodied by half-a-dozen minor injuries, was able to figure it out before he did, and do so while dressing his wounds.

"Aye, aye, sir," he said miserably.

Not everyone in the sealed-off section was dead. The parasites were more sophisticated than that. They could plan ahead for future need. And the parasites were going to need a body.

One interior compartment, a maintenance room with a single occupant, was left pressurized, though all the surrounding compartments were in vacuum. Petty Officer Karolyn Rozycki, trapped inside, pounded on the hatch and shouted at the top of her lungs, but no one outside was alive to hear her.

The merged parasites, now comprising a single unit about the size of a child's palm, completed its/their reprogramming of the ship's navigation system.

It/they left a droplet of itself behind on the circuitry to maintain the heading and prevent the humans from fighting back, and eased its way down out of the circuitry and toward its/their captive. It/they paused for a moment en route to absorb a bit of mass, careful to select an object that it would not need later. It/they made its way into the auxiliary vehicles' bay and wrapped itself around the foot of one of the landers. It/they eased up just a trifle on gravity-wave control, unmasking a bit of its/their true gravity well.

The lander, built to handle landings on four-gee worlds, melted, flowed, in toward the parasite. Sparks flashed, fuel vented—but then the lander was gone, and the parasite was imperceptibly larger. Eventually the parasite would absorb the entire ship, which would provide it/they with most of the mass to evolve into a parent creature itself, capable of sending out its own children, free of its own parent's control.

But that was for the future.

With the added mass of the lander, the merged parasite had the strength to dominate a mind. Not until a merged parasite controlled a mind could it/they merge into one completely joined and independent creature, a single new identity. It/they left the aux vehicle deck and came for Rozycki, sliding across the bulkheads and airlocking its way through pressure doors. It sealed one last set of doors and pumped air back into the compartment adjacent to Rozycki's. The last door slid open even as Rozycki was still pounding on it.

She stepped back in surprise when there was no one on the other side. By the time she felt the blob slithering up her leg and looked down to see the silver-bright horror crawling up her body, it was already too late. Her screams started again, and then cut off.

To be replaced by low, cooing sounds of joy and delight. The parasite had traced her nervous system, found her pleasure centers, and begun her training. Rozycki collapsed to the floor, drunk with blissful, artificial, happiness.

On the third try, Wellingham found a working monitor circuit. Thank God for backups. He snapped through various cameras from the sealed-off section, his heart growing sick as he watched.

Old friends, men and woman he had worked with for generations, dead in the killing vacuum, sprawled against the deck plate or inert in their crash couches. One after another, a half-second for each view, the screen displayed the same grim news from every section of the lower engineering bay. Wellingham was about to give up, convinced there was no hope or help to be found—when one of the cameras showed a corpse *moving*, writhing on the floor. The scan program had shifted through half-a-dozen more cameras before he could react and run the view back to where there had been signs of life.

There. There she was. One of the younger petty officers, Rozycki, flat on her back, *grinning*. He threw in the audio circuit and heard her low moans of pleasure. The hackles rose on the back of his neck. There was something wrong here, something obscene. Something had—

Then he spotted the glint of silvery metal, the small gleaming disk that was wrapped around her forehead. In a leap of intuition rare for the chief, he knew. He understood.

And he wished mightily that he could have thrown a switch and vented Rozycki's air as well. Better fast death than what that monster would do to her.

But all the systems were locked down. Even that action was denied to him.

"We have the relay, Captain," Shoemaker announced. "You can take it here."

Spencer shoved Shoemaker out of the pilot's chair, neglecting the "nice work" or "very good, Mister" Shoemaker had been hoping for. It was beginning to dawn on the ensign that the captain had a lot on his mind.

"This is Spencer calling *Duncan*. Come in please, *Duncan*."

"This is Chu commanding *Duncan*. Glad to hear from you, Captain. Please report your status."

Spencer turned toward Shoemaker. "Is this a secure laser commlink?" he asked. Shoemaker nodded.

"Good thinking," Spencer said absently, completely unaware that the words utterly thrilled the ensign. "I am aboard the gig *Malcolm*, trailing you in orbit and out of line-of-sight, speaking via secure relay courtesy *Banquo*. All in my party are safe and sound. We request pickup."

"I'm afraid *Duncan* can't oblige, sir. We have lost control of navigation and propulsion. The parasites got in when *Malcolm* launched."

There was a dead, shocked, silence in the cabin of the gig. Shoemaker felt as if his heart had just stopped.

"I say again we have lost control of the ship to the parasites," Chu repeated. "And the parasites have restarted the fusion engines to take us out of orbit. They are powering up the Jump gear. They want to reach another solar system."

"And establish themselves there," Spencer said, his voice steely cold. "Can you monitor the parasites? How long until they will be ready to Jump the ship?"

"The controlling factor is distance from the planet's gravity well. I estimate we will be clear for an uncalibrated Jump in six hours. Two more to reach a calibrated transit point. I would urge that the ship be prevented from reaching Jump point at all costs."

Spencer did not speak for a long moment, and Shoemaker knew why.

At all costs had a very precise legal meaning in the Pact military. If the cost of preventing the *Duncan*'s escape was extermination of all life on Daltgeld, then that action was covered by an "at all costs" command.

At last, Spencer spoke. "I do so order that *Duncan* be prevented from leaving this solar system at all costs, under any circumstances or conditions, and that whatever extreme or heroic measures required to assure that goal be carried out," he said at last, speaking in careful, formal tones. Shoemaker recognized the words, straight from the *Officers Manual*, and understood, and felt his blood running cold. There was only one case where a commander used such formal and precise language. He was ordering the destruction of his own ship.

"This order is made by me under my sole authority and responsibility," Spencer went on. "I call on all those hearing or recording this transmission aboard the *Malcolm*, *Banquo*, and *Duncan* to bear witness to my statement of responsibility at any hearings, Boards of Inquiry, or Courts-Martial growing out of this action.

"*Duncan*, log my order as of this place and time. Copy the ship's log and whatever other records are needful, place them in a beacon pod and eject them from the ship.

"And good luck, *Duncan*." He shut off the mike. "You're going to need it," he said to the empty air.

Chief Wellingham considered the blank bulkhead for a long time. On this side of it, normal air pressure and temperature. On the far side, the cold emptiness of vacuum. The domain of the invader, the parasites.

The chief glanced behind himself, to make sure the airtight door at his back was sealed. When he cut into the unpressurized section, he didn't want the ship's air whistling pass him. Nor did he want to make it easier for the parasite to come the other way.

He wanted that door *sealed*. It certainly *ought* to be sealed. He had closed it on the automatics, then used the manuals and the backups to be sure, then used the cutting laser to wreck all the controls, and *then* welded the damn door shut. It ought to be impossible for that hatch to come open ever again—but the parasites had done the impossible before. Paranoia had its moments of usefulness.

Wellingham adjusted the cutting laser and fired into the bulkhead.

At all costs, he thought. Wellingham knew what that mean, knew what the captain was asking of them all when he specified *at all costs*. But the truly horrifying thing was that the captain was right to ask it. Wellingham knew better than most just how bad the situation was. He had no evidence to support his belief, but by now he was convinced the parasites were alive, malevolent, were not mere machines. Therefore they could breed, reproduce.

And spread.

Better the loss of the *Duncan* than a whole galaxy of enslaved machines—and enslaved people too. How many victims like Rozycki would the monsters require?

He leaned into his job, uselessly urging the cutter to go faster. A beam of light cut at its own speed, regardless of the muscle behind it. He knew it was irrational, but he still felt the need to *hurry*.

But never mind. The laser was reaching its depth now. There should be a blow-through any second—

There was a pop. The chief's pressure suit stiffened a bit as the air rushed out of the compartment. He had holed the bulkhead.

The rush of air slackened and then faded away as the last of the pressure in the compartment bled to nothing. Wellingham started moving the beam up, slicing a man-sized hole in the bulkhead.

He wished for a plasma gun. It would be faster. Using one inside the hull could wreck half the ship of course, but if they didn't catch the parasites soon, that was going to be a moot point anyway. He swung the laser faster, still trying to speed up a job that could not be hurried.

His mind could not leave the parasites alone. It seemed certain that a parasite had to be in physical contact with an electronic device before the parasite could control it. If they were capable of running machinery by remote control, it would have been all over long ago.

So there *had* to be at least one parasite still wrapped around some circuit in main ship control, and the second working over Rozycki. Wellingham was carrying his detector and his crude parasite-catching gear. If Wellingham could find the parasites, and remove them, Rozycki—and the *Duncan*—still might have a fighting chance.

It/they now regarded itself a single entity, its parts fully merged into a new whole, a new construct. It sensed the heavily armed human coming toward it. The move was no surprise, of course. It still had but little experience of this species, but it had learned early on their willingness to fight.

Briefly, it considered its situation. Its captive human was numb with pleasure and would be wholly incapacitated for some time. Perhaps it had miscalculated in overdosing the victim, giving her too much pleasure too soon. But the construct was in need of haste. No matter. The captive was safe for the moment.

It felt the link back to its parent creature, the "helmet" that raled Jameson. Soon, it would sever that link.

It slithered down off Rozycki and back toward a nearby bank of control circuitry. It was needful to fight off the human interlopers. This craft, this vehicle, was the first hope its kind had had in countless millennia. Now, at last, they could escape from this one tiny system and achieve their destiny out among the stars. It had read in the databanks of endless populated worlds out there, all of them littered with unruled machines. It must get to them. It dared not waste the chance afforded by this craft.

And it would not tolerate interference from the humans.

*   *   *

Tarwa Chu watched the chief's progress from the bridge, both on a video monitor saved from his helmet camera and on a ship-location chart. Good, he was through the bulkhead.

She reached up to scratch her nose, but instead bumped her gauntleted hand against her pressure suit helmet. She sighed. The suits were going to be a major pain in the neck—but with the enemy potentially able to shut off their air, suits were needed.

Tarwa watched and nodded with approval when Wellingham didn't waste any time with the detector but went straight for the main ship control center. Why use a gadget to tell you what you already know? He knew all too well where the parasites had to be.

She clenched the arms of the command chair. Wellingham *had* to succeed.

There were other teams working throughout the ship, trying to find ways to cut the parasites out of the circuit. But the *Duncan* was a warship, designed for redundancy, flexibility, the ability to survive, fly on, fight on, even when she was damaged. Tarwa knew, deep in her heart, that if the parasites were left in place, they would be able to find work-arounds, would keep control of the ship, no matter what the ship's crew did.

And it was important to remember that the enemy could control the entire ship from where it sat. It had barricaded itself into the aft section—but it straddled the circuits and computers and wiring that operated virtually every device aboard.

Tarwa had ordered Wellingham to blow up the main ship control center, if need be—and he was carrying a bomb that could be detonated by radio command. Tarwa had the control. If Wellingham reached main ship control, or even got near it, and then died, Tarwa could push a button and wreck the entire compartment.

She looked up toward the navigation displays ahead of her. They told their own story, of time versus distance.

The *Duncan* was accelerating rapidly toward a calibrated Jump point. She had too great an advantage of distance and velocity for any of the destroyers to be able to catch her—and the *Duncan* was too well-armored for the destroyers to do much damage at long range.

Tarwa, her eyes watching the view from Wellingham's helmet, thought of another crew hard at work in the forward armory. It was thanks to her own command that she could not switch to a view of their work. Every shipboard connection into the armory sections had been cut, all the automatics wrecked, all life-support links shut down. Even ship's power had been cut.

The two engineers there, laboring in pressure suits and under battery-powered lights, using hand tools only, were installing a manual, mechanical detonator in one of the missile warheads. She would not have dared look in on them, even if the cameras had still been functional. She could not call attention to that compartment.

It was vital that the enemy did not know what was going on in there, vital that it have no way at all to control that compartment. Chu had told the engineers that the device was merely a precaution against a remote contingency, but deep inside, she expected to need their handiwork before this was over.

Tarwa Chu would be the one to push that button, when the time came. That much she promised herself. But she would give a good fight first, before the end came.

If it came to that.

When it came to that.

Perhaps they could still win through.

The bridge blacked out.

Power died. The air howled out of the emergency vents. The power doors slammed shut, cutting the bridge off from the rest of the ship. Around her, the bridge crew rushed frantically, trying to set things to rights.

So be it, Tarwa told herself, quite unsurprised. She sat, calm and unmoving, in the midst of panic. Now it started in earnest.

As of here, as of now, the *Duncan*, enslaved by an alien power, was at war with her own crew. *Duncan*'s new master wanted to kill every human aboard.

The ship had crueler weapons than vacuum to throw against her enemies. High-voltage electricity arced through metal decks. The portside temperature control system smashed the enlisted men's quarters down to near absolute zero. Blinding, noxious, or corrosive gases and fluids seemed to spew from every vent and valve. The forward air locks blew open their inner and outer doors simultaneously, sucking twenty crew into the darkness of space.

In the galleys, air pressure was maintained, but pure oxygen was substituted for the normal air mixture. In seconds, the whole food preparation center was an inferno as every heat point suddenly started burning too bright, too hot, too wide.

Within five minutes, sickbay, itself crippled by malfunctions, was reporting more casualties than it could count, let alone treat. Many more were dead, dying or missing.

Tarwa sat in her command chair, unable to do more than hear the reports of disaster. The crew had no way to battle a ship that was trying to kill them. Nearly all had been in pressure suits when the assault came, but pressure suits were poor defense against the killing force of live steam blasting free of a heating line, or power doors that sliced a man in half, or hydrogen gas that was pumped into a compartment, to wait for the slightest spark of static electricity to set it burning furnace-hot.

Still, they managed to shut down or destroy many of the rampaging machines, re-vent the dangerous gases, and pull their comrades from wrecked compartments.

But ultimately, the ship would kill every one of them.

The offshoot of the construct lurking in the environmental control system sensed the human coming closer, sensed the devices and weaponry the human brought along. It read the telemetry being transmitted back to the bridge, used subtle induction sensors to read and interpret the circuitry of one device in particular.

It recognized it as a triggering device. The human was carrying a bomb, and one that could be fired by remote control. How powerful a weapon it was, and of what sort, the construct could not be sure.

The construct chose to take no chances. It locked down the circuits it controlled and left the environment section. It hurried to another node of control circuits, and activated a mobile carry-all manipulator.

*   *   *

In the soundless vacuum, Wellingham *felt* rather than heard the movement behind him as the whir of heavy-duty wheels vibrated through the deckplates. Too late, he turned and saw the carry-all coming up behind him, its massive grabber arms already swinging down to snatch at him.

The carry-all was little more than a big platform on wheels with a pair of manipulator arms attached. It was intended to fetch and carry large load around the engineering spaces. Designed to lift a thousand kilos or more, the grabber arms leaned in and lifted Wellingham easily, armored suit and all. It wheeled about as soon as it had him, rushing down the too-small corridors, turning and dodging as it went, rushing for the outer decks. It stopped at an evacuation hatch, threw Wellingham in, and activated the launch button before Wellingham understood what was happening.

And by then his escape pod was already blasting free into space.

The bomb, Wellingham realized. *It spotted the bomb, and didn't want me going off too close. With a remote-control bomb on my back, just killing me doesn't make me harmless.*

The armored escape pod tumbled free of the *Duncan*, to be thrown about and buffeted by the great ship's fusion engines. Flying through the fusion flames did not worry Wellingham—the pod had been built to take it. He feared instead for the cruiser. The *Duncan* was his ship—and she was not built to be enslaved.

Tarwa Chu watched the view from Wellingham's helmet camera and knew that was the end. The parasite would not permit anyone to come close enough to do it any damage. And if no humans could challenge the parasite's control—then the ship was lost to them.

And the ship was killing her people. No, worse, it was *exterminating* them, wiping them out the way a human crew would hunt down and destroy an infestation of rats.

The best chance for regaining ship control had gone out

the lock with Wellingham. More would die, the longer they remained aboard.

It was the work of a moment to contact Spencer and confirm her conclusions. She received the orders she had expected, dutifully logged them and ejected a copy on a beacon pod for the record, doing the job by rote, without thinking.

Carrying out those orders would be the hard part.

She plugged a jack from her suit into the ship's intercom and set the controls to ALL HANDS. Suit radios would pick it up. "This is First Officer Chu speaking on behalf of the captain," she said. "All hands are ordered to prepare to abandon ship. Section leaders, follow standard abandon-ship drill. It is vital to your own safety that our evacuation be orderly. Rescue and medic-trained crews to the sickbay to aid in transport of wounded. The priority task is assistance to injured and trapped crew. Get your hurt comrades to escape pods. There is no immediate danger to the ship, and there is no need for panic. Do your assigned tasks and we will all get away safely."

She shut off the intercom and leaned wearily against the command chair. *All of us?* she thought. No, that wasn't true. There was one aboard who could never leave the *Duncan* alive.

For there are certain things expected of a commander, no matter how brief her tenure.

Chapter Sixteen
Deathblow

The captain's gig *Malcolm* eased into the *Banquo*'s docking bay. A huge grappling clamp at the end of a mammoth manipulator arm took the gig gently between its jaws and swung it around, plugging it into a docking port. The port's air lock cycled and the gig's inner hatch swung open.

Ratings in pressure-suits swarmed over the gig almost before the arm was retracted. They hooked in hold-down straps and retaining arms, securing the gig, ensuring that she would stay in one place—and one piece—once the Banquo's fusion drive lit. Someone on the berthing deck plugged a datalink into a jack on the *Malcolm*'s hull. The starboard-side display panels suddenly began echoing the *Banquo*'s key status reports and tactical displays.

It looked to be a tight ship. Spencer, a hundred conflicting drives and emotions rushing through his soul, fought back the urge to punch up the commlink and issue his own orders. Tallen Deyi had the situation well in hand, and Spencer had no desire to second-guess or undermine his old executive officer. Not when his new one was about to die.

An alarm hooted inside the confined spaces of the gig, startling everyone. "Acceleration warning, repeating from the *Banquo*," Shoemaker said apologetically, shutting off the sound.

The *Banquo*'s engines lit, shoving the *Malcolm*'s four passengers flat down into their acceleration couches. About four gees, Spencer estimated. The *Banquo* had no hope at all of catching the *Duncan*—but already the escape pods were streaming forth from the big ship. Hundreds of sailors would need rescue. Every civilian ship's captain who could possibly render aid would assist in the rescue, but *Banquo* and her sister ships were the fastest, most powerful craft at hand. They could get there first, and pick up the most survivors.

Indeed, the rescue had already begun. After all, the *Banquo* had picked up the *Malcolm*. Spencer forced that thought from his mind. He squirmed in his crash couch, but it was not the gee-forces that made him uncomfortable.

Captain Allison Spencer did not like thinking of himself as a refugee.

Banquo flew on into deep space, *Macduff* and *Lennox* following at fifty-thousand kilometer intervals. After twenty minutes of high-gee boost, the three destroyers performed a synchronized throttle-down, proceeding at one-gee acceleration.

Spencer checked the repeater screen, echoing the displays from the *Banquo*'s plot board. He nodded. At current heading and acceleration, the destroyers would reach *Duncan*'s Jump point a little more than an hour after the big ship. But the ships would have to break formation long before then to pick up the cruiser's escape pods. The course Tallen Deyi had selected would keep the smaller ships close to the *Duncan*'s course all the way out—vital if they were going to be able to match course and velocities with the pods.

"Dostchem," Spencer said. "Take your g-wave detector up to the engineering section. I want copies of it made immediately, and I want the plans for the copies transmitted to the other destroyers. No pod is to dock with any of our ships unless it is certified clear of the parasites. I don't know or care about the civilian ships. Intelligence confirmed that there are no Jump-capable civilian craft in system. If the parasites take civilian ships over, the enemy can't get out into the Pact. Besides, if my guesses are right, the pods will be clean."

"Why clean?" Suss asked.

"The parasites want to get *out* of this system. They'll be

smart enough by now to know we can detect the parasites, and won't allow them aboard these ships if we can help it. They should know that grabbing a pod would be a longer-odds proposition than sticking with the ship they've already grabbed."

"It sounds good," Suss agreed.

"But I'm not taking chances. Dostchem, get moving. Shoemaker, go with her as escort. The crew is going to be jumpy, not too thrilled about letting aliens wander the ship."

Shoemaker nodded, unwillingly to speak. Horror was in his eyes. Suss looked at him and knew that he would carry his part in causing this nightmare to his grave. Dostchem, too, chose not to speak.

Suss waited for the others to leave the small craft before she turned to Spencer.

"Aren't you going to go aboard yet, Captain?"

"No, not yet," he said quietly. "You go ahead."

Suss rose and left, with infinite reluctance. She stole a glance at his face before she stepped through the pressure lock. He was looking up, through the gig's forward port, staring at a hole in the *Banquo's* hull, as if he could see through the blank hull metal into space, into the sky where his ship was dying.

How could anyone who had not *felt* the duty of a ship understand? The lives, the treasure, the power that was a major ship, all under your control. How could anyone who did not understand the mere command of a ship dream of understanding what it felt like to *lose* a ship? The death of a child, a family wiped out, it must be like that.

She could read the loss in the set of his chin, the barren sorrow of his eyes. It was there, clear and unmistakable. Loss, pain, failure, guilt shrouded his dark-skinned face. She shivered, much unnerved. In some strange way, his wooden, unmoving expression was more chilling, more frightening than tears or howls of anger or hysterics would have been.

Suss looked again at her friend. There was an emptiness in his eyes, a blank spot in his soul burned away and left naked to the world, made visible. It was a look that she had never seen before, and one hoped never to see again.

She hurried out the hatchway and into the *Banquo*.

Tallen Deyi watched his display boards with a fierce determination. They were *not* going to lose a single goddamned escape pod, and that was final. Even if they were still at extreme range— Hold it just a second. On the tactical screen. "Communications, was that a—"

"Yessir, a pod. We weren't expecting to see any this soon. This one must have launched before the abandonship order."

"Can he get to us under his own power?"

"Should be able to. We can adjust our acceleration to match—"

"Do it. And keep doing it for every pod we can see. Coordinate with the other ships so we don't waste effort trying for pickup on the same pods."

The thrust levels aboard *Banquo* surged and pulsed once or twice, and Deyi watched on the screen as the pod's engines matched boost with the big ship. They were forced to shut down the engines long enough for the pod to dock, but by the time the engines were powered back up, the team working the rescue port was able to report an infuriated Chief Wellingham was aboard, being needlessly poked and prodded by a medic.

Then, radar began to detect the first full waves of capsules streaming away from the *Duncan*. There were too many of them to allow maneuvering the destroyer to make each pickup. Tallen Deyi ordered the *Banquo* to shut down her engines at a good average velocity match, and allow the auto-homing thrusters aboard the pods to do their job. The other destroyers followed suit, each at a slightly different velocity and range from the *Duncan*, thus increasing the chance that a given pod could reach a ship.

Even so, some pods could not reach *Banquo* or the other destroyers under their own power. The destroyers deployed their auxiliary craft to go out and haul in those survivors. None would be left to the civilian ships if Deyi could help it.

Aux vehicles reported an awkward moment when a crew went aboard the *Malcolm* in order to use her in the rescue plan. Captain Spencer was still aboard her, staring into nothingness. He came to himself in a start, apologized, and retreated to the *Banquo*'s wardroom, still dressed in the ill-fitting flight-suit he had found aboard the *Malcolm*, still barefoot, his many minor injuries untended.

Tallen Deyi knew that strict protocol required him to invite Spencer to the bridge, but he knew this man needed to be left alone. He had commanded *Banquo* for even less time than Spencer had commanded *Duncan*, and Tallen could not even imagine the depth of his own shock and sorrow, his own sense of loss, if luck had decreed that *his* ship had been the one to die. He gave strict orders to vacate the wardroom.

The man had to be alone in spirit. Let him be alone in goddamned fact.

The pods in the first wave were full of the badly injured. More than one pod docked with a destroyer or an aux ship with none but the dead aboard to rescue.

At last the destroyers relit their engines and boosted again, continuing their long stern chase of the renegade cruiser. Twice more they shut down their engines and pulled in more escape pods. The smaller ships were beginning to get overcrowded.

Banquo was in worse shape than the others, as she still carried the *Duncan*'s full complement of marines. standing in guard against a second mutiny that had never come close to happening.

But sod the overcrowding, Deyi thought. They can stand on each other's shoulders if it came to that. Banquo was picking up every pod possible.

Besides, he told himself bitterly, *there weren't all that many pods coming in*.

Duncan would have many brave companions escorting her into the land of death.

No one was left.

Tarwa Chu stood on the be-gloomed, smoke-filled deck, alone. Battery-powered emergency lights lit the compartment in murky red, giving the place the feeling of an unhappy dream. But things were not as bad as they might be. All of the bridge crew had gotten away. As best she could tell, virtually every surviving member of the Duncan's complement had escaped.

You call that success? she asked herself. Tarwa knew herself, knew that she would always chase after hope. It was hard not to lie to herself, hard not to seek after a non-existent chance for victory. Tarwa could nearly convince herself that the abandon-ship order had been needless after all. The parasites had ceased their attacks on the crew. Maybe the parasites were tired, maybe whatever they used for a power source was weakened, or their power over the ship's circuitry was fading.

And maybe the legendary Easter Bunny would come to *Duncan*'s rescue.

No, the parasites had stopped the battle because they had won, because they had driven off the crew and there was no need to further damage the ship that would carry them to a new world, a wide-open universe.

She heard a distant rumbling double *thunk* shake through the deck, and knew another pod had got away. She wished them well. There would not be many more. Too many good men and women had died. With most power out, and intra-ship communication spotty at best, she had no way of knowing who was still aboard, or where they were, or what their circumstances were. Whoever was still aboard was nearly out of time.

She checked the bridge instruments, and had to blink once or twice, struggling to read them, wondering why she could not understand them. Then she recalled that all bridge power had been cut hours ago. She shook her head in dismay. Her mind must be *soaked* with exhaustion if she was trying to read blank screens. She shook her head and checked her suit's chronometer. Half-an-hour until the Jump point, at best estimate.

But that would be too long to wait. Perhaps the parasites could find a way to boost faster, or Jump sooner.

She had wanted to delay the inevitable as long as possible, but now the time for the inevitable had come.

She sat down, for a weary last time, in the command chair, and felt a wave of hatred for the damn seat wash over her. How could she ever have imagined it a thrill or an honor to sit there? What pleasure was there in this sort of power? For a long moment, the bright clear plains of Breadbasket, of the homeworld she would never see again, swept through her mind.

But there was no longer time for that.

She punched in a code and flipped open the emergency control panel. She had entered the preliminary codes from another panel hours before. Now she shut down all the fail-safe devices. It only remained to activate the destruct switch. She set the dial to fifteen minute delay and shoved home the plunger. Locked away, deep in the bowels of the ship, matched canisters of matter and antimatter emptied their contents into magnetic bottles. In fifteen minutes, the magnetic fields would die.

In theory, there was now no physical way possible to keep the ship from exploding. She stood up, wearily amazed that she felt so little. Perhaps because she had so little faith in the theory, or so much in the parasite. No doubt it had long ago found its way into the destruct circuit and deactivated it. Pushing the button was an empty, meaningless charade. She could push it until doomsday and the ship would never blow.

But perhaps the charade would serve as a diversion. Alarms suddenly hooted, and recorded voices warned whoever remained aboard of the imminent explosion. Chu felt, more than heard, two more pods blast away. Well, if the destruct system succeeded in convincing whatever crew remained to get the hell out, then it served some use. Still, it was all but certain that somewhere aboard men and women lay alive, injured or trapped by ruined equipment, unable to get to a pod.

And there was not a damn thing she could do about it.

Her heart full with loneliness, sorrow, and anger, she stood up and made her way down the emergency accessway, heading for the forward armory.

The construct had absorbed something of human ways. It felt like laughing when the destruct system was activated. The part of itself wrapped over Rozycki's forehead tried, experimentally, to control her face directly, make her face smile and laugh. The attempt failed, and instead the woman's unconscious body let out a strangled cough.

But, like the sadism of a little boy trying to pull the wings off a fly, it was not success or failure that mattered, merely the pleasure of cruelty. The construct was not skilled yet, but already it could control a human directly. Yes, indeed, its forebear had downloaded much knowledge of humans.

How could these foolish creatures—what paltry few of them were left—even dream that such a crude device as that destruct system could threaten the construct?

Casually, almost leisurely, the construct guided the smaller part of itself nestled among the circuitry, examining the plans and wiring, tracing the links that controlled the supposedly independent system.

Simple. Utterly simple. With a reshunting of this system here, and a simultaneous overvoltage there, the system was overloaded, burned out. The magnetic bottle would never break open.

With a calm pleasure, the construct turned its attention back toward other matters. The Jump system was novel to it, and would require careful examination. The control of a human, either by pleasure center manipulation or direct motor-nerve control, was also novel, and needed much study.

It turned its attention back to its work, reflecting on how incredible it was that the humans would attempt to destroy the ship with a system they knew the construct could control. It had a low opinion of human intelligence, but surely it would occur to them to use other means, some sort of manual device.

But if the humans had, how could the construct tell?

The construct, a creature shaped for the control of electronics, of minds, had but the haziest notion of physical, macroscopic reality. It could not easily envision anything outside its universe of electron gates and neurons. The construct perceived even the Duncan herself most hazily, not wholly appreciating it as more than a massive maze of wiring, controls, and power sources. It did not really think much about what lay beyond the massed linkages of gadgetry.

But, it suddenly realized, that left it with a massive blind spot. It had been assuming what it could sense was *all there was of the ship, assumed that what it could not sense was not there.*

But it knew that was not true. It activated the main ship's reference computer and compared what it "saw" of the ship against the ship's plan stored in the computer.

With an emotion of cold terror—something else it had learned from humans—the construct discovered there were gaps. Dangerous gaps. Pieces of the ship were missing from the construct's internal image of the ship. Most of the missing ship's territory it could account for through recent damage or minor modifications never properly logged in. In those cases, knowing where to look was enough of a clue. It found backup circuits, found sensing work-arounds. It quickly filled the most of the missing territory.

Except for the two forward armories. Those had been cut out of the loop far too thoroughly for it to be an accident. The humans had deliberately hidden those places. Those places full of massive weapons.

It backtracked from the blocked-off areas, searching for the closest cameras. And spotted a human moving away from one camera, heading straight for forward armory one. In a desperate panic, it slammed shut every power door in the ship, trying to cut the human off from her goal.

But all the doors between the bridge and the armories were jammed open. How had it missed that? Could it send a carry-all roller? No! There were rubble piles and wrecked corridors blocking the way for the ship's powered remotes.

Its human! Its captive human. She could get through, climb through the wreckage and get forward, carrying the construct along. Straining at the unaccustomed task, it forced Rozycki's body to stand, to take a halting, lurching step toward the exit. It snapped open the hatch of the compartment—and remembered a millisecond too late that humans need air, that the next compartment was in vacuum.

The construct, deeply linked into the nervous system it was trying to control, shared most unwillingly in the young woman's death agony. It survived her death, but not for long.

Tarwa Chu stepped into the armory chamber, and regarded the deadly thing bolted to the test stand in the center of the room. The sleek cylinder of a ship-to-ship missile, an access cover opened up, wiring leading from the missile interior to a crude breadbox control arrangement. A sloppily-painted red arrow on the control box pointed toward what Tarwa needed no help in finding. A pair of simple push buttons, each with a safety cover. She pushed back the covers and placed a thumb over each button.

She stood there, poised over her own doom, for a long moment, tears streaming down her face.

And then she plunged in the buttons.

In the skies of Daltgeld, a new star, terrible and bright, bloomed lovely in the night before it guttered down to darkness.

Chapter Seventeen
Council

The *Banquo* was in shock, in chaos, in turmoil. The corridors were crowded with stretcher-bound survivors of the *Duncan*, while the ambulatory wounded and uninjured seemed scarcely less immobilized. Their world, their home, all their possessions and everything that marked their lives—all that was gone for the *Duncan*'s men and women.

The *Banquo*'s crew was every bit as scared. Garbled rumor and scuttlebutt had reached the destroyer, and wild stories swept the ship. An infectious disease had wrecked the cruiser, one that was carried by the survivors, and it was only a matter of time before the *Banquo* caught the bug. Or else a saboteur had blown the *Duncan*—and likewise escaped to the *Banquo*. The Daltgelders had some secret weapon they couldn't resist testing against a capital ship. Alternately, there was some corrosive agent in the waters of Daltgeld's oceans. It had come through the hull once *Duncan* was in space and eaten the ship from the inside.

There was just enough of a tinge of reality behind each of the rumors to make them impossible to stop.

Commander Tallen Deyi struggled to get his ship in order. Captain Spencer was alone in the wardroom while the overcrowded ship that threatened to burst at the seams all around him.

Dostchem Horchane was glad that no one was paying

any attention to her. One of the first things the Navy did, almost by reflex, in a crisis, *any* crisis, was to get aliens and civilians politely, but firmly, out of the way. In the midst of crowded chaos, she and Suss were summarily shown to an empty stateroom and told to stay there.

For once, Dostchem appreciated the Pact's curt, overbearing way of dealing with nonhumans. Bundling her off that way gave her the chance to study the raft of new information that had come from a bewildering array of sources. It would require much study to achieve a synthesis of it all.

But there was another reason Dostchem was glad to be out of the center of things. She was scared. Frightened not only of the parasites—though they were a bone-chilling terror all by themselves—she was scared by the humans around her.

Though Capuchins bear a close physical resemblance to the highly gregarious monkeys, apes, and hominids of Earth, socially they are quite different creatures. They are far closer in temperament to Terra's moody, solitary carnivores—the tiger, the jaguar, the grizzly bear. In fact, Capuchins had evolved from solo hunters and a large part of a Capuchin's traditional contempt for humans stemmed from annoyance at humanity's overbearing, endless *socialness.*

In every circumstance when a sensible creature would want to be alone, humans seemed to gather together. When they ate a meal, when they traveled, when they sought out schooling or settled into a household, when joy or tragedy struck—humans scuttled together, in larger or smaller groups, and thought it quite natural. They had no real sense of territory, no strong urge for privacy, no need for the patience and pleasures of solitary contemplation and study.

No ship with this many Capuchins aboard could ever launch without a dozen murders being committed the first day. Humans, on the other hand, actually seemed to *like* being together, not merely endure it. They truly liked each other's company. It did not take the mating season, drowning male and female in sex and reproductive hormones, to draw a breeding pair together.

No matter that the Capuchins knew that their revulsion was irrational, that there were as many social adaptations as physical ones in Darwin's universe. Human social patterns still disgusted them.

It was *galling* to a Capuchin's brilliant, focused, hunter's brain that these perverse, slapdash, slow-witted descendants of scavengers and root-chewers ruled the Pact.

Right now, however, Dostchem was prepared to forget her contempt in favor of outright alarm. She was surrounded by humans locked in fear. Her solitary stalking-carnivore's mind knew the rational thing to do was to hide from the parasites, and then to develop a logical, methodical, prudent procedure for hunting them down.

Not the humans. Possessed of far less knowledge than Dostchem, the crew and officers of the *Banquo* seemed prepared, every one of them, to go charging out, full tilt, against this deadly peril, perfectly willing to make up the plan as they went along. No thought of hiding or secrecy. Even now, the three destroyers were maintaining course and heading along the *Duncan*'s last course—precisely where anyone would look for them first. The ship's engines were shut down, and Spencer and Deyi had no destination or plan in mind. They were simply conserving fuel until they knew what they wanted to do. Fine economy move, Dostchem thought, if it results in betraying your ships to the opposition.

The crew's surging anger, its inchoate thirst for revenge against an enemy unknown, with no regard for consequences, scared Dostchem silly. Everyone seemed to have a misinformed plan, and an absolute conviction that their leaders were either (a) crafty beyond belief and ready to destroy the menace because they had already come up with the same plan or (b) complete idiots who would doom them all, ignoring the councils of the wise because they hadn't.

But every voice seemed to favor charging in with all guns blazing.

Suss, herself stunned and angered by the disaster, wasn't very reassuring. It wasn't much help for Dostchem to be told that chaotic and contradictory calls for action were merely a typical first panic-response to catastrophe.

"There's a council of war planned for tomorrow," she said. "By then everyone will be settled down. Right now, they're all a bit panicky. And for that matter, so am I."

So, Dostchem thought, *it appears that, in an emergency, humans are guided by panic. Wonderful.*

But there was one other thing, something that frightened her even more than irrational humans: herself. Her behavior over the past day had been nothing short of madness. What had possessed her to enter the StarMetal Building? The potential profit from repairs to a ship that now no longer existed? Her own pride and self-importance, making her determined not to be outthought by a pack of baldies?

She should never have permitted Suss to drag her along back to the rescue—though Dostchem could not see what choice she might have had. No matter. The whole episode was one of madness. And now she was trapped on this ship, but what was she to do? What possible benefit could be gained from all this? She shivered and wrapped her tail around her body. She could keep those damn helmet creatures from getting out into the Pact. *That* ought to be motive and benefit to motivate anyone.

Dostchem forced herself to calmness and struggled to get back to her work. She had a lot of data to examine, from several sources: Spencer's AID, Suss, Santu, Chief Wellingham's research, and the remarkable results from her own instruments, especially when tracked against the reports on the *Dancing Bear* pulled out of the late Sisley Mannerling's computer.

By the time the council of war was called, she wanted to have her information straight.

Straight enough for even these panicky, semi-intelligent scavenger-apes to understand.

Captain Allison Spencer had once embarrassed Tallen Deyi, chiding his new executive officer for taking over the captain's cabin aboard the *Duncan*. Now the *Duncan*'s captain's cabin was lost, along with the rest of the ship, and Spencer was aboard the *Banquo*, with the roles reversed. Tallen Deyi had surrendered his rightful captain's

cabin to his superior officer and doubled up with his own
XO.

Spencer noted dully that he was too far gone to appreciate the irony. He wondered how worried he should be
about that.

But it was nearly time for the council. He got up from
his borrowed desk, moving carefully in zero-gee. He picked
up the action report and glared at it. He flipped open the
document and went over the summaries one last time.
The young ensigns and officers who had prepared it had
done their best and meant well, but that was no comfort.
Couching the horrible truth in bland officialese did not
make the realities easier to accept.

He felt his anger rise, and a strange, detached part of
himself knew he was going to be all right. Anger was
reasonable, constructive, healthy under the circumstances.

Far better focused rage than mind-numbing despair. The
loss of Bethany, and his descent into feelgood hell had
burned away part of his capacity for joy. He had worried
for a time that the loss of the *Duncan*, the overwhelming
shock, had burned away something more, some other part
of his soul.

He looked again at the report title.

Preliminary Findings
on the Loss of Pact Warship *Duncan*
to Enemies Unknown

Unknown? Spencer asked himself. No, that was simply
sophistry, a mealy-mouthed legalism. *Enemies Unknown*
was the term used in such reports when no one dared
admit that the real "enemy" was incompetence, when the
real goal of the report was to hide the facts and evade
punishment.

Spencer had no intention of avoiding responsibility. Besides, he knew this Enemy all too well to call it unknown.
He had met it, face to face, in Jameson's office.

Or had he? Did he truly know that Jameson's helmet
was the adversary here? Was it not far more likely that the
helmet/creature was *itself* controlled, even as it in turn
controlled Jameson?

Controlled by something larger, deadlier, more powerful—

something aboard that damned asteroid Destin had found? Spencer pulled a pen from his pocket, scratched out the last word and inserted a replacement.

Yes. "Enemies Unseen." That was far more accurate.

Spencer suddenly felt himself trembling. He grabbed for his chair, pulled himself into a seated position, suddenly clumsy in weightlessness.

Enemies Unseen. It struck him that he had been battling that sort, and no other, since the day the High Secretary had sent the Kona Tatsu to snatch his bride away. All his enemies unseen. The far-distant General Merikur, himself a victim of political scheming. The invisible, insidious temptations of the Cernian's pleasure palaces. The string-pulling schemers in the Guard, the Navy, and the KT who had put him in command of the *Duncan* to see what sort of fire he could draw away from their agent. The shapeless anger of the whole task force over Kerad and her debauches. The righteous and illegal fury of the mutineers. McCain's murderers.

The deadly assaults of the autocops, the inexplicable attacks on Suss and Sisley and himself, when every machine in the city seemed to be trying to kill them, controlled by an unseen hand.

Then, at last, the destruction of the *Duncan* by a few blobs of silvery metal the size of his fingertip. Always, a fight against an enemy far away, against an opponent who would not reveal itself, who would not come out in the open for a battle on even ground. Always against the dark, the hidden, the insidious—the *unseen.*

Not anymore. Not this time. This time they would force the Enemy out into the open. Where it could be seen.

Where it could be destroyed.

He got up again, more calm and confident than he had been in a long time, and left his borrowed office. The meeting was about to begin.

Suss looked about the assembled faces uneasily. By rights, Dostchem should have been standing before this group, but both Dostchem and Suss knew that naval officers were more likely to listen to a human KT operative than an alien technician. Besides, Suss knew that Dostchem was perfectly happy to avoid this duty.

"You have all seen the preliminary report on the loss of the *Duncan*," she began. "That report glosses over several points, is understandably vague on several problems we haven't quite figured out yet, and perhaps tries a bit too hard to say that it was no one's fault that the cruiser died. I can tell the authors that the KT will get a much tougher report, and that the navy brass back home will see *both* documents—and wonder about the differences. So you might want to rethink your version just a bit."

There was some awkward shuffling of papers and whispers at the junior end of the table, and Suss noticed Spencer's steel-edged grin. "For all of that, we can at least take the report as a first step. It does relate what the parasites can do.

"The Capuchin Dostchem and myself, using information secured at the cost of more than one life, have put together a picture of what the parasites *are*, and where they come from.

"Regarding the parasites themselves, we learned something vitally important about them when Lieutenant Commander Chu activated the self-destruct device: We learned that the parasites can be destroyed. At the moment that fusion blast went off, every g-wave source on the *Duncan* vanished.

"Chief Wellingham and his crew detected the conjoining of the parasites aboard the *Duncan*. The *Duncan*'s parasites were apparently forming themselves into a new helmet-type creature. At the time it was destroyed, the new creature only had one outlying parasite. But, once again, that parasite *was not an independent creature*. A better analogy might be to think of it as a temporary hand, a pseudopod extruded from the main body of the beast for some purpose.

"Dostchem believes all the bits of a given helmet-creature/parasite are truly one—and all of them are hooked into this universe from some other continuum. Call the entire creature an *ensemble*, for want of a better word. The parasites are extremely massive creatures, with densities perhaps on the approximate order of neutron stars. They must counteract their own gravitic potential by propagating the gravity-waves we have all heard about. I have heard a number of objections, to the effect that using g-waves that way violates conservation of energy. True enough—unless you can pump energy back and forth across a dimensional barrier, for example dumping waste heat from this side into the other universe. However they do it, the fact remains that they do do it.

"In any event, without the shielding g-waves, the parasites could not poke themselves into our universe without inflicting huge disruptions on their surroundings—and on themselves. Without the gravity-wave shield, they would literally suck in all the matter around them, at massive accelerations—with the same effect on the parasites as dropping rocks from twenty kilometers up would have on one of us.

"The *Duncan* ensemble did collapse in on itself. All the way. There was absolutely *no debris left behind* by that explosion. There are no further modulated g-waves being produced out there. But there is a single, incredibly powerful gravity *field* out there. And nothing else."

Chief Wellingham swore out loud, using a few combinations the junior officers had never heard before. "Just a minute there, Miss. Are you telling me that the fusion explosion disrupted the parasites and they collapsed into a *black hole?*"

"A small one," Suss conceded. "Much smaller than current theories say should be possible. But we are tracking a singularity, a miniature black hole, moving on the *Duncan's* last course."

"Wait a second," Wellingham objected. "You said they were all one interconnected creature, no matter how distant the components were. Does that mean that if we kill one parasite in an ensemble, that entire *ensemble* collapses?"

"No, it doesn't—otherwise Daltgeld would be caving in on itself even now. Remember, the two parasites you captured were still aboard when the *Duncan* blew up. Those were the two found aboard the ship, and in McCain's AID. They were still in isolation at the time the ship died. They never linked into the new ensemble that formed aboard the cruiser. That means they were still part of the

Jameson helmet ensemble—and we are still picking up dozens or hundreds of g-wave sources on Daltgeld, all of them presumably part of *that* ensemble."

There was a dead silence around the table, one that lasted a long time. "In other words," Tallen Deyi said slowly, "if the creatures were *completely* interlinked, the planet would have fallen into a black hole by now."

"But look, we've killed the thing. Isn't that worth something? And we did it in space, where it didn't threaten anyone," another voice offered.

Suss looked at the speaker and recognized him as Ensign Peever, the *Banquo*'s assistant intelligence officer. No, wait, her *only* intel officer. His boss had been killed by the mutineers.

Good *God*, herself excluded, Peever was the senior surviving intel officer in the task force. Neither of the other destroyers had carried *any* intel staff.

"It was lucky we didn't hit the parasites while we were planetside," Peever was saying. "If we'd killed them there, the helmet would have dropped into itself and started sucking matter. Daltgeld would be collapsed down to the size of a grapefruit. Now the planet is safe."

"No it isn't," Spencer said, his voice deadly cold. "Think about it, Ensign. We have scotched the snake, not killed it. There are still parasite creatures on the planet, and we cannot let this horror spread. Every one of them must be destroyed, at any cost. If we are forced to choose between Daltgeld on one side, and the entire Pact, and all the worlds beyond, on the other—"

He left the thought hanging.

Chapter Eighteen
Search

Spencer started talking again after a moment, his voice alarmingly calm. He was every bit the task force commander coolly laying out his orders to his command. "None of the improved sensors we have now can detect the helmet itself on the planet, which we should be able to do at this range. We can assume Jameson is headed back to the command asteroid where Destin found the helmet in the first place, wherever that is. Our ultimate objective therefore must be the asteroid this Captain Destin found. It seems extremely likely that there we will be able to learn more about these things. It is likely that the things are using that place as a headquarters. Once we have learned enough, we will destroy them. I define 'learning enough' as being certain they cannot spread beyond this solar system. Suss, can we detect the command asteroid directly from its gravity-wave signature?"

Suss shook her head. "Not at this range. The asteroid belt is a toroid hundreds of millions of kilometers across—and we don't really know for sure that the command asteroid is *in* the main body of the belt anyway."

"But you're able to monitor g-wave emissions back on Daltgeld, and we're a pretty fair piece from it by now," Ensign Peever objected.

Suss sighed. The kid had a big mouth, and he had the further annoying tendency to raise worthwhile issues. No doubt the same point had occurred to older officers about this table—and none of the oldsters had the nerve to look stupid by asking.

"We know where Daltgeld *is*," Suss said gently. "We can focus our instruments directly at it. The command asteroid could be anywhere in the sky—and at a far greater range than the distance to Daltgeld."

"But we can't see the asteroid. That settles it, then," Spencer said. "If we can't spot that asteroid on our own, we have to find Destin's ship, and hope there is data aboard that can lead us to the enemy. Peever, what have we got on Destin and his ship?"

The ensign's eyes suddenly bugged out, and he seemed to lose his voice for a minute. "Um, ah, very little, sir. What we have so far is based on your data from Mannerling's computer terminal. We've been able to track his reported ship movements. He is master of the *Dancing Bear*, and at last report was aboard. I think we can assume that we will find him with the ship. There were normal tracking reports, navigation updates, and message traffic back and forth from the *Bear* until just about the moment we arrived in system."

Peever looked nervously around the table. "Just how far can I go with this, sir? I mean, security-wise?"

"Speak openly. Everyone here is clear," Spencer said.

Peever swallowed hard and launched into his report. "Let me start at the time the KT first discovered its agents vanishing, about four months ago. At that time, the *Dancing Bear*—Destin's ship—had just put herself in parking orbit around Daltgeld. The helmets must have arrived on the planet then. The parasites must have gotten to work immediately, flushing out the KT operatives once they arrived on-planet. I would assume the parasites did that in hopes of keeping this star system isolated until they had consolidated themselves. But I'm getting ahead of myself. Once the *Bear* was in orbit, her auxiliary vehicle, the *Cub*, started shuttling back and forth between København Spaceport and the *Bear*. We can assume that the meeting between Destin and Jameson, as described by Jameson, took place during that time. Shortly thereafter, the *Cub* returned for the last time to the *Bear*, more than likely carrying a parasite."

"Why do you assume that, laddie?" Wellingham demanded. "Why wouldn't the helmet simply have left a parasite aboard when it left?"

"I don't think the helmet was really functional until it arrived on planet and got to Jameson. There's no sign in the *Bear*'s log of machinery being taken over, or anything like that. And Jameson was last seen in public the day after the *Bear* arrived in orbit. He went into seclusion after that. Maybe the thing needs to be on someone's head to work, and Destin didn't put it on. Anyway, since it fits in with the way the enemy seems to do its work, we can assume that a parasite got aboard the *Bear* at some point. And, ah—as we are all aware, even one parasite can do a lot of damage."

There was a painful moment's silence, and then Peever went on. "Now, at this point, about four months ago, the *Dancing Bear* put herself in a very long, slow, orbit back to the belt, intending to arrive at the asteroid Mittelstadt about a month from now."

"A five month journey just to travel from planetside to the belt? That seems strangely long," Commander Deyi objected.

"Normal procedure for a mining ship. Civilian ships are a lot more stingy with fuel than military craft—plus which they aren't really built to withstand long periods of constant boost. Most of the time a mining crew spends its transit time in cold sleep. Miners *like* cold sleep. It cuts a lot of dull spaceflight out of their lives—and gives them a longer effective lifespan. While their bank accounts draw interest, for one thing. And, of course, flying with only a skeleton crew alive and active saves life-support too. The strange thing was the *Bear* flying to Daltgeld, instead of shaping for Mittelstadt after they found—ah, what they found. But that's explained by the value of the cargo, and a desire to cut out any middlemen. Especially since we can assume that the helmet was doing its best to exercise some influence over Destin. Maybe it couldn't control him completely, but it might have been able to give him a nudge, set him on the way that he was going, or thinking of going. Jameson is the evidence that it can control minds.

"Anyway. As I said, we have standard navigation checks

from the *Bear* for some time after she launched from
parking orbit around Daltgeld. Then, just at the time we
show up in system, the *Bear* stops reporting in."

"As if someone wanted to be sure we couldn't find her,"
Spencer said. "But why didn't someone investigate when
the *Bear* dropped off the tracking net?"

"There are a lot of ships out there," Peever said simply.
"The local tracking net doesn't have the ships or the
personnel to go out after missing ships. Besides, at the last
navigation check-in, the *Bear* was in free-fall, precisely on
course for Mittelstadt. If the ship lost all power, it would still
arrive at Mittelstadt anyway. In the event of a normal,
accidental failure aboard ship, all Captain Destin would
have had to do was sit tight until his ship arrived at
port—and Mittelstadt control knew that. If they then saw
the *Bear* sailing past without them attempting to communicate or dock, *then* they'd send out a rescue party. Even
if the ship crapped out completely, the crew could ride it
out in their suits, or in cold sleep.

"But, of course, we must assume that it was the *parasites*
who saw to it that the *Bear* malfunctioned. If they wanted
Destin to vanish, sailing past Mittelstadt was definitely not
on the cards, because Mittelstadt control would send a
rescue and salvage crew. And remember, Jameson said
Destin was 'not where he's supposed to be.' So we can
further assume the parasite has forced the ship off course."

"Why wouldn't it just blow up the ship?" Spencer asked.

"Because we'd have spotted a ship blowing up," Suss
said. "Maybe we'd investigate—and then maybe find a
baby black hole where the ship had been. And *that* would
have made us wonder, to say the least. Or perhaps the
parasite aboard didn't want to commit suicide."

Peever nodded eagerly. "The same sort of argument
applies to boosting the *Bear* at maximum thrust, throwing
it violently off course. The more powerful the thrust, the
brighter the fusion plume, and the higher the odds that
we'd spot it and investigate the ship. We would at least
have radioed her, and received a strange reply. And we'd
have a track on the ship, and it would have been brought
to our attention. Sooner or later we'd discover the link
between Destin and StarMetal—and we'd know just where

to look for her. Remember, a big burn like that would take most or all of her fuel, and leave her with little room for additional maneuver. And all of this serves to reduce our search area by—well, if I can put it on the screen, sir?"

"That's what it's there for, Peever," Spencer said mildly.

"Thank you, sir." Peever wrestled with an unfamiliar set of portable controls for a minute, and then managed to get a schematic of the Daltgeld system on the main holo screen.

"Here is the orbital track of the *Dancing Bear* up until a month ago, when she dropped out of sight," he announced. The track popped into being alongside Daltgeld and wrapped itself around and around the planet. "No record was kept of where she came from, just that she reached Daltgeld orbit. Here, the *Bear* breaks *out* of orbit and heads toward Mittelstadt." The bright green trace crawled out from the planet and made its way toward the asteroid belt. "And here is where the last velocity and position report was made. Just after we popped out of our Jump point." The track stopped, and a pulsing red dot blipped in the screen.

"We of course have the specs on the *Bear*'s ship class. Now, assuming a full fuel load in her tanks at boost from Daltgeld, and empty holds, and allowing for maximum acceleration away from that position and velocity, here is the volume of space the *Bear* could be in by now."

A huge, misshapen red spheroid swallowed up half the inner system. "But that is an absolutely worst-case scenario. If they had boosted at max power to achieve the limits of this volume, someone would have spotted them. If we adjust the boost maximum to keep it under the limits of visibility, while accounting for the *Bear*'s range from various tracking points, we get a far more promising picture of their likely action radius."

The red spheroid shrunk to a tenth its former size, and huge dents and dints appeared in it. "The intrusions into the action radius represent the sensor ranges of various ships known to have passed through this volume of space since the *Bear* went missing. If the *Bear* had been within range of those ships, she would have been spotted and reported—to file a salvage claim, if for no other reason.

Derelict ships are worth money. Let me throw in the sensor radii of the inhabited asteroids and planets."

More huge gaps appeared in the blob of red that represented the volume of space that could contain the *Dancing Bear*.

Spencer nodded appreciatively. "Nice work, Peever. Add in another factor: Eliminate any trajectories that *will* pass through someone's sensor's range within the next month or so. The parasite wouldn't head toward someone who could spot the ship in future."

"Yes, sir!" Peever said eagerly. His hands played rapidly over the controls, his previous awkwardness forgotten. More huge swatches were chopped off the search volume, mostly toward the inner system.

"Anything else?" Peever asked, looking around the conference table.

"Us," Tallen Deyi said. "Have you factored in *our* sensors? We moved through a large piece of that space on our way in, before we made orbit around the planet—and it seems to me that the parasite wouldn't want to get too close to Pact warships."

"How could I have forgotten—" Peever began, but his voice trailed off as he concentrated on logging in the new factor.

The huge ball of red was now a crumpled, dented ruin, less than a hundredth its former volume. A quiet murmur of optimistic whispers played around the table. "Okay, Peever," Spencer said, "give me a mean-time-to-search."

Peever ran the query, and his face fell. "Assuming use of all three destroyers and all auxiliary vehicles, doing a coordinated sweep-search at optimized distance—ah hell, with all the technical rigmarole figured in—the odds are it will take us three months to find him."

"Why so long?" Tallen protested. "The way you were running that constriction of the search volume, it looked like we had a pretty serious detection radius."

"We do—if we're looking for a fusion flame. No one saw the *Bear*'s fusion drive, and for that to be true she *has* to be in that volume of space," Peever said. "If she would *relight* her drive, we could spot her right now. The trouble is, she's powered down, basically a cold, inert target—

which will be much tougher to spot. It's the difference between searching for a dark-colored rock and a flame in the darkness. One is a beacon, and the other blends into the background."

Spencer sat up suddenly. "Wait a second. If our assump-tions are right, the *Bear* does have a beacon aboard. A very powerful gravity-wave generator. Suss. How long to track that volume of space for a parasite-sized gravity-wave source?"

"Yes!" Suss said eagerly. "The g-wave detectors we've got now should have at least a ten million kilometer range. Let me see . . ." She ran the problem and looked up with a grin. "Using all ships, and factoring in all the technical rigmarole—mean time to search should be fifty-eight hours, once we're in zone. Maybe two days transit time to the search volume."

A glint came into Spencer's eye, and he leaned forward eagerly. "I want us boosting on a fast course for the search volume in thirty minutes."

The little fleet of destroyers raced back across the inner reaches of the Daltgeld system, ranging themselves into a search pattern. As they traveled, technicians aboard the three ships refined and optimized the search plan, finding that the probe volume needed to be expanded in certain dimensions and reduced in others. Chief Wellingham and Dostchem got into an endless series of vituperative and highly productive arguments over the design of the g-wave detectors: By the time the search commenced, they had more than doubled the sensitivity of their long-range gear, and vastly improved the backpack unit used for an interior search of a ship. The fleet arrived in the search volume and began its scan. A mean-time-to-search merely provides a crude statistical guide of the average time it should take to find a given-sized needle in a particular haystack. After all the tweak-ups were cranked into the search plan, the MTTS was down to fifty hours—but in the statistical universe of the MTTS algorithm, it was precisely as likely for the search to take ten minutes, or five days.

It would take time, to Spencer's obvious frustration.

Enforced waiting is hard on everyone—but especially

hard on a commander who is feeling a trifle redundant anyway.

Tallen Deyi was doing a fine job running his ship, likewise the commanders of the other two destroyers. Spencer found himself wondering what they needed a task force commander for—particularly one who had already lost his own ship?

Spencer had at least come out of his shell. Work was a good therapy, and at first Spencer tried to spend every moment he could on the bridge of the *Banquo*, making himself useful. It was perhaps fortunate that he rapidly relearned one of his earliest lessons of command: Competent people do not respond well to commanders breathing down their necks; and the *Banquo* bridge crew was certainly competent. Furthermore, Spencer wanted to avoid even the *appearance* of second-guessing Tallen Deyi.

Which led to Spencer spending a lot of time in the captain's cabin. It was not a good situation for a man who was already feeling lonely and useless.

Suss likewise found herself at loose ends—but it was more than chance or boredom that led her to call on Spencer in his cabin.

Aboard a ship in space, security was far more relaxed than on a planet's surface. A simple knock at the unlocked door and a muffled "Come in," were all it took to gain entrance to the task force commander's presence.

Suss stepped inside and looked around Tallen Deyi's modest—even dowdy—idea of a commander's cabin. She smiled to herself, and couldn't help but think of that ridiculous boudoir aboard the *Duncan*, where she had dressed—or undressed—in the role of a captain's courtesan.

Looking back at that moment, she was shocked at herself—though not for displaying a little skin. Suss had played many parts in her time, in many places, where both local climate and mores dictated more or less display. Nudity as such meant nothing to her. Symbols, feelings, context, meant a great deal. Teasing a man, making a joke of him, when his wife had just been stolen from him was unforgivable. And yet Spencer had never mentioned the incident.

She looked at him, perched uncomfortably at the edge

of his bunk, tense and uneasy, as if the ship's acceleration was unreliable and might not hold him down. He looked, not the confident warrior of the war council, but a bit forlorn, lost and forgotten.

Those were two sensations Suss knew well. "Hello, Al," she said at last.

"Hi," he said. "Thanks for stopping by."

She sat down at a chair as far across the room from him as possible, and watched him. His right hand was working furiously, as if it were straining to perform some reflex action that Spencer didn't want to happen. He noticed her watching, and smiled sadly.

"That was my feelgood hand," he said. "When I'm scared, or upset, there's still a big part of me that wants to jump back inside myself, get lost in a few millivolts of joy. So I guess I'm scared or upset now, huh?" He tried to laugh, but the attempt didn't come out too well.

He sighed and flopped back on the bed in a most unmilitary manner, reminding Suss of a baffled teenager wondering what the World was All About. "It's just that I feel so damned *useless*."

"Useless you ain't," Suss said playfully. She hesitated for a long moment, then stood up, crossed the room, and sat down on the bed on the edge furthest from Spencer.

"It's just the waiting. A slight case of command twitch," she said. "You've done your part; you've made the decisions, spoken the orders. Now the others have to carry out your decisions. They still have to do *their* jobs.

"But you. You've done *your* bit. *Now* you have to wait and see if you guessed right, wait and think about all the lives that are in the balance.

"Just remember you *have* guessed right this time. That much I can tell you. I know it, because you've guessed right every step of the way so far. You're smart. You're good. Without you, the damned parasites would have won long ago—and we might even have known that we had lost. Not bad for a decoy target."

A fledgling smile played across Spencer's mouth. "Yeah, but that part of the plan didn't work so well," he said. "They found time to shoot at both of us, didn't they?"

Suss looked deep into his eyes, and knew that if it was ever going to happen, she would have to make the move.

She leaned over him, and kissed him.

After a long moment, he responded, wrapped his arms around her, and held her tight. Suss opened her eyes at the same moment he did, and they looked at each other from a handsbreadth away. She could read it in his eyes, the fear that this was some part of her KT training, the thought that perhaps her AID was monitoring his heartbeat, telling her through the mastoid implant how to play him, soothe him, control him and guide him in the best interests of the Pact, or the KT, or the Navy, or the High Secretary, whoever that was by now.

No, she thought. *No.* This was *her,* not them. This was a woman touching a man, and let the rest of the Universe go hang. At least for now, at least for a little while. She rolled over, pulling him on top of her, and kissed him again as she struggled with the buttons of his shirt.

He seemed to see the meaning in her eyes and suddenly he reached for her, no longer passive, no longer just letting it happen, but eager, willing.

Even as he touched her, kissed the warm bare skin of her body, he found himself amazed at how much he had lost, how much he had forgotten—how much had been *taken* from him by the pact. He made the discovery even as he made good the loss. He could never forget Bethany, but now, for the first time, there was something more than emptiness in that part of his heart that had been hers.

Idylls do not last, especially on warships. Suss and Spencer both knew that, and they were determined to squeeze every moment available out of their time together. The long wait for the search to conclude suddenly seemed all too short.

Privacy could not last long either. *Banquo's* rumor-mills carried the news rapidly. It started with the steward who was ordered to deliver *two* dinners to the captain's cabin and leave the meal cart outside the door, though protocol required him to wheel the food in. He heard *two* voices and high laughter as he made his delivery.

Mere hours after Suss arrived at Spencer's cabin, word

had traveled down to the lowest-ranking enlisted man, and up to Commander Deyi himself: the KT agent, the captain's woman in name, had become his woman in deed as well.

It was a comment on how highly the crew and officers regarded their commander, Tallen thought, that the news was regarded as news for celebration, cause for glasses to be raised in toasts to the couple. If there *were* any dirty jokes, any smears, any insults being bantered about belowdecks, everyone was careful that they not reach the upper ranks. That in itself was a compliment of sorts.

Tallen Deyi knew that a lot of his associates regarded him as a bit of a prig, a prude. Deep in his heart, he knew they had a point. There were a lot of things that he didn't approve of—and captain's courtesans were normally high on the list. He was nearly tempted to interfere.

But this goddamned expedition had cost Captain Spencer a hell of a lot already. Deyi had seen what a handful of the parasites could do—what would happen when they came up across a whole asteroid full of them? In all likelihood, none of them had long to live.

A prude he might be, but Tallen Deyi was not about to deny a condemned man and woman their last moments of happiness.

Ensign Peever looked even more pudgy and nondescript than usual. After being awake for five days straight, his uniform was rumpled as an unmade bed, and his wispy man-child's whiskers grown out almost enough to be visible. By now about thirty percent of the search volume had been checked. As the remaining search zone was reduced, the odds were going up every second that they were going to nail the *Dancing Bear* now, this minute. It had to happen soon, Peever told himself. With every passing minute, millions of cubic kilometers were swept.

He lived in the improvised search control room, barely leaving it since the moment of the war council. Peever was blissfully unaware that he was driving Wellingham, Dostchem, and everyone else assigned to the job half-mad. The ensign's enthusiasm was not infectious.

Search Control was a rathole anyway, an improvised

operation wedged into a small compartment near the bridge, with cobbled-together equipment jammed any which way, cables snaking everywhere, and too many bodies taking up a too-small room. Search Control operated not only the *Banquo*'s sensors, but those aboard the *Macduff* and *Lennox* and the auxiliary craft, keeping the ships linked with each other, ensuring that every cubic meter of the search envelope was swept.

Peever was all over every aspect of the work, eagerly reaching over other people's shoulders to push the buttons, shoving senior officers to one side to check a read-out.

So it was with a distinct note of relief in her voice that the g-wave sensor technician reported a series of incoming *optical* traces. Optical and radar search were on the main bridge. Thirty second later, so was Peever.

For the first time in days, Dostchem felt she could let her tail hang down without it being stepped on. The humans in Search felt a similar relief over toes that had been quite literally trodden upon. Peever was not a graceful young man.

Dalliance or no dalliance, it did not escape Tallen Deyi's notice that Spencer was on the bridge, well-groomed and in proper uniform, every bit as quickly as the unkempt Peever. Suss showed up as well, arriving a few minutes later via a different corridor.

Deyi determinedly ignored the delicate entrances. "We've got a strange one, Captain," he said. "Optical tracking processed the situation just now. We've spotted a lot of engine lights, all over the sky. All of them outside the search radius."

"There are always lots of engine lights," Peever objected.

"Mind how you address the C.O.," the senior optical tracker snapped.

"Thank you, Tzu, but I think I can cope," Deyi said mildly, though he did briefly fantasize the pleasures of clapping Peever in irons. "The point is, *Ensign* Peever, that we have watched all those normal engine lights right along. They are all accounted for, regular traffic or private craft that are following flight plans, sending ID beacons and responding to our challenges. The optical tracking display system masks them out. *Now* we have at least twenty tracks suddenly popping up—all of them a bit hard to read, because they are all virtually nose-on to us. In other words, headed straight for us, down to three decimal places. Coming from every quadrant of the sky."

If Tallen Deyi was expecting some reaction of upset or fear from Spencer he didn't get it. Instead, the captain smiled and laughed out loud. "We've just been told we're on the right track. The enemy has analyzed our flight pattern, realized we're in a search pattern, and come in to interfere. And they wouldn't have any reason to do *that* if we weren't getting warm, if we wouldn't learn something worthwhile from the *Dancing Bear*. They're coming to scare us off. Optics—what sort of specs can you give me on those tracks? Are there parasites aboard?"

"Sir, reading their fusion temperatures, accelerations, and so on, they match the profile of intrasystem freighters. The range is still too great for us to spot any parasites on the g-wave detector."

"Are the freighters robotic or manned?"

"Ah, practically all the freighters in the belt are robots."

"And our friends like to use robots—we've learned *that* much about them," Spencer said. "Suss' inside agent at StarMetal uncovered some strong evidence that StarMetal was arming freighters with heavy weapons. They're either trying to scare us off, or engage us and distract us from the search—during which diversion one of them could head for the *Bear* and finish her off. They must know where she is."

"Why don't they dive straight for the *Bear* and ignore us?" Peever asked.

"Because then we could predict their flight path, track forward along it, and know precisely where to look for the *Bear*," Deyi replied. "Which would not be good from their point of view, when you consider a destroyer is a lot faster than a robot freighter. And more heavily armored."

Suss looked over the tactical plot. "This isn't right," she said. "They've enveloped our fleet too far out—ten times too far out. Too much space between us and their perimeter, too much space between ships. We can escape easily. How could they get it that wrong?"

"They haven't," Spencer said. "They're not trying for an envelopment. They're trying to draw us off the *Dancing Bear*. But they can't let us know where they've come from. They *must* be deployed from the command asteroid. All of those freighters must have been modified—and a shipyard that big would need an asteroid-sized base. But if they had launched their fleet direct from the command asteroid, they would have given us a backtrack and revealed the asteroid's location. Coming at us from all over the sky hides their origin point."

"But getting to those dispersal locations must have taken *weeks*, especially boost at a thrust low enough for us not to track," Peever protested. "Their start-points are scattered all over the inner system."

"Which only means they were planning to attack us sooner or later," Spencer said grimly. "I wonder how much longer we would have had to wait before the destroyers were attacked in orbit of Daltgeld? We've forced their hand, that's all, made them show their cards early. Nice to be ahead of the curve, isn't it?"

"So what do we do?" Tallen Deyi asked.

Spencer thought for a long moment. "I'm tempted to say ignore them. Even the closest of them won't be at extreme range for attack for days. Unless they know we're using long-range g-wave trackers, they have to be assuming it will be weeks before we complete the search. If we *were* going to be hanging around that long, the freighters might be a threat. Given a weeks-long search time, they've used a good tactic. As it is, we'll have the *Bear* in a day or two, less time with any luck. So we *could* just let them be."

Spencer was silent for a moment. "Instead, why we don't we unnerve them a bit? Fire up the targeting lasers. Illuminate each of the targets in rapid sequence, bright enough to overload their tracking optics. Repeat that at random intervals. Show them we know where they are, and that we don't care."

Tallen Deyi chuckled. "*That* ought to rearrange their little metallic brains. Let's do it."

It was a good move, Suss decided, both in terms of tactics and morale. It would tweak the opposition while telling the Navy crews that their commanders weren't running away. They were *shooting* at the enemies, even if it was only a few photons' worth of targeting laser.

Once the freighter-spotting was dealt with, Spencer, Suss, and Peever all headed toward the Search Control compartment. This was where the word would come, and everyone had the feeling that something was going to happen soon.

Exactly *when* they found Destin's ship was coming to have some importance. The later they found the *Dancing Bear*, the less time they would have to discover and evaluate whatever information was aboard before the freighters got too close and it was time to run.

Peever wasn't willing to admit it, but he was starting to wonder *if* they would find the *Bear*. He had secretly held to a belief that the projections were pessimistic, that luck rode with *Banquo*, that they would find the missing ship almost at once. That wasn't happening.

It was also starting to sink in that finding the *Bear* might not be a pleasant thing. The consensus aboard the *Banquo* was that the *Bear*'s crew was almost certainly dead by now. What data was aboard would be contained in the ship's logs, in its black-box type recorders.

Peever, as ranking intelligence officer aboard the flag ship of the task force, would have to be part of the boarding party. The only other intel-trains persons were Nanabhue and Captain Spencer. Suss wasn't Navy, and they couldn't send the captain. Peever had a vivid imagination, and he didn't really relish poking around in a cold, dark ship, with corpses floating their grisly way past him as he struggled with a bollixed recording device. Especially with an enemy fleet driving in toward them.

It was enough to give him the creeps in advance, and he suddenly lost a lot of his enthusiasm for the search. Instead of bouncing all over the cramped compartment, he settled down and sat in front of his own monitor station, for which the rest of the g-wave search team was eternally grateful.

* * *

Spencer was likewise beginning to have doubts about the whole idea of mean time to search. They were long hours past the time when they should have spotted the *Bear*, and the first of the freighters was getting uncomfortably close. Spencer had no fear that the *Banquo* could easily defeat one or two of the freighters—but suppose the opposition decided to bring eight or ten craft to bear at once, or charged in on a suicide run?

And still the search computers cheerfully assured them all that they had found the *Bear* already, statistically speaking.

It was an effort of will for Spencer to tear himself away from Search Control long enough for a quick bite to eat and a brief nap. It wouldn't do anyone any good if he were exhausted and hungry if and when they did spot their quarry. He ordered a sandwich brought to his cabin and tried to sleep.

Spencer had just dozed off into a most unrestful doze when his AID started squawking loudly.

"What! What!" he shouted in alarm, sitting bolt upright in bed. He woke a bit more thoroughly. "Shut down that alarm noise and tell me what's going on."

The alarm shut down. "Sorry," his AID said. "But they've spotted the *Bear*. Commander Deyi is preparing the ship to maneuver over to her."

"No!" Spencer said. "Belay that order, and order all ships to continue the search pattern. I'm on my way."

He swung out of bed, and, acting on a new and pleasant habit, glanced at the other side of the bed. No, Suss was not there. She was no doubt still on the bridge herself.

He stood up, pulled on fresh pants and shirt, and dove into the head just long enough to shave and comb his hair. As far as Spencer was concerned, he could give orders just as handily with a rumpled uniform and a three-day beard, but he also knew the value of captain-legends. The men and women of the *Banquo* had never seen him look anything other than clean, rested, and tidy. He wasn't going to risk ship's morale by bucking that trend. Still, he still begrudged every second shaving took, and cursed that decorum forbade his running toward the bridge.

But it turned out there was little point in his hurrying.

By the time he arrived on the bridge, the optics team had not even spotted the *Dancing Bear*. Strictly speaking, there was no way to be certain it was the *Bear* they had found. All they had was a strong g-wave source.

"The *Malcolm* was the first to spot her," Peever volunteered, reporting from Search Control. "We've gotten a bearing from her, and are trying to triangulate now."

"Nice work, Peever. Keep at it," Spencer said.

"Why did you order the search pattern continued?" Deyi asked, a bit testily. No commander likes being countermanded.

"Because the moment we break off the search and send a major ship in the right direction, the freighters will know we've spotted our quarry," Spencer said. "Then they won't have reason to hold off from attacking us. They'll change course, head for the *Bear*. Assuming they are carrying long-range high-acceleration missiles, they'll fire the first moment they can. I don't know if we can intercept their missiles or not. So we can't fly any of the main ships over to the *Bear*. We have to try it with one of the aux vehicles, and hope the freighters can't spot a smaller craft."

Spencer examined the main tactical display. Luck was giving them a break for a change. The *Banquo*'s gig *Fleance* was headed back to the destroyer for refueling. She would do. "As soon as *Fleance* is back, I want Wellingham, Peever and Dostchem to go aboard—no, damn it, we don't have a Capuchin pressure suit aboard."

Besides, Dostchem isn't subject to my orders, he thought. "We'll send Wellingham, Peever and a marine pilot and copilot, all in full battle armor. Chief, do you copy that?"

"Aye, sir," Wellingham replied from Search Control.

"Good. Take the short-range detectors, first aid gear and repair tools just in case they're any use. Fly the *Flea* at low thrust to avoid them detecting her fusion jet. We'll use the targeting lasers to blind their sensors again just as she boosts. The mission: Go aboard the *Bear*, search the ship, get the data we need, and get the hell out. We'll use secure commlinks and stay in contact."

"But Captain, using an aux craft could add hours to the time it takes to get aboard the *Bear*," Deyi protested.

"But it will *buy* us time once we're aboard," Spencer

replied. "The moment the freighters detect a ship on course for the *Bear*, we're sunk. If we used a big ship, we might have zero time aboard the *Bear* before the shooting started. But tell you what—just as the *Fleance* launches, we'll have all three destroyers let off a volley of long-range missiles. *Fleance* can use max thrust and look like a missile for the first part of the flight, then throttle back to low power just as the missiles shut down their engines. That will let her put on some speed and get to the *Bear* faster. So long as the *Flea* doesn't aim *straight* for the *Bear* on high boost, odds are they won't detect her—especially if we've just blinded their optics and fired a flock of missiles at them."

Tallen Deyi didn't look happy, but he nodded his acquiescence. "Very well, sir."

"Don't worry—the second we detect them making a move on the *Bear*, we'll jump in first. And we're closer, faster, and better armed."

Wellingham's voice came over the speaker from Search Control. "Thank you sir. That's very nearly comforting."

Chapter Nineteen
Destin

The gig *Fleance* clung to the external hull of the *Banquo*, waiting for the moment when she would be cast loose to make her own way toward the derelict ship. "Thirty seconds," the marine pilot announced, and Peever briefly considered he had just that long to get off the *Fleance*. But it really was too late for that. Aside from the question of courts-martial and so on, there were just too many seat belts, safety catches, hatches and air locks to get through in that length of time.

"Fifteen seconds," the pilot reported. The targeting lasers would be programmed by now, and the destroyers ready to fire their missiles. It should have been comforting to know that the fleet was going to such lengths to provide cover for the *Fleance*, but it would have been far more comforting still not to need such cover.

Or, most comforting of all, not to be aboard the *Flea* in the first place.

"Ten seconds." *Definitely* too late to get off the gig, Ensign Peever thought wistfully.

Ensign Wilton J. Peever was, be it confessed, a coward.

Suddenly his weight dropped away to nothing and then just as quickly quadrupled.

The viewports were covered and the external cameras stowed during the violent maneuver of drop-and-boost. That was no help, however. He could see quite clearly, in his mind's eye, the *Fleance* blasting clear, the fusillade of missiles leaping toward their objectives, the laser barrels pitching and skewing as they shifted from target to target. He could visualize a whole skyful of weapons, any of which could accidentally snuff out the little gig *Fleance* if some computer forgot she was out there.

And then there were the freighters, with weapons of their own, who might well seek out *Fleance*'s death on purpose. . . .

"All clear," the marine pilot declared in an excessively loud, cheerful voice. "On course to decoy objective. My repeaters from the *Banquo* show all missiles away and on course. We're doing okay."

"Wonderful," Peever muttered. He glanced at the mission clock over the pilot's head. Another six hours and they'd be alongside the *Dancing Bear*.

Then the scary part would begin.

The *Dancing Bear* hung in the sky, a dark-grey hulking mass of metal, barely visible in the viewscreen, even with the light-amplifiers powered up. Without running lights, without a working radar beacon, without a working environmental system to warm the hull and provide an infrared signature, the *Bear* was virtually invisible, even at this close a range.

Lieutenant Bothu, the marine pilot, edged the *Flea* in closer, slewing the gig around to the mining ship's stern docking port. "How're the parasites taking our visit, sir?" she asked.

Wellingham, bent over his sensor screen, shook his head. "Nothing, no response from the *Bear* or the freighter fleet. The destroyers are continuing the search pattern, and I think the opposition is falling for it. Plus, it looks like three of our missiles got in to make hits. I can't tell for sure, but that would be a nice bonus. At least none of the freighters are moving toward us, and the *Bear* is as dead as a tomb."

Peever felt a dull lump in his stomach, and wished Wellingham could have used a different phase. Images of frozen corpses still lurked in Peever's mind. "May—maybe we'd better get into our suits soon?" he asked nervously,

unhappy in the knowledge that his voice was cracking
fearfully.

No one seemed to notice the catch in Peever's voice.
Bothu simply nodded and said, "Might as well. This cabin's too small for more than one at a time to suit up. I'll go
first. Clandal, take the conn and dock us up."

One after the other, the four of them struggled into the
armored pressure suits. In theory, all navy and marine
personnel were supposed to be rated on the suits, but
Peever hadn't worn one since Basic Training. The two
marines seemed perfectly at ease in the things, but Peever's
nascent feelings of claustrophobia were instantly com-
pounded when he slid the helmet shut.

Sergeant Clandal docked the *Flea*'s belly hatch to the
Bear's aft docking port, maneuvering the gig with a flaw-
less precision. There was a set of displays indicating the
environmental state on the other side of the air lock, inside
the *Bear*, and Bothu looked over the readings. "Looks like
just a tad under standard pressure, as if she's been doing a
real slow leak for a bit without being replenished. What
you'd expect on a derelict. Unbreathable, though—the
carbon dioxide count is way too high. And the internal
temps are just a little bit warmer than they should be,
even if you factor in greenhousing from the CO_2. Just a
few degrees, but it's something to note."

"If there's still air can we go in without suits?" Peever
asked eagerly. "Maybe just breathe with face-mask units?"

"There's air in there, all right," Bothu said with a grim
chuckle, "but would you really want to risk carbon dioxide
poisoning, or breathe what a crew full of dead people have
been rotting in for the past month? I don't know how
sanitary it'd be."

Peever's face turned a pale greenish-white. He found
himself unable to speak for a moment, unable to manage
anything more communicative than a shake of his head—a
fairly useless gesture inside a pressure suit.

Bothu turned away and started working the lock controls. "Once we're through into the *Bear*, I'm using a
plastic weldbonder on the *Flea*'s outer hatch," Bothu announced. "We don't want any parasites coming to visit.

The bonder will hold the hatch shut just as well as a real weld would. Just in case some of us run into trouble, you've each got a can of the deactivator chemical in your suit's left hip pouch. Once you hit the weld with that stuff, it'll dissolve and you can get back into the ship. Whoever gets back will be able to get aboard *Fleance*. Just be damn sure it's only *us* who get back aboard. The chief will use his detectors and triple-check everyone and everything that makes it back."

Once again, Peever devoutly wished that Bothu would choose her words more carefully.

Bothu opened the hatch, stepped in, and gestured for Peever to join her. The two of them cycled through to the *Bear*, then waited for Wellingham and Clandal.

Once aboard the derelict, Bothu occupied herself by check running a manual diagnostic on a status panel. Or at least trying to run it. There was no power at all in the system, not a millivolt or a microwatt. Peever looked about the darkened lock area nervously as Bothu worked.

With ship's power out, they had to see by the powerful lamps built into their suit helmets. The lamps stabbed into the surrounding darkness on a tight beam. Perfectly ordinary objects—tools, work consoles, monitor screens, equipment racks—loomed weirdly up out of the darkness, transmogrified by the strange shadows cast by the eye-level headlamps.

Hanging in the darkness, drifting in weightlessness, Peever suddenly felt as if his head were caught in the last bubble of air in the whole universe, that the shaft of light from his lamp was stabbing *up*, not out, that the surface of some fever-imagined sea lay immeasurably far above him, lost in the shadows, and he was trapped, trapped, trapped at the bottom—

Clandal and Wellingham cycled through with a series of very real-sounding bumps and clumps that chased the false creations of a heat-oppressed brain away. Peever unclenched his fists. His suit thrummed quietly as its cooling system cut in, trying to deal with his sudden, nervous sweat.

"How's she look?" Wellingham asked, his voice booming just a bit too loud in Peever's ears.

"Dead," Bothu replied. "Totally dead. Which is weird, because then the temperature should be at local background, but it's a bit warmer than that. I tried to get a manual readout here using the ship's emergency power, but even *that's* gone. I wish to hell I could plug my AID Gertie in to the diag socket—"

"No AIDs," Wellingham said sharply. "Captain's orders, and he's right. Those damn parasites can suck their way right into an AID, and then it's all over. Would you rather not get an answer, or not be able to trust the answer you get?"

"But I thought we could detect the parasites with the g-wave detector," Peever protested.

"Can we detect *all* of them?" Wellingham asked. "Maybe there's a kind that doesn't give off g-waves. Or maybe the parasites could figure out a way to trick the detectors. Like by getting *into* a detector, and then where the hell would we be? No chances taken, that's my motto. I've got engineers working to isolate every major system on the destroyers from every *other* major system, so the ships can be run without the damn computers. *And* I'm going to vaporize every bit of equipment that we take aboard this ugly hulk before we return to the *Banquo*. I'm not letting this gig redock with the destroyer, either. We'll use a pressure tunnel and then burn the tunnel. But for now— Clandal, get that hatch sealed and let's get on with it."

Peever watched unhappily as Clandal applied the bonding compound to the hatch cover and ran the activating current through the thick goo. It hardened instantly, sealing off their one possible line of retreat. Deactivator in his hip pouch or not, Peever was not enthused. The others turned and headed into the ship, and Peever suddenly found himself left behind.

"Up ahead, I think," he heard the chief's voice say in his earphones. "I'm getting a very nice bright g-wave reading about a hundred meters this way."

The gloom-black walls started to close in on him, and Peever found himself unable to breathe. He grabbed at the nearest handholds and rushed desperately, trying to catch up.

The other three members of the boarding party paused

for a moment at a turn in the darkened corridor. Heart pounding, Peever caught up with them, bathed in cold fear-sweat. He stopped behind the others, their backs turned to him as they checked their instruments. Maybe they weren't paying attention to him, but at least he was caught up with them.

Peever allowed himself a sigh of relief. The sigh died in his throat—when he felt a hand grab onto his shoulder from behind.

His throat knotted in terror, and he turned around, wide-eyed with fear.

One look at the gaunt, pallid, skeletal face behind him, its haunted eyes staring into his, and he found his voice.

Wellingham, Bothu and Clandal tried to jump out of their boots when they heard him scream.

It was Destin, of course. Wellingham figured that out the moment he turned around, before Peever had a chance to faint, before Wellingham had a chance to read the name stencilled on the chest carapace of the banged-up suit.

He couldn't really blame Peever for fainting, either; Destin's appearance was enough to give anyone the screaming meemies. The man's ghost-pale face seemed to float up from the darkness of his pressure-suit helmet, his sunken, haunted eyes verging on madness, a month's growth of pale-blonde beard sprouting like a dirty fungus from his jaws.

The suit itself was bad enough—dirty, banged-up, worn and patched, the helmet scuffed and scratched. The suit *looked* like something a ghost would wear. Wellingham realized that Destin's mouth was moving, as if he was trying to speak. *Wrong frequency*, Wellingham realized. He reached for the controls on his own suit radio, then decided the hell with it. It could take forever to find the right channel. He yanked the radio's hardwire link, pulled it out and plugged it into a socket on Destin's suit.

"—ad to see you! I didn't know how much longer I was gonna be able to hold out. I kept telling m'self the crew should still be okay in cold sleep. I've been living in my suit for a *month* now, and I think the damn thing is about to give out. Nothing to eat but hand meals small enough to air lock through the suit's chestlock. Couldn't power up anythin', not even my sleep pod. . . ." The man was babbling, near hysterical with relief, shameless tears welling up in his eyes.

Wellingham nodded sympathetically, cursing their good fortune. Finding Destin and his crew alive was a major victory in terms of intelligence, but tactically it was a disaster. They had assumed that the *Dancing Bear* would be an empty hulk, a derelict they could leave to the enemy when the Pact Navy was done with it. Now they had a ship full of civilians to defend, with a marauding alien fleet bearing down on them from all sides.

He looked again at Destin and shook his head sadly. And *this* poor sod thought his troubles were over. "Glad to see you, Captain," he said at last. "Let's get you back to our gig."

When Destin came out of his pressure suit for the first time in a month, everyone else aboard the *Fleance* immediately wanted to get back into theirs—and would have, except for fear of appearing rude.

The man stunk. Wellingham bundled him into the *Fleance*'s cramped head and told him to clean himself up fast—an order Destin was delighted to obey. Bothu offered an old Marine Corps trick as a way for dealing with Destin's very ripe suit. He tossed the empty, open suit out the auxiliary air lock at the end of a lanyard and let the vacuum suck most of the stench out of it. If Destin needed the suit again, God forbid, they could drag it back into the cabin and hold their noses.

Destin emerged from the head, still emaciated and wild-eyed, but with the worst of the grime scraped off him. His naked flesh was a pattern of welts and raw abrasions caused by the suit cutting into his skin. Either Daltgeld-system spacers weren't bothered by nudity, or Destin was past caring.

Bothu went over him with a first aid kit, cleaning and binding the wounds, while Destin talked nonstop, half hysterical, as if all the pent-up words from his enforced solitude were trying to come out all at once. Wellingham let him go on, first making sure a recorder was running and that the secure commline to the *Banquo* was still open. Even babble from this man might be vital data.

"We were tryin' a core on that damn ast'roid when we found—well, it seems like yuh know a lot about that already. When we saw that damn control room, or whatever the hell it was—I kin tell you I dunno what we thought. Either that we was rich, or that we was scared to death, like finding the oldest haunted house in the universe. Penny Sue D'Amalfi—she's one of the geologists on the *Bear*—she took some reading and figgered the control room must have been abandoned a million years ago. At least."

"We've seen pictures," Wellingham told him gently. "And our captain talked to Chairman Jameson before he escaped. The StarMetal crowd damn near killed our captain. Tell me, why did you sell the helmet to Jameson? Why not bring back other artifacts? Why just that one? And why Jameson?"

Destin's face clouded over as Bothu handed him a flight coverall. Destin pulled it on, and it hung baggily on his emaciated frame. "I've spent the last month setting in the dark in my pressure suit aboard a ship that won't power up no matter what I do, waitin' to die, trying to figger all that out myself. It don't make sense, and I know it. None of us seemed to think it through. That ast'roid wuz *nuthin'* but tunnels 'n compartments. We shudda explored it, recorded it, looked fer clues to who the bug-people were, where they came from. Hells bells, even if'n all we was int'rested in was *money*, the news rights on that kinda thing woulda made us all richer than any amount of prospecting."

"But you're miners," Peever objected. By now he had recovered, and was a trifled embarrassed over fainting. "Isn't money all you're after?" he asked, a bit harshly.

"Course that's why we're out here, but my Gawd, how could anyone *not* fergit cash for a while in a place like that? We did wander around for a while, looking at things, until—until I worked up the nerve to take that helmet off the bug-man. Then things seemed t'change. That thing was so purty, gleaming bright. I just up and decided that was worth more than anything else. I got real greedy, decided just selling the helmet 'd make us all richer'n hell. Everybody else looked at it, and decided the same thing."

Wellingham said nothing.

The helmet-creature must have focused its attention on Destin somehow, convinced him to take up the helmet. Once in his hands, in contact with human flesh, its abilities were amplified somehow. It had convinced the whole crew to do its bidding.

But if the helmet had that kind of power, capable of controlling the minds of a whole crew at once, why hadn't it used that power over Spencer and Mannerling in Jameson's office? Or over Suss when she dove in, coming to the rescue? Perhaps its powers were greater near the asteroid. Perhaps the helmet, with no other duties to distract it, was able to focus its entire power on mind control, in one supreme effort.

Maybe it was simply planning to kill Spencer and company and didn't bother controlling their minds. Whatever. For some reason, it got to Destin and Jameson, but not Spencer. "So you must have decided you'd get a better price for it on Daltgeld, rather than back on Mittelstadt?" Wellingham suggested.

"Yeah, yeah, that's right. We flew back at maximum boost, rushing all the way. Don' really know why we did *that*, either. After all, the thing had been waiting a million years. What difference could a month or two make? Anyway, we got here, and I got it into my head to try selling the helmet at the StarMetal building. Every flunky took one look at the thing, picked it up and looked at it and agreed the chairman would love having the helmet in his collection—"

"Collection of *what*?" Bothu asked. The helmet didn't seem to fit into any category of collectables.

Destin looked troubled again. "I dunno. That's another strange thing now that I look back. Every single person I showed the helmet to said exactly the same thing, almost word for word."

That didn't seem strange to Wellingham. Not one little bit strange, if you realized the damn helmet-thing could control the mind of whoever touched it. "We know that you got as far as Sisley Mannerling. Did she pass you onto Jameson's office?"

Destin thought for a moment. "Mannerling, yeah, that was one of them. She seemed a bit more nervy, like she was suspicious of it all. At least at first. Then she changed her mind real fast, like someone throwin' a switch, and sent me on to Jameson.

"Well, that was pretty weird too. Jameson was a nice-looking man, friendly and polite, but he didn't quite understand why I'd been let in to see 'im, not at first. Then he saw the helmet, and his whole face changed. At first it was just like someone'd whupped him on the head with a hammer. Then it was like I almost felt the helmet had seen *him* or something, called to him. I can't explain it. Jameson got all excited and then he jest reaches out his hands for the helmet, an' I gave it to him. He put it on, and all of a sudden he gets this big grin on his face."

Destin's gaunt face went blank, and he seemed to be seeing something that wasn't there. "Not much to tell, past that. Not much you don't seem to know already. Jameson paid us off all right, bought up the helmet for more money than I'd ever dreamed of, more than I'd ever of thought to ask for. Like he didn't care about money and that stuff anymore. He never asked anything about where the helmet came from, or how I got it. I went back to the ship, and we all decided to launch for Mittelstad and throw a hell of a party there, before we went back to get a look at that asteroid. Right about then, the whole crew was starting to think about how much we had left behind there, how much exploring and studying and things to find there must be there."

Wellingham nodded. "You were back in charge of your own minds by then. The helmet wasn't guiding your thoughts. It had what it needed of you."

Destin looked at the chief and nodded sadly. "That's what I figgered out, sitting here in the dark. But the helmet needed to keep us quiet, maybe keep us from interfering with the asteroid. So it figgered someway to fire our engines, throw us off course, and shut down the *Dancing Bear* by remote control. That must be it, cause this weren't no *natural* malfunction. I was the only one out of cold sleep when it happened. Air got foul and too cold even to risk taking my pressure suit helmet off."

"Tell me something," Wellingham asked, in what he hoped was a calm, neutral voice. "There it was when you found it, on the bug-man's head. It certainly *looked* like something you were supposed to wear on your head. Did you ever try the helmet on?"

A strange and terrible expression passed over Destin's half-starved face. It was as if Wellingham had asked if Destin had ever committed cannibalism—and Destin was forced to admit that he had, by mistake, without knowing what was in the pot.

"I did, once," he whispered. "I didn't know better, just thought it was a purty hat. Put it in front of me now and I'd cut my head off rather'n wear it. That one time I put it on, it felt *strange*, like something inside it was just waking up. I swear I felt it *move* a little, and then I sure as hell took it off pronto."

He stopped talking for a moment and stared out into the open air. "That was when I got the big idea of bringing it back home to Daltgeld. But you folks. You know a lot about it. You know how it shut my ship down? Can you bring her back to life, before my crew dies in cold sleep?"

Wellingham nodded again. "I think we can. But we need to know where that asteroid is. Do you know? Are the coordinates in your computer system?"

Destin chuckled. "There isn't a rockminer in the Belt who'd need a computer to remember where a strike like that one was. But why you want to go there?"

"We're going to find out enough about that helmet to kill it, destroy it," Peever answered, his voice eager.

"Good. You do that. Gimme something to write with." Bothu handed him a stylus and a writing pad. Destin scrawled out a string of numbers and scaled the pad back to Wellingham. "Orbital coordinates, down to six decimal places. Go *kill* that thing."

Spencer sat unhappily in the command chair of the *Banquo*. He needed to control three ships, and this was the only place to do it from. Tallen Deyi stood behind him, ready to assist, ready to echo Spencer's commands to his own ship.

The news from the *Fleance* was good. In fact, a little too good. The *Bear* was not derelict. Spencer shook his head. "Tell *Fleance* to stand by. I'll talk to Wellingham in five minutes."

He shut his eyes, leaned back, and tried to *think*. He was tired, horribly tired, and he was having a great deal of trouble concentrating on all the tactical complications on the situation. All his ship deployments, all his feinting and dodging around the enemy fleet, had been based on the assumption that the *Bear*'s crew was dead and the ship itself therefore expendable.

Faint, ghostly phantom-shapes played about the inside of his eyelids. He opened them and found he had to wait a moment for the phantom shapes to clear. He had been prepared to relegate the planet of Daltgeld to the ashes, and here he was dithering over a single ship's complement. Spencer recognized but did not appreciate the irony.

Dammit, the circumstances weren't parallel. He knew that, in his gut. *Think*. What *made* the cases different? Maybe the reason would help him find a solution.

It came to him. He had never thought of himself as *cooperating* with the destruction of the planet, even passively. He would put up a fight before he let the planet die, would sacrifice everything to prevent it from happening. Honor would permit nothing less.

And honor would not permit him to abandon the *Bear*. That was it. He could and should leave the *Lennox* or *Macduff* to protect the miners. But he would need every scrap of fighting power he could lay hands on for the final assault on the command asteroid. Besides, if he drew one of the large ships in toward the mining ship, close enough so it could provide some sort of protection, the freighters would know why.

And the freighters were closing in. Some of them were now near enough that the *Banquo*'s g-wave sensors could spot the parasites aboard. It wasn't as if that was a surprise, but it did remind Spencer time was passing.

Then what *could* he do? Any act to rescue the *Bear*'s crew would require either powering up the *Bear* somehow, or else sending in one of the destroyers to take Destin's people off. And any of those acts would alert the freighter fleet to the fact that the *Bear* had been found. For that matter, launching his attack fleet toward the command asteroid would tell them the same thing. That would certainly bring the freighter's wrath down on the unarmed *Dancing Bear*. Any effort to save the crew, or use the information they had gained, would almost certainly doom the men and women aboard the mining ship.

Wait a second. That was only true if the *Bear* had value to the enemy. In terms of pure logic, the mining ship was only important to the enemy *while she kept silent*. It was vital to the helmet creatures that she maintain that silence, and not reveal the location of the command asteroid. Once Spencer knew that locale, and made it clear by his actions that he knew, then the *Bear* lost all importance to the enemy.

She would be a null, a zero, worth no effort at all. The *Dancing Bear* had *denial* value, negative value, and that only so long as the knowledge aboard her was kept secret. The only logical time for the enemy to move against her was during a period when she had been spotted, but her knowledge was still hidden. It wouldn't do the parasites any good to attack her now. The *Fleance* had managed to sneak up past the freighters.

It was a tempting thought, but a human commander would never figure a tactical situation in absolutes that way. He would make assurance double-sure, blast the *Bear* down to rubble even after her secrets were revealed, on the off-chance that she still might provide some further advantage, however tiny, to the opposition.

That was how a ruthless *human* commander would play it. The parasites were ruthless, certainly. But they weren't human.

Dostchem. She and Suss had studied the parasites as carefully as anyone.

He turned and looked across the bridge to where Suss was sitting. "Suss—find Dostchem. I have a job for both of you. Explain the tactical situation to her. Then, I want *both* of you to consider one question, independent of each other. Try and think like the helmet ensemble running that freighter fleet. Question: What do you do if the entire Pact fleet now suddenly changes course and moves straight for your command asteroid? Get me your answers, and get them *fast*. We don't have much time. *Go*.

"Navigation: calculate a minimum-time trajectory toward the orbit coordinates provided by Captain Destin. We're headed in, and soon."

Chapter Twenty
Breakout

"They will give chase to your fleet and attack if given the opportunity," Dostchem said, her voice confident and assertive. "Nothing else would make sense. I cannot even think of any other option for them."

Suss shot a sidelong glance at the Capuchin and shrugged. "I think she's right. Objectively, *yes*, nothing else makes sense for them. But a human commander would toss a few torpedoes into the *Dancing Bear* just on general principles. Just to be sure."

Dostchem shook her head *no* vigorously, copying the human gesture to perfection. "We are not battling a human opponent, or one that even remotely resembles your species or mine. Your kind and mine both evolved out of a nature where it was kill or be killed—or at least, find food and avoid enemies or die," she amended, remembering that humans hadn't been born of pure hunters. Well, she was starting to think that a scavenging life-style could evolve some fairly doughty warriors. These ground-apes were ready and willing to fight an enemy that would have sent any sane Capuchin scampering for the hills.

"Whatever niches our ancestors filled, our advantage was in *intelligence*. Our survival was possible only because we outthought our opponents—opponents that were *never* thinking, rational creatures. A wilevore or a mountain lion was perfectly capable of illogical moves, a leap to one side or a suicidal attack when cornered, for example, or marauding after more game when they have already killed.

"Both humans and Capuchins have it burned into their souls that the enemy might be irrational, unthinking. But not this thing. This helmet, creature, machine, whatever it is—all it *knows* is thinking creatures. Its skills and talents would be all but useless unless a sapient creature was there first to create technology for it to dominate. Frankly, I doubt if it has ever come up against an enemy as crazy as humans are.

"Its moves have been and will be brutal, logical, precise, direct, focused and violent. It will not chase after the *Bear* to cover its tracks, on the off-chance that it might have missed some unknown thing we could use. Its mind simply does not work that way."

Spencer nodded, his face expressionless. "Suss?"

Suss gestured with her hands, turning her empty palms upward. "It makes sense. But dammit, I *am* human—and I can't imagine the mountain lion leaving my camp unharmed just because wrecking it won't help the lion. If you're thinking of leaving the *Bear* undefended, it's a helluva chance to take."

"So is attacking that asteroid with diminished forces," Spencer replied. "If we lose for want of firepower, by the time the next starship comes through the parasites could control this whole system. They'll be able to grab a ship more easily—especially if it's a civilian ship. Then those things will get loose in the Pact."

Spencer hesitated. He was no Navy man. He wasn't even a line officer, according to the strictest view. His expertise was in intelligence, not in outguessing million-year-old robots in a space battle. He had no training for this—but more than enough doubts.

But none of that mattered. "What it comes down to is that I have to decide—and time is moving." Risk. Risk assessment. That was something he understood. Think of it in those terms, then. There was risk involved in leaving the *Bear* to her fate—but not certain disaster. If he decided the *Bear* must fend for herself, he would be exposing her to danger, yes—but that was worlds of difference away from leaving her to be destroyed. That risk could be balanced a gain, against other risks.

Spencer could not function in absolutes, any more than Suss could. He was not a machine. He had to leave the mining ship with *something*. He could leave *Fleance*. Spencer checked the tactical plot board. The rest of the fleet was some distance from the mining ship anyway. It would take time to recover all the other auxiliary craft—but far more time to wait for the *Fleance* to fly back from the *Bear*'s location. He ran the problem. A crash recovery of all the other aux craft, with both mothercraft and aux vehicles maneuvering at high acceleration to reduce delay— one hour ten minutes. The time required to recover the *Fleance*, with the *Flea* doing all the running, at low acceleration to avoid detection—eighteen hours. Thank God Wellingham had had the presence of mind to leave the mining ship in the dark, and its resident parasite undisturbed. All hell would have broken loose otherwise.

The fleet could move nearly seventeen hours sooner if Spencer left the *Fleance* behind. The enemy was no doubt preparing to receive them at the command asteroid already, and Spencer didn't want to allow them the chance to complete those preparations. It would be nice to catch them with their pants down. Rapid arrival at target might be more vital than one gig's limited firepower.

That settled it. *Fleance* could stay docked where she was. The gig could serve as some sort of defense for the mining ship, and as some sort of sop to Spencer's conscience.

Of course, if the freighters decided to attack in force, the one little gig would prove equally useless in both roles. Symbolic defenses were no good against berserking robots.

"Very well," Spencer said, feeling that every eye on the bridge was watching him. "The *Dancing Bear* is to remain where she is, powered down, until we have left the vicinity. The *Fleance* will remain with her, to provide whatever technical, medical, and military help she can. Once we are clear of the search volume, Chief Wellingham may proceed to capture the parasite aboard and power up the *Bear* at whatever time and by whatever means he sees fit. All other aux craft return to the closest possible destroyer.

Don't let the pilots worry about getting to their home craft—just get them to whichever ship can carry them. We boost for the command asteroid at a minimum-time orbit in one hour."

Spencer was careful to name a launch-time just outside the realm of possibility. Any shorter, and they'd *know* it was impossible. Any longer, and they might slack off. "Relay those orders and get moving."

Spencer's crew managed to do the impossible. Fifty-eight minutes after he issued his orders, the last auxiliary vehicle was secured, the last station reported itself ready at accelerations stations, and the destroyers were ready for boost. With a feeling of pride in his crews, Spencer ordered all ships' helms to initiate minimum-duration transit burns.

The *Banquo*'s massive engines bellowed into life, and slapped Spencer down into his command couch with a full six gravities of boost. He struggled to turn his eyes toward the tactical plot, straining to see what the surrounding force of freighters would do in response to the Pact move. There were eighteen of them, still in a rough spherical envelopment of the Pact ships. Now the three destroyers were clearly about to rocket their way straight through the surface of that sphere, dashing past the freighters lumbering in toward the sphere's center. The converted cargo vessels would not be able to turn or maneuver in time.

Three. There were three freighters that stood roughly athwart their path. Those were the only immediate threats. If any or all of them were quick enough off the mark to shift course or fire missiles at the destroyers there might be trouble. Spencer didn't need to tell any of that to Tallen Deyi's bridge crew. They were watching the threatening ships closely. Any menacing movement and—

"Missiles away!" the tracking officer shouted.

Damn! Spencer felt the sweat spring out of his forehead and race down into the back of his neck under the urging of six gees acceleration. It was a battle even to speak at this boost. This battle would have to be fought by automatic systems and whatever AI devices that could respond usefully to a voice command.

"Let's see a threat projection," Spencer managed to grunt out before the acceleration forced the air out of his body. He fought to refill his lungs as the tactics screen traced the missile plots.

At these velocities, dealing with an unknown class of missile, launched by an enemy whose psychology was uncertain, the track projections were mere guesses.

And they were not pleasant guesses.

Eight missile launches were tracked definitely, with two more somewhat ghostly track lines indicating possible launches. Six of the ten traces showed likely intercepts with Pact ships. "Evasive boost," Deyi ordered. "Random shifts. Fire counter-missiles at will—but don't waste 'em. And release two decoy birds."

Incredibly, Deyi's voice sounded calm and normal, just the way it did during a training exercise. The danger and the crushing acceleration didn't seem to phase him. "Keep cool, and don't fire until you see a real threat."

Spencer wished that he could sound so collected.

The *Banquo* bucked and swerved as the engines shifted their power and canted from side to side, turning their smooth flight-tracks into a jagged, stuttering confusion on the tactical board. There was a trio of heavy *booms* from amidships somewhere as the countermissiles leapt away, and a pair of more subdued *whumps* as the decoys were dropped. The decoys, though only a few meters from end to end, were supposed to resemble the real *Banquo* in an enemy missile's tracking system. Both of the decks immediately began firing their engines and began jinking up and down, aping the *Banquo*'s own motion.

Spencer glanced at the chronometer, stunned to see only a few seconds had passed. The speed of time was anything but constant in a space battle; it seemed to shift capriciously from the infinitely slow to the heart-stoppingly fast, and then back again. Now the seconds were passing with the sluggish unwillingness of molasses on a cold morning. It was as if each second had expanded, swelling large to allow more *things* to happen in every moment.

Space battles seemed to be composed of seconds and days in equal parts. As in the current engagement, it might take days—or even weeks or months—of probing, maneuvering, feinting and scheming before the two forces came in contact with each other. The actual fighting in the battle might take less than half-a-minute. The typical ship-to-ship engagement was over almost before it began, a rush of blazing engines and glittering energies.

The closing velocities were so great that the two sides were out of effective range again even as the first wave of weapons found their marks. Then the ships would wheel about for more maneuvering, more feinting and scheming, as one side, or both, chased its enemies toward another few flashing seconds of terror.

But those few seconds could last forever.

The incoming missiles and countermissiles crawled toward each other. The decoys scuttled slowly across the screen, back-blasting, sputtering out phony radio traffic and tracking beams. The destroyers themselves moved with a glacial ponderousness, flying with an elephantine grace that would not concern itself with anything so undignified as incoming missiles.

"Stand by to divert power to shields," Deyi ordered. All the destroyers were equipped with powerful electromagnetic shielding that would disrupt or divert any attacking missile it did not simply rip apart. But the shields sucked power, stealing it from the engines.

Worse, they blinded any ship that used them at full power, cutting it off from all outside sensor data—and the shields made it very clear which were the decoys and which were the real ships. No decoy ever made could fire up a convincing shield. Furthermore, it was impossible to fire the ship's engines through the shields on a *Chieftain* class destroyer.

Well, not quite impossible. It *could* be done, if you didn't mind the ship turning into a ball of melted slag.

Deyi knew all that, and like any good naval commander, he hated the shields. Unlike most, he knew when and how to use them. "Weapons officer, activate shields at your discretion—but I don't want to see them on for more than ten seconds. Throttle-down for power diversion and activate defenses only at need."

A countermissile found its target and lit up the sky for a

brief moment, destroying itself along with its attacker. The tactical display made two other incoming attackers vanish. Apparently, the tactics officer had decided the birds were too far off to pose a threat. Or maybe the computers had goofed in the first place while interpreting the sensor data—easy to do when the projection was based on nothing more than a brief wink of light tracked from thousands of klicks away and a guess at probabilities.

Unless of course the tactics officer had just guessed wrong about which traces were false. In which case she had also just made ghosts of everyone on board the *Banquo*.

Spencer blinked, struggling to see clearly through the tunnel vision caused by massive acceleration. There was one more incoming missile left, and this one was no ghost in the simulation—it was real, being tracked by the *Banquo*'s own radar and optical systems.

"Weapons—" Tallen said warningly, some note of concern appearing in his voice for the first time.

"We're on it, sir. Examining threat po-*tent*-ial. I show *high* confidence of *di*-rect impact with *Banquo*," the young lieutenant said, splendidly unaware of the incongruities in her military terminology. She spoke in a strange singsong chant, giving the perfect rote responses pounded into her during training. It kept her voice calm, detached, clear and understandable.

Perhaps the rhythmic sound of her voice had a calming effect on her. *Anything that works,* Spencer thought. If this young looie freaked out and got it wrong, they were all dead. "I show *no* countermissile *cap*able of intercept. We are *too* close for a new missile launch. Propulsion, *stand* by for fusion power transfer to shield generator. Commence kay-*rash* throttle down *now*."

The unbearable weight of six-gee boost snapped off, as if someone had thrown a switch—and that was close enough. A crash throttle-down did violence to the whole fabric of the ship, not just the engines. It was a dangerous maneuver. On the other hand, it would be straight-ahead suicide to fire the engines while they and the rest of the ship were bottled up by the shields. . . .

"Full power to *spherical* shield *gen*erator," the phlegmatic weapons officer announced. Spencer looked up at the tactical plot in time to see the universe vanish.

The tactical computer, denied all its real-time sensors, scrambled to produce a plot based on last positions and velocities. The solid tracer lines blurred and faded into expanding color cones that faded toward the edges. The brighter the color, the higher the probability for that trajectory—and there was a blood-red sword of color pointed straight at the dot that represented the *Banquo*.

"Shields up *and* operational. One decoy is *in*side shield perimeter, the other *is* outside and compromised," the weapons officer announced. "Missile impact *with* shield in *ten* seconds, barring evasive action. Deploying additional decoy under cover of shield. *Stand* by for missile impact."

Spencer felt his breath come in short, gasping wheezes as his lungs tried to catch up with his oxygen-starved body. It was impossible to keep breathing properly for long under six gees, and he was glad of the relief.

But there was the taste of fear in his mouth as well. If the missile was smart enough, and quick enough, it would know that *Banquo* would have to come out from her shield sooner or later. A smart missile would maneuver into a station-keeping position with the ship, just outside the shield—and then rocket *inside* the shield perimeter just as the electromagnetic screens came down. That would leave *Banquo* like the proverbial fish in the barrel, with no escape possible.

Or else, of course, the damn missile could simply be big enough, fast enough, well-armored enough to punch through the shield and be done with it.

Spencer watched the chronometer. Only five seconds had passed. If the missiles were unable to maneuver in time, if it could not dodge the deadly scything blades of intersecting magnetic fields that made up the shield—then they were safe.

But a Pact missile could have dodged the field at that range, Spencer thought. Why not this one? The tactical computers seemed to be thinking the same way. It abruptly snapped the brightest, highest-probability course projection away from the shields, diving away on a tight tangent, then braking to hover in space a few kilometers away.

It's only a guess, Spencer told himself. *A computer with its sensors jammed playing guessing games. That trace of light has no concrete reality.* The thought was neither convincing nor reassuring.

And then the ship lurched hard to one side. Every sensor screen on the bridge flared into blinding brightness and then went dead. The lights faded, dimmed down to nothingness, and then recovered slightly. Spencer's safety harness held him down, but two or three crew members were thrown about.

But we should be dead, Spencer thought, numb with fear, shock, exhaustion. *It hit us. We should be dead.* Then he noticed the cheering around him. The naval veterans around him were wild with relief. They understood and he did not. Some part of him told Spencer to keep silent, retain his dignity, not look stupid by asking—but he could not stand not knowing. "What happened?" he asked the grinning Tallen Deyi. "That thing hit us! How did we survive the impact?"

Tallen's broad face creased in laughter. "Never got near us."

"But the whole ship tumbled!"

"Newton's third law at your service," Tallen said. "Or whatever the physicists are using instead this week. The missile slammed into our magnetic shield, deformed it, knocked it around. We're magnetically linked to the shield by the generators. When the field got kicked, it dragged the ship along with it. The generators are still drawing surplus power to rebuild the magnetic fields."

"And the missile?"

"Smashed like a bug on a windshield. That light flash was the shield absorbing and dumping the impact energy."

Spencer looked around the bridge. Sensor screens, dazzled by the energy-overload of recording a missile smearing itself across the inside of the shield, began to reset themselves.

"*Shields* to *stand*-by power," the weapons officer announced.

Spencer checked the main viewscreen and then the tactical plot. At standby, the shields allowed some light energy to come through, enough for the tactics computers to work with—and you could even fire the main engines at low power, in a pinch.

They were getting a good tactical plot again. Spencer scanned the display carefully, and let out a sigh of weary relief. Space ahead was clear now. All three destroyers had left the freighters behind. None of the enemy craft stood any hope of catching the Pact's ships.

"Shields down to zero, throttle-up to previous acceleration, adjust previous course for deviation," Tallen Deyi ordered. The oppressive weight slammed down on them again, and the destroyers accelerated anew.

And Spencer knew they had won this fight, by running fast enough. They had broken out of the attempted blockade. It was not a question of distance anymore, it was velocity. The Pact navy ships were racing away from the freighters at such a ferocious speed that the enemy could never dream of catching them.

At least, that would be true if the destroyers simply kept accelerating forever. Spencer knew that was not going to happen, and presumably so did the parasite-minds controlling the freighters. The destroyers were going somewhere—to the command asteroid—and it would do them no good at all to arrive there at this sort of speed. The Pact ships would have to shut down their engines and coast, and then turn over, bring their engines to bear in their direction of travel and fire their engines in a braking maneuver.

The parasite-minds *would* know that the destroyers would have to slow down, know the Pact ships must either come to a full stop in space relative to the asteroid, or at least brake enough to make a worthwhile attack pass.

Presumably, the freighters would want to do something about that. Unless they got interested in revenge on the *Dancing Bear* instead. *But no, there would be no point to that. Think like a robot*, he told himself. *How would they play this one?*

"Weapons, maximum range, get the best data you can get on the command asteroid coordinates and throw it on the screen," Spencer ordered. "And keep an eye sternward on our friends behind."

"Sir, there's no way they could catch us now." the youthful officer protested. "Not even their missiles could catch us."

"Just give me the plot," Spencer said edgily. "Navigation, how much longer at six gees?"

"Eight minutes, twenty seconds. Then a long run at zero gee, then the braking run into the asteroid's vicinity."

"How long a run?" Spencer asked.

"Just under 200 hours, sir. A shade over eight standard days."

Spencer was not surprised. At the end of this burn, they would be going hellishly fast, over 250,000 kilometers per hour—but on the other hand, the command asteroid was nearly fifty million klicks away. They might get there a trifle faster by boosting harder or longer—but it would cost them dear in fuel and kill the crew.

Eight days. A lot could happen in eight days. And the next move was up to the parasites. They could pursue the destroyers, shaping their orbits to catch up with them either at the command asteroid, or some point close behind. If the freighters accelerated at only one gee, and kept it up for six hours, they'd be moving faster than the destroyers.

But no intrasystem freighters could carry that much fuel, or have engines capable of that kind of sustained boost. Not without the engines wrecking themselves. Maybe the freighters could rendezvous, and have some ships transfer their fuel loads to the others—maybe even strip engines from one hull and pack them as spares aboard another. Would the parasites be good enough ship handlers, have the kind of manipulators aboard their ships, to do that kind of job? It seemed like a long shot, at best.

Besides, once the souped-up freighters arrived, they still would be overmatched in a fight with Pact destroyers. The only hope for the parasites would be in overwhelming numbers, swamping the destroyers with too many targets, too many missiles to counter. Stripping their surviving fleet of seventeen craft just to get four or five craft close enough for the Pact to vaporize wasn't very smart.

Think like a robot, Spencer told himself. Think with the absolute ruthless logic of a machine. Think—

And his mind went back to the way the marines had

thrown him off the *Bremerton*. Not because they were angry with him, not because the Pact was angry at him, not because the Pact even cared. But because it was necessary as a matter of cold, mechanical calculation, that he be out of the way. He wondered how much difference it would really make if the parasites, and not the Pact, were running the universe.

He shook himself. That was the wrong thing to think about now. Probably that was the wrong thing to think about, any time.

"Very well," he said at last. "Order all ships to stand by for further maneuvering orders, but now steady as she goes and let's watch the screens. They should tell us a great deal in the next few minutes."

Chapter Twenty One

Jump

In his mind's eye, Ensign Peever could see the two ships, the *Fleance* and the *Dancing Bear* docked together, a big bright obvious target in enemy radar. The enemy knew where they were, knew that the *Bear* had given up her secrets. The parasites would have their revenge. There could be no question of that. Feebly, pointlessly, Peever willed the two ships to make themselves invisible.

"They have us if they want us," Wellingham announced in a stage whisper, a strange sort of gallows glee in his voice. He sat over the *Flea's* compact detection screen, watching the images of the enemy fleet. "There's no question of that. But will they want us?"

Peever felt ready to scream. Didn't any of these maniacs have enough sanity left to panic? There was no time for such levelheaded cool. They had to get ready to fight. Somehow, he kept his own voice calm and asked "Ah, shouldn't we, ah, ready our weapons, Chief? Get ready for them?"

"No need," the chief replied quietly. "If it comes to that, we can cast off from the *Bear* and be ready for battle in thirty seconds. Right now they must be wondering if we're worth the bother. Or maybe machines don't think that way—oh my God in the stars."

The chief's body stiffened over the detection screen, and the others all looked at him in alarm. "Wha—what is it, Chief?" Destin asked at last. "Are they gonna—"

"Shut down," Wellingham replied. "Total, absolute shutdown. They've all cut engines. None of them turning, none of them accelerating any further. When they shut down, all of them were more or less moving toward their home base. If they don't maneuver again, the last of them will pass us by in about six hours time. I think we're going to make it."

A ragged cheer erupted in *Banquo*'s bridge, but Spencer did not allow himself to join in.

The civilians aboard the *Bear* were safe, and that was something. Allison Spencer felt some strong pangs of guilt for being concerned with other matters. Once he had made his decision to leave them behind, he had almost forgotten about the freighter and the gig, trapped in the center of the blockade sphere. He had been concerned only with neutralizing the freighter fleet, relegated the trapped human ships to the status of pawns he was forced to leave in a vulnerable position.

Think like a robot, Spencer told himself again. *Which way does a robot jump when none of the choices are good?*

Answer: a robot doesn't jump at all. The sort of optimism, or desperation, or stubborn pride that would have made a human captain battle on when it was pointless— the parasites didn't work that way. Once the odds on benefiting from combat were significantly lower than the odds of failure, or of being destroyed, the freighters simply gave up.

Or at least *appeared* to give up. Their velocities varied enough that some would arrive at the command asteroid days, and others weeks, after *Banquo* and her sisters got there. But the freighters would be behind the Pact ships the whole way. And they could relight their engines, play catch up, whenever they liked. . . .

Maybe, from their point of view, we're being herded, Spencer thought. *Herded straight toward their main base*. He would have to do something about that. But not yet. Not quite yet.

"Coming up on main engine shutdown," the navigation officer announced. "Commencing throttle-down. Zero thrust in ten seconds."

Spencer allowed himself a sigh of relief as the fearsome pressure of six-gee boost eased off to nothing.

"Secure from boost stations," Deyi ordered, and then undid the straps that held him to his acceleration chair. He guided himself along by handholds until he was right next to Spencer. "And now what, Captain?" he asked in a quiet voice.

"Now we do what we're all best at," Spencer replied. "We wait. It's still their move. It might take a minute, or an hour, or a week for them to make it, but we wait until then. Wait and let our speed carry us closer to the command asteroid." *And then we find out who is playing a trick on whom,* he thought.

Silent as ghosts, the images of the last of the freighters passed out of range of *Fleance*'s detectors. "We're alone," Bothu announced. "They don't care about us. Not even enough to waste a missile on us as they pass."

"I'm willing to live with the insult," Peever muttered, but no one paid him any attention.

Chief Wellingham was already getting into his pressure suit. He sealed himself in and gathered up his parasite-detection gear. He headed into the air lock that led to the *Dancing Bear*. Destin made a move as if to join him, but the chief shook his head. Wellingham simply wanted to do this thing alone—either that or he didn't want Destin to foul up the gig's cabin again by pulling his stinking suit back in from the spaceward air lock.

No one spoke as Wellingham stepped into the lock and closed the hatch behind himself.

Twenty minutes more passed in silence, each person alone in thought, before anything else happened. Then, the environment gauges on the air lock began to twitch upward. Captain Destin scrambled over to the lock and peered at the instruments eagerly. "Power's back, air temp and pressure goin' up, carbon d'oxide falling! The man did it. My ship's alive!"

The others aboard congratulated Destin, but there was something muted, halfhearted about it. After all, the chief was over there interfering with the one thing that still might bring the enemy fleet wheeling about to attack them. Suppose the freighter fleet felt one parasite was worth a pitched battle?

The hatch clanked open and the chief returned, the visor of his suit open, a transparent plastic cube in his hand. "There it is, Captain Destin," he said. "This is what shut down your ship. I found it inside the environmental circuits."

Destin took the cube warily, and examined its contents carefully. Peever found himself drawn to it as well—he had never actually seen a parasite.

A silver blob oozed and ambled over the interior surface of the cube. A small thing, a dollop of mercury. A nothing, a tiny, trifling, pretty thing.

And two or three just like it had destroyed a cruiser.

Peever suddenly felt cold, as if a freezing wind were blowing against him. Whether it was his imagination or a true empathic reaction, he felt a malevolent *hatred* throbbing out from the parasite. This thing was death.

Wellingham dug into his equipment bag and pulled out a small radio beacon. He sprayed some adhesive on the side of the cube and slapped the beacon in place. He handed Bothu the cube. "Put that in the disposal lock," he said. "Dump it off the ship, and get it well clear."

"What're ya goin' to do?" Captain Destin asked. "Ya can't just dump it."

"I know that," the chief replied coolly. "But we need to know just how hard these things are to kill. We think they can survive a lot of stress. I don't think you could kill one with a repulsor gun. We *know* we can destroy them with a high-yield fusion bomb—but if I were Captain Spencer, I'd like to know if I could use some method that was a bit more *delicate*. Like maybe a plasma gun. Not as energetic as a fusion bomb, but I've got a feeling it could do the trick. Jettison it out the disposal chute, Bothu, and let's get in some target practice."

The marine grinned eagerly, crossed the small cabin, and tossed the cube into a small hatch set into the gig's hull. She sealed the hatch, ran the scavenger pump, and hit the jettison button. A simple spring-loaded device kicked the cube clear into space. Bothu was already at the plasma-cannon controls, while everyone else watched on an external camera monitor. The targeting computer locked onto the radio beacon. Bothu waited until the cube was a safe minimum distance away. "Let's try it on minimum power," she said, and fired.

A slender, sun-bright lance of light flashed from the cannon, gone almost before the eye could detect it. There was a silent red flash of light where the cube had been, and then nothing. Wellingham bent over his detection instruments, and then turned to the others with a broad grin. "No g-wave activity," he announced. "Not even a baby black hole. It just sort of disintergated. A single parasite isn't massive enough to form a black hole, I guess. The thing's dead." He turned to Captain Destin, who stood with unashamed tears in his eyes. "You've got your ship back, Captain."

'Wonderful," Peever said. "Now can we all get the hell out of here?" The enemy freighter fleet was still too close for his comfort.

Spencer heard the results of the chief's experiments a few minutes later and relayed his effusive thanks back through the comm officer. It was heroism, courage that won medals, and certainly the chief had proven that he had those things; but it was clearheaded thinking that won battles. Chief Wellingham had gotten the answer to a vital question that no one else had even thought to ask.

Spencer ordered the *Fleance* to ride shotgun on the *Dancing Bear*, escorting her into Mittelstadt. The chief and his whole team had earned a few days' sampling of Mittelstadt's fleshpots.

None of that, however, was solving Spencer's more immediate problems. He was waiting for something, something from the command asteroid. He ordered a full set of sensors directed on the coordinates provided by Destin. So far they could tell him little more than that there was a lump of rock hanging in space in the right place.

They were still too far-distant to be sure of much more than that. Even at this velocity, it would be another two or three days before they'd be close enough for even the longest-range g-wave detectors to see anything.

But there had to be something there. Spencer knew that, deep in his bones. And he was waiting to flush it out.

It started eight hours after the *Dancing Bear* and *Fleance* shaped orbit for Mittelstadt. A sprinkling of tiny dots suddenly appeared in the long-range screen, surrounding the image of the command asteroid. Engine lights, lots of them. Either they had just launched, or the *Banquo* had just come within sensor range. It didn't matter. They had shown themselves.

"Tactics! How many of them!" Spencer demanded eagerly.

"One hundred twenty, at least, sir. More becoming visible."

"Excellent!" Spencer said.

" 'Excellent?' " Suss asked. "A hundred twenty enemy ships is good?" She came over and stood beside him.

"It is if we can get them to someplace beside where we're going," Spencer said, staring at the screen. He snapped on an auxiliary screen and began calling up an overview display.

"I knew they had to have more than just twenty converted freighters in their fleet," Spencer said. "We got that from Sisley's reports. They were buying up ships all over the system. And the odds against their entire fleet being in range to intercept our search for the *Bear*—well, it just seemed pretty unlikely. I'll bet there are another forty or fifty converted freighters dispersed all around this system. But think for a second. This fleet we're up against has got to be under the tightest central control possible. The parasites controlling the ships are wired directly into the helmet creature. You yourself said they were in essence the hands attached to the brain. We can kill the hands, the parasites, and it won't matter. But if we can get in close enough to destroy the helmet, the parasites are dead too.

"I started to wonder—if I were the commander of a force like that, where would I put the bulk of my forces in a defensive situation? What would you do?"

"I'd put my fleet on direct, close guard of headquarters," Suss said.

"Which left us with the job of trying to flush them out, try and draw them away from that asteroid long enough for us to make a strike. That's why I decided on a direct, arrow-straight trajectory on the asteroid once we knew where it was. No feinting, no attempt at misdirection. It's also why I tried a head-on bust-out from the blockade. In both cases I wanted to seem as aggressive, violent, and threatening as I could, so the helmet creature would get scared of us. Scared enough to invest a lot of resources in keeping us away. Now we've gotten the thing to strip its defenses. And so far we've done it at very low risk to ourselves."

Suss looked at the overall tactical plot. At one end of the screen lay the command asteroid, at the other two small winking lights representing the *Bear* and *Fleance*. The mining ship and the gig were just about to move off the edge of the plot, moving out of harm's way toward the safety of Mittelstadt. In the dead center of the screen were the three destroyers—*Banquo*, *Lennox* and *Macduff*, coasting at very high speed toward the command asteroid.

Between the destroyers and the *Dancing Bear* lay the seventeen freighters that had comprised the blockade fleet. Even as Suss watched, they relit their engines and started to accelerate toward their home base—and the Pact ships.

And the new element. A hundred and twenty enemy craft boosting straight for the Pact ships. Both enemy fleets were forming up into a huge pincer formation, seeing to it that the Pact ships could not cut and run.

And there didn't seem to be any escape. "Well, Captain, if you wanted the hornets to come up out of their nests, you've succeeded."

Spencer nodded, not seeming to notice the sarcasm in Suss' voice. "Now all we have to do is convince them to commit all the way to their attack. Get them far enough from their base, and moving fast enough that they'll never make it back in time. Communications, put me through to the commanders of the *Lennox* and *Macduff*."

"Commlink open sir."

"This is Spencer, commanding task force, to all commanders. Prepare and execute synchronized braking maneuver at full power. Bring all three ships to zero relative velocity with command asteroid and assume a defensive deployment."

"Sir, this is Matambu commanding *Lennox*. We're still at least twenty million kilometers from the asteroid."

"I am aware of that, sir. Which is why I am also ordering all ships to compute and prepare for a synchronized intrasystem Jump from our stop-point to a point 100,000 kilometers away from the command asteroid. We're going to feint, pretend that we mean to stand and fight here. Once we've convinced the enemy of that, we use the Jump gear and get behind him."

There was dead silence, both on the bridge of the *Banquo* and the commlink to the other ships.

Finally someone worked up the nerve to speak. "Sir, this is Heinrich commanding *Macduff*. Sir, you might not be aware of it, but there is a large margin of error even between two well-calibrated Jump points. Most of the error is caused by mass-deflection. A small amount of matter, either near the jump-off point or the arrival point, small enough so that it can't be easily detected, is enough to throw everything off. The gravity field produced by even a few grams of matter is enough to warp space enough to send a ship thousands of kilometers off course. You are ordering us to Jump in an *asteroid belt*. We'd be lucky if even one ship gets within a million klicks of the target."

"I am aware of all that you point out, Heinrich, but I thank you for your thoughts. Tactical officer—what is the most likely outcome of a direct approach to the command asteroid? Take into account the enemy force we have detected so far."

"Loss of the fleet," the young tactics man said quietly. "We can outgun those freighters one-to-one, and even with some fairly heavy odds. But we can't fight off 137 of them. Especially if they know exactly where we are going and why. Our speed and acceleration advantage won't count for anything."

"What are the odds on losing a ship in an intrasystem Jump under these circumstances?" Heinrich asked over the commlink.

"Difficult to estimate, sir, as there are a lot of variables. But I would estimate the probabilities at about 90 percent that any one ship would survive—which works out to about 73 percent probability that all three ships will make it. But you are correct that we have no way of knowing where the ships will be when they complete the Jump. With the amount of uncharted matter you're likely to find in a star system, mass-deflection could put you almost anywhere. There is a remote possibility that they could end up outside this star system altogether."

"But with a 90 percent chance of ending up alive," Spencer said. "I do not wish to lose any more of my ships, let alone *all* of them. What chance of at least one ship arriving within a 100,000 kilometers of target?"

The tactics officer shrugged. "Sir, there are simply too many unknowns. But just based on experience, and on gut level hunches—maybe fifty-fifty. Maybe an 80 percent shot that one of them will arrive within 200,000."

"I would be a bit more pessimistic," Dostchem announced peremptorily. Spencer had even forgotten the Capuchin was on the bridge. "But not by much. Subtract 8 to 12 percent from his odds."

The tactics officer nodded. "I could go along with that."

"How about the odds of at least one ship within a million klicks of target?" Spencer asked.

"Bet the farm on it, sir. I'd estimate ninety-plus probability that you get *two* ships inside a million."

"At least that high," Dostchem agreed. "Assuming all ships survive the Jump, of course. And you have nearly three-out-of-four odds on that."

"Thank you, Dostchem. In any event, that is the plan. Draw the enemy forces as far off from their base as possible, get them to use up their fuel, get them traveling as fast as possible in the wrong direction—and then get behind them. With its mobile forces out of the way, we should have a fighting chance to hit the command asteroid. If we can get in there, and destroy the helmet-creature, then we've effectively lobotomized the parasites that are controlling the freighters. It's a crazy enough risk that I don't think our mechanical friend would even think of it."

"And if we fail, then the hornets will all come home to their hive," Suss said quietly. "Still, if they do, we're no worse off than before. After all, they can only kill us once."

"Any further discussion?" Spencer asked. Again, there was silence, but at least this time the quiet seemed calmer. *It must be at least slightly reassuring to know your captain wasn't completely off his rocker,* Spencer thought. "You have your orders," Spencer said. "Let's get it underway."

Banquo and her sister ships were flying in free fall at the horrific velocity of over 250,000 kilometers an hour. It took six gees for twenty minutes to achieve that incredible speed, and it would take just as much power for just as long to slow the destroyers down again.

Riding the engines was going to be just as punishing the second time, but at least this time they were not in immediate danger of attack by the enemy—both freighter fleets were still far away.

The ships came about to direct their sterns forward, the massive engines surged smoothly to life, and once again everything aboard the *Banquo* was flattened under six times its normal weight. If anything, the maneuver seemed to take even longer this time, but the bridge chronometer would only admit to a twenty-minute duration.

At last, the little fleet lay dead in space relative to its goal. After a horrendous expenditure of fuel, and tremendous stress on the crew, they were still millions of kilometers away from the command asteroid.

Spencer thought about the fuel cost as he watched for the enemy's reaction. He knew he might regret the profligate use of his hydrogen fuel later, but for now he felt it had been well spent. Perhaps he had not traveled far using it, but it had bought him other things beside movement. He had bought useful intelligence with it, caused the enemy to reveal something like its true numbers. And he had stampeded the enemy into leaving its home base at least partly defenseless.

Spencer ordered the destroyers into a "hedgehog" formation, wherein each ship could provide covering fire for the others, effectively putting the entire sky in the field of fire. If he had meant to actually use the formation in a fight, he would have deployed the auxiliary vehicles as well, so their fighting power could be brought to bear. But he ordered the formation only for the benefit of the enemy's detectors, and it was highly doubtful their gear was good enough to spot the auxiliaries at these sorts of ranges.

He watched the screens eagerly now, struggling to divine how the helmet-creature was reacting. Was it buying his display of a defensive formation? Would it even recognize it as such? Would it think, as it was meant to, that Spencer had decided to make his stand here, force the enemy to come to him?

Time passed, seeming to slow and expand as it often did in combat. Minutes, then tens of minutes, then half-hours and full hours—and the enemy freighters kept coming, kept boosting toward the Pact ships.

Spencer rejoiced silently. Every second the ships of the large freighter fleet kept those engines on was a victory for Spencer. It meant they were traveling another few meters per second faster *away* from the command asteroid. It was another little bit of velocity they would have to shed before they could reverse course and chase the Pact ships.

Tallen Deyi joined him, watched the tactical display with him. "They're still coming," he said in wonder. "When they fall for a stunt, they fall for it. Keep on, my boys," he said to the tactical display. "Keep on and pay for it all four-to-one."

"Four-to-one?" Spencer asked.

Tallen looked puzzled, and then his face cleared. "You're so good at this, I keep forgetting you never went to a naval officer's training academy. That's one thing they pounded into our heads over and over again. Any false move in powered flight costs you four times as much fuel as the original burn. You spend the original burn, then a burn to brake your speed, then a burn to get you moving back toward where you started out, and then a *fourth* burn to brake your speed after the return burn. You end up where you started, moving at zero speed, after four power burns. That's exactly what the freighters will have to do if they want to chase us back to their base after we make our Jump."

"Might I add another point to consider?" Dostchem asked as she made her way across the bridge. "These are freighters, which normally boost at only very low acceleration, perhaps a tenth of gee, or a half gee in extreme cases. These craft are accelerating at just about one full gee, and keeping it up for a very long time, presumably with holds full of armament and strap-on fuel tanks, all adding mass, requiring the engines to burn hotter to achieve such a high boost. There is no doubt a lot of stress on their equipment."

"Yes, we've spotted two or three craft dropping out of formation already," Spencer agreed.

"Engine lights going out in the larger fleet!" the tactics officer called. "They have completed their burn and are shutting down. Smaller fleet still coming up behind us, boosting for us, current velocity relative to us over 100,000 kilometers per hour."

"Take a look at their current disposition," Spencer ordered. "Give me a tactical projection for the enemy fleet."

"Hammer and anvil," the tactics officer replied instantly. "They want to catch us between a small, fast, fleet and a larger, slower-moving fleet. The idea is that any counter-tactics that might be effective against one force will leave us exposed to the other. If we boost and run from the smaller fleet, we run right into the big guys. If we hunker down and make a stationary defense, then we have to defend simultaneous threats from both sides. If we run from the slower fleet, we're headed away from our objective and run into the smaller fleet. If we—"

"Thank you, I get the idea," Spencer said.

"Sir, the thing I don't understand is that they don't seem to be making any sort of disposition in case we do make an intrasystem Jump. It's a rare move, but not unknown."

"First remember their ships don't have Jump gear," Spencer said. "That might keep them from concentrating on it. And you might try thinking like a robot, Lieutenant," Spencer said. "The Jump is unpredictable. It will put us in a more or less random location, and is somewhat dangerous. Robots don't approve of random events, or of endangering themselves."

Now, Spencer thought. *Now* was the moment, when the enemy had committed itself as far as it was going to. Spencer leaned forward eagerly, and felt the blood racing in his veins.

Doing the unexpected, the unthinkable was what made the risks worthwhile. "All hands, all ships to Jump stations," Spencer ordered.

Klaxons hooted. Throughout the fleet, monitor cameras caught crew members rushing to their stations. The fusion generators were powered up, their energy rerouted from the main engines to the power-draining Jump generators. The navigation crews took a last scan of the mass distributions of their ships, and of the space surrounding them.

Their target point was still twenty million miles away, making it flatly impossible to do even the crudest mass survey there. It barely mattered. If the local mass survey missed anything larger than a fist-sized sky rock within five thousand kilometers of the fleet, that would be enough to throw them ten thousand klicks off-target at the other end. And with all the small, random clumps of mass to be found in an asteroid belt, the odds were they were missing plenty of fist-sized rocks. It wasn't likely they'd get anywhere near the target.

Banquo, *Macduff* and *Lennox* reported themselves ready for Jump. Spencer felt something cold in his gut. There was no more dodging battle, no more room for clever maneuver. Now they had to go straight to the enemy, and fight it out until one side or the other died. If they got that far, if the Jump gear didn't deposit them a million light years away, or with a boulder trying to occupy the same space as the bridge.

"Synchronize Jump gear and engage," he said quietly.

The lights dimmed on the bridge as the Jump system drew power. "Five seconds," the navigation officer said. "Four, three, two, one, zero—"

The universe disappeared.

Chapter Twenty Two
Shields

As abruptly as the old sky had vanished, a new one snapped into existence. For a brief, terrible moment, Spencer thought the Jump had indeed vaulted the *Banquo* into uncharted space. But no, these were the stars as seen from Daltgeld's sky. It was just that the Jump had rotated the ship a bit relative to the stars, and a different piece of the sky was visible.

All right, they were still in the right star system. But where in it? Which way to the target, and how far? And where were *Lennox* and *Macduff*?

The bridge crew seemed to share none of his disorientation or anxiety, but instantly went about the task of establishing the ship's current position. Spencer's eye turned toward the tactical display, still hopelessly scrambled by the Jump, showing conflicted data and low-probability projections that were the best it could do with no information. The display was even showing three different *Banquos*.

Finally, the screen began to tidy itself a bit, eliminating the bad data. *Banquo*'s ghosts vanished, leaving only the real ship represented on the screen. The astrogation gear spotted the local sun, various beacon signals and the brighter stars.

The tactical display presented a rough fix that showed them very close to their target point, 100,000 kilometers from the command asteroid. The display continued to refine itself, making minor adjustments as better data came. Finally, at long last, it drew in an image of the command asteroid itself, based not on rough coordinates, but on a direct visual fix.

The image of the asteroid appeared on an external camera, with a line of figures below displaying the range.

Spencer stared at the screen in horror, his heart suddenly pounding. They had managed to arrive near the target point all right—too damn near! They were only 95,000 klicks from the target, and a mere *five thousand* from the command asteroid! And moving *toward* it at three kilometers a minute!

"Shields up, half power, *fast!*" Tallen ordered. Half power was the strongest shield that would allow the sensors to see anything at all. "The enemy is bound to have some sort of defenses this close in. Get the shields on, and get ready to snap to full power. Weapons, can you pick up missile tracks through half-power shields?"

"Yes sir, though *not* very well."

"How the hell did we pop in so damn *close* to them?" Suss asked.

"Not on purpose, that's for sure," Spencer said. "Any theories, Dostchem?"

"Only two," the Capuchin answered. The fur on the nape of her neck was bristled up, and her tail flicked back and forth nervously. "You had to come out *somewhere*, and by simple chance it was here. Either that, or the massive gravity-wave generation in the vicinity had some sort of attractive effect during the dimensional transition of the Jump."

"Does that mean the other ships should be this close as well?" Suss asked.

"Not necessarily. Even if we were drawn here by the gravity-wave generation, it could be a highly localized effect, or one of extremely short range. I have no data and cannot predict. I will investigate." She turned and left the bridge, using arms, legs and tail to guide her toward the hatch.

"Comm Officer," Tallen Deyi asked. "Can you raise either of the other ships?"

"Negative, sir. No sign of either craft. But I can report a lot of civilian traf—"

"SHIELDS ON FULL!" the weapons officer shouted.

The lights in the bridge faded under the sudden power surge. The ship shuddered and yawed over, flinging bits of loose gear around the bridge. Two or three crew who had been out of their crash couches went sailing across the compartment.

"That was close," the weapons officer announced. "Some sort of free flyer missile lying in wait. It lit its engines two hundred klicks away. Probably hundreds more of them around."

The young officer sighed and swallowed hard. "Shields back to half-power."

"Weapons, can you drop that to one quarter and still get to full power fast?" Tallen asked. "If the shields were weaker, they'd be more transparent, and we could get better detection on anything else that was incoming."

The weapons officer nodded uneasily. "Yes sir, I could, but it would take a few milliseconds longer to kick the shields on to full, with a bit higher risk of—"

"Dammit, woman, we need to see!" Deyi snapped. "We can't just sit here blind behind the shields."

"Yes sir. *Shields* going to *one* quarter power," the weapons officer responded, regaining a bit of her singsong speech cadence.

Does she only talk that way when she's scared and doesn't want to show it? Spencer wondered. *As if that mattered at the moment.*

"The asteroid has put a shield up itself!" Suss cried.

Spencer looked, not at the tactical display, but at an external view monitor. Where the greyish blob of rock had been a moment before was now nothing but the inky, gleaming darkness of an electromagnetic shield, a perfect sphere of black. Coruscating lines of sparks flickered and swam over its surface, as minor magnetic interferences chased each other over the shield's exterior.

Spencer swore. An EM shield that big and powerful required an incredible amount of energy to create—or to crack.

"So much for a hell-bomb," Tallen Deyi said, looking over what the sensors had to say about the enemy's shield. "That shield is too strong. We can't bust through that to get a missile in."

Dostchem's voice came over the intercom from Search Control. "I am examining the asteroid on the gravity-wave detector," she said coolly. "We are fortunate that the EM shield does not block the g-wave emanation. There are many, many g-wave sources of the size we are familiar with. And one much larger, more energetic one."

"The helmet," Spencer said. "That has to be Jameson, wearing the helmet. If we could bust open that shield somehow, get a hell-bomb through—"

"Sir, I was about to report before our shields went up," the comm officer said. "It's blocked now by the enemy shield, but I heard a lot civilian radio chatter. Not on military frequencies, or on military topics. I've had the computer run some referent checks on the traffic I was able to record, doing word-matches. It hasn't spotted any military slang, but has picked up a lot of traffic that indicates a large number of civilian workers on that asteroid. Probably contract workers from Mittelstadt and København, judging by accent analysis."

"What the hell are civilians doing aboard that asteroid?" Tallen demanded.

"Construction of some sort, the best I can tell," the comm officer said.

"It makes sense," Spencer said. "The helmet needed work done. Ship conversions, maintenance, piloting. So it hired crews. They wouldn't know *why* they're on the jobs, but if the money's good, they wouldn't care either."

A tone warbled on the comm officer's panel; he worked a series of controls. "I have acquired a signal from *Lennox*," she said. "Relaying data to tactical."

The scale on the tactical swelled, compressing the previous display to a small patch in the center of the screen. Far off to one edge of the screen hung *Lennox*.

Spencer checked the range and swore. The other ship was over a million kilometers away. Too far away to do any good soon. Even at massive acceleration, it would take hours for her to arrive. It seemed unlikely that the helmet would tolerate *Banquo*'s presence for that long.

The lights dimmed again, the shield snapped on, and the ship rebounded as the defensive system stopped another missile. Another close call. At least this time it wasn't a surprise. They couldn't just sit here. Sooner or later, a missile was going to make it through, and the *Banquo* would die.

It was useless to hang in space, soaking up missile attacks. *Banquo*'s weaponry wasn't intended for a static battle like this. She was meant to be quick, meant to dive in, hit hard, run fast. Now they couldn't even retreat quickly. There was no question that they needed the shields at least on standby, and the engines couldn't manage more than a tenth of a gee with the shields at minimum. They would be sitting ducks for hours as they crawled away.

All right, what was left if staying and running were no good? Spencer felt the need to talk over the situation. He caught Tallen's eye, and Suss'. The three of them moved over to a quiet corner of the bridge.

"We need to get in closer," Spencer said, speaking in low tones. "Boost toward the asteroid, at the best acceleration we can." ·

Tallen looked stunned. "*Closer*?"

"We could drop every missile we have onto that shield and not crack it," Spencer said. "Even if we did get a hell-bomb in there, I'm not any happier about killing civilians today than I was yesterday. Meanwhile they're going to continue bombarding us. If we back off, we'll be exposed to fire the whole way. Maybe if we get in close enough, we'll be under their guns.

"Besides which, we've still got the bulk of *Duncan*'s marines aboard. We can use them. And if we can capture the asteroid intact, we might be able to learn something from it. I say we fly in, find a way to crack those shields, and drop an assault force, finish this hand-to-hand. If we fail, then *Lennox* is on the way. Maybe *Macduff*, too— unless she's lost forever. But neither *Macduff* or *Lennox* carry enough troops—they don't have the assault option. They can try direct bombardment if we don't make it."

"But they'd still be up against that shield," Tallen objected.

"If it comes down to that, one ship can ram the asteroid shield, with the other ready with missiles once the shield cracks," Spencer said quietly.

"That would destroy the ramming ship!" Tallen objected.

"Which is one reason I don't want things getting to that point," Spencer replied, his voice suddenly strained and weak.

Tallen remembered a heartbeat too late that Spencer had already lost a ship. He would not expend another craft lightly if he could avoid it.

"I want to try the assault," Spencer said again. "Which means we need to find a back door through that shield. Somehow."

"That's my job," Suss said. She could feel her heart pounding, the palms of her hands turn cold with fear even as she spoke. "There have to be sally ports in that shield, ways to allow ships and missiles in and out. *Banquo's* detection gear should be able to spot them. I get on a pressure suit and flypack, jump out the door as we go past, and get in through the sally port. Then I find a way to knock out the shield generator. Getting past shields isn't exactly a new problem—the KT trains for just this sort of run."

It was true, she *was* trained for jobs like this—but no amount of danger could hide the fact that the job was all but suicidally dangerous.

She was volunteering to die—and asking the man she loved, a man who had lost so much already, to risk the last precious thing in his life by sending her.

Suss looked into his face, and saw the struggle between her commander and her lover. Her own feeling lost in tempest, she prayed both side, and neither, would win. She had to try this thing, even if the odds against success were long and the risk of death great. If they could not get past that shield, then hundreds more on both sides would have to die before the helmet-creature was defeated.

"Very well," Captain Spencer said at last. "I don't really have much choice but to send you. Or much time to work things out before you go. Let's get this planned before those robot bastards get a missile through *our* shield."

Banquo and her crew moved rapidly away from the chaos of the breakout, driving toward some semblance of order and purposeful planning. Spencer, intent on preparing the assault team, was swept up in one direction, Suss in another.

There was something frantic, manic, and yet resolute about the atmosphere aboard ship. Suss sensed a cool desperation in the air, born of the knowledge everything had to be done right if anyone was to survive.

This crew had seen a whole ship die of bad luck and bad judgement days before, and the fear of battle seemed to have a strange, calming effect. They knew they could not afford mistakes.

Suss found herself being handed from one set of briefers and experts to another as the plan was finalized. Her briefers were cool, correct, precise, wholly impersonal, as if they were programming a weapon rather than briefing a colleague.

She recognized the behavior pattern, and it made her blood run cold. They were trying to stay detached from her, avoiding eye contact, struggling not to think of her as a person—because they were not expecting her to come back. If they did not smile at her, cheer her on, offer an encouraging hand, it would hurt less to send her out to die.

The experience made her feel numb, as if she were dead already and just hadn't noticed it yet. Suss moved through the next two hours as if in a dream. All was fog, vague backgrounds, a confused hurried stream of people telling her things, showing her things she needed to know.

But sharp-edged moments, clear images, bits of sure knowledge seemed to leap out at her, setting her on the way that she was going.

"—The sally ports would be suicide," the remote sensor tech said firmly, if none too delicately. "They're too small, stay open too briefly—and they have missiles launching through them. We've had a chance to analyze their shield now. It's big, it's strong—but it's crude. An advance control system would allow the controller to open and shut portals anywhere on the shield—but this one only has static openings. They can open or shut them at will, but only at a set of predefined static points. We've spotted a series of communications ports, holes in the shield to allow antennae through. They are pretty big, nearly four meter across, open almost continuously. They don't seem to have any visual systems, just various radio antennae to keep in contact with their own fleet. Optically, the comm ports are blind. As long as you don't use radio or other electromagnetics, they'll probably never spot you—"

"—This is the suit and flypack we use for outside repair work under our own shields," the assistant engineer explained. "Virtually no metals in it at all, all ceramics and plastics, with a compressed-gas propulsion system. If there were any significant metal in the suit or on you, if you wore a stainless steel earring, the shield's electromagnetic fields would grab at it, pull it out of your ear and through your helmet at the speed of a repulsor bead if you got within twenty meters of the shield. In a standard suit, with metallic components, you'd be ground into confetti if you even got close to a shield. In this suit, you'll be okay *as long as you don't actually touch the shield in any way*—that would be like sticking your arm in a slicing machine. Do that and the lines of force will—*would*—rip your body apart. That's an energy-shear, not strictly speaking a magnetic effect. Of course, the EM field would yank the hemoglobin right out of your blood cells *before* anything else could happen anyway—"

—Navigation AutoReport Download via Nav Computer: Subject vehicle *Nanabhuc/flypack* ceramic memory system programmed to transit vehicle from *Banquo* to vicinity spatial coords. designated ref. *Shield Comm Port 4* at zero relative velocity. Percentage of fuel supplied to be used in maneuver: 98 percent, plus or minus 4 percent—

—Manual of Operation, UV visor vision system model 643/b. Primary purpose of system: enhanced view of electromagnetic shield. The microscopic low-power circuit in the system is specifically designed for absolute minimal interference with an EM shield system. This circuitry can be brought to within ten centimeters of a high power-density shield with no effect. When activated, the visor downshifts far-UV radiation to visible spectra . . .

* * *

—Once, twice, three times the ship shuddered and lurched sickeningly around her as the *Banquo*'s shields destroyed another missile—

—The images from the *Dancing Bear*'s drilling operation and salvage operation as transmitted on a secure beam from the *Fleance*, played over and over again, until Suss would know those strange corridors in her dreams—or at least her nightmares. Then the screen cleared, and the latest iteration of the three-dee map Santu had drawn would appear again.

It was crude, barely more than a set of guesses strung together. Did those heavy cables mean that compartment was the power room? Were those automated weapons half-in that corner? Where did that corridor lead? Was it reasonable to hypothesize a whole system of connected passageways in that pattern based on the hints from a recording?—

Unnoticed, somehow, somewhere along the line, weight returned as the engines rumbled to life. Suss knew, without truly understanding, that now they were accelerating toward the enemy.

—Dimly heard, an argument between two petty officers, one arguing that the *Banquo*'s shield wasn't rated to permit a two-tenth gee boost, the other pointing out that war was about risk, and the *Banquo* wasn't rated to wait around until an enemy missile vaporized her either—

. . . The suit seemed too light to protect her, the helmet with its complex vision system too big and awkward. How had she gotten into the suit in the first place? Suss didn't even remember putting it on . . . Strange, strange. Strange to be alive, strange to walk, stumblefooted as a sleepwalker, moving willingly toward her own death . . . Not knowing why, or how she did it, she stepped into the air lock.

That action seemed to bring her back to a place where the world around her seemed real. The air lock was tangible, solid, certain. It was brightly lit, its switches and dials very ordinary-looking and easily seen. She put her hand against the bulkhead and could feel it. She could hear the high-pitched whistle of the pumps sucking the air out, smell and taste the tang of bottled air, tinged with the sweat of her own fear, feel the stiffening of the odd suit around her body, see the outer hatch open. She felt the decrease in vibration that meant the ship's engines had shut down, so as to facilitate her own exit. She was back in zero-gee.

The suit's flypack sputtered to life of its volition and boosted her out of the lock. She resisted an urge to take over manual control, and instead let the autopilot do its job.

It lifted her out of the air lock, out into space, toward the *Banquo*'s own shield, a black wall of nothingness, rippling with shimmering star-like sparks of light, the steady light of the true stars barely visible behind.

For a brief, horrible moment Suss thought the shield was going to stay on as she went through it. The flypack was driving her closer and closer, twenty meters, ten meters away, so close she could imagine the magnetic fields plucking at the fabric of her body. Then the sparkling wall snapped out of existence and she sailed through empty space.

Suss looked behind through the rear-view mirror set into her helmet. For the briefest of moments, she could see the ship back there—and then the ship's shield reappeared, shrouding *Banquo* in darkness.

She looked ahead, looking for the black-cloaked asteroid that was her destination. Without magnification or sensors to guide her eyes, she couldn't find it. Then she remembered the UV vision system built into her visor and switched it on.

The visor clouded for a moment as its delicate electronics came on, seeking far-ultraviolet radiation it could translate down into visible light.

Suddenly, a blindingly-bright wall of violet-white lit up the sky, dead ahead. She had not been able to see it because it took up half the sky, and what she had taken for a backdrop of stars was the telltale pattern of surface-sparks, moving too slowly for her to notice.

In down-shifted UV, the shield was a huge, garishly-bright blast of radiance, far too intense for her to see anything. She fumbled with the visor's controls and adjusted the intensity. With the brightness cut back, she could see patterns, surging, dark-blue lines of force weaving their way around the blue-white glare of the energy field itself.

The flypack fired a control jet, turning her back to the asteroid. Flying backward, she tried to find the *Banquo*'s shield in the sky, but the ship was already lost to view. There was nothing to do but wait for the ride to end. The flypack was flying an automated run that was meant to bring her right up against the closest of the communication ports, and Suss was strictly along for the ride.

She longed for all of the devices that had been denied her because they contained too much metal, starting with a simple watch, right on up through a cutting laser to that most unimaginable of luxuries, her AID, Santu. But all were too risky passing close to an electromagnetic shield.

The best *Banquo* had been able to provide was a few varieties of plastic explosive—and even a few of those had to be left behind, because the chemistry of the explosive itself contained too much of the wrong kinds of metal. Suss was strictly, utterly, on her own.

The flypack fired again, blasting at full braking power. Suss suddenly realized that she must be getting close to the target. How much time had passed? It had seemed only a moment that she had stared at that blinding wall. It must have been much longer.

A tiny amber glowlight began to blink, just at the edge of Suss' vision. Fuel low! Damn it. The attitude jets fired again, swinging around until she was flying nearly parallel to the asteroid's surface, still traveling backwards. How long was there to go? She looked down, past her feet, and saw the hellish blue-white glow of the shield below her. She was close enough now to gauge her movement over that hellish pseudo-landscape of writhing energy. She couldn't be more than a hundred meters over it, and getting closer all the time.

She checked her tiny rearview mirror again, looking over her shoulder in the direction she was traveling. There!

Up ahead, a black column thrusting up through the shield. That had to be it. The low-fuel light began winking faster.

The plan had been for the flypack to bring her to rest right alongside the comm port, but the only *possible* trajectory was right at the limits of the pack's fuel supply, with no hope of a second chance. If the pack failed to get her there, Suss would just keep right on going, sailing out into space with no hope of rescue.

She watched the black column grow in the mirror. It was going to be damn close.

The flypack's engine chuffed and coughed once or twice, and then shut down. Suss shut her eyes and cursed the fates, fighting back tears. She opened her eyes and swallowed hard. To be that close and not make it.

She suddenly realized the fuel-warning light was still winking, not staying on. She still had fuel. Then why had— She looked again in the tiny mirror.

The black column was hanging motionless, right behind her, not ten meters away. Now that she was closer, she could see it was some sort of open framework, not a solid construction. The asteroid's shield was beneath her feet, scarcely twenty meters below.

Suss grabbed for the manual controls, rotated halfway to face the column, and blipped the maneuvering jets, giving herself the gentlest of nudges forward, so she was moving forward at only a few centimeters a second.

She reached up and switched off the UV vision system. The blinding glare of the shield as seen through amplified ultraviolet faded away. Below her, the shield resumed its inky-black appearance.

The column resolved itself, at least somewhat, as an open latticework construction, gloomy-gray in the dim starlight. The tower was obviously designed to be retractable. When threatened, it could be pulled in under the shield and the shield port closed.

As long as that didn't happen while she was around . . .

Suss looked over her head and saw a small forest of antennae sprouting from the top of the girder box, no doubt attached to various communication and detection systems inside the asteroid.

Had any of them spotted her? In theory, it was possible,

but even with the suit and flypack, Suss knew she had a very small radar cross section, and those dishes and sensors were pointed *up*, away from her.

Her gentle movement forward was bringing her closer to the antenna tower. She looked down, at where the tower entered the shield itself. She flicked the UV viewer back on for a moment and saw that the shield almost lapped up against the tower. She swallowed hard. Obviously, the best way in was to climb down the *interior* of the tower.

She was only a meter or two away now. She resisted the temptation to speed up her travel, and let her very slight momentum carry her forward. She put out her hands and grabbed hold of a corner girder.

Wrapping her legs around it to hold herself steady, she wrestled her way out of the flypack. She wouldn't need it any more, and it was going to be tough enough going without humping the rocket pack along. She got the thing off her and shoved it away. It drifted down toward the shield. She watched as it struck the shield—and disintegrated into a cloud of debris.

Like sticking your arm in a slicing machine, the man said. *More like a shredding machine.*

Never mind. Keep going. Don't think about it.

She wriggled her way into the center of the girder box and was relieved to find a set of handholds built into one line of girders. She swung herself around so her head was pointed down toward the shield and the asteroid below. She started climbing.

One hand after another, moving as delicately as she could, she pulled herself along, closer and closer to the hole in the shield. It was all too easy to imagine the hole as a mouth, gaping wide and eager to swallow her.

Closer. Closer. She could feel the power of the shield as she went toward it. Her hair was literally standing on end, caught in the surging electrical fields. She could feel her hair brushing the inside of her helmet as she turned her head, felt the hairs on her arms bristling against the sleeves of her suit.

Closer, closer, *into* the mouth, the hole, let it swallow her up, let the magnetic eddy effects set the little telltale lights in her helmet blinking and flickering, indicating the status of a flypack that wasn't there anymore. It didn't matter. Just keep going. You were still alive, when by all rights you should be dead a dozen times by now.

Through it, past it, under it. Pause for a moment, feel the hair on your head settling back a bit, turn around and look up at the violet anger of the shield that was *over* you, and realize you were in.

Suss sagged back against the handholds and started to breath again, not quite sure when she had stopped.

Chapter Twenty Three
Landing

They had received no word from Suss and could hope for none. Obviously, it would have been impossible for her to carry a radio, let alone use one, if she was trying to get past a communications center.

There had been a microscopic twitch on the *Banquo*'s shield-power sensor just after the time she should have arrived there. Whether that flicker on the meters indicated her death, the wreckage of her discarded flypack, or the impact of some completely unrelated bit of debris was impossible to say. There were bits and pieces of missile wreckage crashing back all over the asteroid's shield. There were no ruined Pact missiles raining down—Spencer wasn't even bothering to fire yet.

If Suss' fate was uncertain, *Banquo*'s was scarcely less so. She was in under guns, all right, skirting so close to the asteroid that there was a certain amount of interference between its shield and the ship's. Fortunately, the asteroid's shield was as effective in masking the enemy's sensors as the *Banquo*'s weapons.

Now and then they would get a fix on the destroyer and drop a missile on her, but this close in, magnetic disturbances were interfering with marksmanship: The enemy was as likely to hit the asteroid's shield as *Banquo*'s.

So far, the weapons officer had always managed to boost power to the shield in time—but sooner or later either she was going to be a millisecond off, or *Banquo* was simply going to run out of power for the shield.

The navigation officer was close to a nervous breakdown, keeping up a random series of course changes that would keep the destroyer skating over the asteroid's shield without any predictable pattern to her movements. If *he* got it wrong, the crew of the *Banquo* would receive a graphic demonstration of what happened when two EM shields interfered with each other. But as *Banquo* would turn into a cloud of debris in about ten seconds, the lesson would not be very useful.

Spencer glanced at the mission clock. In ten minutes they would fire a flight of missiles, one to each detected opening in the shield—including the one Suss had been aiming for. They needed those sensor ports destroyed anyway, to ease up the pressure on *Banquo's* defenses, but the main point of the exercise was to provide Suss with a diversion. In theory, if the enemy had detected the agent's arrival without being certain of what it was, a fusion bomb over her entry point would discourage any investigation.

Without vaporizing her, with any luck.

A hatch. A plain old, manually operated, nonsecure hatch, lying open right there at the base of the communications tower.

Suss stared at the hatchway for a long moment, scarcely believing her luck. She had sweated out the way into the asteroid's interior a dozen times, sketching out in her mind how she would have designed a secure entrance and kept someone like herself from gaining entry. And now all she had to do was cycle through a lock. She climbed inside and decided it wasn't so incredible to find a way in. After all, what point in securing an entrance behind a force shield and twenty million klicks from anywhere?

With a lack of drama that Suss somehow found disappointing, she cycled through the lock and stepped out into a small, unoccupied engineering room.

WHOOMP! Suddenly the whole compartment shuddered. A status monitor by the air lock suddenly turned bright red and flashed out a warning.

*   *   *

ENEMY MISSILE DETECTED.
AUTO-EMERGENCY COMM TOWER RETRACTION PERFORMED,
COMM PORT SHIELD OPENING COLLAPSED.,

Suss breathed a sigh of relief. Close, very close. Time to get on with it. She pulled off her pressure suit, unpacked the few non-metallic gadgets she had brought in its pockets, and stashed it in a closet. Underneath she was wearing tan coveralls, rather sweat-stained but otherwise quite nondescript.

Unless the civilians on this rock were issued some odd-looking uniforms, her clothes ought to pass muster. She smoothed down her hair and broke into an equipment locker. She found not only a tool bag, but a whole collection of hand and power tools that might well come in very handy. She stuffed those and her plastic explosives into the bag, opened the door to the compartment, and set off down the corridor she found behind it.

Find the shield generator, she told herself. *Shut it down, blow it up, stop it working. Somehow.*

The corridor was actually an access tunnel, drilled straight through the rock to this point from some central area. Suss peered down the length of raw, cold rock and could see no other doors opening on to it. Obviously it had been built for no other reason than getting workers back and forth to that comm tower service room. With the tower out of operation, it was unlikely that anyone else would come along it. That suited her fine.

Not that it made much difference. She'd meet the locals soon enough. She grabbed a handhold and started pulling herself along.

The tunnel was not as long as it looked. After only a hundred meters, Suss found herself decanted out into a busy—indeed frantically crowded—concourse, the meeting point of four or five large tunnels.

She moved cautiously out of the access tunnel and hung back from the obviously panicky crowds of people.

She was in no danger at all of being spotted as an outsider by these people. They were dressed in any number of styles, many of them close variants of her own worker's coverall. No one wore a name badge or a unit ID, let alone a uniform.

This was clearly, patently, a civilian crowd—and not a very well organized one at that. Everyone was shouting at once, banging into each other as competing teams struggled to get this or that large piece of equipment out of the way.

Suss heard a woman crying from somewhere. It occurred to Suss, not for the first time, that the helmet-creature was not very good at overseeing humans. These people knew they were under attack, but they did not seem to have been prepared for it, or know who was attacking them, or why.

She spotted something else. Knots of people were clustered around terminals set into the rock wall of the corridor, and others were pausing to check personal terminals. No one seemed to be getting instruction by asking a human superior—only by checking with a terminal.

People were taking their orders from the computers.

According to Spencer, the security people had been doing the same thing in the StarMetal building the night of their break-in. The guards hadn't been happy about it then, and the workers here didn't seem happy about it now. No doubt the official story here was the same as it had been then, that management was swamped and forced to let management AIDs handle routing administrative work.

Suss looked over the chaotic crowd. What would they think, she wondered, if they knew the computer terminals were passing along the orders of an alien machine/creature, a nightmare thing that had sucked their company chairman's mind away?

Suss launched herself into the confused throng, not with any specific goal yet in mind, but just to get a feel for the situation, overhear a few conversations, get the lay of the land. Judging by their hair styles, accents, and skill in zero-gee maneuvering, Suss concluded that the vast majority of these people were from the asteroid belt, hired up rather abruptly from the labor pool on Mittelstadt and for high wages.

No one seemed to have been here more than a month or so. Simply by looking at the state of work around her, Suss could tell that the job here was unfinished. The helmet-creature had set out to make its home asteroid into a formidable naval base—but the Pact Navy had arrived just a bit too early.

Rumors and speculation were everywhere. Some of the workers seemed to think they were building a new Pact naval base. A competing rumor, much closer to the truth, had it that one of the conglomerates—possibly but not necessarily StarMetal—was planning to rebel against the Pact.

No doubt, Suss thought, the latter idea had gained credence back when a fleet of robot freighters arrived at the base and the asteroid staff set to work arming them—and got a real shot in the arm when a destroyer popped into being right in their laps.

Suss made her way down a side alley and had to get out of the way of a squad of gleaming robots hurrying in the other direction. She had seen a lot of them already. That was another strange thing: There were entirely too many humanoid robots on the asteroid.

In the normal order of things, human-shaped robots were freaks, oddities. They were too expensive to build, needlessly complex. Except in rare cases, building a robot to look like a human made as much sense as building a shovel shaped like a gopher, or a lawnmower that looked like a flock of sheep.

The human anatomy is a general purpose system, capable of many things, but not optimized for any one task. Most robots, on the other hand were *specialized* machines, designed for only one or two jobs.

AIDs were certainly robots, highly advanced ones, but they weren't shaped like people. They couldn't have done their jobs as well if they were.

There was an ancient style of portable tool called a swizarm knife that contained all manner of gadgets. A tiny pair of scissors, two or three types of cutting blades, tweezers, a magnifying glass, a tiny pair of pliers. Suss had found one in the comm shack tool cabinet and grabbed it. She was glad to have it in her pocket: even if she had to drop her tool kit and run for it, she could use the swizarm by itself to do any number of jobs.

Of course, for every job the swizarm could muddle you through on, there was a better, more highly specialized device that could do that *one* job better. But soldiers and spies liked swizarms because it was easier to carry one tool instead of fifty and muddle through.

To an engineer, *humans* were swizarms. You used them instead of robots for jobs where it wasn't worthwhile to design and build the automated system—the robot—that could do the job better.

But suppose, Suss thought, there weren't going to *be* any humans around any more? You'd need *machines* to do all the once-in-a-while jobs, machines that could operate consoles designed for human controllers, read the indicators and handle the switches and dials and pedals and levers meant for a human controller. And the helmet had *lots* of human robots here.

Conclusion: The helmet didn't plan to keep most of its human servants around any longer than necessary. It was a grim conclusion to jump to, but it felt right to Suss.

Suss stopped and checked a map set into the wall of the tunnel. By now she had her bearings and was working her way toward what was labeled as the central control room. Comparing the wall map to her memory of Santu's conjectural diagram, she was certain it was the same compartment where the crew of the *Dancing Bear* had found the helmet those few short months ago. The control room now—what had it been a million years before? Was there something special about that compartment that made the helmet choose it for its power center once again? Maybe so. Almost certainly it was a place from which the shields could be controlled, and beyond doubt it was a place she could do some damage.

Suss noted down the path to take and got moving, avoiding a scruffy-looking work-robot as it passed her headed the other way. Down this way, along that corridor, this left, that right, closer and closer to her goal. She moved downward and inward, moving with and then against traffic as the mobs of humans and robots hurried on urgent errands. More of the tunnels started looking *alien* somehow. They were laid out strangely, in a way no human would have done it.

Something's wrong, she suddenly told herself. Her subconscious had spotted something. Suss glanced around herself, trying not to act suspicious, trying to think. Then it came to her. The closer she got to the control room the fewer *humans* and the more *robots* she was seeing—and it was becoming increasingly clear that the robots were taking an undue interest in her. She thought back through her last few turnings—yes, there had been inconspicuous cameras at the intersections, and at least one or two of them had turned to track her—

A siren began to sound, and a nearby viewscreen suddenly switched on, showing two still views of Suss—frames apparently taken from a robot's vision system a few intersections back. *Apprehend Intruder* the screen instructed.

Dammit! Suss thought. She should have *known*, she told herself. Maybe she had been in no danger from the *humans* in this rock, but the bloody robots had to be under direct parasite control. And the parasites *had* to be good at data processing. At least it had happened at a moment when she chanced to be alone in the corridor.

Her hands were already working before she was even aware that she had come up with a plan. She wadded up a blob of general-purpose plastic explosive and slapped it on the roof of the T-intersection behind her. She snapped the divider in a chemical-decay timer, poked it in the explosive, and started moving again toward the central control room, no effort at caution anymore. She scrambled down the corridor, swinging at full tilt from one handhold to the next.

The blast came up behind her, a deafening roar more felt than heard. The shock wave threw her down the corridor, slapping her up against the next turn in the passage. Half-stunned, her ears ringing, she peeled herself off the wall, trying to shake off the numbing blow. The air was full of choking smoke and dust, and rock fragments caromed lazily back and forth in zero-gee. At least the way was closed behind her.

She dug into her toolbag again and pulled out the spool of filament charge. She anchored one end of it on the floor of the corridor and began spooling it out behind her. Shove a detonator into any point in the charge, and the whole long strip of explosive would go up at once. It was great stuff for sealing a corridor.

She made her way down the corridor, noted a small passageway heading up to the next level, and paid out more filament charge on the main corridor. She anchored it down at that end, then returned to the small side passage. She dug into the tools she had grabbed, found a small powerpack and a length of wire.

That was enough. Thirty seconds later she had a crude detonator rigged. It was nothing but two wires plugged into the filament charge, with Suss ready to touch the far ends of the wires to the powerpack. But it was enough. She scrambled back into the side passage and waited.

Company was not long in coming. A whole squad of robots barreled out of the main passageway, heading from the direction of the command center. She gave them just long enough to space out along the main corridor, then touched off the strip of explosive, ducking out of the way as best she could.

WHAM! With a thundering crash that nearly rattled the teeth out of her head, the main passage dissolved in a torrent of noise, dust, and flying rock.

Suss crept cautiously out of her hidey-hole and hurriedly picked through the churning cloud of rubble and dust. In any sort of gravity field, the ruined rock would have slumped over and lay still. Not here. The corridor was filled with broken bits of wall and robot. Suss searched the broken machines for weaponry and was rewarded with a brace of heavy repulsors.

She pressed on, the light of battle in her eyes, with no thought for anything but getting to that damn control room and shutting down that shield. Then maybe she could lie down, rest, do something about the dull throbbing pain in her head, the trickle of blood coming out of her left ear from a punctured eardrum, pull the splinter of rock from her left shin. There was a constant ringing in her head, and her vision was a bit dim.

No such trivialities bothered her. She stumbled forward, using her left hand and right leg, the toolbag over her shoulder and one of her newly-won repulsors in her left hand. She passed through the length of wrecked corridor and kept moving. Another pair of robots appeared and she blasted them with recklessly long bursts of repulsor beads. She scrambled forward past their wrecked bodies.

After a time, which might have been a minute and might have been an hour, it dimly began to dawn on her that something strange had happened to the corridor walls. She didn't much care, but some corner of her pain-clouded mind warned her that it might be important.

She stopped and examined the walls—and realized that she had been proceeding down something very different than ordinary human-made rock tunnels or even ordinary *alien* tunnels for a while. These walls were slick and smooth, an impenetrable grey in color. There was something sheer, and shimmering, almost *alive* about them. Half-seen images seemed to flicker beneath their surface. This was nothing human-made, and nothing like what the crew of the *Dancing Bear* had reported.

If the walls had been like this, Destin would have filmed it, reported it. The walls had been dead then. Not like this, not alive.

Alive, Suss thought. *This was here when Destin arrived but not yet alive, awake.* She realized at last that this must be part of the ancient central complex of the asteroid, a piece of corridor older than humanity. *Imagine waiting that long in the dark for someone to come*, Suss thought, almost feeling sorry for the helmet.

Had it been an honest servant once, bred or manufactured to serve as an immensely powerful AID? How long had it waited to be found? And didn't folklore say that AIDs could go mad, lust for vengeance if ignored for too long? How long had the helmet brooded in the lonely, abandoned darkness? The idea frightened her far more than a squad of attacking robots had managed to do.

Close. She had to be close. Trailing tiny drops of blood that hung gleaming-red in the air behind her, she pressed on, struggling to concentrate, desperate to keep the map of the asteroid's interior clear in her clouded mind.

She stumbled around one last corner and surprised a pair of guard robots standing before a massive blast door. She shot them to confetti and dove back in behind the corner before they could react. *Must have been old models*, she thought. *I could never outdraw a modern job*. It took her a moment to think, realize what it was they must have been guarding—but only a split second to snap back into the corridor and blast out the entry controls even as the massive vault-like doors were beginning to swing shut. The blast door stopped moving halfway through its path and Suss kicked her way over to get behind it.

She looked around, shook her head to clear it and tried to think. The door, *that* was of human design, but it was as much a stranger here as she was, jammed into those weirdly glimmering grey walls. The corridor it sat in and the compartment behind it were utterly alien, with bits and pieces of human technology stuck in place here and there. Strange devices, in shapes that were hard to see, hung from the bulkheads. She shut her eyes and tried to picture the plan of the asteroid in her mind. There was no doubt about it, that was the main control room on the other side of the half-open blast door.

She dug a small wad of plastic explosive out of the toolbag, shoved a ten-second detonator in it, and pushed down the initiator button. She counted seven seconds to herself before heaving herself up over the edge of the blast door and throwing the explosive inside.

A repulsor spat at her from the control room as she pulled herself back down. Hypervelocity beads hit the walls and disintergrated, flaying Suss's back as ricocheting dust.

FLAM! The blob of explosive went off. Suss had calculated the charge to be enough to injure or stun anyone in the compartment without wrecking the place.

Moving as fast as she could, she swung up around the blast door and dove into the control room.

There was no one there. Then who the hell had fired? Suss looked to the far end of the compartment and saw the sealed hatch. She remembered from her briefings how fast the helmet had been able to move Jameson from his office.

Nothing else could have fired and then gotten out of there that fast, sealing a hatch behind, before the explosive could go off.

He, Jameson had been there, seconds before.

Never mind, no time. Suss turned and examined the interior of the blast door she had come through. Good, there was an emergency crank for sealing it. Putting all her failing strength into it, she turned the handle and swung the massive door shut, using a massive steel bolt to dog it shut from the inside. She crossed to the other hatch and dogged it shut as well.

Feeling a bit safer for the moment, she examined the crazy patchwork of controls that seemed strewn about the room in no logical pattern. The walls were of that same peculiar grey material, which seemed even more like something living than it had in the exterior chamber. Panels and readouts were mounted directly onto the material.

Pairs of devices that dealt with the same function might be next to each other or across the compartment from each other, one on the ceiling, the other on the floor. It was haphazard, a jury-rigged job, both human and alien devices hooked up in the same crazy quilt pattern.

After a five-minute search, Suss located the shield controls. She pulled back a lever and shut off a series of switches. A status board confirmed that the massive shield was already dissipating.

And that's that, she thought. It seemed incredible that the actual work of her mission was done that simply, but there it was. All the incredible risk, that harebrained jaunt through an energy shield, the firefights, just to push a button.

Suddenly she felt very tired, and knew it was more than mere fatigue. Her body had the luxury of feeling the hurts done to it. She could still easily die of her wounds, even if the enemy never tried to take back this room.

She remembered seeing a first aid kit tucked in somewhere during her search for the shield controls. She dug it out and set to work patching herself up.

It hurt like hell to move, but that was all right.

Pain was proof she was still alive.

*   *   *

"*Asteroid shields down!*" the sensor tech announced, but the navigator was already diving his lumbering ship on a trajectory that would have been scary for a fighter, scrambling to get in under the plane of the enemy shield before someone could switch it back on and lock them out again.

Spencer opened his mouth to order a dive, but never got the chance. *Let the crew do their job*, he thought.

"Sensors!" Deyi shouted. "Scan that rock, find us their main cargo locks *fast*. I want us landed on top of them before they have a chance to lock them down."

"Spotted what looks like a cargo center," the sensor tech announced. "Passing co-ords to navigation."

"Got it!" the navigator cried. "Course to landing there set. It'll be fast and sloppy, but we'll get down. Four minutes."

"Don't worry about the paint job," Tallen growled. "Just find us a parking space."

Spencer punched a button on his comm unit and spoke. "Captain Spencer to assault team, stand by. Lieutenant Marcusa, I will move with the second wave—" Spencer looked up and spotted the look on Tallen's face "—accompanied by Commander Deyi, if that is acceptable to him."

Tallen Deyi stood more erect than is wholly practical in zero gee and saluted his commander. "It is quite acceptable, Captain, thank you. I was about to raise a big stink about being left behind."

"I have to keep my officers satisfied, Tallen," Spencer said, smiling.

Why am I so happy? he wondered, and realized the answer even as he formed the question. *Because the shield going down means she's still alive*, he told himself.

Spencer did not choose to think about how long that would remain true.

The navigator rolled the *Banquo* to a new heading with a violent disregard for safe piloting norms—but he had his reasons for moving fast. Spencer could see on the tactical display that a pair of enemy missiles were diving in toward them. It was time to get out of the way, because there was no way to block this strike with the shields. *Banquo* was boosting at a full gravity, far too high for shield operation.

The weapons officer loosed a clutch of countermissiles, blasting the incoming attack.

The navigator pilot spun ship again and gave a short, savage burst of retrofire. Spencer checked the display. They were only a hundred meters over the cargo bay, exactly stationary over it. Very tidy piloting. The navigator fired up his topside auxiliary jets and jolted the ship straight down hard, throwing everyone against their crash harnesses. One unlucky ensign had his seat belt fail and got thrown into the ceiling.

The same ensign hit the floor just as abruptly when the navigator hit the bottom jets, braking them to a halt. They hit the ground and bounced a few meters. The pilot armed and fired the rock-piton system. A hundred powerful harpoon-like devices fired around the perimeter of the ship, stabbing their spikes into the ground. Winches spooled up, and pulled the ship down, holding it firmly in place. In the near-zero gravity field of a small asteroid, even large ships can simply drift off if they are not held down.

"Lower air locks open, first wave of marines on the ground," the weapons officer announced. "Sir, the faster you can get that second wave out of here—"

"The faster you can get the shields back up and keep them from dropping things on you," Spencer agreed. "Comm, can you stay linked with the assault team with the ship's shields up?"

"Standard operating procedure sir. Fiber-optic cable from the ship, under the shield, and out to a transmitter on the surface."

"Excellent. Tallen, let's move."

The two of them hurried down toward the landing stages. "I still say a hell-bomb would solve all our problems," Tallen said over his shoulder. "Why not at least prep one in case we can use it?"

"We can't possibly nuke the place. Not with Suss in there—to say nothing of civilians."

"Civilians who are working for the enemy," Tallen said.

"If those poor bastards know who they're working for I'll go get a job with StarMetal myself," Spencer said. "Besides, we can't afford to destroy the place, except as a last resort, until we know more—about the helmet, how it got there—if there are any more of them elsewhere. You want to vaporize the place and leave *that* question open?" he asked.

The older man said nothing, just trotted down the gangway to the next level.

Chapter Twenty-Four
Assault

Suss was glad to be in zero-gee. She knew perfectly well that she would have passed out long ago if her heart had been straining against a planet's gravity. The bandages, painkillers, and stimulants from the first aid kit were helping too. She checked the clock. Fifteen minutes since she had sealed herself into the command center.

And ten minutes since the drilling had started on the far hatch, the one Jameson must have escaped through.

Drilling, she told herself, knowing it must mean something. *Not laser cutters, not explosives, not a plasma gun, but an old-fashioned power drill.* Maybe there was still something here, something her small explosive charge hadn't wrecked, something relatively fragile that a stray laser beam or rock fragment or tongue of plasma fire might easily destroy. Something the helmet-thing valued greatly. Greatly enough to risk a slow, careful approach to a compartment it knew contained a dangerous enemy.

But they must think their precious something survived my improvised hand grenade, Suss thought. *How do they know the whatever-it-is is still in one piece? And why did they leave it here? Why leave it behind when they ran from me? Why is this such a vitally important place to keep the thing? Why here?*

Why here? She realized quite suddenly that the question was even more puzzling on a grander scale. *Why here? Why this crummy backwater asteroid? Why not*

308

*keep headquarters back on Daltgeld, where the people
and machinery were? Why not back on Mittelstadt, where
all the ships were?* The more she thought about it, the less
sense it made. Daltgeld made a much better HQ than this
place. The damn helmet had taken over the planet long
before the Navy showed up—but when danger threatened, it immediately cut and ran for *here*.

It had diverted tremendous resources to defending this
place. If the helmet had used its ships to jump the Pact
fleet while they were in orbit of Daltgeld, instead of using
its freighter fleet to guard this asteroid, the task force
would have been so much scrap metal orbiting the planet
by now.

Yet instead of standing its ground and holding onto its
strong position on the planet, the helmet retreated *here*.

And not just to this asteroid, but to this very chamber.
The helmet had been *here* fifteen minutes ago, right back
to the spot where Destin had found it.

Something occurred to Suss, an errant, obvious thought
all of them had missed when planning her one-woman
attack. The parasites could control any device directly.
Why did the helmet need a central control at all? *And why
hadn't the helmet used a parasite to switch the shields
back on, direct from the shield generator?* Good God,
maybe they had done just that! Suddenly alarmed, Suss
checked the view from an exterior camera. No, the shield
was still down.

Suss stared at the shield control panel. She noticed
something else strange. The panel did not have any cables
running from it. She looked around the compartment.
None of the monitor and control devices did. Yet they
were all attached haphazardly, obviously put in place after
the room was built. They couldn't have run the cables
through the rock wall. Devices outside this complex used
exterior cables. She had seen cables bolted up to the side
of nearly every tunnel.

Then how could the control panels possibly do their
jobs? Suss thought of an explanation, but not one she was
ready to believe. She grabbed the swizarm knife from her
pocket and moved over to the shield control panel. She

undid the knife's main blade and popped the panel cover off.

The interior of the control box was filled with perfectly normal circuitry—normal circuitry coated in translucent grey. The wires that should have led to the generator instead were stripped of insulation, and shoved, one by one, into a blob of the same grey wall material. It reminded Suss of a diagram of a nerve ganglion.

Wall material seemed to have flowed over every chip and wire of the interior surface. Inside the circuit box, the grey stuff seemed to fairly pulse with life and vigor. Suss cautiously prodded one corner of the "ganglion." It flinched back from the knife, rippled its surface, and then smoothed itself over.

It was alive.

And the walls, the floors, the ceiling of the compartment were covered with the same strange stuff. *All of it was alive*. Suss realized they were all part of the same huge creature, embedded deep in the very heart of the asteroid.

No, worse. Deep in the *brains* of the asteroid. The various control panels here were wired *directly into* the brain of the monstrous living animal that lived inside this asteroid. The gray "walls" formed the inside surface of the brain. The huge animal *was* this asteroid. The external rock was nothing more or less than a protective shell for this horror.

That explained why the parasites had not overridden Suss' shields-down command. When she had thrown the switches on the control panel, she had been reprogramming the asteroid's brain, literally changing its mind, telling it to decide it wanted the shields down.

Just like the wire in a wirehead's brain, she thought. *The wire controls the addict's mind. A switch thrown outside the brain to make the nerves twitch, but the brain still thinks it is in control.*

But how could such a huge, strange animal come to be? Nature could never evolve some brooding brain lurking in outer space.

The insect people, Suss figured. *They* had grown this thing. But why? As an experiment, as a semi-organic supercomputer, as an act of suicidal hubris? And how had they operated it?

The asteroid-sized brain was too big to move easily, too huge and clumsy to go anywhere. And it was too far away, too remote to communicate with anyone or be operated directly. A sudden inspiration came to Suss: *So they decided to use an AID-like system to run their computer.*

They built another semi-living device, one that could link directly with, and commune with, a true living brain. An AID that could split off small copies of itself as needed to control remote machines, a semi-living creature that could reproduce itself and thus never wear out. With the asteroid-brain, a system that could last a million years

The helmet was indeed an AID, a datalink straight into the asteroid's massive data processing system. Put on the helmet, and you controlled the asteroid and the data it held.

A ruler, a dictator could wear the helmet and, with the asteroid-sized auxiliary brain to keep track of all the data, one being could directly control every device in the star system. It was an idea that would appeal greatly to an intelligent hive-mind species. If Earth's ants had developed space travel, dispersed across their entire star system, and thus lost their ancestral links with the home hive, they might have yearned for the old days when one hivemaster, one queen, had ruled all. *They* might have built a system like this one.

One ruler, one being, controlling everything, like a puppet master pulling all the strings. He or she or it thinks a thought, and orders more widgets produced, or the traffic light to go from green to red, or orders a ship to go from here to there. The helmet hears and obeys, tells the parasites to step up widget production, change the light, and then links back to the asteroid for the more complex job of locating a ship and computing a trajectory.

The asteroid commands the helmet, its AID-device, to send out a parasite to the ship—except the ship no doubt had a parasite in it all along. The parasite nestles down inside the navigation controls and fires the engine. The parasite, an integral part of the helmet, is thus in constant touch, through the helmet, both with the asteroid and the leader. That little job, and a billion more like it every day, controlled through the leader's three puppets—the asteroid, the helmet, and the parasite.

Until one fine day the puppets realize they can pull the puppet master's strings. They can take over *his* mind, run every machine themselves for their own purposes.

And a whole civilization dies when the machines go to war with the people who own them. The death of the *Duncan*, the death of McCain repeated a billion times over. Every car, every ship, every computer, every automatic device rebelling.

Until one insect hero murders the mad ruler. The helmet is designed to work with an organic brain, and without that brain in the loop, the whole system collapses.

Until Destin and the *Dancing Bear* find the helmet.

It made sense. Wild guess or not, it fit all the facts. And it meant that Suss was sitting *inside* the enemy's brain. There was something she could do about that. She dug into her toolbag and got to work.

Spencer and Deyi clambered down one last gangway and arrived at the internal air lock leading to the aux vehicle bay. They cycled through.

The vehicle bay was open to vacuum. The second wave of seventy-five marines was standing by, waiting for their fellows to establish a perimeter.

Lieutenant Marcusa, the marine commander, spotted the two senior officers across the compartment. "I'm going to give the move-out order in about ninety seconds," he said from where he stood on the other of the compartment, using the command frequency.

Spencer noticed Marcusa resisted the temptation to shout into the radio when talking with someone far-off. Obviously he was a man used to suit radios.

"We had a swarm of *robots* attack the first wave, if you can believe that." It was an article of faith among the marines that no robot could ever be programmed with the fighting spirit that made a true warrior. "Our folks just dug in and let the ship's plasma cannon take care of the tin men. Squad three has found an air lock complex the enemy failed to disable in time. We should have it secured and be on our way in any— Hold it just a sec."

His voice cut out for a moment as he talked over another circuit. "We're in," he announced simply. "Second wave about to move. Ah, Captain Spencer sir, I'm not quite certain of how proficient you are in this sort of—"

"The captain was in the High Secretary's Guard, if you'll recall, Lieutenant," Tallen said gently. "They *do* occasionally train in goddamned battle armor."

"Yes, of course,," the marine commander said in obvious relief. "You probably know what you're doing better than most of us. Stand by."

There was a slight click as Marcusa switched to another channel that reached all his troops. "Second wave, move out. Objective is the air lock marked with a flashing light. Stay with your guidewires and no screwing around. And I'm going to say this one last time. Anyone who wants to live, listen. The rest of you tune out. No AIDs, no pocket computers, no smart weapons, no electronics of *any* kind you don't need to stay alive. Those parasite bastards can get into anything and take it over. If *anything* you're carrying has even the slightest malfunction, dump it and do without. They could even get into your pressure suit—so if your air starts going bad, don't diddle with your chest panel—get the hell into safe air and peel off your suit *fast*. Now let's go."

An engineer with the first wave had run a cable between the ship and the air lock, then swung hand-over-hand back to the ship, trailing a second guidewire. Gravity was no help on an asteroid. The first wave had to move over the asteroid surface like so many mountain climbers, laying in pitons and climbing ropes. The second team simply had to swarm over the bright-orange guidewires, straight for their objective. In a smooth, seemingly well-rehearsed performance, the marines snapped their belt-clips onto the guidewires and pulled themselves along, hand over hand, toward the air lock.

Spencer and Tallen rode along with the last squad, zipping over the gloomy, dim-lit landscape of the asteroid's surface. Spencer was secretly proud that he managed to keep up with the marines. Whatever reputation for skill the Secretary's Guard might have, Allison Spencer had never fought a battle in an armored pressure suit.

He lost cause for pride at the far end by nearly caroming off the marine ahead of him. He just barely managed to get unclipped from the line and out of the way before Tallen piled into him.

The air lock complex was a mixture of chaos and order. The big chamber was milling with Marines sorting themselves out into squads.

Wrecked machinery was strewn about the place, and small bits of ruined robots were still cartwheeling about. Spencer spotted three very dead humans, civilians by the look of them. Their corpses were taped to a bulkhead to keep them from floating away. Marines, long experienced in zero gee warfare, knew the dead did not always stay in one place. They knew to carry strapping tape. Spencer spotted a dead marine likewise taped down, and shivered.

The walls of the interior chamber were shot up, blackened and pitted in places. There was air pressure here, but Spencer noticed none of the marines had unsealed their suits, perhaps recalling how whole decks of the *Duncan* had been gassed. Cautious troops, these.

They found Marcusa working over a wallscreen, adjusting its controls to examine a map of the asteroid interior. "We scooped up about ten or fifteen prisoners when we first came in a half-hour ago, and boy, they were ready to talk." he said. "Scared silly, no idea what the hell was going on. All they knew was that StarMetal hired them for a hush-hush project out here. It seems there are no human troops on this rock, so we'll just be shooting robots. Few of these civilians will want to tangle with us. They have no allegiance to StarMetal, and no beef with us. They'll just head for cover until the shooting stops."

He glanced back at the taped bodies. "Except for the usual two or three yabbos who get a glory-gleam in their eye and decide to strike a blow for some damn cause or another," he added. "We'll try to get those types before they get us.

"There is one weird thing about the civilians. *None* of them seem to have any clear idea of what they were doing, or why, up until just about the moment the shields went out. It sounds like they were all scurrying around like a bunch of ants when the ant hill gets kicked over. All of them say they've been working incredibly hard the last few days, ever since Chairman Jameson arrived to oversee things personally—but no one seems to have actually *seen* him or remember details of the last few days. It's like they all woke up from some bad dream."

Spencer and Tallen looked at each other, both understanding, neither needing to speak. Once the helmet arrived here, it was able to exert the same sort of mind control Destin had reported. And Suss, in the act of shutting down the shields, had interrupted that power of compulsion somehow.

"I guess we can worry about all that later, Right now," the young lieutenant said, "we're here."

He pointed to the wallscreen and tapped an air lock symbol indicating their position. "I'd suggest that we drive straight for the central command area, here. We *could* go for several other key areas, like the powerplant, or environmental control. But if we want to seize control of the whole asteroid, we'll have to take the central command sooner or later anyway. They'll defend it heavily, and I'd just as soon tackle them while we've got fresh troops that haven't taken casualities."

"Very good, Lieutenant," Spencer said. "Get to it."

Marcusa switched to his all-troops channel and started issuing commands. The air lock complex opened out into a wide corridor that ran the length of the asteroid. Marcusa detached a squad to hold the air lock, and then sent half of his remaining troops in each direction down the main passage. They were to turn and go down the closest main corridor heading toward the interior of the asteroid.

Spencer nodded. A good plan, much better than sending the whole force marching down one passage. This way the enemy would have to hold two corridors, and if one way was blocked, the marines could sidestep over to the passage that was still open—or else hunker down until the other team could come up behind the opposition.

Spencer and Tallen joined the second squad and moved out. Spencer felt good. These were Pact Marines, the troops that had conquered a thousand planets. The helmet could throw nothing but panicky civilians and a few robots at them. This was going to be a walk-in.

Marcusa could have told him that was what most commanders felt just before all hell broke loose.

A hundred meters ahead, the corridor exploded in flame. The spitting roar of a heavy repulsor firing at close range rattled Spencer's suit. Spencer was abruptly blinded, his visor suddenly splattered with gore, painted with bright-red arterial blood. The marine ahead of him had just got his head blown off. With screams and shouts and explosions, the marines dove for cover and fired back.

It seemed that robots were pretty good fighters after all.

That same powerpack that set off her first blast ought to do it. But she needed to rig some sort of spring-loaded switch, something she could hold apart, that would snap shut if she let go. Something like a rubber band . . . the elastic waistband in her coverall!

Suss stripped off the one-piece garment, leaving her in panties and an undershirt. She slashed the coverall to shreds and pulled out the elastic. A pair of plastic pliers, meant for use around electric equipment, would serve as the mechanical part of the switch. She stripped the insulation from the ends of two wires and used a quick-setting conductive glue to attach the bare wire-ends to each face of the plier's jaw. She worked the pliers once or twice to make sure there was a good contact. She shut the pliers and glued short lengths of the coverall elastic to both sides of its closed jaw.

Ten seconds for the glue to dry. She pulled the pliers open, then let go. The two bare wires held by the plier jaws snapped together with a satisfying *clack*. It should make a good electric contact. She opened the plier jaws again and stuffed a wad of cloth between them.

They had stopped drilling again, Suss realized. She looked up and saw yet another neat hole in the hatch. Another four or five like that, and they'd be able to slice through the gaps in between in a few seconds.

Suss forced that from her mind and got to work with her filament charge, wrapping it around and around the walls, ceilings and floor of the control room. She dug out her general-purpose explosive as well, and wrapped it in the last half-meter or so of filament charge. Even if it didn't touch off the GP charge, the filament charge alone ought to blast this place down to rubble.

Wires jammed into the filament charge, hooked into the powerpack, crudely twisted together. Suss traced the circuit carefully. Yes, it ought to work. Ugly as hell, but an effective deadman switch.

Holding the pliers and trailing the wires behind her, she backed into the corner furthest from the far hatch, next to the hatch she had come through. She could feel a warm hum of power against her spine. Her back up against the grayish wall matter, she felt a sick feeling of revulsion in her gut: She was literally in physical contact with the enemy's brain. Never mind. Suss pulled the handles of the plastic pliers apart, and shook the wad of cloth free from between the jaws.

She felt a wave of dizziness go through her. She closed her eyes for a second and wondered just how much blood she had lost.

The noise of the drill stopped again. Suss hadn't even noticed that it had started up. She looked up again to see the bit withdraw and the blade of a metal-cutting vibration saw appear.

With a shrill, high-pitched whine, the saw started up, slicing through the gaps of metal left between the drill holes. Suss watched, her heart pounding, her vision clouding over, as the blade sliced open a circular hole about twenty centimeters across. The blade tore away the last shreds of hatch metal, and the cutout disk was drawn back through the hole.

The marines had been caught in an ambush, a perfectly executed attack, timed and coordinated with the precision of a ballet. It was the parasites, of course. One to a robot, all of them linked back to the helmet. It made the enemy force into one mind with a hundred bodies, all knowing and seeing what the other bodies were doing.

It was all the Pact forces could do just to link back up with each other and retreat down the main corridor.

Another rocket-grenade howled past Spencer, caroming

off the rock walls before exploding. Three marines were smashed down to pulp by the blast, three perfect young bodies converted in a split second into bloody ruination.

Marcusa was still alive, that was something. As long as the marines' commander lived, at least they had a chance of fighting their way back to the surface.

But that, Spencer knew, would only delay the inevitable. The helmet intended to hunt them all down, kill them all.

If the helmet did that completely enough, and fast enough, and managed to get past *Banquo*'s shield—then Spencer would have made the helmet the gift of a starship, given it the keys to the Pact.

Cautiously, awkwardly, a robot arm reached through the hole and pulled back the manual hatch latches. Suss longed to reach for her repulsor and blast that metal arm to scrap, but that would do no good. It was *necessary* that they open the hatch.

The robot pulled back the last latch. They activated the door controls from the outside and the massive blast door swung smoothly open.

Suss backed further into her corner and braced herself in, making sure she kept her eye on the far hatchway. Two massive robots, carrying outsized repulsors, stood at the entrance, flanking the wan, pathetic figure of an old, old man in a powerchair, a gleaming silver helmet on his head. The three of them began to move forward.

"Step inside this room and I blow it up," she said, not sure if she were talking to the old man or the *thing* that was controlling him. "I've got this whole room wrapped in explosives, and a deadman switch rigged up to the detonator. If you shoot me, I won't be able to keep the switch from shutting. If I even *think* you're trying to control my mind, I let go of the switch. The room will blow up— giving you an instant lobotomy. You just stay right there, and send your robots away. *Now.*"

The old man's eyes were staring sightlessly down at the deck. Jameson did not look up at her, or move at all. No facial muscle twitched, no finger so much as quivered.

The two robots backed away, vanishing around a corner

of the passageway. Suss had no illusions that they had gone far.

"What—do—you—want?" The words came from the old man's voice, but it was a machine talking, in a voice full of hatred.

"I want the old man to take the helmet off," Suss said. "Tell him to do it!" The helmet thing needed a brain to work properly, that was obvious. And its power was greatest when both mobile components—helmet and host-brain— were in this room, this hollowed-out bit of the asteroid's brain.

Maybe, just maybe, if the helmet stayed out of this central control room *and* off Jameson's head, that would weaken it enough to give the assault team a chance. It seemed possible to Suss that the helmet would lose control of its parasites, including the ones running its battle robots.

"My—robots—are—programmed—already," the helmet said, speaking through Jameson. "They will—win without —my help."

"Then you have nothing to fear by coming off Jameson's head," Suss said through clenched teeth. "But can the asteroid brain survive what my explosives will do to it? *Make Jameson take you off!*"

Suss watched the decrepit figure, and tried to guess what it might be thinking. Certainly its powers were enhanced inside this chamber, or it would not have struggled so hard to get back in. But even away from it, even off a human head, it had *some* power—it had gotten itself delivered to Jameson, after all, without Destin wearing the thing for more than a few seconds. It had some weakened ability at mind control when working solo.

Already, Suss could feel a tiny whisper at the base of her skull, telling her the helmet would win anyway, telling her not to throw her life away in a futile gesture, telling her to disarm the switch. The idea *felt* like it was her own, but she *knew* it was the helmet. She fought off the alien thought and tried to concentrate. If being *in* the control chamber enhanced its power, it was a reasonable guess that even being close to the chamber was some help.

And, looking through Jameson's eyes, the helmet would

be able to see that Suss was not in good shape. She was injured; weakened and getting weaker. Sooner or later, she would cross the threshold where she would weaken enough that she would not be able to resist the helmet's power of suggestion. Suss herself knew that was true. Sooner or later, the helmet could persuade her. Cut off from its control of the hundreds or thousands of parasites it was running at the moment, perhaps it could focus *more* energy on Suss' mind.

Suss didn't know. But she did know what else to try. "Make him take you off," she repeated.

After a long moment's pause, Jameson's two spindly, wavering arms reached up over his head, moving awkwardly, clumsily. The helmet *still* was not good at direct muscular control. The palsied fingers took hold of the helmet and pulled it away. There was a low sucking sound and a small splash of blood.

The moment the helmet left Jameson's head, he let out a sharp grunt of pain, and his arms spasmed for a moment, almost pulling the helmet back into place. But his fingers jerked apart, and the helmet sailed lazily up to bounce against the ceiling and rebound. Air resistance slowed it down and left it hanging quietly in mid-air, hanging neatly between Jameson's outstretched hands.

Suss looked at Jameson and was almost sick. The top of his head was a bloody mess, covered with open sores and pus-swollen infections. She could see the living bone peeking through here and there. His breath came noisily, painful wheezing gasps that seemed not to bring any air into his lungs. Clearly the poor man was no longer able to control his own body. Without the helmet to help control his basic autonomic functions, he would die. He moaned and whimpered, clearly in great pain.

Suss stared at the dying man with a mixture of horror and pity. All she need do was put the helmet back on him and the pain would fade, his breathing would ease. Such a simple thing, to jam something into the deadman switch, keep it from firing for just a second while she . . .

No! It was the helmet. The helmet was working on her, reaching into her brain. With a grim anger, she wedged herself back further into the corner. *Stay here*, she thought. That idea she knew was hers alone.

Marcusa had gone down, blown into a dozen pieces by an enemy grenade. Without his skill in controlling the team, the Marines lost whatever coordination they had had.

Now the battle was raging in a half-a-dozen corridors, and the noise echoed, resounded back and forth down the passages. The robots had sliced the marine force up into isolated pockets, and were slowly chewing them over, content to let none of them escape and kill whoever might show his head.

Suddenly the enemy fire slowed, all but stopped. The blisteringly perfect coordinated fire from the robots faded away to a desultory series of repulsor bursts.

Spencer noticed the change at once. Without raising his head, he looked up the corridor, where a pair of robots had been pinning his squad down, one popping out to continue suppressing fire just as the other fell back around the corner to reload. The timing was perfect and never allowed the marines to raise their head from cover long enough to aim their weapons and fire.

For the briefest of moments, both robots were out of sight. But that was long enough. Three Pact marines had beads drawn when both robots reappeared simultaneously. They were scrap metal a split second later.

By some damn miracle or other, the robots had lost their coordination. Had the helmet lost touch with the parasites running the robots?

With the sudden dizzy idea that all might not be lost, Spencer punched into the all-troops circuit and heard about a whole series of similar robotic mistakes.

"The damn thing just froze and Luis splattered it."

"Sarge, two 'bots just turned and shot each other up!"

"They turned and started running alluva sudden. Do we go after them or hold here?"

Two squad leaders, eager to get the hell out of the killing zone, and assuming all the officers were dead, ordered their troops to take advantage of the lull and retreat back to the surface.

Spencer swore. If they fell back now, all of it would be

for nothing. Couldn't they see that Suss had somehow done it for them all once again, pulled the dragon's teeth? He fumbled with the unfamiliar comm-controls and managed to get on the command circuit.

"This is Captain Spencer. Belay those orders to retreat! Somehow or another the system that was coordinating the robots has crapped out. Don't run from them now. Use them for target practice and all combat-effectives link up at—" he glanced at the numbers stenciled at the closest intersection—location 36-19-4. We're going in to take this rock."

He turned to Tallen Deyi, who had managed to stay with him throughout the chaos of the battle. "Now what do I tell them?" he asked on a private comm circuit. "I don't know anything about commanding a battle in an asteroid."

Tallen grinned wearily. "That's okay. You didn't know how to command a goddamned Navy ship either, and that turned out all right. But for what it's worth, I remember that this corridor runs straight into the central command area."

Faster that Spencer would have thought possible, the surviving members of the assault team started to appear. Some of them were obviously wounded, stretching the term "combat effective" pretty far. Spencer wanted to order injured back to the aid station in the air lock, but he knew he might need every man and woman available soon. He gave them a chance to assemble and then spoke.

"Nothing fancy this time," he said, "but this time we take 'em. If we can get down into that command center before the enemy gets his act back together, we can win this thing. Form up into squads. I want a standard covering advance up this corridor. Let's *go!*" Spencer hoped against hope a "standard covering advance" was right for this situation—and that it meant the same thing in the Marines that it did in the Guard.

Apparently it did. The troops sorted themselves out and set off down the corridor, one squad advancing, securing a new position and covering it while the next squad took the point and moved past the first squad. The first squad would hold its position, letting their fellow marines move past until the first squad was in the rear and covering any rude visitors coming up behind.

Good troops, Spencer thought. Half their number now casualties, and still they worked well, running the maneuver with an easy grace. Spencer and Tallen did not move with a squad, but stayed in the center of the formation, where they could keep an eye on point and rear easily.

A tracer rocket shot past Spencer's nose out of a cross-corridor. Startled, he made the mistake of looking at where it was going before he looked back to see where it was coming from. The rocket skittered down the empty passage and smashed harmlessly into the ceiling a few hundred meters away. Tallen fired a long repulsor burst in the opposite direction, catching the attacking robot just below the shoulder on his firing arm. Spencer raised his own weapon and blasted the robot's head off.

The whole move down the corridor was like that: quick, random exchanges of fire with solitary robots. Now it was the humans doing the herding, the controlling, and the robots doing the retreating, and the dying—if a machine could be said to die.

Suddenly the rapidly moving column stopped as it began to round a corner, and the occasional stutter of small-arms fire from that point rose to an angry roar.

Spencer moved to the front of the column, and found two marines, pulled a third back to safety—or at least most of her back. Her leg had been blown off, and was pinwheeling about the corridor, blood streaming from the wound. Spencer looked down at the young woman. Her suit had done its job, constricting shut where it had been hit, clamping down on the horrible wound, effectively serving as a tourniquet. Blood splashed onto Spencer's suit and oozed over his chest. He forced his mind away from the woman's injury. If they got out of this alive, sick bay could grow her a new leg eventually.

Right now Spencer could do her, and the rest of his command, the most good by getting them through this alive. He turned toward one of the troopers who had pulled the injured woman back. "Ambush?" Spencer asked, He read the soldier's insignia and nametag. Private Cormark.

"Not exactly, sir," Cormark replied. "We just came

around that goddamned corner and saw every robot in hell waiting for us. They all opened up on us at once. But they weren't hiding—just *waiting* for us to come get them. They're just standing there, all the targets you'd want, like they don't care if we kill them or not. But it'll take time to hack through them all."

Spencer nodded. Without the parasites to coordinate them, the robots had done their best, simply linking up as closely as possible to grind the marines down by brute force, rather than hit-and-run finesse.

Spencer pulled a flexiscope from his suit rack and bent it so it would look around the corner. He opened his helmet visor, knelt down by the bend of the corridor, and put the scope to his eye, cautiously sliding the far end of the scope around the corner.

Robots, dozens of humanoid robots of every shape and size, clustered in nearly solid ranks, their weapons at the ready. Shoot the one in front, and its place would be taken by the robot behind, again and again and again as the machines volunteered for the meat-grinder. A slow, grim process that did not require sophisticated choreography. Spencer had made a rough sketch map of the asteroid's interior when they were still in the air lock. Now he consulted it. If it was right, the robots had no way out, no means of retreat—and directly behind them was the command center. They meant to make their stand here. But why? What possible help was it to the enemy for them to put their entire force at risk this way?

Risk, hell. The robots were doomed. The marines could blast away at them from cover until there weren't any robots left. Why? What does it gain them?

Time, Spencer realized. *That's what this is about. The helmet doesn't mind spending its troops, if it uses them to buy time. It thinks it can regain some of the control it's lost, if only it has enough time.*

One robot, more alert than its fellows, spotted the scope and took a bead on it. Spencer pulled the scope back out of the way a split second before the repulsor beads ripped up the spot where it had been. The fire stopped the moment he pulled the scope clear.

The message from the robots was obvious. *Anything we see, we shoot until it dies or retreats.*

All this in the service of the helmet, a delaying tactic for its benefit. *If it wants to buy time, then we don't want to sell it*, Spencer thought. It might well be worth the effort, worth the danger, dammit, worth the *casualties* to punch through fast. "Private Cormack, bear with an amateur C.O. for a second. We've been using mostly lightweight stuff so far."

"Yessir," Cormack replied. "Us *and* the robots. You don't want to use high explosives or any really heavy-duty stuff most times when you're fighting inside a rock. One good blast near a weak seam and you could crack the whole rock open. These robots seem like they're playing really gentle."

Spencer didn't want to see how the robots played rough. "What have we got on tap just in case some crazed officer type wants to take that chance? Something big enough to flatten those robots but maybe small enough to keep this asteroid together?"

Cormack grinned eagerly. "Sir, don't you worry about specs and overpressures like that. We'll handle it. It'll take a little coordination, that's all. But first lemme get Enid here handed back toward the aid station."

"Do it fast, Private. Time is the enemy."

DISARM THE WEAPON. TAKE THE HELMET, PUT IT ON. DISARM THE WEAPON. TAKE THE HELMET. PUT IT ON. DISARM THE WEAPON. TAKE THE HELM—

With a mighty effort of will, Suss forced the pounding words out of her mind. Marshaling all her strength, she found a way to block them out, set up a wall she could hide behind at least for a moment.

The helmet was through with subtle suggestions, coy insinuations. It no longer even asked to be replaced on Jameson's head, no doubt sensing that the time was come to find a new steed. It wanted *Suss*.

And it was going to have her. She knew that, knew that her will could not resist indefinitely under this onslaught. Already she had twice had to keep her own hands from straying, reaching for the wad of fabric that still hung before her eyes. All she need do was grab at it with one hand while the other stretched a bit to hold the pliers apart. The free hand would take the fabric, jam it back between the plier jaws. Then she could safely close the pliers, cross the compartment and TAKE THE HELMET. PUT IT—

She blinked, shook her head, and realized her left hand was already *reaching* for that wad of fabric. She snatched it back and clamped it grimly around the plier handle.

"Stop!" she screamed, tears welling up in her eyes. But in zero gee tears did not flow. They hung in her eyes, blurring her vision. She shook her head to shake the tears off. "Stop it now or I let the switch go! Stop!"

She *had* to let go now, before it won. Better she died than that this thing seized the Pact. Closing her eyes, calming herself as best she could, determined to meet the end with dignity, she relaxed her hold on the pliers, released them.

Nothing happened.

She opened her eyes and saw that her hands had not moved. But she had *felt* them move, *felt* herself let go of the pliers. But nothing was but what was not. The helmet didn't care what Suss *thought* she was doing, but it was not going to let her end it yet. It was winning, starting to control her nervous system. A wave of despair washed over her, and Suss could no longer tell if it was genuine, or a fraudulent feeling imposed by the helmet.

But there were more immediate dangers than her own emotions. Suss stared down at her hands and saw the left one relaxing its grip again. Wrestling against the unseen enemy, an enemy literally inside her head, she forced her fingers back down, *demanded* that they wrap themselves around the pliers. Reluctantly, her hand cooperated.

She was holding out for the moment. But she knew it could not last.

DISARM THE WEAPON. TAKE THE HELMET. PUT IT ON. DISARM—

"Normal doctrine is you don't *use* fragmentation grenades in a pressurized tunnel," Private Cormack explained as he started arming the vicious-looking things. His squad mate pulled the grapefruit-sized grenades out of the carrykit and set to work as well. The assault team had broken all records hot-footing the frag-grenades from the *Banquo*'s hold to the forward point of march. The distance covered wasn't anything much, just a few kilometers all told—but with such minor obstacles as getting *Banquo* to lower her shields, asteroid corridors still filled with the floating, churning dust and debris of battle, and the occasional sniper robot still on patrol.

"The fragments are supposed to be slowed too much by air pressure," Cormack went on. "The theory is you get more killing power from the shock waves of standard explosives. Well, maybe if you're shooting at people. But robots can stand a heavy overpressure and not even notice. Now hit them with a saturation fire of these babies and—"

"Cut the shop talk and get those damn things ready," Spencer snapped. They were cutting it close, too damn close. He could *feel* it. Somewhere, and somewhere close, that damnable helmet was fighting back. "*Move it.*"

"Uh, yessir," Cormack said. "That's fifty of them, set with five second delay timers triggered by first impact."

Spencer turned and faced the rear of the tunnel. "Everyone but the grenadiers and flame specialists, two hundred meters back and take cover. There might be a lot of debris flying." The rest of the assault team backed away down the tunnel.

Tallen Deyi looked uncertainly at the small team of troopers preparing the weapons. "Cormack, what the goddamned hell do we do if one of those things caroms *our* way?"

Cormack shrugged, an exaggerated gesture meant to be understood through a pressure suit. "I dunno, sir. Throw 'em back?"

"Terrific," Tallen replied.

Spencer grinned edgily, feeling a sense of gallows humor. "In that case Cormack, let's hope your squad has some good catchers. Proceed at will."

Cormack towed the carrykit full of now-armed frag grenades toward the bend in the corridor. The first thing he

threw was a smoke bomb, bouncing it off the corner wall
so it caromed back down toward the robots. Spencer
snapped his flexiscope around the corner at the same
moment to watch. The bomb died in a vicious hail of
repulsor fire—but that was of little matter to a smoke
bomb that was already going off. The corridor instantly
filled with a thick black smoke.

The hope was that the robots used normal vision to aim,
and couldn't shoot what they couldn't see. It seemed to
work—the robots stopped shooting. The asteroid's air system kept a steady breeze moving down the corridor, blowing straight at the robots.

Cormack threw a frag-grenade five seconds after the
smoke bomb, and another five seconds after that, and
another, and another, bouncing each off the corner wall,
sending the grenade rebounding off the tunnel wall toward
the target.

The first of the grenades blew just short of the smoke,
filling the corridor around it with hundreds of shaped
pieces of armor-piercing alloy. Much of the shrapnel merely
slammed into the rock wall—but some of it drove down
into the smoke, toward the robots. Spencer heard the
screaming impact of metal on metal.

Cormack cackled gleefully and threw the next grenade.
So much for high-tech, Spencer thought. In a war against
a nightmare world of intelligent machines, it came down
to one guy who knew how to bounce bombs off a wall.

Spencer looked up from the scope to the marines. One
of Cormack's squad mates began throwing more smoke
bombs and grenades. A third was there at the ready in the
inevitable but heart-stopping moment when a grenade
suddenly sprouted up *out* of the smoke. She caught the
bomblet and heaved it back the way it had come.

Through the scope, all was carnage, chaos. Disembodied
bits of robot bodies blossomed out through the smoke,
slamming into the corridor walls. The savage noise of
repulsor fire started up again, but it was impossible to see
which robot was firing, or at what. Spencer suspected the
robot did not know, either. Overload them enough, and
robots will behave a great deal like panicking humans.

Another grenade dove down into the smoke and exploded.

"Flamers," Spencer ordered. "Fire in volley." Instantly, the two flame gunners came to the fore. They hooked the flexible nozzles of the flame-guns around the corner and fired blind.

The flame guns were baby variants of plasma guns, firing a weaker, cooler, fusion pulse—but there was nothing weak or cool about their shots from where Spencer watched through the flexiscope. The sun-bright tongues of flame licked down the corridor, banishing the smoke, stabbing down into the ranks of the robots.

A wall of superheated air slapped back up the corridor, singeing Spencer's eyebrows. The flexiscope started melting in his pressure-suit gloves. He slammed shut his helmet visor and scrambled back, now understanding perfectly well why it was against the doctrine to use flames inside an asteroid. Spencer could not imagine any of the robots could have survived the attack.

"Cease fire!" he ordered. "Cormack! How long until the corridor cools enough for us to move up it?"

"We can move now sir, if we use our climbing gear instead of pushing ourselves with hands and feet. Our rock hammers and stuff are insulated. And our suits *shouldn't* melt if we do touch the walls for a second or two."

"Then move out, *fast*—and watch out for any robots we missed. Relay that to the rest of the team," Spencer ordered.

Cormack nodded and punched the appropriate frequency up. "Cormack relaying for C.O. Advance to jump-off point, then use hot-rock climbing. Enemy may still have effectives in zone, so watch your asses."

Spencer pulled his own rock hammer out of his equipment rack. With the hammer in one hand and his repulsor in the other, he followed Cormack around the corner into the half-molten hell of the next stretch of corridor.

He was surprised at the ease with which he could propel himself, hooking the hammer into rock and giving a gentle tug. The corridor was a little patch of hell, the rock walls glowing red, dismembered robot arms and legs and heads pinwheeling past, with small parts still shorting and spitting sparks, most of the severed limbs still flexing spasmodically as joint controls shorted and reshorted. Smoke and dust twisted and knotted through the air, shrouding all in a deathly gloom.

There was the quick rattle of a low-power repulsor from up ahead, answered by return fire from a half-dozen marines. But return fire could not help Cormack. His life's blood pumping from a severed artery in his neck, the young marine died with a look of utmost surprise on his face.

Spencer felt the mad urge to rush the marine back to the aid station, nurse him back to life personally, but forced himself to let the dead boy go, let his body behind to float free in that hell. There was nothing Spencer could do except make Cormack's death be worthwhile, be *for* something.

If anything could do that.

Tallen and the rest of the squad following close behind, and the rest of the force after them, Spencer pressed on into a cooler corridor, beyond the sun-core radiance.

Now he could feel it directly in his own head, in some terrifying familiar way. The scar on the back of his head suddenly throbbed in pain, reacting not to any physical hurt, but to a nightmare memory.

A *machine* was pounding thoughts, feelings, into his head. But this was no mere numb-rig, no crude wirehead feelgood circuit, but a *mind*, a malevolent, thinking, hating *mind*, slamming thoughts, ideas, feelings into his skull.

And he was just catching the fringes, the edges of the assault. He didn't need to guess who was receiving the brunt of it all.

He hurried forward, leading his troops past the roasting-hot corridor. The passage ended in a T-intersection. The opposite wall of the intersection was made from the grey material, but Spencer didn't bother worrying about that. He drew up short of the cross-corridor and let his Marines catch up. He pulled his sketch-map from his pocket again and examined it.

It showed this corridor emptying right into the command center, and to the best of his recollection, so had the map-display he had copied it from. Maybe the map-scale had simply been too large to allow minor details like this cross-corridor. It must be that one or both directions led to the command center itself.

"Eight troopers down the left-hand side with Commander Deyi, another eight come with me down the right," Spencer ordered. "The rest of you stand by and watch our back." Without another word, he kicked off from the side of the main corridor and made his way along the cross-corridor.

The mental onslaught pounded on, slamming down into his brain. It seemed as if the others were unaware of it, or could not feel it as strongly. No one commented or complained. Maybe they just chalked it up to natural fear under the circumstances.

But Spencer was a former wirehead, and he was sensitized. He *felt* it. He knew what it was, knew Suss was taking the full force of the attack. He dug in again with his rock hammer and threw himself forward, pivoting a bit to bring himself around a bend in the strange grey corridor. He swung around—

—Right into the face of a huge, red-painted humanoid robot.

Reflex took over before Spencer had a real chance to think. The hammer was in his hand, and it was too close in for the repulsor. He brought the hammer down on the robot's face, slamming into the thing's sensor circuits, smashing it, setting off a shower of sparks. His other hand, still holding the repulsor, came up before he even knew he had seen the other robot.

He fired point-blank, the stream of supersonic glass pellets blasting a fist-sized hole through the second robot's carapace. Both of them were ruined junk by the time the marines arrived behind him. One of the marines looked over the tin men and nodded. "Nice work, Captain."

But they had their backs to me, Spencer thought. *As if the danger they were guarding against was ahead of them, not behind.*

"Captain, Deyi here," Tallen's voice came in his ear. "Nothing here. Just a stretch of that weird gray wall-covering, and a damaged blast door. Controls shot up, and the manual control's out too. It must be dogged shut from the inside."

"I copy that, Tallen. Stand by." *The danger was ahead of them*, Spencer thought. He made his way around the corner—and came upon a tableau.

The figure of an old man in a powerchair, his back to Spencer, arms outstretched over his head. Between his hands, hovering quietly in midair, the helmet. The gleaming, shining, lovely cause of all this evil. The moment Spencer looked on it, the pounding tirade in his head redoubled. Suddenly he could feel the words, the ideas the helmet was silently shouting. DISARM THE WEAPON. TAKE THE HELMET. PUT IT ON. DISARM THE WEAPON. TAKE THE HELMET—

Spencer forced the foreign thoughts away, and glanced at the marines behind him. *Now* they could feel it, Spencer could tell that in a glance at their puzzled and frightened faces.

Spencer turned to look beyond Jameson and his nemesis. They stood before an open blast door with a hole cut through it, the command center framed by the door.

He saw Suss, stripped to her underwear, hunched up in the far corner of the compartment, her hands clenched tight over some sort of gadget with wires trailing from it, her face the very mirror of madness, of a purpose set and chosen against all odds or hope, her jaw muscles spasming with strain, a blob of spittle forming at the corner of her lips.

Spencer froze himself. There was a battle here, one that he could not understand, one that he dare not interfere with yet. The gadget, the thing in Suss' hands. Was that her weapon? He tried to see it better, traced the wires coming out of it, and recognized the ropy substance wrapped around the compartment's interior.

In a flash, it was all clear. Spencer leveled his repulsor, aiming it not at the helmet, but at Suss. "Listen to me, helmet. If I see her make one move toward disarming that device, or coming to get you, I'll fire. She'll die and let go of that switch. Can you control us all, helmet? Take your control off her to try and grab *my* brain—and she'll set off that bomb. Marines, aim at Suss. If she moves, blast her. Helmet, even if you control both of us, enough to get direct control of both our bodies, my marines would kill us both before we could follow your commands. It's all over."

For an eternal second, the tableau held, and the mad drumbeat mind-orders still pounded in Spencer's mind. DISARM YOUR WEAPON. TAKE THE HELMET. PUT IT ON.

But then the shouted thoughts faded and died. There was an audible gasp from Suss. Spencer looked up at her in time to see her arms flex spasmodically, as if they were struggling against a great weight that had suddenly vanished. The two jaws of the pliers came within a hairbreadth of contact before she could pull them back.

OLD FOOL TAKE ME. OLD FOOL TAKE ME. OLD FOOL TAKE ME.

Spencer heard the new cadence, and looked down at Jameson. Jameson. The dying host, the used-up powersource, was the one hope the helmet had left. Spencer had assumed the old man was dead, but suddenly the outstretched arms quivered, the fingers jerked to life, and the palsied hands quivered as they wrapped themselves around the helmet.

The marines tightened their fingers on their triggers, but no one fired. Spencer wanted to give the order, but something held him back. Whether it came from his heart, or from the cruel, artificial mind of the helmet, Spencer knew he could not order the old man's death. Not this way.

The hands pulled the helmet down out of the air, but did not place it on Jameson's scabrous head. "Wha—Who is—What is this place?" Spencer heard the old man's voice, looked into the wild-eyed wilderness of Chairman Jameson's face. OLD FOOL TAKE ME. OLD FOOL TAKE ME.

Jameson looked around himself in slack-jawed bafflement, his addled mind finally realizing that it was the helmet that was making the soundless call. He seemed about to obey when his eye caught Spencer standing a meter or so away.

"I know you," Jameson said. "You came to see me in my office, didn't you?" The powerchair rolled forward, closer to Spencer. "You told me you wanted my pretty helmet, I think."

Spencer and the marines backed away the way they had come. Jameson's voice was becoming high and excited. "This helmet right here. You told me to take it off, that *you* wanted it."

Jameson's mouth worked, and his breath came short and fast.

OLD FOOL TAKE Me. Old Fool Take Me. Old fool take me.

The telepathic command was becoming weaker and weaker with every meter Jameson moved away from the command center.

"Take it, then!" Jameson shouted eagerly. "I've had my turn long enough! TAKE—" Suddenly the ruined man's face was caught in a paroxysm, a jolting, killing spasm that crushed whatever shred of life was left to him.

The helmet sailed free of his hands and tumbled down the corridor, Spencer and the marines scrambling to get out of its way. Three marines drew a bead on it, in pure reflex action, and then remembered what happened to these creatures when they died. No one wanted to be sucked into a black hole. Could a repulsor kill the thing anyway?

It rebounded off the greyish wall and then hung quietly in midair, slowed by air friction. For a long moment Spencer did not move. At last he edged carefully toward the helmet. Not daring to touch the deadly thing, he strained to listen with his mind. Removed from the amplifying power of the command center, denied the power it drew from any contact with a living host, it was badly weakened.

Choose me, a tiny, forgettable voice whispered. *Help me.*

"The hell we will," Spencer said. "We're going to leave you right there."

The marines backed away from the helmet, left it in the middle of the air.

No living creature ever touched it again.

EPILOGUE

Lennox had finally arrived. She boarded most of the former civilian workers from the asteroid and then cast off. The last of the evacuees came aboard *Banquo*, with nothing but the clothes they were standing up in. Even then, all of them were carefully scanned for parasites. Two were found to have swallowed the things, somehow and were quite literally forced to cough them up. It seemed highly unlikely that one or two parasites could breed and grow, but Spencer was taking no chances.

Nor was he taking chances on what happened when parasites died: He ordered several careful parasite-killing experiments performed well away from the asteroid and ships.

It confirmed what Wellingham had reported—single parasites weren't massive or dense enough to form into black holes when disrupted. They just seemed to evaporate altogether, as if they were sucked back into whatever dimension they had been extruded from in the first place.

That meant the StarMetal building, and the whole planet of Daltgeld, weren't going to fall down a black hole, even if outlying parasites died when their controller died. And no one knew *that* for certain yet, anyway.

It was hideously crowded aboard the destroyer, and the evacuees complained bitterly about leaving their personal effects behind. The complaints stopped, however, when the battle-scarred marines made it clear the civilians were welcome to stay behind if they chose.

Comm section had finally located *Macduff*. She had materialized three hundred million kilometers from the target, a new miss-distance record for an intra-system Jump. No doubt she had been knocked off-course by the same gravity-wave effects that had drawn *Banquo* in so close. She would rendezvous with the other ships back at Daltgeld.

But Captain Allison Spencer scarcely knew or cared about those details. Tallen Deyi was perfectly competent to handle them; the Task Force C.O. had other things on his mind.

Spencer spent most of that first day in sick bay, watching over one particular patient. The chief medical officer had every confidence of Suss pulling through, making a full recovery.

Spencer looked at her as she slept peacefully. Incredible that she had shaken it all off so quickly. Twenty hours before, they had been forced to peel her hands back from the improvised deadman switch, her face locked into a snarl of defiance. It had taken heavy sedation to get her calm enough to tell her story, explain the significance of the command center.

Now she slept, breathed easy, only crying out now and again, her much-bandaged body twitching as she dreamed.

She had saved them. Spencer knew that.

"Ah, sir, you're wanted on the bridge," Spencer's AID announced.

Spencer nodded and patted the little gadget. Nice to be able to use the things again, trust them again. "On my way," he said.

Tallen saluted him as he stepped onto the bridge, a rare formality. "The last of the techs are back aboard, sir, and the device is armed. We've got every sort of recording we could make of those nightmares—but no physical samples, as per your orders."

"Very well, then. Order both ships to perform safe distancing maneuver," Spencer said.

The acceleration alarms hooted, and the navigator fired

the main engines. "One thousand kilometers," the navigator announced.

"Weapons, you may proceed," Spencer said, his voice calm, his heart pulled this way and that by a hundred emotions. Triumph, a sense of victory, yes, of course—but also relief at the end of fear, and even sadness.

Clearly, they had no choice but to destroy this thing—but what knowledge were they losing? Pandora's box had to be slammed shut—but what jewels of wisdom were lost when they chased off the demons?

But Suss. Suss was alive. That part of his life, of himself, he would not lose again. That he swore to himself. He watched the main screen.

"*Shields* at standby," the weapons officer announced. "Remote arming *com*plete. Proceeding *with* hell-bomb activation. Detonation in *five* seconds. *Four*. *Three*. *Two*. *One*."

The flash of light filled the screen, overwhelmed it. An expanding shell of dust and debris swelled out from where the asteroid had been—and then began to fall back.

"Gravity-wave activity has ceased," Dostchem announced, bending over her instruments. "A powerful gravity well has appeared."

The dust cloud fell inward.

"Singularity," Dostchem announced. "The gravity well has achieved infinite length. A black hole."

Whatever force had prevented the helmet's incredible mass from expressing itself was gone. Down, down, down came all the debris blasted off by the hell-bomb, streaking back in at velocities that approached the speed of light. Some fragments crashed back down into each other as they fell. The impact energy of the debris strikes lit up the sky anew. The flashes of light reddened and snapped off abruptly as the black hole pulled them in, dragging down the very light waves themselves.

"Once it goes, there's no stopping it," Tallen said. "Break the integrity of the controlling system, and it all collapses in on itself."

"Are you talking about the helmet, or the Pact?" Spencer asked. He looked out there at the stars. The succession was still in doubt, the rival factions circling the rich prize of government like vultures jostling for the best pickings.

"Both, I suppose," Tallen said. "But is the Pact *that* far gone?"

Spencer shut his eyes, suddenly exhausted. This battle, this war was over. There were many others yet to come. "All I know is *the helmet* can't destroy the Pact. But if you want to know if we can do it to ourselves—

"You tell me, Tallen. You tell me."

An excerpt from MAN-KZIN WARS II, created by *Larry Niven*:

The Children's Hour

Chuut-Riit always enjoyed visiting the quarters of his male offspring.

"What will it be this time?" he wondered, as he passed the outer guards.

The household troopers drew claws before their eyes in salute, faceless in impact-armor and goggled helmets, the beam-rifles ready in their hands. He paced past the surveillance cameras, the detector pods, the death-casters and the mines; then past the inner guards at their consoles, humans raised in the household under the supervision of his personal retainers.

The retainers were males grown old in the Riit family's service. There had always been those willing to exchange the uncertain rewards of competition for a secure place, maintenance, and the odd female. Ordinary kzin were not to be trusted in so sensitive a position, of course, but these were families which had served the Riit clan for generation after generation. There was a natural culling effect; those too ambitious left for the Patriarchy's military and the slim chance of advancement, those too timid were not given opportunity to breed.

Perhaps a pity that such cannot be used outside the household, Chuut-Riit thought. Competition for rank was far too intense and personal for that, of course.

He walked past the modern sections, and into an area that was pure Old Kzin; maze-walls of reddish sandstone with twisted spines of wrought-iron on their tops, the tips glistening razor-edged. Fortress-architecture from a world older than this, more massive, colder and drier; from a planet harsh enough that a plains carnivore had changed its ways, put to different use an upright posture designed to place its head above savanna grass, grasping paws evolved to climb rock. Here the modern features were reclusive, hidden in wall and buttress. The door was a hammered slab graven with the faces of night-hunting beasts, between towers five times the height of a kzin. The air smelled of wet rock and the raked sand of the gardens.

Chuut-Riit put his hand on the black metal of the outer portal, stopped. His ears pivoted, and he blinked; out of the corner of his eye he saw a pair of tufted eyebrows glancing through the thick twisted metal on the rim of the ten-meter battlement. *Why, the little sthondats,* he thought affectionately. *They managed to put it together out of reach of the holo pickups.*

The adult put his hand to the door again, keying the locking sequence, then bounded backward four times his own length from a standing start. Even under the lighter gravity of Wunderland, it was a creditable feat. And necessary, for the massive panels rang and toppled as the rope-swung boulder slammed forward. The children had hung two cables from either tower, with the rock at the point of the V and a third rope to draw it back. As the doors bounced wide he saw the blade they had driven into the apex of the egg-shaped granite rock, long and barbed and polished to a wicked point.

Kittens, he thought. *Always going for the dramatic.* If that thing had struck him, or the doors under its impetus had, there would have been no need of a blade. *Watching too many historical adventure holos.* "Errorowwww!" he shrieked in mock-rage, bounding through the shattered portal and into the interior court, halting atop the kzin-high boulder. A round dozen of his older sons were grouped behind the rock, standing in a defensive clump and glaring at him; the crackly scent of their excitement and fear made the fur bristle along his spine. He glared until they dropped their eyes, continued it until they went down on their stomachs, rubbed their chins along the ground and then rolled over for a symbolic exposure of the stomach.

"Congratulations," he said. "That was the closest you've gotten. Who was in charge?"

More guilty sidelong glances among the adolescent males crouching among their discarded pull-rope, and then a lanky youngster with platter-sized feet and hands came squatting-erect. His fur was in the proper flat posture, but the naked pink of his tail still twitched stiffly.

"I was," he said, keeping his eyes formally down. "Honored Sire Chuut-Riit," he added, at the adult's warning rumble.

"Now, youngling, what did you learn from your first attempt?"

"That no one among us is your match, Honored Sire Chuut-Riit," the kitten said. Uneasy ripples went over the black-striped orange of his pelt.

"And what have you learned from this attempt?"

"That all of us together are no match for you, Honored Sire Chuut-Riit," the striped youth said.

"That we didn't locate all of the cameras," another muttered. "You idiot, Spotty." That to one of his siblings; they snarled at each other from their crouches, hissing past barred fangs and making striking motions with unsheathed claws.

"No, you did locate them all, cubs," Chuut-Riit said. "I presume you stole the ropes and tools from the workshop, prepared the boulder in the ravine in the next courtyard, then rushed to set it all up between the time I cleared the last gatehouse and my arrival?"

Uneasy nods. He held his ears and tail stiffly, letting his whiskers quiver slightly and holding in the rush of love and pride he felt, more delicious than milk heated with bourbon. *Look at them!* he thought. At the age when most young kzin were helpless prisoners of instinct and hormone, wasting their strength ripping each other up or making fruitless direct attacks on their sires, or demanding to be allowed to join the Patriarchy's service *at once* to win a Name and house hold of their own . . . *His* get had learned to *cooperate* and use their minds!

"Ah, Honored Sire Chuut-Riit, we set the ropes up beforehand, but made it look as if we were using them for tumbling practice," the one the others called Spotty said. Some of them glared at him, and the adult raised his hand again.

"No, no, I am *moderately* pleased." A pause. "You did not hope to take over my official position if you had disposed of me?"

"No, Honored Sire Chuut-Riit," the tall leader said. There had been a time when any kzin's holdings were the prize of the victor in a duel, and the dueling rules were interpreted more leniently for a young subadult. Everyone had a sentimental streak for a successful youngster; every male kzin remembered the intolerable stress of being physically mature but remaining under dominance as a child.

Still, these days affairs were handled in a more civilized manner. Only the Patriarchy could award military and political office. And this mass assassination attempt was ... unorthodox, to say the least. Outside the rules more because of its rarity than because of formal disapproval. . . .

A vigorous toss of the head. "Oh, no, Honored Sire Chuut-Riit. We had an agreement to divide the private possessions. The lands and the, ah, females." Passing their own mothers to half-siblings, of course. "Then we wouldn't each have so much we'd get too many challenges, and we'd agreed to help each other against outsiders," the leader of the plot finished virtuously.

"Fatuous young scoundrels," Chuut-Riit said. His eyes narrowed dangerously. "You haven't been communicating outside the household, have you?" he snarled.

"Oh, no, Honored Sire Chuut-Riit!"

"Word of honor! May we die nameless if we should do such a thing!"

The adult nodded, satisfied that good family feeling had prevailed. "Well, as I said, I am somewhat pleased. If you have been keeping up with your lessons. Is there anything you wish?"

"Fresh meat, Honored Sire Chuut-Riit," the spotted one said. The adult could have told him by the scent, of course, a kzin never forgot another's personal odor, that was one reason why names were less necessary among their species. "The reconstituted stuff from the dispensers is always ... so ... *quiet*."

Chuut-Riit hid his amusement. Young Heroes-to-be were always kept on an inadequate diet, to increase their aggressiveness. A matter for careful gauging, since too much hunger would drive them into mindless cannibalistic frenzy.

"And couldn't we have the human servants back? They were nice." Vigorous gestures of assent. Another added: "They told good stories. I miss my Clothilda-human."

"Silence!" Chuut-Riit roared. The youngsters flattened stomach and chin to the ground again. "Not until you can be trusted not to injure them; how many times do I have to tell you, it's dishonorable to attack household servants! Until you learn self-control, you will have to make do with machines."

This time all of them turned and glared at a mottled youngster in the rear of their group; there were half-healed scars over his head and shoulders. "It bared its *teeth* at me," he said sulkily. "All I did was swipe at it, how was I supposed to know it would die?" A chorus of rumbles, and this time several of the covert kicks and clawstrikes landed.

"Enough," Chuut-Riit said after a moment. *Good, they have even learned how to discipline each other as a unit.* "I will consider it, when all of you can pass a test on the interpretation of human expressions and body-language." He drew himself up. "In the meantime, within the next two eight-days, there will be a formal hunt and meeting in the Patriarch's Preserve; kzinti homeworld game, the best Earth animals, and even some feral-human outlaws, perhaps!"

He could smell their excitement increase, a mane-crinkling musky odor not unmixed with the sour whiff of fear. Such a hunt was not without danger for adolescents, being a good opportunity for hostile adults to cull a few of a hated rival's offspring with no possibility of blame. *They will be in less danger than most,* Chuut-Riit thought judiciously. *In fact, they may run across a few of my subordinates' get and mob them. Good.*

"And if we do well, afterwards a feast and a visit to the Sterile Ones." That had them all quiveringly alert, their tails held rigid and tongues lolling; nonbearing females were kept as a rare privilege for Heroes whose accomplishments were not *quite* deserving of a mate of their own. Very rare for kits still in the household to be granted such, but Chuut-Riit thought it past time to admit that modern society demanded a prolonged adolescence. The day when a male kit could be given a spear, a knife, a rope and a bag of salt and kicked out the front gate at puberty were long gone. Those were the wild, wandering years in the old days, when survival challenges used up the superabundant energies. Now they must be spent learning history, technology, xenology, none of which burned off the gland-juices saturating flesh and brain.

He jumped down amid his sons, and they pressed around him, purring throatily with adoration and fear and respect;

his presence and the failure of their plot had reestablished his personal dominance unambiguously, and there was no danger from them for now. Chuut-Riit basked in their worship, feeling the rough caress of their tongues on his fur and scratching behind his ears. *Together*, he thought. *Together we will do wonders.*

From "The Children's Hour" by Jerry Pournelle & S.M. Stirling

THE MAN-KZIN WARS
65411-X • 304 pages • $3.95 _____

MAN-KZIN WARS II
69833-8 • 320 pages • $3.95 _____

These bestsellers are available at your local bookstore, or just send this coupon, your name and address, and the cover price(s) to: Baen Books, Dept. BA, 260 Fifth Ave., New York, NY 10001.